Once, Twice, Three Times an Aisling

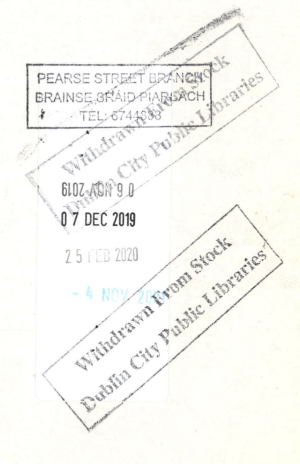

Once, Twice, Three Times an Aisling

Emer McLysaght & Sarah Breen

Gill Books

Gill Books
Hume Avenue
Park West
Dublin 12
www.gillbooks.ie

Gill Books is an imprint of M.H. Gill & Co.
© Emer McLysaght and Sarah Breen 2019

978 07171 8164 3

Copy-edited by Emma Dunne
Proofread by Susan McKeever
Printed by CPI Group (UK) Ltd, Croydon CRO 4YY

This book is typeset in Stone Sans 12/18pt.

This book is a work of fiction. Any references to historical events, real people or real places are used fictitiously. Other names, characters, places and incidents are products of the author's imagination, and any resemblance to actual incidents or persons, living or dead, is entirely coincidental.

The paper used in this book comes from the wood pulp of managed forests. For every tree felled, at least one tree is planted, thereby renewing natural resources.

A CIP catalogue record for this book is available from the British Library.

5 4 3 2 1

ABOUT THE AUTHORS

Like Aisling, Emer McLysaght and Sarah Breen are from 'down the country': Emer from Kildare and Sarah from Carlow. They met in 2003 while studying journalism in Ballyfermot College of Further Education and formed a firm friendship. The character Aisling was conceived in their Stoneybatter sitting room in 2008, when they pulled together the many traits, characteristics and quirks of a very particular type of Irish girl: one they identified around them and one they identified with. They started the Oh My God, What a Complete Aisling Facebook group shortly after. It now boasts almost 50,000 members. *Oh My God What a Complete Aisling: The Novel* was a break-out number one bestseller, receiving high praise from critics and fans alike, and *The Importance of Being Aisling* won Popular Fiction Book of the Year at the Irish Book Awards. They are currently working on the fourth book in the series.

Emer McLysaght has worked extensively in journalism and radio. She writes a column for *The Sunday Business Post*. She lives in Dublin and drives a Nissan Micra, like a good Aisling.

Sarah Breen's background is in print journalism, specifically magazines. She lives in Dublin and dreams of the day Oasis will reunite.

Praise for *Oh My God, What a Complete Aisling* and *The Importance of Being Aisling*

'A day-maker – the cure for cynicism and whatever else ails you.'
SUNDAY INDEPENDENT

'Hilariously funny, but often very moving too.' **JOHN BOYNE**

'Oh lads! This book! There aren't enough words for how much I love it. It's feckin' HILAIRE and very touching.' **MARIAN KEYES**

'Everyone in Ireland was reading *Oh My God, What a Complete Aisling* this Christmas and I got thoroughly swept up in the hype, devouring it in a couple of sittings. It's been called "An Irish Bridget Jones" – and that should give you an idea of what you're dealing with. It's sweet and it's funny and it's moving.' **LYNN ENRIGHT**, *THE POOL*

'A loving ode to a certain type of Irish woman that's hilarious, comforting and warm. A hot water bottle of a book, if you will.' *THE DAILY EDGE*

'An utter ray of sunshine. Now that I've finished the book, I miss Aisling so much that it hurts. It's funny. Proper funny. Actual, literal, LOL funny. I laughed. Out loud. On the tube.' *RED MAGAZINE*

'There's a little bit of Aisling in all of us.' **THE SUNDAY TIMES**

'One of the funniest books I've read in twenty years.' **PAUL HOWARD**

'One of my fave novels of 2017. It really does remind me of Marian Keyes.' **LOUISE O'NEILL**

'Funny, charming, reminiscent of *Eleanor Oliphant is Completely Fine*.'
THE INDEPENDENT

To Ciara and Gav, the soundest of sounding boards.
Doireann is one lucky gal.

PROLOGUE

I was checking for moths in the back of my wardrobe when I found it: my teenage diary. Well, one of many. There are three boxes of them under my bed, and another few in the attic too, but this one must have escaped my rigorous filing system. Mammy used to be at me to bin them, and now it's to recycle them, but you never know when you might need a trip down memory lane.

Ever since Majella got engaged we can't stop reminiscing about our old school days. You'd think she was dying, not getting ready to tie the knot. Of course, she was over like a hot snot when I told her I'd found the rogue diary, mad for a bit of nostalgia and a chance to reminisce on how skinny we were.

The year on the cover is 2005 but I could have already guessed that due to the sheer volume of Westlife pictures sellotaped all over it. I was sixteen. Transition year. The height of my Shane obsession.

'That reminds me, I did my Junior Cert art project on the evolution of Nicky's hair,' Maj says, lying back on my single bed. 'Got a B too. I must dig it out and show Pablo. He's become a bit of a fan.'

Majella sailed through school, somehow managing to be friends with students and teachers alike, while also being a bit of a rip. I don't know how she got away with it. She didn't go to a single PE class, and the one time she convinced me to mitch, I got so nervous my stomach went funny and I spent the entire forty minutes in the girls' cloakroom – I might as well have been in the sports hall doing the bleep test. To this day I still have to make sure I'm near a toilet if I'm stressed. It seems like a lifetime ago, but at the same time, not much has really changed. Even Westlife are back at it.

I can faintly hear Mammy downstairs shouting at *Liveline* as I flick open a random page – 19 February. 'Aisling woz ere' is scrawled around thirty times and I remember I was experimenting with the tail on my *g* that year. Straight? Curly? It looks like I was undecided. I still think the hearts above the *i*'s are quite funky.

'You always did have lovely handwriting, Ais,' Maj says approvingly.

Practice makes perfect and God knows I was trying to be perfect. I flick again.

'Ooh, what's this?' I say with a smile. 'March 23rd. Majella Moran is NOT MY FRIEND. Majella Moran BETRAYED ME. Majella Moran BETTER WATCH HER BACK.' The words are scrawled in block capitals. I rack my brains trying to remember what I was on about. 'Was that the time you told Baby Chief Gittons my 32AA bra was "absolutely swimming" on me?' I ask.

Majella looks pensive. 'Can't remember, bird. That doesn't sound like something I'd do?'

'Oh, you did. But it was only because I decided Sinéad McGrath was going to be my best friend and I gave you back that friendship bracelet you got me in Tramore.'

'You wagon!' She swats me with a rolled-up copy of *Wedding Belles* magazine. I saw 'Always the Bridesmaid?' on the cover and couldn't leave it behind me in the newsagent's in Dublin last week. The woman at the till had asked was I the bride or the bridesmaid and I told her and we ended up talking for fifteen minutes about the best way to transport The Dress. Helping to transport The Dress is one of a bridesmaid's most important duties and the woman in the shop – Helen was her name; we nearly swapped numbers – told me she once booked an extra seat on a flight to Palma for The Dress. Needs must and all that. There was quite a queue behind me at that stage and I definitely heard a few tuts so I had to take my magazine and let people pay for their chicken fillet rolls. As I was walking out, the woman called after me, 'You sound like a great friend, Aisling. I hope all brides have an Aisling in their lives,' and I was pure delighted until she roared, 'And your time will come too,' as I skirted the postcard stand on the way out the door.

I turn the page in the diary again and we're greeted with what looks like an essay. The heading across the top, underlined several times, reads '30 Things I Must Do Before I'm 30'. Oh Jesus, I remember this. I was trying to pluck up the courage to buy a packet of pads in the chemist in Knock when I overheard Kelly Kennedy and Linda Dalton from sixth year reading out an article from *Cosmopolitan* about goals to achieve before that particular milestone. I was afraid to even look at *Cosmo* on the shelf in Filan's newsagents in case I accidentally picked up a sex tip.

'"Have savings." Maybe if I stopped spending all my babysitting money in Topshop.' Kelly had laughed, leaning on the counter while Linda took bottles of Sun-In out of a box. The whole school had gone bonkers for the stuff and I was nearly tempted myself until Deirdre Ruane turned her fringe bright orange. I dropped the pads and skulked out. When I got home, I decided to do up my own list. Right in this very room, actually.

Majella takes the diary out of my hand and scans the page. 'You're not doing too badly at all here, Ais.'

'Really? Read me out a few there.'

'Okay. "Number one: buy something in Topshop."'

'Check! It was a pair of sunglasses. Fifty per cent off because I got them on the eighth of December.'

'"Number two: go on an amazing road trip with your bestie." We've definitely done that.'

'We were only in Kildare Village last week. So, yeah, check.'

'"Number three: read *Moby Dick*."'

'I have it. I've started it.'

'"Number four: buy my own car."'

'Well, I went in with Daddy on it.'

'"Number five: do the Women's Mini Marathon."'

'Check. And I have a number of T-shirts to prove it.'

'"Number six: shift Prince William."'

Maj grimaces a little and we look at each other and say in unison, nodding, 'Prince Harry instead.'

'His manners are just as good, I'm sure, and he'd treat you like a queen,' Majella says confidentially. 'No less than you deserve.'

She runs her finger down the page. 'Not too shabby at all, Ais. Assuming you're going to finish *Moby Dick*, given that Harry *and* William are taken and since you can no longer meet Pope John Paul, you're twenty-seven out of thirty. I'd be happy with that. Very happy.'

'What's the last one then?'

Majella takes a deep breath. '"Number thirty: get married. Preferably to Shane Filan."'

I paste on a smile. 'You never know. There's still a couple of months to my birthday.'

CHAPTER 1

Even though I've pressed myself up against the window I can't get more than one bar of signal. Two if I stick the phone outside, but that's no good because then she can't see me.

'Ais, what am I looking at here? Are you wearing … a jersey? All I can see is fields. Hold still!'

The reception is shite. I could blame it on Sadhbh being in Tokyo but I know the problem is more than likely on my end. The Japanese are notoriously technological. Meanwhile, the 3G goes entirely if there's so much as a stiff breeze in Ballygobbard. You can only get 4G in two spots in the village and one of them is in the local postman's front garden. Pat Curran is forever running people who've hopped the wall to download a podcast. I must admit I did once tip over the wall myself. Colette Green, Ireland's foremost fashion and beauty blogger, had just posted about her new line of fake tan on Instagram, and while I've never been a slave to the tan myself, I am a slave to Colette, particularly since she made the trek down to Ballygobbard during the summer and put my humble little café, BallyGoBrunch, on the map. Her Insta might be all hashtag vegan but she definitely horsed into at least three of our award-winning sausages. We had an influx of what Majella would call 'Insta huns' for weeks afterwards and, to be honest, the café has been buzzing ever since – I'm dead on my feet every evening. Running the place is harder than I ever imagined.

The broadband is so bad it's reminiscent of the dial-up we got installed in 1999 after Daddy saw a programme about new technology making it possible to watch your cows calving online. Mammy still goes pale when she thinks about the waste of money and the fact that it took four days for a full picture to load and by that time the calf would nearly be talking to you. It did nothing for Ballygobbard's local reputation as 'BallyGoBackwards' and is probably why we were always more keen on just calling it 'BGB'.

'Obviously I'm wearing my county jersey!' I exclaim. 'It's homecoming day!' I manoeuvre the phone down to my chest, moving it left to right so she can see.

Sadhbh squeals and hoots. 'Oooh yas, mama. Show me the goods.'

Honestly, for a girl whose wardrobe palette rarely hovers above pale grey and brown or what she calls 'pebble' and 'ecru dune' and who can't bear to be in the same room as milk not squeezed from nuts, Sadhbh can be a fierce Majella sometimes.

'Homecoming day, of course!' I can just about make out enough of Sadhbh to see her slapping her forehead. 'I'm all over the place. We just flew in this morning and I don't know if I'm coming or going. The lads were fuming they couldn't find a telly in Tokyo showing the match. Tell me all.'

Sadhbh's GAA etiquette wouldn't be up to much but I appreciate her enthusiasm.

'So, there's a big parade this evening and a street party –'

'Okay, but let me just double check,' Sadhbh interrupts, 'the county *didn't* win the All-Ireland final?'

'No,' I say happily. 'They were absolutely slaughtered. But sure that hardly matters.' I can't help beaming proudly. 'We had four BGB Rovers and two Knocknamanagh Rangers players represented on the pitch. We'll hardly see the likes of it again. The All-Ireland final, like! The county team hasn't been in an All-Ireland final since 1954!' Knocknamanagh is a few miles from Ballygobbard and usually our biggest rival. But to have both towns represented on the same team in the final meant all grudges were temporarily on hold.

'Was it brilliant?'

I pause for a second to think back over the previous day. Somehow, my little village café had ended up sponsoring the team jerseys. Mulcahy Feeds had been the sponsor for years but pulled out a few months back when Johnnie Mulcahy's son didn't get picked for the squad. John, my ex-boyfriend and newly appointed county-team selector, had pleaded for my help and I agreed to put a bit of money behind them in exchange for having the BallyGoBrunch name emblazoned across the jerseys for this year's championship.

'It was brilliant,' I tell Sadhbh, nearly setting myself off again. Myself and Majella had nearly had to be hospitalised for dehydration in the swish corporate box specially reserved for sponsors in Croke Park the previous day. Our emotions got the better of us several times between the BallyGoBrunch jerseys being beamed into every telly in Ireland and the fancy prawn sandwiches and seemingly never-ending glasses of Prosecco. I'm nearly sure I saw Chris de Burgh! I don't know what state we'd be in if the county had actually won. Of course, I had half of Ballygobbard onto me looking for a dig out with a ticket. Mad Tom Doyle offered to do a bit of landscaping around the café in exchange for one but he was brandishing a strimmer at me at the time which had Eamon Filan's name spray-painted on the side of it so he'd clearly stolen it. He got a ticket somehow anyway because he was on the big screen in Croke Park multiple times before throw-in, helicoptering his top over his head. Loves an auld day out, so he does.

Seeing John down on the pitch with the team was strange. I wanted to text him from the box, but it might have been a bit much. We're officially 'friends' since we broke up earlier in the year, but every time I see him I feel as awkward as ever. Majella says it's nearly impossible to be friends with your ex, but with me living in BGB and John back home from Dublin every weekend and with about forty-seven mutual friends, we just have to suck it up. Give it a year and we'll be flying, I've no doubt. I caught sight of Megan, the girlfriend, in the stands behind him yesterday. I mean, no human alive is that particular shade of biscuit-fragranced orange, even with all the holidays primary teachers get, but she is very pretty and John seems very happy with her. I'm happy for them.

'The whole team is having lunch up in Dublin at Croke Park and then stopping off at two hospitals on the way home,' I explain to Sadhbh, dragging the brush through my hair. 'There are rumours that Dessie Connolly from Knocknamanagh has the healing touch after he saved that final goal.' It was a pity he hadn't saved the four goals he let in before that one, but sure, look, isn't it the taking part that counts?

'Okay, and is the whole team coming to BGB then?'

I've the phone held straight in the air in the eleven o'clock position and finally I can see Sadhbh more clearly on the screen. She's leaning back in a huge chair with a cocktail in her hand and I'm fairly sure there's an indoor waterfall behind her. This is her life now, since The Peigs started their stadium tour around Asia. She's moved – 'pivoted' was the word she used, I think – from HR to handling all the social media for the band, but it's all done from her phone so she spends a good portion of her time hanging around five-star hotels listening to audiobooks while Don Shields, her boyfriend and the band's ridey frontman, does interviews and gets ready for the night's concert. Well for some! She loves all the travel but her artsy Instagram tends to baffle me with its photos of a bit of a building or a blurry tree or an old man she doesn't even know with no caption. Whatever happened to a good old-fashioned 'hot dogs or legs' or 'today's office' update? Classics.

'The six Ballygobbard and Knock lads are having their own smaller homecoming on BGB Main Street,' I explain as I dig around in my jewellery box for something a bit dressy. 'Open-top lorry, speeches, the whole shebang.'

'But just to reiterate,' she's laughing now, 'they didn't actually win?'

'No. Annihilated, so they were. A shocking defeat. A complete –'

'Okay, okay. I get it.' She nearly spills the cocktail, laughing. 'It's a big deal.'

'How are you getting on anyway?' I ask her, untangling two necklaces. I can't believe I know someone who's jetting around the world with a famous band. Up until recently the only fame I'd known was BGB's own Leslie Cahill falling off his chair on *Winning Streak*.

'I'm great. It's so nice to be able to travel with Don and we all have such a laugh together. The record company really looks after us, which makes everything chill. It's so funny the people who are crawling out of the woodwork, though. People I haven't seen in years are suddenly sending me Facebook messages in case I can get them tickets for something. One girl I barely knew in school asked if The Peigs could play at her sister's fortieth. The neck of her!'

The idea of The Peigs squashed into the corner of a function room while drunk aunties slosh their Bulmers on them is too much to bear. They've been on the *Late Late* twice!

I hold up a pair of earrings beside my face and point my phone at them. 'Are they too much?'

'Hmmm.' Sadhbh takes her time analysing the earrings as best she can, biting her lower lip. She takes fashion very seriously, even if it's only accessories. Me and Sadhbh are like chalk and cheese, and I will never expect her to be at one with the GAA culture that flows through the veins of every BGB-ite, but ever since we became roommates in a swanky Dublin apartment last year we've been the best of friends, no matter how many times she's tried to get me to buy a 'neutral poncho'.

'They're very … dangly,' she decides eventually. 'Have you got something smaller? Maybe a delicate hoop?'

I do another quick search through my jewellery box: I've a few nice Newbridge Silverware pieces, a gold cross on a chain I got for my Confirmation and some bits from Penneys, as well as the two identical Pandora bracelets I've stashed in a little velvet pouch. No hoops though.

'I don't,' I admit. 'Should I just take them out altogether? Now I'm worried I look underdressed.'

'You're very het up about the earrings,' Sadhbh says coyly. 'Is there any other reason you want to look particularly nice? A … James Matthews reason?'

I instantly blush and of course the picture goes the clearest it's been for our entire call.

'Aha, *there* it is,' she squeals. 'How is the handsome devil? Still erecting things all over BGB?'

James Matthews is the developer who bought and renovated the abandoned building just outside BGB village that houses BallyGoBrunch and the three apartments above it. We've been 'doing a line' – as my mother mortifyingly called it on the phone to Auntie Sheila recently – since the night I reopened the café after an awful break-in and James literally charmed the knickers off me with his lovely smile, impeccable manners and multi-pocketed work trousers. I blush just thinking about it.

'Ah, look at you. So cute!' Sadhbh squeals and I nearly pull a muscle in my knees with the cringing. 'So, what's the story with you two? He's *sooo* nice,' she continues, pulling a fresh drink in front of her and muttering what I assume is 'thanks a million' in Japanese. I advised her to fire up the Duolingo before going and I'm delighted to see she took my advice. Nothing says 'chic global traveller' more than being able to order your cervezas in the local tongue. I should know, I've been to Spain twice.

I take a deep breath before answering her. I don't want to be getting her hopes up. She's a fierce romantic at heart and I've managed to avoid too much chat with her about James so far. 'There's no story, really.'

'Ah, go on, there's always a story. Isn't he such a ride?'

He is a ride. She's right. I still can't quite believe he fancies me.

'Yes, but there's really no story. Sure, he's leaving in a few weeks.'

'Oh *nooo*, is that still happening?' Sadhbh looks as dismayed as she sounds.

'Yeah, he's signed up to that job back in England as soon as the build at Woodlawn Park is finished, and he's hardly going to stay in BGB for me.' James has been overseeing the Woodlawn Park housing development in Rathborris for the past six weeks but it's onto the final phase.

'Stranger things have happened.'

'No, no, no. It's just a bit of a ...' I have to pause to make myself choke out Majella's word for it. '... a fling.'

Sadhbh nearly comes off the chair as the word 'fling' leaves my mouth. I don't really blame her. I'm not exactly the 'fling' type. I can definitely count on one hand the number of lads who've seen me in the nip. She fumbles with her phone and it's a moment before her long, elegant neck ricochets back into focus. She's one of the few Irish women I know who could actually get a tan, but she's so hell-bent on avoiding wrinkles that she rarely exposes herself to the sun. Such a waste.

'A fling. In Ballygobbard. I've heard it all now,' she says, composing herself. 'Would you not try make it work long distance or something, though – no? He was so mad about you that night you got together. It seems like such a shame.'

I feel like if James was into trying long distance, he would have said something already, and it's not like *I* can ask him to stay. I don't know if I can even imagine him staying at this stage anyway. I've known about his work commitments from the get-go. He told me the morning after we first got together that he had work lined up back at home. He said he'd love to keep seeing me even though it might not be a good idea since he wasn't going to be there that much longer. He was so noble saying it that I felt like I was in one of Majella's bodice-ripping novels. I was weak for him. But he's leaving and I can't be a goose about it. And I'm certainly not moving to England, although I do enjoy the challenge of a currency exchange. BallyGoBrunch is taking off so well and is so hectic and I barely have time to fit James in as it is. Sadhbh *is* right about him seeming mad about me though. We went to the new cinema in Knocknamanagh the other night and we were like teenagers – not that I'd ever done anything of the sort as a teenager, seeing as there was no cinema within a twenty-mile radius. The new Knock cinema has only one screen and seventeen seats and has been showing the same film since it opened three weeks ago, but it's quiet and dark so we could shift in the back row with no eyes on us. Mammy asked me what the film was about the next day and I had to make up something ludicrous about Tom Cruise punching a shark. Mammy has only been to the cinema three times since the nineties and two of those were *Mamma Mia* films so it's easy enough to cod her. Meanwhile, I've stayed in James's place for the past–

'Five nights in a row Majella says you stayed with *him* this week. You're mad about him too,' Sadhbh teases. Bloody Majella and her big mouth. James lives in one of the apartments above BallyGoBrunch and on the floor above him is the entire Moran clan, plus Pablo and Willy, their jack Russell. They're squashed into the two-bed apartment while they're waiting for their family home to be habitable again after the fire. The things I've heard through the ceiling .My BallyGoBrunch business partner Carol Boland's place is across the hall from James. It's all very, very cosy. A bit too cosy. But it's just hard to resist James when I go up to his apartment to say hello after closing the café and he has the two glasses out for the wine. It's a bit exciting, this fling business. And it's nice to have someone to cuddle up beside. It was one of the main things I missed about John – falling asleep with my head on his chest watching *The Office*. No better feeling.

'I'll say no more about it now.' Sadhbh finally cops via my silence that I'm not giving her anything more on the James topic. 'But you're seeing him every night of the week and I think you're really going to miss him and you'll regret letting him go when he leaves. That's all.' She waves her hand across her face in an 'I'm done' motion and I breathe a sigh of relief and hope that she's wrong. 'God, there's nothing like a good fling, though, is there?' she adds. 'So wrapped up in each other, counting each other's freckles.'

My freckles are a great source of torment to me. How could she? 'What's going on with the house,' I say, determined to change the subject,

'The builder is in now. Hallelujah!' She whoops and raises her drink in the air, and I can just imagine the Japanese taking pictures of this mad Irishwoman to send to their friends and aunties. Sadhbh and Don had been in a bidding war on an old fixer-upper in Dublin for when he eventually gets off tour. Last I heard she'd been on the phone to the estate agent for three hours going up in €50 increments. Her strategy to annoy the other bidders into submission must have worked.

'Ah, Sadhbhy, I'm delighted for you! When will you be moving in?'

'The renovation should be all done and dusted by Christmas.'

'Ah, what a present! I can't wait to see it!'

'Speaking of presents,' she's adopted a coy tone again, 'what do you want for your thirtieth?'

'Ah, nothing, nothing. I want no fuss,' I say, shaking my head vigorously and meaning it.

'It's your thirtieth! Of course I'm getting you something.' Sadhbh smiles. 'Do you know who buys great presents, I bet? James Matthews.'

My eyes fall on the two Pandora bracelets in the jewellery box. Both identical and both from John, two Christmases apart. Not his finest moment, gift-wise. I choose to ignore Sadhbh's hint about James and she mercifully carries on.

'And Majella says you're not having a party? Not even a night out?'

'No, I'm grand. No fuss. I've enough to be doing.'

My birthday. My thirtieth birthday. It's next month and I have no interest in it. It's such a grown-up number and half the time I still feel like I'm a teenager asking Daddy for lifts and lusting over Shayne Ward with Majella. She wrote Shayne so many letters she got a solicitor's one back. She framed it.

And now Maj is engaged and Sadhbh and Don have their house and I'm back living at home with my mother, involved with a too-good-to-be-true man who's about to leave. I suppose I'm just not where I thought I'd be and I'd rather not draw attention to it. Plus, life has been hectic these past few years and I definitely thought Daddy would be at my thirtieth making sure nobody gave me the bumps. It's a good job, really, that I'm single and nowhere near getting married. The thought of walking up the aisle without him … No, I'm going to keep the head down and maybe buy an eye cream.

'Are you sure, Aisling?' Sadhbh cajoles. 'You should mark it. Thirty is a milestone. You had Pablo jump out of a cake for Majella's.'

I thought he'd be wearing more clothes to be quite honest.

'I'm sure. I don't think I'm quite ready to accept being thirty, Sadhbhy.'

Sadhbh brings the phone up close to her face. 'You're a successful businesswoman, you've looked after your mum, you've great friends and you've scored the most eligible bachelor in town. I'd say that's pretty good going heading into a new decade.'

I blush again and begin my 'stop that now's and my 'bye, bye, bye-bye, bye's but as I look around my childhood bedroom, I can't help feel like turning thirty single and in a single bed just isn't worth celebrating.

CHAPTER 2

'**A**h you'll have to do *something* Aisling,' Sharon calls behind her as we elbow our way back from the bar in Maguire's which is completely rammed, a sea of county jerseys. 'Thirty is a milestone, like.'

Is there something in the water today or what? First Sadhbh, now Sharon, and just an hour ago I got an email from a gym I joined four years ago when I was working in PensionsPlus, reminding me once again that my birthday is hurtling towards me. I had to pack it in at that gym after just one Pilates class, which I signed up for thinking it would be lovely and gentle to ease me into my new life as a fitness fanatic. I was expecting to lie around in a room festooned with linen curtains, maybe with some candles and whale song in the background while I imagined wheat fields and natural yoghurt. Instead I was tortured for forty-five minutes and couldn't walk for four days. I had to pretend I was happy to work through lunch at my desk because getting up out of the chair was such an ordeal. Gwyneth Paltrow has a lot to answer for. I'm still tormented by the three months' membership I lost on that gym, but after needing the help of the Pilates instructor and the gazelle beside me to get up off the ground, I could never go back.

'Carol will do you a cake,' Sharon says, setting the drinks down on the table and nodding at Carol, who nods back enthusiastically. She does a great cake, to be fair to her.

'What time are the lads due in at?' Sharon asks, pushing her voluminous blonde curls back over her shoulder. She's a wizard with the GHD but I suppose she wouldn't be BGB's foremost (and only) beauty-salon owner without the skills. In the few months I've known her, I could count on one hand the times I've seen her less than 100 per cent glam, and this evening is no exception. I could never get away with the tight red dress she has on under her jersey. My hips have always been a great trial to me, but Sharon shows off her ample curves like a pro.

'Seven, I think. Any sign of Majella?' I crane my neck looking for my best friend but instead catch an eyeful of Mad Tom up at the bar, top off again. It is warm, even by September standards, and outside the village is a riot of colour thanks to the bunting taught between telephone poles and the incredible job the Tidy Towns committee did with this year's hanging baskets. I must remember to pass on my congratulations to Tessie Daly. There's an ice-cream van doing a roaring trade outside Strong Stuff, Sharon's beauty salon, and Eamon Filan has speakers in front of the newsagents-slash-funeral-parlour pumping out the nineties dance hits. The atmosphere is electric and the kids are all up to ninety, dabbing and whatnot. It's almost as exciting as the time a horse trainer from outside Knock won the Grand National and they closed Main Street for a full day to parade Dexy's Midnight Galloper through the town. The poor horse had to go into retirement it was so wrecked. Still, though, a mighty day.

As I scan the pub for Maj, I'm keeping an eye out for James too. He said he'd probably head in for the festivities with some of the lads from the building site and for some reason I'm feeling anxious. We haven't done a whole heap of socialising together in BGB, and if my hand was forced I'd have to say I'm just not that keen on being seen out and about with him. I don't need people thinking we're a big serious item, especially when everyone is so mad about him and his manners. Me and John's break-up was big news and I don't want the Bowls Club and the entire Zumba with Mags class talking about us and feeling sorry for me when James is gone.

'Was it busy today, Carol?' I ask, relaxing back into my seat, no sign of either Majella or James. I took today off from BallyGoBrunch at Carol's insistence after working twelve days in a row and then going straight from behind the counter to Croke Park for the match yesterday.

'A steady stream.' Carol nods. 'We ran out of sausage baps at the takeaway counter and Noel grated his knuckles into the coleslaw but no other emergencies.'

She'd deny it but Carol and her secret sausage recipe are the real reason BallyGoBrunch is such a roaring success, if you ask me. She battled with her bully husband over that recipe and now both she and it are free of him, Carol Boland Sausages are trademarked and the recipe is patent pending. I'm a 49 per cent stakeholder in CBS and we sell so many packets of them in the café that we've outsourced their production to a small factory in Kildare. Carol is delighted with their standards and it's freed up a good bit of space in the fridge. The space in the fridge is one of many things that wakes me up worrying in the dead of night. That and Noel the kitchen porter's knuckles in the coleslaw. In fairness, Noel works brilliantly alongside Carol and we're delighted with Karla, our new front-of-house whizz kid from Rathborris. She has a real way with people and is great for upselling desserts, and she gives me a bit more time to spend in the office wrangling invoices and wages and orders for our new catering sideline – wakes, Confirmations, twenty-firsts. You name it, we'll cater it.

'Oh, thank Christ, there you are!' Majella's hand comes snaking through the throng surrounding our table and she grabs my arm and pulls herself towards me like she's clawing her way out of quicksand. She's managed to keep an impressive hold on a pint she must have acquired along the way.

'You made it!'

She looks very shook. 'I almost didn't get into the town at all. The Tidy Towns committee are on perimeter security detail and I nearly had to show Murt Kelly my passport to get through the cordon.'

'Is Murt Kelly not your godfather?'

'He is. The power went to his head. He wouldn't let Dr Maher into his own driveway. And I'm nearly sure I saw Tessie Daly frisking Billy Foran.' Majella winces as she rocks back and forth on the balls of her feet. 'I didn't even get a chance to get home and change out of my work gear. I don't know how much longer I can wear court shoes for, Ais. Bunions run in my family, you know?'

Majella's the new deputy principal at St Anthony's in Santry and went completely berserk buying work suits and pencil skirts in Dunnes so she looks the part. She's already gone through seventeen pairs of American Tan tights and school is only back a week. She said Pablo hid in the en suite for half an hour after she put her fingers through three pairs in one morning, such was her rage.

Sharon and Carol shove up on their bench and she goes to sink in beside them, but changes her mind and stands up on it instead, roaring over the heads towards the bar. 'A round please, Felipe. Working women over here in need of a drink.'

I just about stop myself from reminding her it's Monday and a literal school night tonight for her. Although, even though she's only just back, she seems to be making a real go of this new role. She did some serious prep over the summer and is flat out organising sub teachers and making sure she can still leave early enough to catch the four o'clock Timoney's bus Down Home every day. She buys Double Deckers for Tony Timoney to keep him sweet so he'll wait for her if she's a few minutes late. If you miss the four o'clock you've to wait for Tony to drive all the way down to BGB and all the way back to Dublin to collect you.

Felipe makes a gesture which looks rude but, not being Brazilian, we can't be sure. He's very proud of his culture so we never question him. He roars back at her. 'We are all working, *pequeño*. Wait your turn.'

Majella brandishes one court shoe at him and he holds up his hands in mock defeat and starts putting our order together.

'Any sign of Pablo?' Majella says, scanning the pub as she sinks down. According to Sharon, Pablo actually passed through Maguire's like a whirlwind just before I arrived, grabbing as many bodies as he could. He was shrieking something about crowd control and Murt Kelly, which now makes much more sense. Pablo's very impressionable and Murt must have put the frighteners up him. I suppose you can't be too careful when it comes to public safety. I was once at a free St Patrick's Day Brian Kennedy performance up in Dublin and I'm amazed there weren't fatalities when he threw his leprechaun hat into the crowd. I nearly had the ankles taken off me by a girl from Ballina who kept screaming that he was her second cousin once removed. Daddy had warned me to mind my bag and keep my wits about me when he dropped me and my cousin Doireann off, but I wasn't expecting a near-death experience. I wonder if Sadhbh and The Peigs are dealing with similar madness in Japan – knickers walloping them in the face and what have you.

'We'll have to head out after this one, Ais.' Majella nudges me with an American Tan toe. I've been invited onto the VIP viewing platform on Main Street for when the heroes arrive and I'm bringing Maj as my guest. She was at me to bring James, but the thought of parading him on a literal stage is just too much. Mammy would be straight into Geraldine's Boutique for a hat and I had enough 'when's the Big Day' chats when I was with John to last me a lifetime. Majella, my platonic life partner, will do the job just fine.

She nudges me again, a glint in her eye. 'I've news.'

She's not. 'You're not ...' My gaze flits from her almost empty pint glass to her stomach to her face just as she throws her eyes to heaven.

'Jesus, no, chance would be a fine thing. And also, I'm not wrecking my honeymoon by not being able to drink. Imagine what a dose that would be.'

'Well, what then?'

'I got a call from the Ard Rí this morning. For luck it was little break so I could take it – although, the yard roster for little break is my responsibility, and I swear there are first class teachers who keep swapping and making a balls of it –'

'Majella! What about the Ard Rí?'

I gave Maj and Pablo the Effortless Elegance wedding package at the local fancy hotel as an engagement present. I'd randomly won two hundred grand after placing a drunken bet in Vegas earlier in the year, and I knew it would take them forever to pull the money together living on Majella's income and Pablo's multiple part-time jobs while saving so hard to get a place of their own.

'They had a cancellation,' she breathes through a massive grin. 'Some couple from Dublin had it booked the weekend of the May bank holiday but apparently she's moved to Amsterdam with the stripper from her hen …'

'No!'

'And the whole thing is off! And because my wedding package is already paid for, they've offered the slot to me! I'm getting married next May!' She raises the dregs of her pint and the four of us cheers her as I frantically calculate the months in my head. I mean, as her only bridesmaid, I've obviously been thinking about the hen since the day she got engaged, but now I'll have to go into turbo-speed mode. A bullet of panic rises in my throat and I fight hard to push it back down. It will be grand. I'll just stay an hour longer in the BallyGoBrunch office a few nights a week and research our options.

'Hey, I've a favour to ask you, Ais.' She gives me the puppy-dog eyes I usually see when she's scheming something. 'Will you ask The Peigs to perform at the wedding? They'll definitely say yes to you.'

The bullet rises again. Sadhbh was just giving out about this kind of thing. Their hearts are probably broken with requests and favours like this.

'Even just a few songs. Imagine the glamour,' Majella continues breathlessly.

Of course, Sadhbh is one of my best friends and she and Maj are good pals now too. I suppose I can call Don a friend too, which is completely mad. I still kind of curtsy every time I see him. He and Sadhbh were down in BallyGoBrunch just before they left for the tour and there were girls hiding in the bushes outside and I caught a woman old enough to know better trying to slip his napkin into her handbag. He'd twelve bras signed before he managed to leave.

I suppose Sadhbh and Don will be invited to Maj and Pablo's wedding anyway, so maybe it wouldn't be that much of a stretch to ask the rest of The Peigs to come too. Maj has been a fan since before they made it big so I know it would mean a lot to her. I add talking to Sadhbh about it to my mental list of things to worry about.

'No problem. I'll ask them.' I smile at Maj and she squeals.

'Imagine the craic we'll have bopping along to them with Elaine and Ruby.' Elaine and Ruby are me and Sadhbh's old Dublin flatmates. They had their own wedding on New Year's Eve. Mammy thinks she's the height of sophistication knowing a married lesbian couple and has started watching the *Ellen* repeats every morning on RTÉ in solidarity.

Majella is already singing The Peigs' current hit 'She's the Business' under her breath and smiling away to herself. I can't let her down. I won't.

'Maj, will you tell Aisling she has to do something for her birthday?' Sharon says, accepting a tray of drinks from an extremely harassed-looking Felipe. 'Her thirtieth, like.'

'I'm blue in the face telling her,' says Maj, pouring a pile of €2 coins onto Felipe's tray.

I lift my gin and slimline tonic off and take a refreshing sip. I was forced to drink a G&T at a local networking event for rural women in business. I was shocked, to be honest. I always thought gin tasted like Calpol but it's actually quite delicious and I've transitioned from my traditional West Coast Cooler. They can keep those big fishbowl glasses though. Your whole face gets wet. I prefer a slim jim myself.

'Please, girls. Let me be in my old age. I don't want a fuss.'

'This better not be about getting old,' Majella says defensively. 'I've been thirty for months and I made Pablo tell me this morning that I looked like a foetus. Skin like a newborn's arse.'

'And I'm so far past thirty I can't even see it in the rearview mirror,' Carol pipes up.

'I just don't want a fuss,' I repeat.

I wish I could explain to them that it just doesn't feel like it's happening to me: turning thirty. Where's the adult woman I thought I'd be?

'You've done nearly everything on your list,' Majella announces.

'What list?' says Sharon.

'She made a list when she was sixteen of things to do before she was thirty. Travel the world, that sort of thing.'

'Have you travelled the world, Ais?' Carol asks and I nod magnanimously. Spain twice, Berlin twice, Vegas, Blackpool for Auntie Sheila's fiftieth. Mammy still talks about getting her photo with the cardboard cut-out of Bruce Forsyth.

'Still haven't kissed Prince William – or Harry,' I counter, just as a pair of strong hands land on my shoulder and a smooth voice in an unmistakable English accent says, 'Hello, you.'

Majella's eyebrows shoot up and she nods her head towards James Matthews, 'Next best thing.'

CHAPTER 3

'**W**ell, this is exciting!' James beams as he hurries along beside me through the crowds towards the VIP platform. Majella insisted he take my place after Pablo arrived into the pub traumatised by his brief stint as a security guard. Apparently Mad Tom, who, after losing his licence recently, had attached a makeshift engine to a pushbike, was threatening to do a stunt leap over the pump in the village square and Pablo was tasked with stopping him. Majella is back in Maguire's now comforting him and James was only too delighted to be my plus-one instead. He's had a few drinks with the lads and his arm kept snaking around my midsection in the pub, his breath warm in my ear. Carol and Sharon nearly nudged each other onto the floor. Those chocolate-brown eyes, the curls just touching his ears, that three-day stubble. He really is very attractive. I mean, alarmingly so. The smell of him has made me understand why so many of Mammy's books I read as a teenager described men as 'intoxicating'. All the same, I had to keep fighting off the urge to push him away, mortified, while reflexively sucking in my tummy every time he touched me. I haven't so much as thrown an eye to my Weight Watchers bible in months. And as for going to a class … I'm surprised my leader, Maura, hasn't put up posters looking for me. Bless me, Maura, for I have sinned. I haven't calculated a single Point all summer.

It's fine when it's just me and James alone in his place, although I'm like a whippet getting under the duvet. Out in public, something just feels … not right. The excitement and all-consuming nature of the fling is all well and good, but I feel it's because I know he's going. He's such a dote to me, though. I always wanted a lad who'd buy me flowers and get me thoughtful presents and replace his socks regularly and want to get married someday. James brought flowers into the café for me last Tuesday when Tessie Daly was in getting a quiche and the eyes nearly fell out of her head. The story made it back to Mammy, who has such a soft spot for James that she's close to starting a fan club. She asked me right out if he's my boyfriend and I had to stick my head in the breadbin and mutter that it's not serious and remind her that he's only in BGB short term. I think it's the posh accent and his general handiness that gets her. She definitely has a crush on him. All the local ladies do. He carried Sumira Singh's shopping to the car for her last week and I swear there was an emergency meeting of the Active Retiree's Book Club to discuss it. Sumira runs the nursing home so she had ten litre-bottles of prune juice in each bag. Apparently, he didn't even wince picking them up.

Mammy is also turning a blind eye to my nightly absence from the house. She's relaxed a lot since the early days of me and John's relationship when she'd pointedly leave the spare-room door open and a pair of Daddy's pyjamas on the single bed for him if we got a taxi back together after the pub – a practice John's God-mad mother, Fran, kept up in reverse at her house right up until we broke up for good.

I grab James's hand as we push through the crowds and he laces his fingers through mine. My heart gives a little ping. Mortification aside, I will miss him when he's gone. Sadhbh got into my head earlier about it, and Colette Green posted 'It's better to have loved and lost than never to have loved at all' on Instagram last night after her Gucci belt was robbed from the gym and I couldn't like it fast enough. It all feels a bit romantic and tragic, although I know I'm not in love with James – I've only been in love once, and I know what it feels like.

News that the team's arrival is imminent has spread through BGB and everyone has now taken to Main Street for a gawk. We squeeze past Cyclops, John's friend and dependable Knock Rangers centre back. He's also Sharon's boyfriend and is headed to Maguire's to get her, He had his eye on her from the day she arrived in BGB with her freshly signed lease and a suitcase of hairdryers. They're absolutely dotey together and he's already moved into her flat above the salon. Maj teased her about moving fast but Sharon just shrugged and said, 'I'm thirty-two – what am I waiting for?'

James and I crab-walk along the side of an ice-cream van pumping out the 99s and head for the VIP section, which is really just a raised platform guarded by Tessie Daly in a high-vis vest. Already the crowds are clamouring for the attention of guest-of-honour Devon Dempsey, who was recently featured bouncing on a trampoline in a Bord Bia ad. He's only five but was just brilliant on that trampoline – a real star. He's waving from the platform and posing for snaps and I debate for a second making an excuse and sloping away so James and I won't be on display for the whole town, but Tessie catches sight of me and roars my name.

'Hiya, Tessie,' I call up to her over the din and the music. Jesus, she has a clipboard and all. I go to inch past her up the steps and she stops me.

'Name?'

'Tessie. It's me, Aisling. You've just called me over. And you've known me since I was born.'

'Security is very tight here today, Aisling. Now, name?'

James stifles a laugh and she glares at him as I sigh. 'It's Aisling.'

She studiously runs her finger down the list. It's a small platform. The list can't be that long.

'Ah yes, here we are. Aisling, plus one. Off you go.'

James flashes her a smile as we push past and she visibly swoons. 'Tell your mother I'll be in this evening to collect my loaf tins, good girl,' she calls after me hoarsely.

Mercifully, the seats on the platforms are in rows, and I resist the urge to rush Devon for a selfie and instead pull James onto a fold-out chair at the back. All the other local VIPs are on the platform, including Marty Boland, the town's prize-winning butcher and Carol's bully ex. I try to catch his eye to give him a filthy look but he avoids my gaze. Skippy Boland from Solas FM is there too and Imelda Patricks, winner of this year's Pride of BGB. Her talent was playing 'Riverdance' on the glockenspiel and it went briefly viral on YouTube.

'What would it be like if they'd actually won?' James asks in an amused tone, resting his hand lightly on my knee.

'Honestly, I don't want to even think about it. Carnage.'

'There's been so many kids around all day. They didn't …?'

'Oh, they did. They closed the school.'

He chuckles. 'I mean, I'm not complaining – I can think of worse ways to spend a Monday evening. But it's just a bit … mad.'

'Do you not have community spirit over in England?' I ask, genuinely interested.

James and I haven't talked a huge amount about his background because there just doesn't seem to be much point, and he doesn't offer a lot of information. I know he's in the building trade, obviously, and it's a big-bucks family business. But other than that he's a bit of a closed book.

'Of course we have community spirit,' he retorts, slightly indignant. 'Buckleton's annual village fête is always very well attended. It's the highlight of the cricket club's social calendar, and the cricket club is Dad's pride and joy!'

'Buckleton sounds like a name you made up,' I tease.

'You're one to talk. Ballygobbard. BallyGoBackwards, BGB.' He elbows me in the ribs and I have to nod and concede that he has a point.

'Okay, so what's Buckleton like then? Do you have your own town pump? Is there a Mad Tom?' I jerk my head towards our own Tom, who has now scaled Marty Boland's butcher's shop and is threatening to stage-dive from the roof into the assembled roaring crowd, a can of Guinness in each hand. Marty, true to form, is puce with rage, shouting at him to get down.

James regards all this with amusement and says thoughtfully, 'I don't know that we have a Mad Tom, but there is a village green and a school and I believe Mrs Simmons still runs the post office.'

'And what happens at the village fête?'

'Well, I haven't been in a few years, but I'm guessing they still have the Morris dancing, a tombola, cream tea, that sort of thing. All very civilised.'

Cream tea sounds like something I'd be very interested in, to be fair. The rest sounds straight out of an Enid Blyton book. 'And what was school in Buckleton like?'

James shifts in his seat. 'I didn't go to school in Buckleton.'

I know James went to boarding school as a teenager because his brother Harry was in the same class as Ben Hatton, brother of Niamh Hatton and member of the overbearing Protestant family who have lived across the road from us all my life. Niamh from Across the Road has been a source of great envy and pain-in-the-arsery since childhood. I was never more envious than when Niamh got a Chernobyl child when we were fourteen. Sent from the Ukraine for a summer's worth of Irish fresh air, Natasia's arrival was truly the most glamorous thing to ever happen in BGB. They used to say that the months spent in Ireland would add another ten years onto their lives, and Natasia is a pilot now and looks like a model so I think we can definitely take credit for some of that. And, of course, the world is so small that Harry Matthews is now going out with Natasia.

'Primary school, though? Did you not go to primary school in Buckleton?'

James just shakes his head and squints into the low evening sun. 'They must be nearly here, surely?'

His clenched jaw makes it fairly clear that he has no interest in talking about it any more, and I drop my next planned line of questioning about his Irish granny – I know for a fact his mother's mother was born in Dublin. Luckily I don't need a new topic of conversation because there's an ear-splitting honk and a Ballygobbard Agri-Sales lorry comes into view around the corner. 'The Boys Are Back in Town' is blaring from its speakers and the crowd goes absolutely wild as the lorry snakes its way up Main Street. The boys are indeed back in town, and I can't help myself: I jump to my feet and push to the front of the platform, jostling with Devon Dempsey for space, the little shite. The lorry comes to a standstill right in front of the platform, with the six BGB and Knock players and their WAGs on the exposed trailer at the back, egged on by the crowd, jumping up and down and spraying cans of Budweiser at each other. All that's missing, genuinely, is the trophy.

John is up there among them too, looking proud as punch in his snazzy county zip-up. 'Put 'Em Under Pressure' blares out over the speakers. It's the wrong sport and the wrong decade but nothing gets a crowd going like an Italia '90 anthem. James looks on in bemusement as the crowd roars along – 'Olé olé olé olé, olé, óle. We're all part of Johnny's army.' With that, John is shoved to the front of the gang on the lorry and jostled by the players. You'd swear he was the county manager, such is the reverence they show him. I feel a swell of pride for him. His commitment to training with the Rangers was sometimes an issue in the eight years we were together but look how it paid off for him. He helped pick a team that got to an All-Ireland final and even got to put some of his friends on the pitch too. What a moment for him.

Just then, Knock Rangers' centre forward, Baby Chief Gittons, catches my eye and gives me a little wave. We're almost level, him on the lorry, me on the platform. Without warning, he bends down and hops off the lorry bed. He runs over to the platform and calls up to me. 'You should be up here with us!' His face is flushed with excitement and probably a few pints. He gives James a half-wave. 'Sorry to interrupt ye but ...' He turns back to me. 'You should be up here with us, Missus BallyGoBrunch.' He gestures at his jersey. 'Hup now.'

Me? On the lorry? Christ, no. I'd never be able to scale it. 'Ah no, Baby Chief, I couldn't –'

'Mon outta that, Ais. Get up there!'

The lads on the truck behind him catch wind of what he's at and start shouting my name and waving me on. I look down at Baby Chief's face again and, with the gin inside me and the excitement of the occasion, I turn to James and pull an 'I'm sorry' face, and he just points me towards the platform steps and says, 'Have fun.' I jog down the steps, past Tessie Daly, and duck under the cordon along the side of Main Street just as she clocks me.

'*Security breach!*' she roars to nobody in particular, and then calls after me, 'Don't forget about the loaf tins.'

Baby Chief has already clambered back up onto the lorry, and he instructs me to put my foot on the back tyre so he and fellow Rangers player Titch Maguire can haul me up. Not my most graceful moment, and I wonder just how many people on the viewing platform catch a glimpse of my knickers. John helps me to my feet and we stand awkwardly together for a second until he turns around and pulls Megan through the gaggle on the lorry towards him. She lifts her hand shyly at me and I mouth 'Hiya' back and the lorry lurches forward and I catch sight of James just before he moves out of view. Titch hands me a plastic cup of something and roars, '*Wave!*' And so I wave.

****

Half an hour and a pint and a half of fizzy wine later my ears are ringing as I wait my turn to exit the back of the lorry, arms sore from waving and feeling like maybe *I* played in Croke Park yesterday. A hand comes up to help me down and it's John's. I take it and give him a warm smile. 'That was some craic. Thanks a million.'

'Ah, thank *you*, Aisling. We couldn't have done any of it without you, sure.'

And he's reaching up again and manoeuvring me out of the way and Megan hops down behind me. He slings an arm around her shoulders and she gives a wave and they head towards Maguire's.

I reach into my bag and pull out my phone, suddenly exhausted by the emotions of the day, the hectic past few weeks at BallyGoBrunch, and the late nights at James's. There's a text from him to say he's gone home and to join him if I fancy it. There's a photo from Majella from inside Maguire's. Pablo's wearing a sombrero in the county colours and Sharon is dancing on a chair. I debate following John and Megan in. I debate going to James's. But, really, I just want a bit of peace and quiet so I go home, to my own single bed.

CHAPTER 4

The following night Mammy is sitting at the kitchen table with a fresh blow-dry, wearing a new blouse I'm pretty sure is straight out of the window of Geraldine's Boutique. I'm immediately suspicious, especially as she's been so busy with the eco farm and has barely even brushed her hair in the past few weeks. Mammy and Constance Swinford, formerly of the Garbally Stud, have gone into business together, turning a large part of our family farm into a modern petting-zoo-cum-boutique-campsite complete with farm shop that sells everything from jam to fresh-pressed apple juice to beeswax candles. Heavy on the notions. They're currently in tortuous negotiations with an unreliable Mongolian yurt consultant who's dragging his heels on delivery. Constance is like a force of nature; she ran the stud for years after her husband died and up until she and Mammy got thick as thieves was known as 'The Posho' in our house. Now, Constance has sold the stud and she and Mammy are rejecting retirement to welcome tourists and hen parties and school tours to stay in their yurts and pet their piglets and sample their farm produce. More power to them.

'Are you going somewhere after, Mammy?'

'God, no, love. Where would I be going at nine at night on a Tuesday?' She holds up a beslippered foot to prove her point as I flick on the kettle.

I'm still feeling fragile from yesterday's celebrations and have a light dose of The Fear, even after slipping off so early. Not everyone-hates-me levels, more a vague feeling of dread that even two sausage baps and a bag of twice-cooked crisps earlier couldn't help me shake. It's not an unfamiliar feeling. Sometimes you just can't put your finger on it.

'It's just … you look very done-up to talk to Paul. That's all.'

My younger brother has been living Down Under for a couple of years now. Although he Skypes regularly, this is the first time I've seen her get dressed up for the occasion.

'Aisling, he's met someone!' she says, looking positively giddy. 'He said she might be there the next time he Skypes.'

So that explains the sweep of green eyeshadow and the fact that Mammy appears to have dusted the entire kitchen. It's big news, to be fair.

'Have you the computer on?' I say with a sigh.

It's alarming the number of times she's told me Paul can't get through to her on the Skype and I've found her looking at an inky black screen like she's staring into the abyss.

'I do,' she huffs. 'Haven't Tessie and myself started a new course over in Knock Town Hall? Introduction to Computers. Although, I told Tessie I already know as much as I want to about those yokes, but she gets a discount if she brings another person so muggins here was drafted in.'

Even I have to admit that the older I get the more baffled I am by computers and the like. It took me a good week to get the hang of the little card reader I had to buy for the café, and the teenager in the shop specifically told me it was 'idiot proof' (his words). I can't imagine what I'm going to be like at Mammy's age. Oh, to be a fly on the wall at Introduction to Computers when the instructor tries to explain the difference between Wi-Fi and Google, but I suppose I should be supportive.

'Fair dues, Mammy. I'm sure it will come in handy with the business.'

I'm about to ask her if there might be a free spot in the class when the familiar *bing-be-boo-bom-bom* tone of an incoming call makes the pair of us jump and That Bloody Cat screeches across the room and out the door like greased lightning. I hit Accept and watch as Paul's big dopey head fills the screen. Then I adjust our camera so he can see us and not just the bockety ceiling light.

'G'day, lads,' he says, waving around a fork with a piece of black pudding hanging perilously from it. 'What's the craic?'

'Hiya, pet,' Mammy says with a wave. 'Is it just yourself? I was hoping ...'

Paul smiles. 'It's not, actually. I have someone here that I'd like you both to meet.'

Mammy gasps and instinctively places her hand on my forearm to steady herself. She was worried Paul would never find love again after he had a bad break-up with the left back from the BGB Gaels camogie team a few years ago. I did suspect there was a Sheila on the scene, especially after his weekly WhatsApps about how to cook steak (seven minutes each side, just to be safe) had started to taper off. But I didn't think it was serious enough to be introducing her to the family.

He looks off to the side of the screen and starts beckoning frantically. Mammy's grip on my arm increases to the point where I have to pry her fingers out of my flesh.

'Mammy, Aisling, this is Hannah,' he says proudly, moving up on the couch and patting the empty cushion beside him. Hannah, a little slip of a thing with long curly blonde hair, sidles on to the screen and waves like a deer caught in headlights. She looks a bit like Kylie in her heyday, minus the gold hot pants.

'Hannah!' Mammy screeches. 'Paul has told me so much about you! I'm so delighted to finally set eyes on you, love.'

Paul has always been her favourite – she lets him ring the landline and reverse the charges sometimes. They've obviously been chatting about his love life on the sly.

'Hiya, Hannah,' I say, raising my mug of tea at the camera. 'And sorry for your troubles.' I wink at Paul so he knows I'm only messing. He's not a bad brother, to be fair to him, and I know heading back to Oz after our first Christmas without Daddy last year was hard on him. Of course, he has the GAA club to keep his spirits up, and if Facebook is to be believed, himself and the lads from BGB over there with him are taking their continued mission to drink the Irish pubs around Melbourne out of Bulmers as seriously as ever, so I can't let him off too easily. Hannah laughs nervously.

'So where did you two meet?' I ask.

'Hannah manages the Tricolour around the corner. It's kind of like our sitting room.'

'Paul got five numbers in the pub lottery. I had to ring and tell him he'd won himself twelve pounds of Clonakilty Black Pudding. He was delighted,' Hannah explains in an unmistakable Cork accent. Mad – I had her pegged as an

Aussie. She could easily pass for one with that healthy glow and the big white teeth.

'Talk about my dream woman.' Paul throws his arm around her shoulders. 'We've been together ever since.'

'Ah, isn't that lovely.' Mammy beams. 'Isn't it, Aisling? Like something out of a film.'

'It is,' I say. 'And you're from Cork, is that right, Hannah?'

'I am,' she says. 'Cork city. The true capital!'

Oh, here we go. I've only really been pally with a few people from Cork – two of the receptionists when I first started at PensionsPlus, and a cousin from Bantry I met at Martina Cloghessy's hen who was able to mould a penis out of Play-Doh with her eyes closed – and they were all pure obsessed with the place. I thought nobody could love their county more than me but I was wrong.

'A beautiful part of the country,' Mammy says with a smile. 'Maybe we'll get a chance to go down there sometime –'

I tap her bare ankle with my foot to cut her off. Christ, they've only been going out a couple of months and she's already angling to meet Hannah's family.

'Have you been in Australia long, Hannah?' I say, changing the subject.

'Coming up to a year now. I'll have to head off and do six months of regional work soon, but it should be good craic. Me and the girls are going to rent a camper van. Some of them are already panicking about not being able to bring their straighteners.'

I notice a shadow passing over Paul's face and I'm surprised. He knows the rules with the visa – he did fruit picking himself. He's obviously head over heels.

'Maybe I'll convince Philser and the lads to go too.' He laughs. 'Be nice to get out of the city once it gets hot.'

'Paul, you're only in the new house a few months,' Mammy says. 'And didn't you sign a year-long lease? I don't want you to go losing my deposit, now.'

'I won't, I won't,' he says. 'It was just an idea. I'd be mad to leave the promotions company, anyway. We'll be flat out at events once summer comes.'

Paul's main source of income has been dressing up in a Mr Tayto costume handing out bags of crisps. The Ozzies are, by all accounts, gone mad for the stuff, and his authentic Irish accent is a big draw. Myself and Majella are counting down the days till Alf Stewart appears in the Summer Bay bait shop with a bag of cheese and onion.

'I suppose you heard all about the big homecoming yesterday, did you?' I say.

'Jesus, yeah.' Paul picks up Hannah's hand. 'This one had to talk me out of booking a ticket home for it. John said at one stage Mikey Maguire was letting people pull their own pints.'

'When were you talking to John?'

'Last night. God knows what time it was there – he was well on.'

'What did he want?'

'Not much. He rings the odd time.'

'I didn't know that.'

'You two were going out for, like, forever, Ais. Ye might have called it a day but myself and himself are still friends.'

'Hannah, John was Aisling's ex-boyfriend,' Mammy says quietly by way of explanation. 'A local lad. Centre forward on the hurling team.' And then she lowers her voice a whisker. 'You'd miss him around the place.'

I shoot her a look but Paul keeps talking. 'He said he's giving up the selector job? One season was enough and he has work and the girlfriend to factor in.'

'Ah, that's a shame,' Mammy says.

That's the first I've heard of it. It's weird to be getting information about John second hand from Paul like this, and from the literal other side of the world. I'm not sure how it makes me feel. Jealous, a bit. His stories aren't my stories any more, though. That's life, I suppose.

'Are your parents missing you, Hannah?' Mammy interrupts.

Hannah and Paul exchange a sad smile. 'Well, my dad died six years ago this July, so it's just my younger sister and my mam.'

'I'm sorry to hear that, love,' Mammy says gently.

'Cancer,' Hannah replies and we all just nod silently.

Then Mammy gets her second wind. 'It's an awful thing. God love you all. Tell me, how hot is it at the moment? You're making sure to wear factor every day, aren't you, Paul? Even when it's cloudy?'

Mammy's obsession with the Australian weather continues. She's forever looking up the UV index and emailing Paul articles about the danger of skin cancer. She's convinced he's living in an oven, even though I've tried to explain that the climate in Melbourne isn't *that* extreme.

Paul reassures her that he's an adult and has figured out how to work a hat, and then Mammy launches into a barrage of updates about the yurts and the new beehives and how

Constance Swinford is training as a yoga teacher so they can offer retreats and how all the stretching and bending has done wonders for her arthritis. Before we know it, we've been talking for an hour and it's time for Paul to transform into Mr Tayto and head off to work.

Once we say our goodbyes and the laptop is securely closed, I turn to Mammy. 'It's nice to see him in such good form, anyway.'

'I'm made up for him, Aisling. She seems like a lovely girl, and the head of hair on her too. I haven't seen him this happy in ages. Long may it last.'

Mammy takes off upstairs and I sit in the silence for a while, thinking about Paul's big smiley face. It's a mighty feeling, that rush when you first meet someone. Like there could be an apocalypse happening around you and only the two of you would survive in your love cocoon with your tins of soup and what have you. I think of James and feel a pang of guilt for leaving him last night, especially after he texted me three times today. I've definitely enjoyed being in the cocoon with him this past while. I make myself really sit with the thought for a while. How will I feel when the bubble is burst and he's gone? I think one of my favourite inspirational-quote accounts was giving me a sign earlier when I was scrolling through Instagram on my brief lunch at BallyGoBrunch. It said something like 'You need to let one summer and one winter pass before you let love in again'. It spoke to me. The bubble will burst, and I'll let it. I just don't think I'm quite ready to let it in yet.

CHAPTER 5

I have a standing appointment with Sharon in Strong Stuff for a blow-dry every Saturday morning. It's the most glamorous thing I've ever done. Me! A standing appointment! Even though Saturday is BallyGoBrunch's second-busiest morning (we can barely keep up with the demand for sausages and potato farls on a Sunday), Carol insists that she can manage with the extra help from our part-time waitress, Paula, and Karla's extremely capable people-herding skills.

It was always my dream to be pally with a hairdresser, to walk into a salon and for everyone to know my name instead of looking me up and down and then trying to sell me a €30 bottle of shampoo. And, sure, you can't say no after they shame you about your split ends.

No, Sharon's approach is much more relaxed. She has no problem with my devotion to Herbal Essences as long as I let her put in some kind of conditioning masque once a month. She's also opened my eyes to the wonders of a good wax down below, so, really, coming in for a blow-dry once a week is the least I can do.

'Hiya, Aisling. Sharon is just finishing up with a client in one of the treatment rooms. She'll be about ten minutes.'

Caitriona, one of the young Ó Súilleabháin twins, is manning the reception desk wearing something with fishnet sleeves and looking like she could pop into a nightclub at any minute. It's hard to believe we survived without a beauty salon in Ballygobbard for so long. Between hair, waxing, tanning and nails, Sharon now has three employees and is tipping along nicely.

'No problem, Caitriona,' I say, helping myself to some magazines and waving hello at Deirdre Ruane who's getting her upper lip waxed across the room.

'Actually, some of those are a bit old,' Caitriona says with a smile, taking a stack from one of the hair stations and passing them to me. 'These are all this week's. Now, it's Slimline milk and two sugars, right?'

'That's right.' I nod happily. Sharon also offers tea and coffee with a Lindor on the side. (Two Weight Watchers Points each – I looked it up the second she told me she was getting them in. She wasn't a bit interested but it might be vital information for some of her clients.) She also does Prosecco after four at weekends. Truly a class act.

I'm flicking through Dáithí Ó Sé's holiday pictures in *RSVP* magazine – Dáithí on a boat wearing a captain's hat, Dáithí in chinos leaning against a Vespa, Dáithí looking wistful at sunset – when Caitriona interrupts with my cuppa.

'Ooh, have you seen who Emilia Coburn is going out with? I nearly choked on my Lindor.' Sharon did mention she's haemorrhaging Lindors alright.

Emilia Coburn's granny was from BGB. Well, if you're talking to someone from Knocknamanagh they'd tell you she was from Knock. The truth is, the farm Kitty Coburn owned before she died straddles both townlands. But the actual *house* is definitely on the BGB side, so we've claimed her. They might have two ATMs and the new cinema, but we'll always have Kitty Coburn. Long story short, Emilia used to come here on her summer holidays as a child and now she's one of the world's hottest actresses after popping up in the new *Star Wars*. She's hounded by paparazzi and is rumoured to be a shoo-in for an Oscar next year for some period drama she's in with Keira Knightley. The whole village is very proud, despite the fact no one really remembers her. Everyone still has an Emilia story, though, and it remains the most exciting thing to have happened to the parish since Mad Tom went viral for mowing the word 'shite' into a hay field and it was picked up in a satellite photograph and printed in the *Bangkok Post*.

Caitriona takes the magazine from my hands and deftly flicks to a page that contains a handful of incredibly grainy photographs. It's hard to make out what exactly is going on in them, but if the captions are to be believed, it's Emilia canoodling in a French hotel swimming pool with Ben Dixon. As in, Ben Dixon the new James Bond!

'Ben Dixon!' Caitriona squeals, jabbing at the pics with a pink ombre jewel-encrusted nail. For all intents and purposes, the blob in the picture looks like a Friesian calf but I know *RSVP* wouldn't lie to us.

'Can you believe it?' Sharon teeters across the salon in her signature six-inch heels and draws me in for a hug. 'I'm shaking, hun. Apparently they've been together on the sly for months. Ben Dixon knows we exist!'

Sharon is originally from Waterford but since opening Strong Stuff has taken to being a BGB local like a duck to water. Next thing she'll be on the county council.

'Fair dues to Emilia, all right,' I say. 'I didn't even know himself and Ariana Grande were over.'

'Oh, that was ages ago,' Sharon says, holding the magazine under a light and studying it carefully. 'Jesus, the arse on him. He's unreal in those swimming shorts – you can tell he does all his own stunts.'

'Er, hello?' Caitriona goes, raising her eyebrows. 'What about Cyclops?'

At the mention of his name, Sharon smiles. After everything she went through with her ex, Frankie, it's been pure life-affirming to see how Cyclops worships the ground she walks on. And if her unbroken record for attending Rangers matches is anything to go by, the feeling is mutual.

'You can tell your brother that if Ben Dixon ever shows up in BGB he might have some competition,' she says with a smirk.

Caitriona laughs. 'Another Lindor, Ais?'

****

Three hours later I'm pulling in to the BallyGoBrunch car park, admiring my curly blow-dry in the rearview mirror – Sharon always gets a great bounce into it – and I'm surprised to see James's jeep parked in its usual spot. When I left him this morning, he said he'd probably be working late but I could call over tonight if I wanted. A booty call, Majella's waggling eyebrows would call that. And, sure, why not? Carpe diem – isn't that what Sharon's wrist tattoo says? I've decided to enjoy him while he's still here, even though his revelation last night that he's never buttered a Marietta biscuit had me truly shook. He's never even heard of a Marietta biscuit! I've been keeping a little mental tally of reasons why we would never work to make things easier when he goes, and that definitely went on the list.

The jeep door swings open and his tall frame emerges.

'Hello, stranger,' he says as I open my car door.

I can barely meet his eye. He was only kissing me goodbye a few hours ago. 'You're finished early.'

'A few of the lads have been struck down with man flu so I decided we should all call it quits. We're already a good bit behind on the landscaping and paths – what's an extra day or two?'

His brown curls are shining in the sunlight, and I'm delighted my hair is looking so well, I must say. And I have on my CC cream, which is a new thing Sadhbh sent me. Tinted moisturiser I'd have called it, but what do I know.

'Do you want to …?' He nods his head in the direction of the apartment entrance, around the side of BallyGoBrunch's main door.

'Ah no, I'm just dropping a few things off and then I've to go up to the New Graveyard and do Daddy's grave.'

Mammy is tied up viewing a timber climbing frame in the shape of a combine harvester for the eco farm's all-weather playground, so I've been dispatched with hoes and planters and strict instructions to shine the headstone until I can see my face in it.

'Oh?' He looks confused.

I haven't said much to James about Daddy, apart from the obvious. I might start crying and there's just no need for that.

Best to keep my emotions in check. I don't want any rivulets down my CC cream.

'Do … what to his grave, exactly?'

'Clean it up. It has to look its best for the Blessing of the Graves.' I was already forced to explain the Leaving Cert results mass, the Blessing of the Schoolbags and the Prayers for the New Succulents House in Knocknamanagh Garden Centre after James got hold of the parish newsletter and had a few questions. He still looks a little perplexed, though. 'It's on next weekend. There's an open-air mass and the whole village will be there. Sure, everyone has *someone* who's dead. Competition is fierce around here when it comes to grave maintenance.'

'Oh, I see. Important work then!' I can't tell if he's amused or not. Grave pride is no laughing matter. 'Well, I'm not doing anything – let me help. I'll bring a few tools.'

He already has the boot of the jeep open and is transferring a shovel and some gloves into the boot of the Micra before I can object. It feels a bit intimate or something to be bringing him to see Daddy, but I'm just too tired to put up a fight – I was on my feet for about twelve hours yesterday after Karla got a bit of chilli in her eye and had to go home early. The perils of spice.

James folds himself into the passenger seat of the Micra and I head out of the car park and turn left, away from BGB and towards the graveyard. I always get a lump in my throat on this drive, thinking about the same journey we took two years ago. It's a short trip but already silence has filled the tiny car, and it feels a little claustrophobic. What do you talk about to the man you fancy and are sharing a bed with and who is very nice to you but is leaving town in a few weeks, when you're on your way to clean your dead father's headstone? I'm not sure Colette Green, or anyone else for that matter, has any advice for this specific problem.

I reach for the radio dial, and James pipes up. 'Was he religious then, your dad?'

I think for a second, surprised at how delighted I am to be asked about Daddy. With every day that passes I feel like he's thought about and talked about less and less. 'Not especially, no,' I admit.

'Oh.' I can tell by that 'oh' that James is slightly confused. I wouldn't blame him, really, what with this preparation for the Blessing of the Graves.

'But he went to mass sometimes and I think he had some faith. And so does Mammy. And so do I, maybe. I don't know.'

'Okay. Sounds fair.'

Silence again. And I've never met a break in conversation I didn't feel the need to fill.

'Are your family religious?' I ask James, aware once more of how little I know about them and how little he mentions them.

He looks out the window and shrugs. 'No.'

'Oh.'

'I mean, I had to go to church at school, but my parents weren't into it or anything. They ...' He trails off and I lean forward slightly, willing him to say a bit more. Instead, he points at the sign as I slow for the turn. 'Why is it called the New Graveyard? I got the latest parish newsletter in my letterbox and it said it's celebrating thirty years this year.'

I'm frustrated by the change of subject. There are things about James that confound me and block him off from me – not just his fancy accent and the way he pronounces 'scone' and the Marietta-biscuit revelation, but also this reluctance he seems to have to tell me anything about himself when he knows so much about me. I really just don't know him at all.

'The New Graveyard name just stuck,' I say.

'So where's the old graveyard then?'

'There isn't one. There's just one graveyard. Before this, everyone was buried in Knock.'

'What would happen if I just called it "the graveyard"?' He's smiling now.

'Well, I suppose nobody would know what you were talking about.' I smile back as I pull into the car park.

****

There's already a swarm of people in the graveyard with wheelbarrows and bags of manure and watering cans, flat out. And is that …? It can't be … Yes, that's Attracta Boyne with a power washer. Her poor husband is about to be blasted to kingdom come, God rest him.

James is packing the trowels and compost and cleaning materials from the boot into the big blue IKEA bag I brought for this very purpose. You'd nearly make the trek to IKEA just to get the bag. So versatile.

Daddy is buried on the newer side of the New Graveyard so it's not too tightly packed. There's a lovely tree bending over his grave and it's looking in good shape. Mammy comes regularly enough to pick out any weeds that would dare to show their faces. It needs a few new bedding plants and a good wipe down, though. I lead James towards it along the criss-crossing paths between the plots, pointing out any of particular interest.

'That's Shamey Filan. He was the first man to have a mobile phone in BGB. Oh, and that's Maureen Kelly. Killed by a donkey.'

We reach Daddy's grave and James takes in the granite headstone silently. 'He was young,' he says then, quietly.

'He was.'

We stand there for about thirty seconds and I can tell James doesn't want to move until I do, so I instruct him to put the bag down on the path and I start unpacking my bits. James does as he's told but then stands there a bit uselessly, which is odd for a man who is usually so capable.

'You could wipe the bird shite off the back of the headstone, maybe? The tree looks lovely but it does have its downsides.'

I hand him a soft cloth and the special cleaning mix William Foley, who helps Mammy on the farm, made up for me. I didn't ask what's in it but he did say it would take the paint off the car so I instruct James to put the gloves on too. He looks grateful to have a job and sets to work. I start pulling out the few weeds that have escaped Mammy's eagle eye and make some little hollows for new plants. I'm not green fingered and it's always been a great trial to me. I can't even make a poinsettia last to New Year's Day. Hopefully these pansies will take.

It's quiet, awkwardly quiet, despite the busyness of the graveyard. The sound of Attracta's power washer is far enough away to be just background noise. I feel like James is gearing up to break the silence but he doesn't know what to say.

'Hiya.'

Another awkward voice breaks it for him. A voice I know well. I spin around. 'Hiya, John.'

He smiles and nods at our equipment, lifting up the watering can in his own hand.

'Doing the grave?' I ask him,

'Yeah, I'm just giving Mam a hand.' He jerks his head in the direction of the older section of the graveyard where his mother, Fran, is giving Attracta evils. 'Getting some water from the tap. For the flowers. Obviously …' He trails off. Jesus, this is painful.

'How are you doing, mate?' James takes off a glove and holds a hand out to John, who has to switch the watering can to shake it. What is it about men shaking hands? They must have done it back when they were in the caves or something. It's so primal.

'Good, man. Not bad at all.' John scuffs his feet on the ground, and a three-second silence hangs in the air like three centuries.

'Just home for the weekend, are you?' My insides recoil as soon as the words are out of my mouth. He comes home every weekend, Aisling, you enormous clod. He's come home every weekend for the last ten years since he moved to Dublin. Fran would go through him if he missed mass.

'Ah yeah. Bit of training. Mass. You know yourself.' He has the good grace to humour me.

'Paul was saying you're finishing up with the county team already.'

John's eyes flick downwards. 'Yeah, I am. I was spending all my time driving between Dublin and here. I was wrecked from it all.'

'Oh. That's a shame. How's work going?'

'Grand. Busy. We have a new microchip coming out in the New Year so it's fairly manic. You remember what it was like the last time,' he says with a smile.

I do. It was about four years ago. He worked twelve-hour days for six months with the rest of the team to get it done, and when the company turned a seventy-billion-dollar profit, all they got was a bag of fudge each and two extra days' holidays. John was livid but I enjoyed it. Fudge is very underrated, and we went away to a hotel in Longford with a hot tub.

James is still just standing there. It's so excruciating that I silently pray for the ground to open up and swallow me, but there's no such thing as a free burial in BGB. Father Fenlon expects a generous donation to the parish development fund or he'll mention you're stingy from the pulpit.

'Megan must be delighted you'll be around more, so.' I don't know why I feel the need to bring her up, but I do. Just to keep her very real.

'Ah yeah, she's happy out. She'll be down later – sure, you might see her if you're out.' He nods first towards me and then James. God, imagine the four of us out together. My toes curl at the thought.

James's phone goes in his pocket, saving him from standing there like a spare. 'Pardon me.' He looks at the screen, frowns and strides four or five graves away to answer.

'Are you–?'

'Have you–?'

John and I start talking at the same time, coming up with more idle chit-chat in an effort to bring this painful interaction to a close. We laugh, and suddenly it's nice.

He tries again. 'How's the café going?'

'Yeah, great. Business is definitely up since the final. The BallyGoBrunch jerseys really did the trick.'

'Jooo-ohn.'

Fran's shrill voice frightens the bejaysus out of me as she marches up the graveyard path behind me. I notice her taking in James but it doesn't break her stride. I was in her good books for so long. I bought so many of her Mother's Day and Christmas presents. I think I bought that scarf she's wearing, actually. When in doubt, a floaty scarf in neutral colours will always save the day. Or a Clarins hand cream. Fran's a nurse so I was always buying her notiony creams to save her dry hands from the constant washing. She's a terrifying nurse, I'd say. Rumour has it she once ran four men who dared to sit down in the waiting room of the maternity wing. Ran them out of the hospital completely. They probably didn't even dare to come back for the births. She's mad about God too, and scandalised by me, no doubt. Here I am with the English fella in the paint-stained trousers doing Daddy's grave. I feel ashamed and I don't even know why. I feel like a stranger to her.

'John, will you get a move on? Hello, Aisling. How's your mother?'

'She's great, thanks, Fran. And how's yours?'

I nearly get sick as soon as the words fall out of my mouth. Sure aren't we only standing 20 feet from where her mother is buried? My eyes flick up to John's face and I can tell he's struggling to keep from smiling. I'm reminded of the time I accidentally called her shepherd's pie 'dry', thinking it was one she'd bought ready-made in Tesco. Fran's eyes narrow but she doesn't acknowledge it.

'The watering can, John?' she directs him, and he passes it to her before she strides off.

'I'd better go and give her a hand,' he says, a cheeky smile breaking out as soon as her back is turned.

'Tell her I said sorry, will you? I forgot. Christ. And stop smiling!'

'I'll tell Granny you're sorry too, will I?' And he laughs and I can't help joining him. His granny was even more terrifying than Fran.

John waves to catch James's attention and bids me a 'bye' as he heads off back towards his granny's grave. James looks frustrated and barely acknowledges it. I've never really seen him looking cross, I realise. He's been pacing while he's been on the phone and is too far away for me to hear what he's saying, but he looks thick as a bull. I tear my eyes away from him. None of my business, really. I take a deep breath to dispel the laugh that's still inside me after the Fran fiasco and get out the scrubbing brush and start working my way around the letters of Daddy's name, clearing out the tiny bits of moss and dirt that have made their home in the crevices. It's soothing. I kind of forget where I am and get a fierce fright when James's voice suddenly booms beside me.

'You're doing fine work there.' He sighs deeply, shoving the phone into one of his many pockets.

'Is everything okay, James?' He looks like everything is far from okay.

'Yeah, it was just Cel– my mum,' he says awkwardly before rearranging his face and saying a bit more brightly, 'being a mum. Am I wearing a coat – that sort of thing. You know mums.'

I do. I bloody do.

CHAPTER 6

I'm sitting in my little office in BallyGoBrunch looking at the growing list of catering orders for next week and trying to make space from nothing on my desk when I hear the familiar *rat-a-tat-tat* of a key against the window. I know before I even look that it's Majella, and I'm glad of the distraction. The workload is getting on top of me this week, even though I'm now setting my alarm for 5.30 every morning. I'm loathe to turn anything down in case our customers start going elsewhere. It doesn't help that I've spent every evening since Majella broke the news about the wedding date working on ideas for the hen party. Sometimes I wish there was another bridesmaid to delegate to, but I suppose I'll be glad it's just me when there's no one to compare myself to in the pictures. And Maj has her own problems too, of course. It's a tight squeeze upstairs in the apartment, especially the way Willy the Jack Russell marks his territory, so she's taken to coming down to me of an evening for a bit of a breather and to reel off the day's complaints.

I nip out and open the back door. She's got an open box of Black Magic – the lowest form of chocolate – in her hands and her mouth is full.

'That bad?' I go, stepping back to let her in.

'Um muum mmumfh fummh fummf, fummf.'

'Come again, Maj?'

'I'm fit to be tied, bird,' she says with a gulp. 'Mammy and Daddy were supposed to be heading into Maguire's for a drink tonight to give us a bit of space, but Daddy's refusing to go now because the bloody *Late Late Show* country-music special is on. Pab cried. He actually cried. Now he won't come out of the en suite. Fuck Philomena Begley anyway.'

'Ah no. Ah God, that's very annoying.'

She stuffs in another chocolate – one of the coffee ones, I think. Things must be very bad. She turns and looks me in the eye.

'I bet you and James are still riding every night, are you?'

'Maj!' She's always fairly forthright, to be fair, but she could at least have bought me a drink first. I did drunkenly tell her when James and I first got together that things were pretty hot and heavy, and she's been gently slagging me about it ever since. Now, though, she looks distraught.

'Well, I mean … I suppose …' The truth is, we can't keep our hands off each other. He told me yesterday that he's booked his flight home for next weekend. While there's part of me that's looking forward to the clean break, I know I'm going to miss him and we're clinging onto that last bit of us 'together'. Maybe I'll throw Maj a few details. She'd love that. 'We're actually –'

'Pablo's gone fierce shy, bedroom-wise,' she interrupts, sitting down. 'Between sharing that tiny flat with my family and his mother in his ear from Tenerife twice a week about saving himself for marriage, he's being impossible. Once the sex dries up, you know, it's the death knell.'

Poor Mrs Pablo. If she thinks Pablo has been saving himself for marriage she's got another thing coming.

'Maybe he just doesn't fancy me any more.' She looks dejected and slides down in her seat a bit, grabbing another chocolate indiscriminately. She's not even looking at the menu!

'Of course he fancies you – I've never seen anyone more mad about someone. Doesn't he get up every morning and cycle after the bus for a mile to see you off to work? It's the thin walls that are the problem, not your relationship.'

Truth be told, half the town thinks Pablo's a few bananas short of a bunch, but he's just bananas for Majella.

She shrugs and reaches for the sweets again, but her face does brighten a bit. She pushes the box in my direction. 'Will you have one?'

I actually retch. I can't help it. Nibbling on dark chocolate is supposed to cure cancer and make the weight fall off you, but I'd rather die, to be honest. Weight Watchers Maura was always telling me to have just two squares to ward off sugar cravings, but two squares of dark chocolate are not a patch on a Snickers, Maura, and you're only fooling yourself if you genuinely believe that.

'You work away there. How was school today?' I enquire.

'Not too bad today, actually. There's a kind of turf war happening with some of the third class boys. They were going at each other like something out of *Love/Hate* in the yard, but I managed to disperse them with a water gun. It's nice to feel like I'm making a difference.'

I'm not sure what the Board of Management would make of her technique but I say nothing.

'Well, listen, now that you're here, I think it's time we started talking about –'

She sits bolt upright, her face lighting up. 'My hen?'

'Your hen,' I confirm, reaching for a folder on the crammed shelf behind my computer and squaring my shoulders. 'Okay, the wedding is now happening sooner than we expected but I've been busy brainstorming. I was actually brainstorming when I should have been ordering toilet roll for the café last week, but luckily James had a few extra rolls upstairs. Timewise, I'm thinking Easter. It's very close to the Big Day, but you'll be off school and there are great deals if we book early. Now, I've obviously had some ideas …'

'Tell me you're getting me a stripper, Ais. You know it's my dream. I'm partial to a guard but I'd take a fireman with a big hose at a push.'

'Ah-ah, I'm not giving away any of my secrets,' I say, patting the folder. 'But before we get started on the details we need to talk location.'

'Gotcha, bird. Shoot.'

'Now, we've both been to our fair share of hens …'

'More than, I'd say.'

I open the folder and flip over the red subject divider. 'Right. How about two nights on the Wild Atlantic Way? I'm thinking surfing and seaweed baths on the first day, and then on the second we can get a man to come to the house and serve afternoon tea in the nip.' I consult my notes again. 'Actually, hang on, he'll be wearing an apron for health and safety reasons. But he'll be mostly in the nip.'

'You hate surfing, Ais.'

'I know. I'm just not built for it.' And the wetsuits. There's no dignity. I had a headache for two days after trying to get into one for Caroline Craven's hen.

'Next! I like where this is going, though,' Maj says, rubbing her hands.

'Okay so,' I say, flipping the purple page divider. 'A weekend in Liverpool. I found a really funky roller disco that serves gin in teacups.' It's cracked what people are up to with gin nowadays. 'And on the second day, we could do a life-drawing class. Again, there would be a naked man.'

'You know I can't bear the Beatles, though, ever since I nearly choked on one of Elaine's Linda McCartney vegan sausage rolls. Just hearing the opening bars of "Hey Jude" triggers my PTSD.'

'What has that got to do with anything?'

'I don't think Liverpool would be safe for me.'

'Okaaay,' I say, taking a deep breath. I want this hen to be the best weekend of Majella's life. She and I have both forked out thousands of euro over the last couple of years for everything from white water rafting in Athlone (we never found the white water) to burlesque classes in Cardiff. The very least I can do is give her the send-off to end all send-offs. And it's my job as her best friend and only bridesmaid. She is being a bit of a tough customer, but I anticipated this and I love a challenge. I flip past the orange and yellow sections in the folder and go straight to green. I think she's going to like green. 'How about going a bit further afield?'

Majella's hand flies to her mouth. 'Do you mean like Vegas? To see the Thunder from Down Under?'

Jesus, I couldn't be going back to Vegas so soon after my escapades there last year. I turn puce every time I so much as see an ad for the place. I actually had to leave the room when Mammy was watching a travel show about it the other night. Angela Scanlon was standing in front of the MGM Grand and everything – the scene of the crime.

'Er no. But what would you make of … Tenerife?' Pablo's home island. Surely it'll be a hit.

'Tenerife? Okay, sell it to me.'

'Well, flights are cheap enough if we go on a Wednesday and come back on Saturday, and of course Tenerife is where I first met Pablo and that's how he came to live in BGB and fall in love with you.' I poke her and she breaks into a reluctant smile. Of course, it was really John who became besties with Pablo on that ill-fated holiday. 'So, it's all very … meaningful. And it could be handy, assuming you want to invite his mam, and doesn't he have a few sisters too?'

'Oh, shit.' Maj slumps back in her chair and throws another fistful of chocolates down the hatch while I'm forced to look away. 'I forgot about the mams. I haven't actually met Juana yet. Outside of Skype, like.'

'Ah, you have to invite the mams, Maj. It's tradition – I couldn't have it on my conscience if we didn't. And your Aunt Shirley has already been on to me on Facebook. There's going to be a fair crowd of us. But, listen, all you have to do is have a good time. Leave the rest of it to me.'

'Right you are, Ais.'

'I actually even looked up the Paradise Aqua, where me and– where we stayed that time. It wasn't exactly luxurious, but it would do for a big gang for a few nights. The website is under construction but I spoke to the manager, a lovely English girl called Flo, and she said it's undergoing a huge renovation and we'd probably be the first guests to stay in it once it's done. She said if we give them a good review on TripAdvisor she'll halve the rate for me. Apparently they're struggling to get past two stars and, to be honest, I can understand why – they didn't even have a double bed for us when I was there. All in, we could be looking at only €220 a head for three nights if we share rooms. Mad when you think it's practically in Africa.'

'That's a bit of a bargain, alright.'

'Isn't it? And the weather will be lovely. You can get a bit of colour and you might be able to hang onto it for the wedding.'

This is my *pièce de résistance*. Majella has had enough fake-tan disasters in her life to be unable to resist the lure of a bit of bona fide sunburn-that-eventually-turns-to-brown.

'Go on. You've twisted my arm, so.'

'Savage,' I say, delighted with myself. 'And as for guest list, so far I have you, me, Sharon, Dee Ruane, Denise Kelly, Maeve Hennessy, Sinéad McGrath –'

'Sadhbh, Elaine and Ruby?'

'Sadhbh, Elaine and Ruby. They wouldn't miss it. Your mam, your Aunt Shirley, Pablo's mam and how many sisters?'

'Two. Maria and Paola. They're both older.'

'Grand. That brings us up to fifteen. Now, your cousins. Who do you want?'

Majella takes a deep breath. 'Karen and Danielle, definitely. And Bernadette. And if I invite Bernadette I'll have to invite Joyce and Avril. Then that just leaves Carmel, Teresa, Ellen and Aine. No, fuck Aine, she didn't invite me to hers.'

'Right,' I say, scratching out Aine's name. 'Aine can go and shite. So that's twenty-three. Anyone else? Anyone from work?'

'Christ no. Oh yeah, better ask Mairead and Fionnuala.'

'Do you think they'd be up for it if they know Sadhbh is going?' Majella's old housemates from the place they shared in Phibsboro are teachers too, and they got a serious land when Maj moved out and Sadhbh briefly took her old room. Between their fondness for buying and labelling their individual milks, and not one of them almond, and Sadhbh's blatant disregard for their rules around the storage heaters, it was quite the culture clash.

'Ah yeah, it was all water under the bridge as soon as she revealed her Peigs connection.'

'Okay, I'll add them in so. That's twenty-five.'

'Is that not a lot of people to keep track of?' Maj looks worried now and I'm feeling a bit panicked myself. I'll just have to be meticulous about all the organising and maybe start getting up at five instead. It'll be grand. And James will be gone so it will be great to have a project to throw myself into, while dodging all mentions of my thirtieth birthday. Majella and Sadhbh, thankfully, seem to have gotten the message and stopped hassling me about it.

'It'll be grand. You know I love this sort of stuff.'

'Are you sure, Ais? We could just go to Maguire's for pints. It'd be far less hassle for you.'

'I wouldn't hear of it. It'll be deadly, just leave everything to me.'

'If you say so.'

CHAPTER 7

I've decided to simply call the WhatsApp group Majella's Hens and I have it fired up less than 24 hours after Maj has agreed to Tenerife. I tried to think of something funny or a pun for the name, but there was nothing happening. Sister Anne was right – I don't have a creative bone in my body, but I am very good with numbers. I did get Noel the kitchen porter to make me up a group icon that says 'We Can't Keep Calm It's Majella's Hen Weekend!' though, so the girls will know this is no ordinary trip.

I've managed to source everyone's numbers, including Aunt Shirley and the Tenerife gang's. Shirley was very suspicious – she likes to do all her communicating exclusively through Facebook, usually via passive-aggressive Minions memes, which she tags people in. And Pablo had tears in his eyes when I asked for his sister's number. He's very in touch with his emotions, to the point where I don't know how Maj puts up with it. I bumped into him in the corridor when I was leaving James's apartment the other morning, and he was actually bawling because the sky looked a bit pink and he said it reminded him of home. I had to tell him to catch a hold of himself.

With the initial guest list, plus six more cousins and three aunts that Majella added this morning after a guilt trip from her mam, we're now at thirty-four hens, but I'm trying not to think about it. I'll just keep going with the organising and hope stress isn't as dangerous long term as the media claims.

'Well, girls, the time has come!' I type into WhatsApp. 'Our Maj is finally settling down with Fab Pab, but we need to give her a proper send-off!' I throw in some champagne, heart and bride emojis. 'We're going to Tenerife from 29 March–1 April.' Sun emoji, beach emoji, palm tree emoji. 'The price is a bargainous €220 pp, including flights, shared rooms and transfers. Let me know if you can make it! I'll share my bank account details tomorrow and if you can transfer a €50 deposit, and post your name as it appears on your passport, I'll get booking before the flights go up.' I finish with a rake more emojis and press Send.

My phone immediately beeps.

'Who is this and how did you get my number? This is a data protection breach.'

Fionnuala – I should have known. God forgive me, but she's some dry shite.

'Fionnuala, it's Aisling,' I fire back. 'Got ur number from Maj. Hope you can come on the 29th!'

'Wouldn't miss it, hun!' Sharon is straight in there, and thank God for that. We're off!

'Hi Aisling, sounds good! Can I get my own room? Will pay extra.' That's Karen, a cousin. I did up a quick room plan this morning and had pencilled her in to share with Danielle, considering they're sisters. But I suppose I can contact the Paradise Aqua and price a single room. I take a spiral notepad out of my desk drawer, write Hen To-Do List with my Good

Pen and underline it twice. Nothing like a list to make you feel in control.

'I'm sure that'll be grand, Karen,' I type.

'Jesus, Karen, you're some pain in the hole. Thanks, Aisling, I'm on for it.' Danielle is in too.

'Me and Ruby are THERE, Ais.' That's Elaine. 'Can you make sure we get a double room, though?'

'No probs, Elaine!' I write 'Remember double room for Elaine and Ruby' on the list.

'Wild horses couldn't keep me away!' Sadhbh is on board too. 'I'll fly from New York to Dublin and meet you all in the airport. Will you book me an extra bag?' I stick 'Sadhbh extra bag' on the list.

'Looking forward to it! Can I get an aisle seat, Aisling?' Shirley, wouldn't you know. I suddenly start to feel very warm.

'I'll do my best, Shirley,' I type, while fanning my armpits. Then I add 'Shirley aisle seat' to the list.

'Lovely, Aisling.' It's Liz, Majella's mam. 'How many bags can we bring and do I need to weigh them? Can I have the aisle seat across from Shirley?'

I bring up the Ryanair website and try and make sense of the current cabin-bag situation, which seems to change weekly. You'd want to have your wits about you. It looks like you can only bring a small carry-on bag, unless you book this Plus thing, which is an extra €20. Honestly, I don't know how Michael O'Leary sleeps at night. What an absolute chancer.

'Ladies, you can bring one small carry-on bag each! Otherwise you can pay another €20 to check a bag up to 20kg!' I type.

'Is that each way, Aisling?' Mairead, who's been known to reuse tea-bags, doesn't miss a trick. I go back to the hellish Ryanair website. It is. It's €20 each way.

'That's €20 each way,' I clarify.

'So it's actually €260 if I want to check a bag?' Mairead replies, adding a money-flying-away emoji, which I feel is a bit unnecessary.

'A small price to pay when you're practically in Africa!' I fire off. 'Plus you get priority boarding.' Then I throw out a smiley-face emoji to keep the tone light.

'Sounds deadly, thanks for organising, Ais!' That's Dee Ruane. 'Maeve is here with me. She's looking forward to it too!' Excellent. They'll share a room.

'Hello, Aisling, Liz's sister Selina here. Will it be very hot there that weekend? I don't do well in the heat.'

I take another deep breath and Google 'Tenerife climate'. It looks like the temperature will be 14–22 degrees at the end of March.

'It'll probably be around 18 degrees, Selina. Lovely!' I reply.

'Selina has left the group.' Oh right.

'Hola, Aisling, this is Paola, Pablo's sister. Thank you for organising the party. My mother would also like to come her mother, her six sisters and eight nieces. Is this bueno?'

I take a deep breath. Make that forty-eight hens.

CHAPTER 8

I had to mute the WhatsApp group. Between Aunt Shirley's increasingly outrageous demands (extra legroom on the plane, a sea view, my reassurance that she'd get a full refund if it was cloudy) and the new Tenerife contingent talking back and forth in Spanish, I was just getting too distracted. And I couldn't risk making a mistake on my VAT return. The last thing I need now is Revenue breathing down my neck. Not that I have anything to hide – I'm very above board when it comes to taxes. If anything I pay too much. Not like Bono or Bob Geldof. I'm devoted to U2, of course, like any self-respecting Irish person, but Bono makes it very hard sometimes.

My phone rings beside me on my old bedroom desk, scene of many's an essay about the causes, courses and consequences of the Easter Rising and some very neat colouring in of the layers of the earth's crust. I've left BallyGoBrunch in Carol's capable hands to get some documents together for my accountant, Patrick. He's Maeve Hennessy's older brother and went very crusty after doing six months in India to find himself. As long as he can find my invoices I don't give a monkeys if he wears shoes or not. I think he tried to make a go of it as a pottery teacher when he came back from Goa but had to pack it in and return to his accountancy roots.

I barely have the phone lifted to my ear and Majella has already started talking.

'Pablo said you asked for his sister's number. So does that mean there's a WhatsApp group?'

Nothing gets past her.

'Majella, you know I'm not going to tell you anything. It has to be a surprise.'

'Ah go on! Did they say they were going to come? I just want to be prepared.'

'All will be revealed in due course.'

'I can't concentrate until I know, Aisling!'

'Stop, will you! You'll never break me. And it's not for ages yet.'

'I found a place in Playa de las Americas that does strippers. Everything is cheaper over there ...'

'Do you not have long-division lesson plans or something to be working on, Majella, for the love of God?'

'Oh yeah, good point. I might learn something myself.' She laughs and then hangs up.

If I didn't know she was only messing I'd be worried. But the truth is that Maj always manages to get great results out of the class as well as being one of those teachers who's not afraid to stick on *Puffin Rock* for two hours on a Friday afternoon. The kids are mad about her, of course.

I stand back and look in the full-length mirror Daddy screwed to the back of my bedroom door in my Leaving Cert year. It's pine, like everything else in the house. Mammy got it collecting SuperValu tokens. I'll never forget her determination.

She got a lamp, too, and a set of non-stick saucepans that are still in their box in the attic. The Good Saucepans, as she calls them. Sure it would be a shame to scratch them. Mammy says she'll part with them when I have my first home. They never appeared when I moved in with the girls above in Dublin so I think I know what she means.

'Aisling, is that James in the driveway?' Mammy's voice is shrill coming up the stairs. I don't think she'll ever not be starstruck by James.

I fly to the window. That's his jeep alright. What the blazes is he doing here?

'You'll have to tell him we're on the way out. If we don't leave now we'll have to park on the GAA pitch and I won't have tyre marks on my conscience!'

The Blessing of the Graves is a highly attended event. Parking will be at a premium. The mass doesn't start for half an hour, and even though the New Graveyard is only a ten-minute drive away out the Garbally Road past BallyGoBrunch, Mammy has been pacing the hallway for twenty minutes anyway.

'Coming!' I roar down to her, as I hear the slam of his jeep door and the crunch of feet on the gravel.

Mammy gets to the front door before me. It's usually reserved for Christmas visitors or Una Hatton dropping off her annual jar of gooseberry jam and staying for a quick boast about what Niamh is up to in New York. But James is foreign and obviously used to sailing in front doors. Mammy probably wouldn't let him in the back anyway, despite his near-constant uniform of work trousers and functional fleeces and the tinsel garlands of Crunchie wrappers decorating the dashboard of the jeep.

She has the door already open when I arrive at the bottom of the stairs, furiously brushing the cat hair off my shumper, and there's James in his Good Trousers. His own hair is glistening from a recent shower and I can smell his woody, lawnmowery man scent from where I'm standing.

'Hello, James,' Mammy booms in her telephone voice.

'Hi,' I wave gingerly from the bottom of the stairs. He knows it's Blessing of the Graves day. Sure didn't he spread the slug pellets across Daddy's little grave flower bed himself? But I didn't mean for him to come with us, and I certainly didn't invite him. I told him I couldn't stay with him last night because Mammy would be up at the crack of dawn fretting about getting there on time and I'd need to be there to calm her down. We barely have a week left together so I was sorry to miss a night, but needs must. What is he doing here?

He runs his hand through his hair and looks at his feet awkwardly and then back at me with a shy smile. 'I thought you might like a lift?'

'Well, isn't that lovely?' Mammy turns around and flashes me two raised eyebrows. 'I can take my own car, sure.'

'Oh, I'll take you both, Marian.'

'Good lad. I'll just get my coat.'

Mammy has insisted James call her 'Marian' since they first met. She insists everyone calls her that, though. But instead of ignoring her and going for the 'Mrs' and going red like most normal people, James has managed to follow her wishes and not cringe in the slightest. I met my old fourth class teacher, Mrs Keating, in the New Aldi and she told me to call her 'Fiona' and I'd sooner have climbed into the freezer with the raspberry roulade.

I feel deeply confused and a bit panicked. Is James really going to come and stand at the side of Daddy's grave with us? This is only our second graveyard mass since he died; before we used to all huddle around Granny and Grandad Reilly's grave, joking with Auntie Sheila and my cousins Doireann and Cillian. It's different now. His absence is so keenly felt. It's too intimate for James to be there. But what can I say?

'You must be busy, James. You don't need to give up your Sunday to go to a mass,' I say as gently as I can.

He pauses and then looks me dead in the eye. 'I'd like to come, if that's okay?' Something about the way he says it gets me and I nod.

'Can I get my Good Coat out of the press behind you then?'

Even after months in BGB he's still mystified by us calling them 'presses' when he insists they're 'cupboards'. I don't slag him about the 'scones' business, though, so I have no time for it.

Mammy comes bustling back into the hall with her handbag. 'Come on, come on, we'll be late.' Her urgency is catching, and James throws open the front door. 'I'll just turn the jeep, ready to go.'

Mammy is about to follow him out when I catch her arm. 'You don't mind him coming, Mammy, do you?'

She tilts her head to the side. 'Not if you don't, pet. I just want you to be happy. He's a lovely boy. Man. He's a lovely man.'

She senses my hesitation. 'Is he still leaving, though, Aisling? Going back to England? I don't want you getting hurt.'

I squeeze her arm. 'I won't, Mammy, I'll be fine.'

'Maybe you'll keep it up when he goes back, the two of you? Sure it's only a hop, skip and a jump over the water.'

I don't want to be getting her hopes up so I just smile and give her a little shove towards the door. 'Come on, There'll be no parking,' I say, and promptly fall over That Bloody Cat as it streaks in the front door past me, hardly able to believe its luck.

****

Between the traffic on the Garbally Road and the battle to get That Bloody Cat back outside so Mammy could set the alarm, there's an army of GAA minors in their club colours directing cars into neat rows onto the pitch by the time we get there. Mammy is mortified. When we eventually get to Daddy's grave, Father Fenlon is already making his way to the trestle-table-slash-makeshift-altar in the centre of the graveyard. As well as his good robes, he has on a new flesh-coloured headset microphone, which allows the entire congregation to hear him go 'for fuck's sake' when he stubs his toe on an errant pot of hydrangeas. There's a shriek of feedback from the PA and The Truck, who's more used to playing eighties hits on his legendary mobile disco, dives for the sound desk. A titter spreads through the crowd. I catch Mammy's eye and we both smother a laugh. I'm glad – I was afraid we'd get sad standing here.

The whole village is indeed out for the mass, or it looks like it anyway, despite the fact that rain is forecast and the sky is slowly turning from a benign shade of white to an ominous grey. To the right is the McGrath family plot. Sinéad McGrath only buried her great-grandmother eight months ago. Angela McGrath died doing what she loved best – cursing at *Telly Bingo* when her numbers didn't come up. She was ninety-nine and the oldest living resident of Ballygobbard. Now the honour falls to Pierce Heffernan, who used to run the abattoir in Rathborris. He's a comparative spring chicken at just ninety-two, but he does smoke twenty Carroll's a day so we'll see how long he lasts.

It's a warm day and beside me James takes off his jacket and my nostrils are filled with that aftershave scent of his. It's divine, truth be told. John never got much beyond Lynx Africa. My eyes flick over to his granny's plot and there he is, head bowed, Megan beside him in a gorgeous floral dress. Fran on his other side, rosary in hand. John looks up and catches my eye and holds it before I have a chance to look away. He smiles and jerks his head towards Father Fenlon, who's taking full advantage of being cordless and is weaving through the graves at high speed in a not entirely respectful fashion, especially for a priest. I stifle a giggle.

'Aisling,' Mammy hisses. 'Your father is barely cold in the grave there.'

'Sorry, Mammy,' I mouth back at her. The time for laughing is obviously over.

Father Fenlon is now going full throttle through the homily and striding around the graveyard, frightening the daylights out of people who are using the occasion to catch up with pals.

'And now the Our Father, unless there's something you want to share with us, Terry Crowley?' Father Fenlon booms, popping out from behind the Crowley family headstone and nearly giving Terry an aneurysm with the fright. Terry, BGB's one and only taxi driver, shakes his head guiltily and Father Fenlon strides off with two altar boys jogging after him.

Billy Foran, whose father is Daddy's neighbour on our left, presses a bag of Werther's Originals into my hand. 'Take one and pass them along, Ais,' he says with a wink, and I dutifully help myself and then hand the bag to Mammy just as the first fat raindrops start to fall.

'… and deliver us from evil. Amen. Ah, feck it anyway,' Father Fenlon says with a groan as people start reaching for umbrellas.

Naturally, I have a handy little Totes number in my bag. It wasn't cheap – €12.99 in Arnotts – but it's lovely and neat and much better quality than the ones you get in Penneys for a fiver. You're only throwing your money away with those. I flick it up and James, Mammy and I all huddle awkwardly under it as the heavens open.

Father Fenlon makes his way back towards the altar, giving instructions about how communion will be doled out and where people should queue. An altar boy is shielding his face and head with a massive umbrella, walking backwards and just asking for trouble. As he heads past the Moran family plot I catch sight of Majella's head peeping above the top of a massive granite headstone. She's helping her dad, Shem, wrestle into a raincoat while Pablo struggles with a particularly wriggly Willy. Suddenly Willy bolts and Maj lets go of the arm of the raincoat. Shem's elbow flies out and shoves the umbrella-wielding altar boy, who falls forward into Father Fenlon, pushing him straight into an open grave two plots over. A gasp echoes around the graveyard and, thanks to the cordless mic, we hear every bump on the way down. I never expected a man of the cloth to have such a colourful vocabulary, but I suppose they're only human too.

There's a stampede to the graveside, led by Shem, who's understandably mortified. James makes a start to go and help but I instinctively stop him. This is local business. There's a bit of a tussle as men start pulling off coats and jackets and tying the sleeves together to make a kind of rope while Father Fenlon, voice as clear as day over the PA, effs and blinds from six-foot under.

Mammy, never one to miss an opportunity to beat the rush, places a hand gently on my forearm. 'Will we go?'

****

We drop Mammy over to Constance's house in Woodlawn Park. They need to discuss stock for the eco farm petting zoo, and I bet they'll raise a glass of something to Daddy too. Constance lost her husband years ago, and having a pal in the same boat is a great comfort to Mammy.

'Where to now?' James asks as we sit outside Constance's. I'm fully aware that her curtains are probably twitching like a tired eye as she and Mammy sit inside and discuss us so I need to make a decision fast. The tradition is that everyone goes to Maguire's after the Blessing of the Graves. Mikey Maguire always gets a band in and many glasses are raised to the souls of all the faithful departed. I wasn't planning on James being there, though. Again, it's such an intimate thing.

Such a local thing. Sure, the whole town loves James, and Sumira Singh might be ready to leave her husband for him, but he's a blow-in at the end of the day. But I promised Majella I'd be there. She wants to talk about whether it's okay to explicitly ask for cash-only presents on the wedding invite. It's a minefield. 'Maguire's,' I tell James. 'And we should still be quick enough to beat the rush.'

I'm right and the pub is only half-full when we arrive. I easily nab us a table down the back while James heads for the bar. It's still bucketing down outside, and the smell of the turf fire fills the air. I check my phone – a text from Majella.

'Daddy had to go in after Father Fenlon. Now they're both stuck. Sweatin for wine xx'

'We're lucky we left when we did,' I say as James passes me my gin. 'It's gone from bad to worse.'

Felipe follows James to the table with a few packets of taytos and places them in front of me. I look at James with delight. 'Good man, I'm actually starving.'

He beams. 'I know you well enough now to not come back without crisps.'

'How many at the graveyard?' Felipe has his notepad out, ready to plan for the influx from the mass.

'Loads,' I tell him. 'Packed. Father Fenlon fell into a grave so people will be in high spirits.' Felipe will love that. Father Fenlon isn't his favourite person since he refused to let Felipe accompany the odd mass with his guitar and some Brazilian hymns. Father Fenlon prefers to stick to 'Bind Us Together' and 'He Is Lord'. Absolute bangers, to be fair.

'Oh, good. Serves him right.'

I knew it. He's delighted.

'You two. You're cute. Cutesy pies. Very nice.' Felipe wags a finger between me and James and winks at us. My cheeks start to flame immediately, and I steal a glance at James and he's gone a bit pink too. James raises his glass slightly at him in a 'thanks very much, now please leave us alone' gesture and Felipe retreats to the bar.

James turns to me and raises his glass again. 'So. I wanted to thank you for allowing me to join your family today. I know I muscled in a bit but ...' He looks upset.

'Are you alright?'

'Aisling, I have to leave tomorrow. Go back to England, I mean. The foreman on a job in Bristol has quit and I have to go and oversee it. It's a bit of a mess.'

'Oh.' My heart drops. He's not supposed to be leaving until next weekend. I wasn't particularly looking forward to a long goodbye, but I also wasn't expecting this. He's about to say something else when the pub door flies open and Majella bails in, followed by Pablo, The Truck, Maeve Hennessy, Sinéad McGrath, Dee Ruane, Cyclops, Sharon and half the Knocknamanagh Rangers hurling team as well as some of the BGB Rovers. Everyone has someone buried in the New Graveyard. They're all soaked to the skin and creasing themselves laughing about the Father Fenlon fiasco while firing orders at Felipe behind the bar. Mikey Maguire passes out towels as Shem Moran walks in to what can only be described as a hero's welcome after his graveside rescue. Majella and the gang squeeze themselves in beside me and James, the noise and damp pushing away the awkwardness. James catches my eye and gives me a tight smile. I shrug at him and mouth 'sorry' but I also feel a bit relieved. He was looking very serious and I'm not sure I'm up for a big sad farewell at this moment.

The pub door swings open again and John and Megan walk in, shaking off an umbrella and sliding out of their coats. Cyclops gives a shout to John and waves him towards us, while Sharon gives him a dig in the arm and Majella shoots me a sympathetic look. Lads can be so clueless. John and Megan have no choice but to join us and Pablo darts around like a whippet sourcing two extra stools for them.

'John, my friend, here! And Megan!' he says, placing them right opposite James and me. Great.

'Lovely day for it.' John smiles as he takes his seat.

'Mighty.' I smile back, wishing the ground would open up and swallow me.

Megan immediately moves on to complimenting Sharon's handbag, which is absolutely tiny and wouldn't even fit a hairbrush but, sure, Sharon likes her bits. Leave her off.

John leans forward and puts his elbows on the table, but then changes his mind and leans back again, clearing his throat and running his hands through his hair. He's feeling awkward too, I can tell. James takes the opportunity to excuse himself to the bathroom.

'Well, Aisling, any plans for the big birthday?' John asks, nearly too loudly, like he'd been rehearsing it. I'm immediately reminded that not only is it my birthday, but it would have been our nine-year anniversary. John was my seventeenth kiss at my twenty-first, a lifetime ago. 'The big three-oh' he continues awkwardly when I say nothing. Majella shoots him a glare and I'm nearly sure she kicks him under the table. I give her a little smile. She's really taken what I said about not wanting a fuss to heart.

'Oh, when are you thirty, Aisling?' Megan leans away from Sharon and towards John, her big blue eyes genuinely interested. Rumour has it she's only just gone twenty-seven.

'Two weeks,' I tell her as James rounds the corner on his way back from the bathroom. He sits down beside me and gives me a sad look, leaning into my ear to say quietly, 'I'd better go. Packing to do.'

'I'll come with you,' I say, starting to gather my things, feeling such a mixture of emotions I could scream given half the chance, and actually glad of the opportunity to get out of there.

'There's no need,' he says, but I'm already pulling on my coat and waving away Majella's confused stare as James puts on his own coat and starts to say his goodbyes to the surprised faces. I can feel John looking at me and I resist for as long as I can before looking down at him.

'Are you okay?' He doesn't actually say it but I can tell that's what he means with just the raise of his eyebrows. Of all the people to be offering eyebrows of comfort.

'I'm grand,' I say quietly and wait patiently for James so I can say my own goodbye.

CHAPTER 9

'**D**id you cry?'

'A bit. Just as he was leaving.'

'Did he?'

'No. I don't think so.'

'I bet he did. He was mad about you, you know,' Majella says matter-of-factly as we scurry through the drizzle from the car towards the entrance. It's the first time I've seen her properly since James's departure. We huddle into the revolving door, which spits us out into the foyer and nearly hurls Majella into a giant plant pot bookending one of four velour couches, all facing inwards in an intimate square. I squeeze between the arms of the couches and sink myself into one of them. Jesus, it's very low. I'll need a medical hoist to get out of it. The nicer the hotel, the more cavernous the chairs, I suppose. And of the two hotels within a thirty-minute radius of BGB, the Ard Rí is definitely on top.

I'm exhausted. I was up crazy early to get some crucial admin done on the hen. The WhatsApp group went quiet enough for a while, but Majella's cousin Joyce has decided she's going vegan for her health, and trying to explain to her that Ryanair don't provide meals, let alone vegan meals, is like talking to the wall. I've added 'vegan snacks' to my ever-growing list. Meanwhile, Pablo's sister Maria has requested that we all wear traditional costumes one of the nights we're in Tenerife, and even though group costumes are almost a given when you're on a hen, I was thinking more along the lines of matching T-shirts – Busty Bernadette, 'Ave a Go Avril, that sort of thing. Majella's already requested Danielle's Gone Doggin' for her cousin Danielle, who was recently spotted leaving a notorious lay-by the other side of Knocknamanagh. She claims she was just stretching her legs and getting her steps in. At eleven o'clock at night while wearing a bandeau dress she borrowed from Maj in 2009 and never gave back? Pull the other one, Danielle. But I've reminded Majella that the mams will be on the hen and Aunt Shirley's blood pressure is at breaking point as it is. And I've asked Maria if she could possibly price forty-eight traditional Tenerifian costumes for everyone locally, because I've looked them up and the volume of the skirts alone made me feel weak at the thought of the cost of the fabric. The very thought of trying to get Busty Bernadette into the little red traditional waistcoat is giving me the sweats.

Majella sinks into the couch opposite me, looking up from her phone, which is permanently attached to her hand these days. 'You must be missing him? You spent a good bit of time together.' She searches my face, concerned, and I sigh and give in. She's mad for the romance now that her wedding is such a reality.

'I do miss him. He was lovely.' I don't tell her that getting all my time back is the only reason I'm able to be with her here today. Between the café and planning the hen and helping Mammy have alpacas and yurts delivered for the eco farm, it's just as well James wasn't Mr Right, but rather Mr Right Now.

'Did I tell you the yurts arrived?' I say, eager to change the subject. Majella has been deeply invested in Mammy and Constance's yurt saga. Gantulga, the Mongolian consultant, made a balls of the paperwork and the yurts were held hostage in Dublin Port for weeks, but now they are safely at the farm and ready to be installed. Mammy rang me earlier and dropped in the news that John is helping out on the team she's pulling together to get them assembled. John helped out a lot around the farm after Daddy died and Paul went back to Australia. Sometimes you'd nearly swear he was Daddy with the old wax jacket and wellies on him.

'They've arrived! Brilliant news!' Majella exclaims, and she's back on the phone, texting like the clappers.

'Who has you so enthralled?'

'Nobody. It's just an email from China. About the wedding dress. It's been dispatched. Happy days. At this rate the wedding will be planned by Christmas.'

Chinese retailers have been getting big business out of BGB residents ever since Skippy Brennan outed Geraldine live on Solas FM for buying dodgy knock-offs and reselling them as 'designer' handbags in her eponymous boutique. There's been an endless stream of packages arriving into the village every day, each one more disappointing than the last. But the stuff is so cheap people keep going back to it like a dog to its sick. Pat Curran, our notoriously lazy postman, is fuming over the increase in his workload.

Thankfully Majella doesn't have to pin all of her hopes on this dress. Word has gotten around that she doesn't have a huge budget and all sorts of offers are coming in. Tessie Daly swore to me the perfect wedding dress had arrived into the charity shop and she'd keep it behind the counter until I could have a look on Maj's behalf. I downed tools immediately and raced in to check it out, but what she neglected to say was there was the distinct smell of tragedy off it. Like, definitely death. When I pointed this out, Tessie got the hump and told me I'd want to put some hanging baskets or maybe a decorative trough outside the café or she'd set her Tidy Towns cronies on me. As for my own dress, there just aren't enough hours in the day for me to go boutique-hopping, so I've been ordering them online, although not from as far afield as China. I'm worn out trekking to the post office to return the packages because it's been dud after dud so far. Majella knows I have a complex about my upper arms so she's said she's happy for me to pick my own dress, and I don't want to show her anything until I'm happy with it, so I've been doing fashion shows for Sharon instead, pointing out every lump and bump and trying not to despair too much.

'You must be our bride, Majella Moran. Welcome to the Ard Rí, ladies.' A singsong voice comes from somewhere behind the massive plant and Lisa Gleeson, who was three years ahead of us in school, steps out from the shadow of its fronds. 'I'm Lisa and I'll be your wedding coordinator. Please, allow me to show you around.'

She's wearing a navy skirt suit with a red neckerchief and acting like me and Majella haven't spent half our lives going to functions in the Ard Rí and that we weren't all on the same Unihoc team the year our school got to the national championships. We were knocked out in the first round but I had it on my CV until I was at least twenty-five. All three of us were actually only here last month for a Scouts table quiz. We just missed out on first prize too – a four-person inflatable hot tub generously donated by Knock Garden Centre – thanks to a particularly difficult picture round. Sharon was bulling, although it's really her own fault for mixing up young Pierce Brosnan and young Gerry Adams. There was no telling her – God knows I tried.

This is Majella's first consultation about the wedding and I was drafted in at the last minute after Pablo got held up servicing a vintage Massey Ferguson in Filan's Garage. I had to cancel my standing appointment with Sharon. Probably for the best that Pablo isn't here – his emotions have been getting the best of him at the mere mention of the upcoming nuptials. Majella casually revealled on the way here that John is going to be his best man. I suppose it makes sense – they are great friends. The stag is going to be in February, and they're staying local in Ballygobbard to keep the cost down for Pablo's brothers.

'Will you do the talking, Ais?' Majella whispers as we follow Lisa into the little office behind reception. 'People always take you more seriously than me.'

Her phone bings and then bings again and she hurriedly puts it on silent.

'I didn't know you'd left the New Aldi, Lisa,' I say, nodding at Maj and giving her hand a quick squeeze. Much like the New Graveyard, the New Aldi has been in situ between Knock and BGB for more than two years now, but once new, always new around these parts. 'Did I not see you guarding remote-control lawnmowers in there last week?'

Lisa lowers her voice and loses the fake smile. 'This is only my second day here, girls,' she says, closing the door. 'I didn't think I'd get it, but apparently no one else applied and they were desperate for a new wedding coordinator. The last one ended up having a nervous breakdown, although the official line is she's on a sabbatical. You didn't hear it from me.' Lisa taps the side of her nose and I immediately remember Lisa Loose Lips was her nickname in school. Clearly not much has changed.

'Would you have much experience with events?' I venture, holding my breath and hoping she was just being modest about the job.

'Not really,' she says with a shrug. 'I'm more used to being on the tills and doing crowd control around the middle aisle on a Thursday. People just can't abide by the two-items-per-person rule. But I've seen *The Wedding Planner* enough times to know it can't be that hard. And I got married here myself.'

She did, too. I was John's plus-one – Lisa's husband, Gareth, used to be the Knock Rangers goalkeeper before Dessie Connolly came along with his giant arm span and usurped him. They ran out of baby potatoes. There was uproar, if I recall.

'Now, Majella, it says here that we have you down for the Country Chic package for 4 May – is that right? It's a Saturday.'

Maj looks over, panic stricken.

'It's actually the Effortless Elegance package, Lisa,' I say evenly.

Lisa starts hammering away at her keyboard while Majella mouths 'she hasn't a fucking clue' at me. 'It'll be grand,' I mouth back. Lisa Gleeson will not make a balls of Majella and Pablo's Big Day. Not on my watch.

'Riiight,' Lisa says eventually. 'Can someone tell me the difference between Country Chic and Effortless Elegance? I've Googled it and our website is not very clear. The packages were just called Platinum and Budget when we booked our Big Day.'

I take a deep breath. 'Do you remember Liam and Denise Kelly's do two years ago?'

Lisa narrows her eyes. 'Was "All of Me" by John Legend their first dance?'

'No, that was Roisin Rice the previous weekend. Liam and Denise had "When You Say Nothing at All".'

'Was that the one where the Ronan Keating impersonator end up shifting one of the groomsmen?'

'That's it,' I say with a nod. 'They were Effortless Elegance. Beeforsalmon. Trio of desserts. Candy cart. Tayto-sandwich buffet. Bar extension. All the extras.'

Lisa is nodding now.

'Aoibheann Laffan's wedding last August. The summer punch reception and dry chicken Kievs?' I say, testing Lisa again.

'Was I at that one, girls?'

'Of course you were, Lisa,' Maj chimes in. 'Go on, you remember. Mad Tom caught the bouquet and one of the bridesmaids ended up knocking out his front tooth. That's why he has the gap.'

A flash of recognition crosses Lisa's face. 'Was the dessert apple tart and vanilla ice cream?'

'Yes!' I half-shout. 'That's Country Chic. See the difference?'

'I do,' Lisa says, nodding furiously. 'Right so, you're Country Chic, Majella.'

'Effortless Elegance,' I roar, slapping her desk with my open palm.

'Yes, of course. Sorry, Aisling!'

Out of the corner of my eye, I see Maj's shoulders drop about two inches. It'll be fine. I'm here and it'll all be fine. She knows that. Ais to the rescue, as always, and I feel my mouth go dry under the pressure of it.

'Can you just remind us again what's included, Lisa?' I say at a more normal volume. Of course, Majella has read the brochure so many times she's nearly memorised it at this stage, but it'll be nice hearing it straight from the horse's mouth – no offence to Lisa.

'Of course! You'll have a Hollywood-style red carpet on arrival …' Maj actually squeals. 'Prosecco reception for guests, or tea and coffee for the older crowd. Floral centrepieces. Six-tier cake. Personalised table plans and menus. Band and DJ for afterwards. Late-night nibbles. A five-course meal. Three glasses of wine per guest at dinner –'

'Will the bottles be left on the table?' Majella asks, her voice high with concern.

'Unfortunately not,' Lisa says, looking at the screen. 'It's a new rule. Apparently they've … I mean, we've, had too many issues recently with things getting out of hand before dessert is even served. Sure you know yourself.'

Majella starts studiously picking threads out of the rips in the knees of her jeans. She knows better than any of us.

'What if she supplied her own wine?' I say, to break the tension more than anything.

Lisa shrugs and picks up her mobile. 'I'm sure that'd be grand. Your wine, your business.'

'And what corkage do you charge?'

'What's corkage?'

'A fee to open the bottles,' I say, again worried that Lisa Gleeson has bitten off more than she can chew here. I'll be the first to admit she was the fastest scanner at the tills in the New Aldi, but planning someone's wedding is a bit more high stakes than making piles of fruit and veg while customers scramble to fire them into their trolleys.

'Ah, I don't think the Ard Rí, I mean, we, would do that now.'

'Should you check?' I say.

'Nah. Trust me. No corkage here. This isn't the Mountrath, girls.'

We all have a little laugh then because the Mountrath, the other local hotel, is definitely a bit of a kip in comparison. Although it is home to the Vortex, the nightclub where I spent every Saturday night from the age of sixteen to twenty-two, so it'll always hold a place in my heart.

'Maybe we'll just go with the waiters serving the wine, will we, Ais?' Majella says. 'You've enough to be doing.'

'It's no problem at all,' I say.

'No, you know, I think it's quite a classy look, actually,' she replies and I must say I feel a bit relieved.

'Anything else you need from me, Lisa?' Majella asks.

'Not really since it's all paid for in full. You're happy with Love Hurts to do the music, aren't you? And then The Truck on the decks from eleven till two before the usual session in the residents' bar?'

I always thought Love Hurts was an odd name for a wedding band but I can't fault any outfit that can segue so seamlessly from 'Mr Brightside' to 'Riverdance', and they supply their own inflatable props. Nothing funnier than a pair of novelty sunglasses or a blow-up saxophone at a wedding.

Majella's eyes glint as she pipes up and nudges me. 'Actually, we might make a change to the musical line-up if that's okay, Lisa. I'm sure we'll be able to confirm soon.'

Oh God. The Peigs at the wedding. I haven't said a screed to Sadhbh about it yet.

'What's this now?' Lisa is all ears at the first hint of gossip.

'Oh, nothing,' I interject.

'We just might have another band lined up to do a few songs is all,' Majella says coyly. 'No one interesting. Definitely tell The Truck we want him, though.'

Majella sounded so certain. I don't know why I can't bring myself to mention it to Don and Sadhbh, but it gives me a small pain in the pit of my stomach thinking about it. The same sharp barbs I used to get in school when there was a maths test looming and the dread made me consider throwing myself down the stairs because a non-fatal injury seemed better than admitting I just didn't get trigonometry. Now, Sadhbh isn't scary at all and Sister Helen was a menace, but the feeling is the same. A bit of dread. Growing and growing. I can't put it off much longer. I'll have to ask her soon.

Luckily the band chat doesn't hold Majella's interest for too long because she's back on the phone smiling away to herself. Pablo, I'm sure. I once witnessed him sending her a text and he actually kissed the phone and whispered, 'Take my words and go to her, little friend.' They're next level.

We plough on, booking Maj and Pablo in for their menu tasting, and are just about to hit the road when Lisa puts a hand on my shoulder and leans in to my ear. 'Your fella, that English lad with the jeep, he doesn't know anything about the Garbally Stud renovation, does he? I heard a rumour they're going to be doing weddings. Bit of competition for us here if that's the case.'

Well, this is awkward. 'Eh … he's not my fella, Lisa. He's actually gone back to England. So I, eh, don't know anything about Garbally, I'm afraid.'

She's not in the least bit fazed. 'No way! I thought you two were dead serious. He was some ride, wasn't he? And such a dote, by all accounts.'

I feel a pang for James. I wasn't lying to Majella when I said I missed him but I'm working on putting it all behind me. I need my summer and my winter to pass and all that. Onwards and upwards. I paste on a smile for Lisa. 'He's a lovely fella, alright, but it was nothing serious. And like I said, I'm no use to you on Garbally.'

'Ah, okay. I was just wondering what you knew. And, sure, aren't your mother and Constance Swinford inseparable since she offloaded the stud? Well, let me know if you hear anything. I'll give you a discount off a photobooth, Maj.'

I don't have the heart to tell her that the photobooth is included.

CHAPTER 10

'Will I cut these into eights or twelves?'

'Eights, good girl. I don't want anyone saying we're mean.'

Carol Boland's sausage rolls are rapidly becoming the cornerstone of BallyGoBrunch's catering wing. We got leaflets done up a couple of weeks ago and did a bit of a social-media push and even more orders have been flying in. The sausages are the big draw at BallyGoBrunch, of course, but the sausage rolls travel so well. She bakes them as one big log and then cuts the flaky pastry into just about bite-sized pieces. The smell of them would drive you bananas. I could eat my fist and here I am with my face twelve inches from a huge batch of them. After my blow-dry with Sharon I had a meeting with Patrick, the accountant, about the possibility of hiring another kitchen porter and bumping Noel up to be more of a sous-chef under Carol. Thank God it was quiet for a Saturday. Then I had to fly out home to meet the lads delivering the polytunnel for the farm. Mammy and Constance are off finalising the soft furnishings for the yurts and they needed me to oversee its arrival. It's a good job too because the chancers were trying to assemble it in the front yard, and I could sense the curtains twitching in surrounding houses and the words 'planning permission' being spoken in tongues.

If there's one thing people in BGB care about, it's planning permission. Shem Moran once tried to get away with an extension on the family's old bungalow and claim it was just a tree-house 'for the kids'. Majella was twenty-seven at the time. Shem should have known the planning permission police would have been out in force. I can't say I blame them. Aunty Sheila's neighbour got away with new dormer windows and she swears he can see her in the bath and claims he did it on purpose. Aunty Sheila's been known to put out the washing in her underwear, so I'd say if he wanted an eyeful he didn't need to go to the bother of major construction.

Anyway, the tunnel is where it should be and the place is really starting to take shape. William Foley took on the task of laying all the paths and walkways and has done a marvellous job, I must say. Mammy and Constance have secured all their stockists for the farm shop – Carol Boland Sausages front and centre, of course. I told Patrick to get on to them about his pottery too. And they've hired four new staff members – one of them is Lisa Gleeson's sister Grainne. She's going to be doing tours and I hope to God she knows more about that than Lisa knows about wedding planning.

'Did you hear? They're going to be doing big events out at Garbally Stud when it's refurbished. Denise Kelly told me.' Carol is packing the sausage rolls into catering trays as fast as I'm cutting them. The local breastfeeding group was in earlier and, while he'd never admit it, Father Fenlon definitely abandoned his cappuccino mid-sip when they started fiddling with their tops. He was looking at my forehead when he was paying and I was fully clothed. Denise Kelly was with the group with baby Cumhall and she told Carol that her husband Liam heard that the work on Garbally was out to tender. Liam works in the county council planning office and has ears everywhere. I must tell Mammy. Might be good news for the yurts.

'That's mad. I suppose, it's a lovely big house and there's loads of land for marquees or whatever. Why wouldn't you just go to the Ard Rí, though?'

'Some people have fierce ideas about themselves.'

She's not wrong. I was at a wedding of one of John's workmates two years ago and they had the ceremony outside. 'Under the gaze of the watchful trees' is what I believe it said on the invitation. It was March and of course it pissed rain and everyone was frozen, and then when they eventually let us into the specially erected tent we had to sit on the ground. 'Help us to honour our engagement trip to India as we dine traditionally and meaningfully.' Listen, they might sit on the ground in India, but when you're wearing your good Karen Millen and pair of nude heels there'd better be someone on hand to reef you up when you need to go to the toilet. I said at the time I didn't think the marriage would last because they were fighting before the starters were finished. Something about her mother falling backwards into a bowl of mango chutney. There but for the grace of God went I, to be honest.

'Your mother will be pleased. It might mean more business for them.'

'That's what I was thinking. Unless the Garbally crowd have their own yurts. I must get on to her to get the dry runs set up and the website running for bookings. It'll be spring before we know it.'

'Look, Aisling, it's half-past. You said to tell you when it was half-past.'

'Oh, good woman, Carol.'

I want to try to catch Sadhbh on the phone before she goes out for the night beyond in Seoul or Singapore or wherever she is now. We keep missing each other and the last I heard Colette Green was going to be meeting up with them on her way back from a trip to Melbourne to promote her jeans range. I was straight on to Paul to tell him to tell Hannah but he said he'd already bought tickets for the pair of them. The idea of Paul at an event to sell skinny jeans is daft to me but, sure, that's what love does to you, I suppose.

I go into my back office to try her but Sadhbh's FaceTime rings out and I'm disappointed but realise I'm also just a tiny bit relieved. I really have to ask her about Don and The Peigs playing Majella's wedding but I just can't bring myself to do it. What if it puts her in an awkward position and she gets thick with me and then Majella gets thick with me? I'll leave it a while longer. Maybe feel her out a bit on it.

'No answer,' I sigh to Carol, mentally reminding myself of the rest of my jobs for the day: drop the takings in the nightsafe at the bank; try to get a handle on the separate WhatsApp group Pablo's female relatives have set up and included me in, despite it mostly being in Spanish and me not having much beyond 'is it very spicy?' in my vocabulary; order new cushions for the BallyGoBrunch window seats. The list is endless. At least it's taking my mind off my birthday, though. My emphatic pleas for no fuss mean just that –

there's no fuss. Maybe I should have organised a *bit* of fuss. As it is, I just have plans with Mammy to sit in and watch *Titanic*. My mother's loyalty to Saoirse Ronan is matched only by her loyalty to Kate Winslet, and it doesn't get much better than *Titanic*. I must remember to get up and put on the kettle when the filth in the car is going on. I can't be in the same room as Mammy when the sweaty hand makes an appearance.

I can't believe I'm thirty tomorrow. I think back to teenage Aisling who made that list in her diary. She really thought I'd be so grown up. I suppose, when you're that age thirty seems like old-lady territory. And now here I am. I get up out of my chair, trying to ignore the ever-encroaching mess of the office. I walk out to the counter. We'll be closing soon and there's just one couple in the corner enjoying their coffees and scones. It's not a bad little place. It is little, though. Despite all I've achieved here, it feels small as I turn thirty. Something is missing. I know if I was to say this to Sadhbh she'd hop off me and say I have all the time in the world to get the other things I want; to meet the person I want to share my life with. But how can I do it in BGB? My mind drifts to James. Was I mad to let him go so easily? Maybe I should ring him. He hinted a few times about maybe doing visits and whatnot. Maybe.

'Aisling,' Carol calls from the kitchen, pulling my out of my funk, 'These sausage rolls are ready.'

****

I drive out to Knock to drop the tray of sausage rolls off at a wake. I don't even know who died, and usually you'd hear that kind of thing around here before the last breath was gone out of the poor divil. Carol took the order, though, and I'm just doing the delivering. The poor man who answered the door was very upset. I get back into the car just as my phone rings. It's Majella.

'The wedding is off, Aisling. There's no way I can wear that … that … rag down the aisle! Promise me you'll take away Pablo's belt and shoelaces when you tell him. He won't take it well.'

The wedding dress from China must have arrived and, from what I can gather between her wails, it looks nothing like it's supposed to. There's actually much more to a bridesmaid's role than just buying willy straws for the hen and guarding the helpless bride on the Big Day. The drama is non-stop.

'I'm sure it's lovely, Maj. You might just need to get it taken in or something?'

'It's not even white! It's mint green! And the bit where my boobs are supposed to go is hanging around my stomach.'

I'm about to say green probably would be a more appropriate colour for Majella to wear on her wedding day than white but I hold my whisht. 'Green has always suited you,' I reply encouragingly. 'And Pablo could wear a matching tie. It'd really set off his tan.' Majella loves boasting about how brown Pablo goes in the sun. It's one of her claims to fame.

'You have to help me, Ais. I'm freaking out here. I knew it was too good to be true but the model in the picture looked so ridey and I just wanted to be a ridey bride too.' She's wailing again now.

'What can I do?' I say. I resist reminding her that the wedding is still months away, although I know that dresses can take a long time to get right. It's obviously not what she needs to hear right now.

'Can I try it on for you with the shoes and the veil?'

'Did you go for the veil in the end?'

'No, but Mammy found my communion one in the attic. I was thinking it might draw the eye up? It's worth a try.'

Jesusmaryandjoseph. 'Don't make any decisions till I get there.'

'No! You can't come over,' she shouts down the phone.

'Why not?'

'Pablo. He can't see me in this yoke, just in case I do end up wearing it. Not that I will. Because I'm freaking out.'

'I can come when he's at work tomorrow then?'

'I won't last the night, bird. I'm going out of my mind with the stress here.'

'Do you want to bring it over to our house now so?'

'Perfect. Daddy says he'll drop me in now on the way to Maguire's.'

'I'll be home in fifteen. Stick the kettle on.'

****

Majella is sitting at the table looking tense when I come flying in the door having driven eight kilometres over the speed limit the entire way. I don't say this often, but thank God the garda station in BGB closed down. Penalty points are my number one fear. Well, after killing someone on that lethal bend outside Knock.

'It'll be grand,' I say confidently, kicking off my shoes. 'Murt Kelly's wife Eileen is a whiz with a sewing machine if the worst comes to the worst.'

Majella smiles a watery smile. 'You just missed your mam – she had to drop something over to Constance. She told me to tell you to feed the alpacas as soon as you got home.'

'Really? I've never fed them before. I'm half-afraid of them.' Despite Mammy's decades of farm experience, it's Constance's years at the stud that have really kept the alpacas going since they arrived at the eco farm a few weeks ago. I haven't gone near them and I don't think Mammy is a fan of them either.

'You have to show them who's *boss*, you see, Aisling!' Constance brayed at me the other day from under her signature Camilla Parker Bowles hat without breaking her stride as she brought the small herd in from the field. Murt Kelly, who keeps a few himself, was giving her a hand and she was honking away at him. 'Here you are now, Muuursh,' she'd brayed, holding a pair of reins out. He was kind of bowing at her, she's that posh.

Majella stands up and heads for the back door. 'Come on, I'm dying to see them. Cute bastards.'

I suppose they are an attractive creature, but up until they arrived on our farm my only experience with them was Niamh from Across the Road cornering me in the pub once to tell me about some time she had spent in Peru. She showed me forty-seven selfies of her with an alpaca and asked me who had the longer eyelashes. I had to lie and say hers were bigger to get out of there.

'Hang on, Maj – where's the dress after all that fuss?' I go, a bit confused.

Majella freezes. 'In my handbag.'

I look at the Orla Kiely on the floor beside her chair. You could barely fit a wallet in it, let alone a wedding dress with a nine-foot train. 'Are you sure?'

'Of course I'm sure,' she says shortly. 'Alpacas first, then dress. 'Mon.'

And with that she's out the back door like a rabbit out of a trap. I stick my feet into Mammy's wellies and catch up with her in the yard. We walk up past the chicken coops and beehives and around the insect hotel and polytunnel towards the fancy new sheds with Majella striding ahead babbling about alpacas and dresses and the merits of compostable coffee cups. I have to jog to keep up with her. The alpacas are very cute, to be fair, and I'm thinking it's good that they've taken her mind off the dress disappointment for a while.

We're just at the gate when she stops and drops suddenly down on one knee. 'My lace is open,' she calls to me over her shoulder. 'You go on into the alpaca shed. Grab me a baby one so I can give it a bottle.'

Confused, I catch hold of the bolt on the shed door and heave it to the right, thinking I don't actually even know what alpacas eat, when suddenly the lights flick on, temporarily blinding me, and about forty people jump out from behind hay bales screaming 'SURPRISE!'

CHAPTER 11

It takes me about thirty seconds to figure out exactly what's going on, and the whole time I'm panicking about the alpacas. Surely the noise will kill them stone dead? But I look around and there are no alpacas, only people smiling and my name spelled out in helium balloons and streamers and banners and basically all the party tat China has to offer. 'Celebration' by Kool & the Gang is pumping out of the sound system.

Faces swim in front of me – Baby Chief Gittons still in his county jersey, I can only imagine the stench; Sharon; Miss Maloney, my senior infants teacher – while Majella presses a glass of Prosecco into each of my sweaty palms.

'*Feliz cumpleaños* to you, Aisling!' It's Pablo. He's wearing his good party sombrero. I'm stunned. Like, really stunned.

'Did you really think we'd let your thirtieth go without marking the occasion?' Maj hoots, grabbing me for a quick selfie. 'You should have seen your face, bird.'

'But what ... where ... the dress?' I stammer.

'I had to think of something that would make you come running,' she says with a shrug. 'I know you take your bridesmaid's duties more seriously than quite possibly anything else.' She's not wrong.

'So it's not green then?' I reply, draining the second glass of fizz while waving hello at Constance Swinford who's striding around purposefully with Grainne Gleeson trotting at her heels, wearing an apron and taking notes.

'Oh, it is. It's desperate. Back to the drawing board. Sadhbh was just saying I could –'

'Sadhbh is here? I thought she was in Singapore this week!'

'I was lying! Happy birthday, bitch!' She appears in front of me and kisses me on both cheeks. This is what three months of international travel has done – she used to be content with constant hugs. I'm so shocked to see her that I barely have time to process the fact that she's wearing a boiler suit. But she is. She's wearing a boiler suit to a party. Not that she doesn't look deadly in it, as per usual, even with the preposterous fur-lined loafers on her feet, but still.

'Oh my god, I can't believe it. Sadhbhy! You're back in BGB!' And then my blood runs cold. I never asked her about The Peigs and now Majella is only twelve feet away. What am I going to do?

'What are we, chopped liver?' I swing around and there are Elaine and Ruby beaming back at me. 'Welcome to your dirty thirties, Ais.' Before I know it, the three of them have drawn me into a group hug and for a split second I screw my eyes shut and breathe in their expensive perfumes and imagine we're back in our swanky Dublin penthouse, sitting around under blankets getting mouldy on Pinot Greej. God, we had some good times in that place, and wasn't life so much simpler? No 5 a.m. starts or cash-and-carry runs or the pressure of paying wages and people's livelihoods and rent depending on me back then. And I was never more than twenty minutes away from a Penneys. I can't remember the last time I was in Penneys. I'm like a hostage to the café sometimes.

'Lads, I can't believe you're all here,' I say, feeling a bit teary. The Prosecco is obviously kicking in.

'Did you really not suspect anything, pet?' It's Mammy, wearing the Going Out Gilet I got her last Christmas.

I look down at my feet. 'I would've put on my good wellies if I did.'

It's her turn to hug me then. I've become very partial to a good Mammy hug in the past year or so. 'Happy birthday, my Aisling,' she whispers in my ear. 'I wish Daddy was here tonight. He'd get some craic out of all of this, wouldn't he?'

'He would,' I sniff back at her.

There's now a swarm of people around me, slapping me on the back, passing me gift bags – very handy, I'll use those again – and telling me I don't look a day over twenty-nine. All the usual birthday craic. And even though I'm right there in the middle of it, smiling and nodding and wiping away the odd tear, it all feels so surreal, like I'm floating above it and looking down.

I think about all the surprise parties I've been an accessory to over the years: Maeve Hennessy's pimps-and-hos-themed twenty-first, Liz and Shem Moran's silver wedding anniversary, Auntie Sheila's sixtieth that was at her house and that she clearly knew about because she arrived wearing more sequins than Liza Minnelli. The convoluted plans and flimsy excuses to get people where they need to be at the right time. The hysteria when word comes through that the mark is on the way. I can't believe that it was all going on around me today and I never copped.

'How was the wake?' Carol Boland calls across the crowd with a wink.

'Was that not a real wake?' I reply, incredulous.

'Noel's brother's house,' she goes. 'We were working on food for tonight on the sly and we needed to get you out of the picture.' Noel is standing beside her, slapping his thigh he's laughing so hard, the absolute sleeveen.

'But there was a hearse parked outside? I talked to that poor man about his dead father for twenty minutes. I ended up saying I'd see him at the burial tomorrow. He cried!'

'The devil is in the details, Ais,' Carol says and then turns back to her chat with Mags from Zumba with Mags.

I wheel around to face Mammy. 'I just can't believe you went to all this trouble.'

'It's your thirtieth, pet. Majella suggested it and Constance and myself thought it would be the perfect opportunity to do a dry run with a crowd to see how we got on in advance of launching the eco farm properly. Sadhbh did all the coordinating from abroad. She introduced me to some great apps. Very handy.'

'Are you even afraid of the alpacas, Mammy? Or was it all a ruse to get me up here to feed them?'

Her face goes stony. 'They're fierce creatures, Aisling. Very cruel eyes.'

Something else dawns on me. 'Is that why everyone was panicking about the yurts arriving on time?'

'Sure where else would we put people?' Majella says. 'I told Sadhbh she could bunk in with me if the worst came to the worst, but that was only because I thought Don would be coming.'

'He's on vocal rest for Tuesday's show,' Sadhbh says apologetically. 'I swear he'd be straight in between you and Pablo in the bed if he wasn't, Maj. He's raging his schedule is so insane.'

'I'll tell you what's insane,' Elaine says, arriving at my side with another bottle of Prosecco and filling my glasses, 'what you've done with this place, Marian. Constance gave us a tour of the yurt village and the yoga space and the nature trail earlier. Ruby actually foraged for food.'

'Blackberries,' Ruby says proudly. 'Straight from the bush. I've never felt more like Bear Grylls.'

'All organic and vegan too, girls,' Mammy says with a nod, even though I'm not convinced she's not a hundred per cent on what either of those two words mean. 'Make sure and tell your pals that if it's a weekend glamping in the countryside they want, they need to come to ShayMar Farm in Ballygobbard.'

'ShayMar Farm?' I don't think anyone around here's named their farm. It's always just Doyles or Ryans or whatever, but I suppose now that the eco farm is a tourist attraction, it needed a name. And this one is perfect.

'That's right, pet. Shay for Seamus and Mar for Marian.'

'Ah, Mammy, that's lovely.' Her and Daddy's names together bring a lump to my throat. She reaches out to take my hand. 'But what about Constance?' I say. 'She's your partner, isn't she?'

'I just couldn't make the Con work, Aisling. She understood.'

'It's fabulous,' Sadhbh says. 'I can't wait to spread the word.'

'Hen parties a speciality,' Mammy says, going straight into business mode. 'Every need catered for. You can book it all online because the website is going to be,' she takes a breath and leaves a dramatic pause, 'transactional.'

'Transactional, Mammy?' I say, surprised.

Majella looks at me and raises her eyebrows. 'Transactional, is it now?'

'Oh yes,' Mammy says proudly. 'It has to be in this day and age, girls. Millennials don't want to be talking on the phone. They want to book their team-building experiences and weekend escapes on their tablets and what have you.'

Sadhbh, Elaine and Ruby all look equal parts amused and impressed.

'Mammy's started a computer course in Knock Town Hall,' I say by way of explanation.

'Honestly, I don't know why I resisted it for so long,' Mammy goes. 'Tessie Daly just wanted to learn how to send a Gmail and I was only hoping to get quicker at my touch typing, but I'm really enjoying it. I'm actually thinking of getting into coding.'

'Well, fair fucks, Marian,' Ruby says, raising her glass. 'You're an inspiration to us all.'

I look down at my wellies and around at everyone else in their finery. 'I might run and get changed.'

'Hang on, Ais!' Majella calls from where she's wiping what I assume is alpaca shite off her boot. How did I not even notice she was dolled up when I arrived? The snakey so-and-so. I hang back for her and she slings her arm through mine. 'You don't mind, do you Ais? I know you said you didn't want anything but you've been so good to me with the wedding and I just –'

'No, no. It's great.' I sigh. 'Do you know what it was? I was just feeling a bit left behind, you know? Single again and living at home with Mammy on my thirtieth birthday. It's not what I had imagined for myself. Remember the diary?'

'I said it before and I'll say it again, twenty-seven out of thirty is a very respectable score. You're flying! And you don't need –'

I cut her off. 'I know, I know. New Aisling doesn't care about settling down and getting the ring and all that, but with James gone now I'm feeling a bit, I don't know, lonely, I suppose. Thank God work is mad enough to keep me busy.'

Majella gives me a big smile. 'I think you'll be just fine. And besides, have you finished *Moby Dick* yet?'

She's got me there. I'll have to renew it from the library again. 'Thirty, Majella. It's so old.'

'It's the new twenty,' she says with a smile.

'I know. And I am grand. Onwards and upwards, eh'?' I squeeze her arm and she peels away from me back to the party.

'Onwards and upwards, bird,' she calls behind her. 'Now go and change those wellies. The state of you.'

I'm walking back towards the house through the yard, which is decked out in fairy lights, repeating a mantra Colette Green said she writes on her mirror and says to herself when she's brushing her teeth.

'I will have patience in the timeline of my life. I will have patience in the timeline of my life.' Now, I think Colette was asking for good thoughts for her scented drawer liners to be stocked in Brown Thomases, but sure everyone has their goals. I break into a little jog, desperate to put on a bit of brown mascara and a slick of Heather Shimmer, not to mention losing the wellies. While I'm at it, I decide to have a quick controlled cry here in the safety of the dark yard. Between panicking about Majella's wedding dress and then the shock of the party, my nerves feel like elastic bands stretched to breaking point. I look behind me and can see all my friends through the big shed window. Pablo is swinging Majella around and going to do himself or someone else an injury. Sharon and Cyclops are kissing on a bale of hay. I let the hot tears fall down my face, my shoulders heaving. It feels good. I turn to head into the house and fix myself up and there's a crunch of footsteps on the gravel. I freeze. Not a bloody alpaca, surely?

'Are you alright, Aisling?'

It's John. Of all people. I swat at my face, wiping the tears away with my palms. It's dark enough that maybe he can't see that I've been crying. Although he's not deaf.

'I was just tightening a few things up in the yurts. Your mother asked me to do one last check. She said there was the party tonight, alright, but I didn't think it would be –'

'Oh no. No. You should come. It's grand. Is Megan …?'

'She's at a hen. Galway, I think. I got a picture of no fewer than three blow-up dolls. My mother nearly saw it. Can you imagine?'

'Jesus. Wigs on the green.'

The following four excruciating seconds of silence threaten to turn into five but he breaks it, thank God. 'Your mother asked if I know anything about websites. She wants to make the eco-farm site transactional.'

John has always been something of a technological guru to Mammy, despite the fact I've told her multiple times he's a mechanical engineer and doesn't in fact work in IT. 'He's in computers,' I overheard her proudly telling everyone at my Granny Reilly's funeral, me and John's first public appearance since we got together at my twenty-first. All my aunts were convinced he was going to be the next Steve Jobs.

'You don't know anything about making websites,' I retort.

'I watched a few YouTube tutorials,' he replies with a smile. 'It's very hard to say no to her. You don't mind?'

'No, no, not at all.'

'Okay. Well, happy birthday, and … look after yourself, okay?'

He crunches away across the gravel and I relax my shoulders down from around my ears. I need another drink. I need another ten drinks. I need another ten drinks and then I need to maybe drunk-text James. Life is too short for this carry-on.

CHAPTER 12

A quick change into my polka-dot tea dress and Good Heeled Boots and four drinks later I'm in much better form. Sadhbh has commandeered the playlist and it's wall-to-wall Beyoncé. Even Mammy is dancing. Maj grabs my hand and twirls me around and around and around – I'll be puking onto a bale of hay if she keeps it up. She spins and spins and I try to focus on one thing to keep from getting too dizzy – a trick I was taught in Irish dancing. My medals are all still up in one of the boxes under the bed. I pick a point above the door of the shed and keep bringing my gaze back to it.

I spin and spin and spin and spin and something catches my eye at the door. Someone. It couldn't be. I rotate one more time and force myself to a stop, staggering slightly and trying to focus.

It is. Standing at the door, in a beautiful blue shirt, is James Matthews, holding a present. I look, dazed, at Maj and she just smiles and shrugs innocently. I look back at James and he smiles nervously and beckons me over. I feel all eyes on me as I try to walk in a straight line towards him, and as I reach him he backs out of the shed door into the relative darkness. We stand and look at each other for a moment before he opens his arms and suggests, 'Hug?'

I'm surprised at the force with which I throw myself at him. I really missed him, I missed those arms – I really wanted to feel them today.

'I was going to text you! Tonight!' I say into his shoulder before pulling back. 'I really was. I was looking forward to it.'

'What were you going to say?' He laughs. He looks relieved.

'I don't know yet. It would have depended on how many drinks I'd had.'

He laughs again and shoves the present into my hands. It's wrapped in blue tissue paper and festooned with an elaborate bow that I'm almost certain Sumira Singh had something to do with. She's famed locally for her prowess with a ribbon. My stomach does a somersault. I wasn't expecting to see 98 per cent of the people I've seen this evening, and I definitely wasn't expecting to see him.

'What are you doing here, James? You didn't come just for the party? We're not –'

'Well, no, not just for the party. That's just a nice coincidence. I got a call the other day that I wasn't really expecting.'

'It wasn't from Liberia, was it? That's a scam, James. They nearly got Joe Duffy himself a few weeks ago.'

'Who?'

'Joe Duffy. From the radio.'

'Is Lassie Brennan not the chap with the radio show?'

'No, you're thinking of *Skippy* Brennan. You've got your telly animals mixed up.'

'I think I have,' he says with a smile and my stomach flips again. 'But it wasn't a scam. It was about a work contract. Here, in BGB.'

I've always loved the way his smooth accent rolls out the letters B-G-B. It sounds so incongruous coming out of his mouth.

'Okay,' I say. 'And?'

'It's the renovation of Garbally Stud, Aisling,' he says. 'I've been offered the contract. The company originally signed on has gone bust. I got the call, flew back, met with them today and they've offered me the tender.'

I'm dumbfounded. I grip the box with my two hands. He carries on nervously. 'If I'm honest, I let them know I was interested weeks ago. I didn't want to leave.'

'What about the work in England?'

'I can hire someone else to cover it. This Garbally job is big and there's a quick turnaround. And, of course, it would mean I'd be back in BGB for the work. But I'd also be back for you, Aisling. I miss you.'

'I miss you too.' It's out before I can stop myself. It's true, I do miss him.

'I won't take it unless you want me to. I like it here. I like you. So much. But I won't take it unless you want me to.'

A hundred things spill through my head. My workload, the stress of the hen, my vow to stay single. But also James and the gorgeous way he treats me and the countless 'what ifs' I thought to myself when we were together. I look into the shed where Pablo and Majella are in a clinch up against the chocolate-fountain table. Mammy read online that hen parties go mad for chocolate fountains so she ordered two and got a free fondue set and she's trying them all out at the party. Elaine and Ruby are talking to

Cyclops, Sharon and Liam Kelly. Liam is showing something on his phone to the others. Probably pictures of the baby. He's awful cute, Cumhall, despite having an abnormally large head. Sadhbh is on the phone making a gooey face. Probably talking to Don.

'You're making me nervous, Aisling,' James says shakily and I realise I still haven't answered him. 'Why don't you open your present?'

I pull off the elaborate bow and find my voice again, asking him suspiciously, 'Did Sumira Singh do this for you?'

He laughs and nods. 'I must admit, she did. She banged on the window of the hire car I was in on Main Street earlier. It was like she could smell me.'

I rip off the blue paper and open the box. Nestled inside is a rose gold Daniel Wellington watch. I gasp. All of my favourite influencers have been parading them around their wheat-coloured houses for months now. I've been deeply coveting one. That's not all, though. There's something else wrapped in more of the blue paper. I hand the watch to James and peel it back and a little 'ah' slips out of my mouth. It's the ticket stub from our trip to Knock cinema. The cute bastard. I throw my arms around him again, pushing aside any doubts and whispering in his ear, 'You *better* stay.'

****

'You're so cute together,' Elaine says approvingly ten minutes later. James and I had re-entered the party to some mortifying squeals, me with my new watch on my arm.

'Cute, but like chalk and cheese,' she continues. 'Like your one and your man – ah, what's their names?' She jigs up and down, trying to jog her memory.

'Brian and Pippa?' I offer hopefully.

She shakes her head, face screwed up in concentration. 'You know them. She's poor and he's dead posh.'

'Harry and Meghan?' I'm feeling less hopeful.

'*Nooo*, ah what is it?'

Sadhbh looks as helpless as me and shrugs just as Elaine's face lights up.

'Doctor Dolittle!'

'The lad who talks to the animals? Thanks a million, Elaine.'

Sadhbh is creasing herself and can hardly get the words out. 'E … E … Eliza Doolittle. *My Fair Lady.*'

'Yes!' Elaine is delighted with herself. Majella points out the window to where James is deep in conversation with Constance Swinford under the lights at the barbecue on the other side of the shed. 'There he is now, with his people. I wonder will you have your own servant when he brings you home to meet the parents in Downton Abbey, Ais?'

'Majella, stop!' Sadhbh laughs. 'James is lovely. There's nothing wrong with a bit of posh. Nothing at all." She nods at the watch and I blush.

'I'm just codding.' Majella slings an arm around my shoulder. 'I'm delighted he's back.'

'You knew he was coming, you snake,' I accuse her, laughing.

She holds her hands up. 'I did. I did. He has good manners, that man. He asked me if it would be okay if he showed up, and after you telling me you were missing him, I said, 'Who am I to stand in the way of true love?' and gave him the green light.'

True love? Steady on, Maj. I look out at James and feel a swell of warmth for him. It's a lot to process, sure. And having to make the decision for him to come back was a lot. I can't just go back on it the way Suzanne Corcoran dropped out of her arts degree when she discovered there was no painting.

'He's going to be a great plus-one for Maj's wedding. He'll look fantastic in a suit,' says Sadhbh approvingly.

That's true. I'd been sort of dreading going alone, even though I know Maj will have me kept busy. It will definitely be nice to have James on my arm.

'Speaking of which, get that ridey boyfriend of yours on the phone there, Sadhbh,' Majella says, nudging her.

A claw of panic grips at my throat as I remember about The Peigs and the wedding. Does Maj think I've asked? Is there about to be a scene?

'He'll be in bed.' Sadhbh laughs.

'He'd better be dreaming about my wedding playlist.'

My breath catches and I watch Sadhbh's face for the inevitable confusion but she just laughs harder. 'He's said under no circumstances will they be covering Ronan Keating.'

'Spoilsport!'

What the–?

Majella clocks my face. 'You were obviously stressed out about it from the moment I asked you, Ais, so I just went straight to the source.'

My stomach loosens ever so slightly. All that worrying for nothing. I really wish Maj had told me.

'Don said himself that they'd love to do it. To my face. Well, on FaceTime.'

'We've been having a lot of clandestine chats to plan your party,' Sadhbh says conspiratorially. 'Don couldn't resist Majella's pitch.'

I'm sure he couldn't. She'll have them at the top table with her and Pablo if they're not careful.

'I've been a Peigs fan since day dot. My loyalty deserves rewards!' comes Majella's mock indignation as she stalks off to the drinks table for a refill.

'I know you have,' Sadhbh calls after her, laughing. And then she leans in to me. 'She asked him to disregard any tweets, Facebook messages or handwritten notes and cards she may or may not have sent him in the past two years "in the spirit of our new and very special friendship".'

'Oh, sure, last time she saw him she was holding his hand for twenty minutes and she didn't even notice. He had to pry it off to go to the toilet. And she definitely put his straw in her bag.' When Majella loves something, she really loves it. 'I'm sure she'll have calmed down by the wedding.'

Sadhbh waves her hand. 'It's no problem. Me and Don were going to the wedding anyway, and the lads are up for playing as long as we can give them a bed.'

'We can give them a bloody yurt if they want one. I was going to ask you about them playing myself but I didn't want you thinking I was taking liberties.'

'We're friends, Aisling. Don't worry about stuff like that. And you're so good to Majella.'

'It's the biggest day of her life. It has to be perfect.'

'And what about you?' She gives me a dig in the ribs and her eyebrows shoot up as she nods out at James, Constance and Mammy deep in conversation. 'What a birthday present, eh?'

As if James has heard her, he suddenly looks up, catches the two of us gawping at him and smiles shyly with a little wave. Sadhbh shrieks and waves back, leaving James laughing as she drags me back to the chocolate fountain.

'Look at you now, with a man like that to round off your thirtieth birthday.' She's piling a paper plate with chunks of pineapple and strawberry to dip into the melted gushes of chocolate, as if she can't even see the mounds of marshmallows there only waiting for their go. 'He's obviously been mad about you since day one, and why wouldn't he be?' she continues. 'You're a catch just as much as he is, by the way, and don't forget that.'

I think about James's shy smile and warm brown eyes and can't help but smile myself. I walk over to the barbecue to rescue him from the two ladies. When I reach him, he has a burger in one hand and a hot dog in the other and Mammy is trying to force a corn on the cob into his shirt pocket.

He smiles gratefully when he sees me approaching and places his food down on a paper plate. 'I'll just go and wash my hands.' He kisses me on the cheek and heads for the new toilet block, only finished on Wednesday, and now I know why there was such a rush on that too.

Constance excuses herself to go and check on the alpacas, which are all still obviously down in the far field, and Mammy starts fussing to put a burger together for me.

'I'm grand, Mammy. We're all full to the gills from the chocolate fountain.'

She puts down the plate and grabs my hand. 'Are you happy, my lovely girl?'

My eyes unexpectedly fill with tears at this and I grab her hand back. 'I am, Mammy.'

'And sure isn't that all that matters?'

I used to think as far as birthday parties go my twenty-first couldn't be topped, but sure, look, things change.

CHAPTER 13

'I'll see you later.' His eyes twinkle and he lowers his voice. 'Wear that little apron.'

I shove James out the door of BallyGoBrunch before Carol hears him, but he ducks back around and gives me a kiss on the cheek. It's been a week and a half since my birthday and we were boyfriend and girlfriend officially after two days, without too much fanfare. He caught me scraping the black off a bit of burnt toast in his kitchen and took the knife off me. 'No girlfriend of mine will be forced to eat burnt toast.' And then he winked at me and that was that. Now, in my defence, I wouldn't have burnt it if he didn't insist on buying €4 loaves of sourdough from the bakery in Knock Garden Centre. I have to really concentrate on not thinking about the 'sour' part when I'm eating it, and the bloody thing is impossible to cut. I got a wedge of it stuck in the toaster. What did the sliced pan ever do to anyone? And at least you know where you are Weight Watchers Points-wise with a sliced pan.

He's off even earlier than usual this morning, getting stuck into this Garbally project. Constance's old house was big but there's a huge extension going into the back of it, according to James. It's going to be used as some sort of fancy private venue. They got the planning permission rushed through, which means there must be a ton of money behind it. The glamour!

I head back into the kitchen where Carol is dipping toffee apples in nuts and sprinkles. Beside her, Noel is hacking at a pumpkin with a paring knife, but I don't think artistic creativity is his strong point, God love him. It's like a massacre.

'Did you flip the sign, love?' Carol doesn't even look up from her toffee-apple assembly line.

'I did. Open for business.'

We got an order for a heap of Halloween-themed food for an office party in Rathborris so she's been at it since five. People will be bringing their kids to the party so Carol's thought of everything. There are spider-web sandwiches on trays ready to go and Noel's already given up on the pumpkin to start adding toasted-almond nails to finger-shaped biscuits. In my day it was a black bin bag, a sack of monkey nuts and a wee prayer that someone wouldn't set That Bloody Cat on fire.

The breakfast rush will be underway in twenty minutes but Carol always has that under control, so I set to work behind the counter refilling her little homemade ketchup jars. The door opens with a cold breeze and in strides Mammy wearing a pair of leather riding boots, despite her well-documented fear of horses. You know that thing where people start to look like their dogs? That's her and Constance.

'Aisling, would you look at what Paul just sent me?' she says, holding out her phone. 'They're as cute, the pair of them.'

I take the phone and start dutifully scrolling through the photos. There must be about twenty of them. Paul and Hannah wearing their respective county jerseys at a music festival. Paul and Hannah doing karaoke in front of a massive Irish flag. Paul and Hannah literally throwing shrimp on a barbie while creasing themselves laughing. And on and on. There's even one of Hannah asleep on the couch.

'Love's young dream, alright,' I say, passing it back to her and placing my hands gently on her shoulders and moving her to the side, out of the way of the small queue forming behind her looking for coffees and sit-down breakfasts. She barely even notices.

'I've never seen him like this before. She's off fruit picking now next week and he's fairly cut up about it.'

'I'm sure he'll survive. Sure, they hardly know each other.'

'According to Skippy Brennan, little Emilia Coburn is engaged to a lad she's only known four months! Romance can happen in a whirlwind, love.'

Mammy has actually convinced herself that she knows Emilia Coburn, even though she hadn't heard of her until Marian Finucane interviewed her on Radio One last Christmas. Mammy is a big Marian fan, but when it comes to local radio her loyalty lies solely with *Skippy in the Afternoon*. It's a hard show to describe: one minute Skippy Brennan could be going head to head with a local county councillor about the dangers of uneven footpaths, the next he's talking to Emilia Coburn's waxer live from Hollywood. All top-notch Mammy content, to be fair.

'Paul is not going to get married to Hannah any time soon, so relax. Look how long he's been in Australia and he still has his watch set to Irish time. He doesn't commit easily.'

'I know that, but he can get a bit obsessed with things. Remember that God-awful phase he went through when he started in the CBS?'

How could I forget? When Paul was thirteen he dyed his hair black and was briefly BGB's only emo, complete with six thousand friends on Bebo. He used to hang around outside Filan's with his earphones in, scowling at people going in to get their messages. I had to pretend I didn't know him. Daddy thought he was going mad altogether and poor Mammy was worn out trying to get the eyeliner stains out of her good pillowcases. Someone suggested he swap his GHD for a hurl and convinced him to start training with the Rangers. He was back to his old self once the dye grew out.

'You have to leave him to it, Mammy,' I say, loading the ketchup jars onto a tray and getting out of the way of Karla, who arrived in a whirl of 'sorry I'm late' and had the apron on and the coffees going before I'd even missed her, to be fair. 'He's an adult now – remember?'

'I know, I know, I just don't want him to get his heart broken.'

Honestly, she'd wrap him up in cotton wool if she could. Mammies and their little boys. John's mother was the same. Nothing was good enough for her little man. I wonder if James's mother is like that. We've been sort of grilling each other nightly to learn more about one another, but he doesn't talk about his parents much. I asked were they wreck-the-heads but he was so tickled by the phrase that he didn't go into it any further. I'm worried how many people at Garbally are going to be called a 'wreck-the-head' in a posh accent by the end of the day.

'Oh, speaking of Skippy,' Mammy is still going but has dropped her voice to a tone I recognise as secretive because it's the same one she uses when she's gossiping about Una Hatton and her low-cut camisoles, 'Sandra Crowley told Miriam Timoney that Skippy was fascinated by the eco farm when he heard about it and he might have Constance and myself on to talk about it.' Miriam Timoney is officially retired but she works part-time on reception at Solas FM so is probably a reliable source. Mammy's whisper has almost turned into a scream by the end of the sentence such is her excitement. Meeting Skippy will be like meeting the pope or Ryan Tubridy.

'Wow, that's brilliant, Mammy! Great for the business!'

The dry run went off without any major hitches. Elaine, Ruby and Sadhbh all stayed in yurts and claimed to have had the greatest sleep of their lives. James and I stayed in one too and he was cursed with a cold shower but it was something to do with an element and it's already been sorted. James was very gracious about it, but I'm not sure Sumira Singh is quite over seeing him flee from the bathroom stalls to the yurt in just a towel on her way to talk to Mammy about cabbage samosas for the farm shop. James told me to tell Mammy that he's available to take a look at any construction bits and bobs. I didn't tell him about John doing the website. There's no need. Mammy and Constance are planning a mid-November opening for the nature trail, and they'll be passing alpacas off as reindeer come Christmas. They should be able to take bookings on the website when it goes live next week, although I can't imagine they'll have many yurt customers until the spring.

'I know. I'll have to see if I can get an emergency appointment with Sharon to get my hair done.'

'Mammy, it's radio!'

'Webcams, Aisling – webcams!'

****

I'm rushed off my feet for the rest of the day. I bring the Halloween party food to Rathborris and deal with the lunch rush with the BallyGoBrunch team. I take four phone calls from Majella about the font for the invitations and whether it should be the same as the menus and one from Lisa Gleeson asking me if the Effortless Elegance package also included a basket of deodorants in the ladies toilets. As if a wedding could be elegant without one.

I make a pit stop at home to collect clean clothes, including one of my two matching underwear sets (Dunnes, €27), to bring back to James's later. I've stayed with him every night but one and have gotten very adept at holding onto my big toilet for when I'm not in his apartment. My stomach has been in better shape.

It's six o'clock when I finally sink onto a stool in the kitchen at BallyGoBrunch. Carol has left a wedge of quiche on the worktop with a note stuck to it. 'For yourself and James.' He's working late over at Garbally and I decide to swing over to him with it. It's Gubbeen cheese and pancetta, and I know he's very partial to both notiony cheese and Carol's shortcrust pastry so I hop into the Micra, balancing the quiche on the passenger seat.

I'm just pulling in to Garbally Stud when I nearly smack the Micra straight into a wall of timber hoarding where Constance Swinford's fancy remote-control gates used to be.

It must be twelve-foot high, with razor wire all along the top. It's dark, but from where I'm standing this temporary wall seems to be running all around the property. A sign hanging just at eye level reads 'NO ENTRY – Trespassers Will Be Prosecuted' and I can see at least three CCTV cameras trained on me. I hop out of the car and start knocking at the hoarding in the hope of finding a door.

Suddenly a tinny voice goes, 'Can I help you?' in an unmistakable Nordie accent. I look up at the cameras and then behind me to where I've left the car engine running and the headlights on. There's no one there.

'Eh, hello?' I say into the dark. 'I'm here to see James. James Matthews. I have a quiche.'

I don't know why I said that last bit. I panicked. Then I see a control panel on one of the makeshift gate-posts glowing as the hoarding in front of me splits in two and opens with a gentle hiss like the doors on the Starship *Enterprise*.

Back in the safety of the car, I make my way down the long, winding driveway at a snail's pace. Behind Constance's beloved old orchard I can see a rake of floodlights, cranes and machinery around the old stable-yard. It seems James wasn't lying when he said it was a massive job.

I pull the Micra around to the back of the house, trying my best to avoid the potholes. Constance would have a conniption if she could see the state of her precious driveway now. She was always very proud of the depth of her gravel. It's mad what posh people care about.

As well as a crew from Dublin, James hired some local lads, including Pablo and Shem Moran, who are smoking in silence when I exit the Micra. Apparently the Dubs are all working sixteen-hour days, six days a week and staying in the Mountrath till the job is done. According to Lisa Gleeson, they're causing havoc in the Vortex when they're not on the site.

'Well, Ais,' Shem calls out when he spots me. 'Have you any interest in a power washer? I have three in the boot there. Be dead handy for keeping the car park beyond in the café clean. Only €80 for you.'

'They had them in the New Aldi for €60 last month, Shem,' I say, narrowing my eyes. 'What do you take me for? Here, there's some quiche in the car if you want a bit?'

'Thank you, Aisling, but no, we must get back,' Pablo says, nudging his soon-to-be father-in-law. 'End of day briefing.'

'How are the stag plans coming along?' I say as they both stub out their fags on the granite windowsill behind them. Even in the dark, I see Pablo go pale as Shem throws an arm around his shoulders.

'Oh, he doesn't know what he's in for. We're giving him a proper BGB send-off. The works.'

'I don't doubt it.' I smile in the dark, wandering off towards the light and noise where I can see James reading architects' drawings off the bonnet of his jeep. His yellow hard hat does something funny to me, and as I get closer, he turns around, takes it off and rakes a hand through his hair in what I would swear is slow motion. A smile spreads slowly across his face when he sees it's me.

'This is a nice surprise,' he says, walking over and kissing me on the cheek.

'I thought you might be finishing up soon?'

'I'll be another half an hour. I'll follow you home.'

The 'home' hangs in the air for a second, and I don't mind it, but I swing away from him anyway because I can feel my cheeks starting to go.

I notice several burly security guards standing around in what appear to be stab-proof vests. I think they might have overestimated the crime rate in BGB. Apart from all the hoo-ha earlier in the year with Sharon's ex, the worst thing that's happened around here lately was Trevor Ruane's dog worrying Billy Foran's sheep. May Lucky rest in peace.

'Excuse me, James – is herself there a friend of yours?' It's the security guard from the front gate by the sounds of his voice. 'It's just she said something about a quiche?'

'It's in the car!' I yelp. Jesus, this place is like Fort Knox.

'I was just checking,' he goes. Then he gives me a nod and walks off, calling 'have a nice evening' over his shoulder. I notice he goes straight to the Micra and peers in the passenger window.

'It's a quiche, not a Kalashnikov,' I mutter under my breath.

'They're very thorough,' James says apologetically, taking me by the hand and leading me towards the jeep. 'Come on, I'll show you why.'

He points to the plans and my eyes nearly pop out of my head. I always thought Garbally Stud was swish, but even to my untrained eye it's clear it's about to become a lot fancier.

James shows me how the house is basically being gutted and extended and the stable-yard transformed into luxury cottages. Not that Constance's horses didn't enjoy the finer things in life, but this looks next level. Words like 'recording studio' and 'wine cellar' and 'private cinema' and 'helipad' are leaping out at me. It reminds me of the golden days of the Celtic Tiger when Irish people used to travel almost exclusively by helicopter and the whole country was off their heads on cocaine. That was when Una Hatton had the decking put in and Mammy started leaving brochures for conservatories around the house. She nearly had Daddy convinced too until I pointed out the cost of heating a conservatory in the winter would be no joke.

'Is that an outdoor swimming pool?' I gasp, pointing at a rectangle to the west of what used to be the slurry pit and is now a spa.

'It has a retractable glass roof but, yes, essentially,' James says. 'It's actually an infinity pool. There's an indoor pool at lower basement level too.'

'And what are all those squiggles around the orchard?' I say, pointing to funny little shapes on the drawings.

'There's going to be an art walk all around the property, with pieces by Louise Bourgeois and Jeff Koons and Banksy.'

Banksy! I've heard of him. His stuff isn't cheap, even when he shreds it.

'They've already started arriving,' James continues, 'hence the heavy security. The paintings for the main house are worth a fortune too.'

'And the circles in the paddock?'

'Bubbles. They're basically clear circular tents so guests can sleep looking up at the stars. Each one will have a private butler.'

'So is it a hotel then or what?' I ask, thinking of the eco farm and everything Mammy and Constance have put into it. Why stay in a glorified tent when there's a bubble with a butler available three miles away?

'I don't think so,' James says, rolling up the plans and sticking them into a cardboard tube. 'They're calling it a private venue, but for what or who I don't know. Nothing's been said to me officially, but a woman in very high heels got a tour yesterday and I overheard her say something about a birthday cake and lots of celebrity guests. Now, will I meet you back at home?' He lowers his voice. 'Should I bring the hard hat?'

CHAPTER 14

'**N**inety-seven-point-six FM. This. Is. Solas. Eff. Em. I'm Skippy Brennan and you're tuned into the home of the Mulcahy Feeds Calving Hour. Coming up between three and four, one lucky listener will be in with a chance of winning a year's supply of home heating oil. I'll be talking to a Knock butcher who found a hedgehog in his car engine – but don't worry, folks, it's got a happy ending. No hedgehog kebabs for dinner tonight. I'll be talking to Councillor Lorraine Doran about planning pitfalls, and Garda Gerry Staunton will be in with his weekly Crime Callouts. Did you see a black Yaris acting suspiciously around the Mullybeg local information map? We want to hear from you. Before the news you heard 10CC and "I'm Not in Love" but I have to say …' Skippy's voice drops to a tone I assume he means to be sexy, '… I am a bit in love with what's in front of me here in the studio this afternoon.'

I can see Mammy's coiffed hair dip and bob through the darkened glass as she demures in the face of the Skippy Brennan charm offensive.

'The business minds behind Ballygobbard's brand new ShayMar Eco Farm and Yurt Resort – welcome to Solas FM, Constance and Marian.'

I'm watching them through the glass from a spinny chair in the Solas offices, granted access by Miriam Timoney to offer moral support and take pictures for Paul, who said he'd try to watch online. Mammy was right about the webcams and she's been up to ninety about her first big radio appearance. She got it into her head that maybe they needed media training and asked me would Sadhbh or Elaine know anything about it. 'Or Don, maybe?' I begged her not to make me ask Don Shields for tips on talking about yurts on Solas FM. Luckily Miriam Timoney took it upon herself to come to Mammy's kitchen and coach her and Constance on the best way to present themselves and the kind of chat Skippy might be after. I caught the tail end of the training session and witnessed Miriam very diplomatically tell Constance that she has a very 'powerful voice' and might practise making it a bit softer. Skippy is well known for having no time for poshos, so the last thing we need is Constance lifting him out of it honking about 'Mongoooaaalian yuhrrts' and the restorative power of 'ashtaaawwwnga'. Constance has definitely become less of an enigma over the past year, but she'll always be like BGB's very own Celia Holman Lee, except with horse nuts in her pocket and straw all over the back seat of her enormous Range Rover.

Mammy and Constance bid their nervous hellos to Skippy and he launches right in.

'So, an eco farm. But just how eco is it, really? How can we be sure it's not just another Hackett's Recycling con waiting to happen?'

Ron Hackett was shamed from a height last year when it emerged that not one bit of the 'recycling' he was charging the residents of BGB, Knock and beyond to collect was going anywhere near a recycling plant. He was dumping it illegally in a sandpit off the Garbally Road. And it later emerged he'd robbed the green bins on night-time crime sprees across two counties. The last thing BGB needs is another environmental scandal. Miriam had warned that with a light story Skippy sometimes likes to go for the unexpected jugular, but right out the gate seems a bit much. And him just flirting with them thirty seconds ago.

'Well, we, eh, we …' Mammy blusters for a second and I feel a sense of rising panic. I will her to pivot instead to her key talking points of solar-powered chick-hatching stations and Foraging Fridays, which they're hoping will bring in school groups and I'm hoping won't have someone in hospital after eating a dodgy mushroom. Bernard 'The Bog' Shefflin is coming in to do the foraging and he basically lives in a hedge so fingers crossed it will be fine.

My phone goes. It's a text from Majella. She said she was going to hide in the toilets at school and listen in while marking spelling tests. 'The louser. I'm boycotting Skippy Brennan from now on.'

That will be hard going. Shem Moran is devoted to Skippy.

Mammy trails off, but before Skippy can go again, Constance pipes up. 'Well, you see, eh, Skippy.' She says 'Skippy' like it's the name of something hawked up by an alpaca. 'You see, we've done our research. We've consulted with farms all over Ireland and all over the world, in fact, and we're confident of our standards. Local farmer Muuursh Kelly will tell you just how rigorous we are.'

Go Constance!

'Oh, I *see*,' Skippy patronises. 'But what's this I have in front of me about imported wood for playground fixtures? An overpowering and unpleasant *smell*?'

Where is he getting this from? This is an ambush! I glare over at Miriam and she shrugs her shoulders apologetically.

'He's in one of his moods,' she whispers. 'The *County Chronicle* got a tip-off that he's been getting Botox and really went to town on him this morning. How the hunter becomes the hunted.'

'That *smell* –' Constance has gone full honk and Skippy cuts her off.

'Mrs Swinford, if we could keep the voices to a dull roar, please?'

Mammy pipes up. Her head had sunk so low I was afraid she had slipped off the chair and under the desk in fright and mortification. 'That smell,' Mammy repeats slowly and calmly, 'was from Engers' pig farm two kilometres away. We get it whenever the wind blows just so and it's been coming and going since long before our eco farm was even a glint of an idea.' She's right. Many's the line of perfectly good washing has been ruined by the stench. 'The wood for the playground came from a sustainable forest in Wicklow and those alpacas belonged to Murt Kelly. Now, have you another question for us, Skippy, or can we tell you about the cabbage samosas?'

Through the glass I can see Skippy holding his hands up and he laughs on air. 'Okay, okay. Just doing my job, holding people to account. The fourth estate never sleeps.'

My God, he thinks he's on Channel 4 news. It's far from Channel 4 Solas FM was reared.

'Okay then, these yurts, tell me about them. Why would I sleep in one and not, say, a lovely hotel?'

****

By the time Skippy has to take a break for the death notices, Mammy and Constance have covered the yurts, the nature trails, the farm shop and the hen-party packages. Skippy had some questions about the compostable willy straws, and Miriam Timoney nearly choked on her tea when Constance called them 'startlingly realistic' and Skippy cut her off and threw to an ad break. I can see the three of them chatting through the window as one of the four death-notice broadcasts of the day goes out.

'Solas FM has been informed of the following deaths. Terrence Foley, The Hastings, Knocknamagh. Reposing at his home from this evening until 10 a.m. tomorrow. Removal to St Brigid's Church ...'

'They used to read them out live, the death notices.' Miriam places a cup of tea in front of me with two Good Biscuits on the saucer beside it. I suppose it's all about the glamorous biscuits in the world of radio and showbiz. 'They pre-record them now, after ... the incident.'

She's only dying to tell me, and I'm dying to hear it, of course. I lean forward and give her an encouraging nod.

'Poor Susan was in there in the studio reading her death notices live, doing her best sad voice when ...' Miriam clutches at her craw. 'Someone here in the office said, "Can anyone else hear that?" And sure enough, there was a song playing over her. Soundtracking her, almost. Live on the radio. While she read funeral arrangements.'

'Was it supposed to be there?'

'Jesus, no. Some clod was in the other studio getting songs ready for his show and he was somehow broadcasting at the same time as Susan.'

'What was the song?'

Miriam looks at me, tragedy in her eyes. 'Chris Rea. "I Can Hear Your Heartbeat".'

****

James is disbelieving when I relay the story to him that evening as we drive towards Knock. Rumour has it they've finally changed the film at the cinema and I've two share bags of Maltesers from Filan's in my handbag.

'Hang on. So they read out who's dead. On the radio?'

'Yes, James.' I'm exasperated. He keeps focusing on that rather than the catastrophe of the song and that Susan had just announced that Jill Noonan had died 'suddenly of a heart attack in her home' when Chris Rea started warbling.

'And then just anyone can go to the funeral? Because it's announced, live, on the radio?'

'Well, it's not live. Not any more.' Was he even listening to my story?

'But it went well anyway? I'm sorry I didn't get to listen. I was battling three very loud power drills and an architect with a very particular opinion about an archway.'

'It did, in the end. Skippy went hard on them at first but they knew their stuff. It will be great for booking, I think. John ...'

I falter over his name a bit and James looks over at me and squeezes my knee. 'It's okay, Aisling. You can say his name. I don't mind.'

Now that we're a proper couple I'm trying to be more sensitive around John and our past together, and I still haven't told James about John doing the website for Mammy. Here goes.

'John has been helping with the website and is monitoring the bookings for the time being, just to make sure it all goes smoothly. There are two groups booked in for March and April already, and loads of emails asking about the Santa experience.'

James doesn't skip a beat but his voice changes ever so slightly. 'Brilliant! And how was work today?'

It was busy. Mad busy. By the time I got back from the radio station Carol was already behind on some catering orders for tomorrow, and for some reason the electricity bill hadn't gone out of the account. But I just want to relax and enjoy the evening. 'Grand. Actually, if we stick on Solas we might catch Mammy and Constance on *Playback*. It's ninety-seven-point-six.'

James flicks on the radio and twists the knob to tune it in, but we're just approaching Knock so we might not catch it after all. The news is still on as James slows down to look for a parking space. We're not the only ones who heard about the new film.

'And finally, on Solas Showbiz, could we be welcoming a Hollywood celebrity into our midst to celebrate a very important birthday? A source has told the *County Chronicle* that –'

James brakes suddenly and exclaims, 'There's one!' And my bag falls forward, packets of Maltesers spilling into the footwell in front of me. I catch it before I lose the two tubes of Fruit Pastilles as well.

CHAPTER 15

The flights to Tenerife kept going up and up, even after I cleared my cookies twice. Well, I didn't clear them, Mammy did. When she first brought it up, I thought she was talking about the Viscounts I hoovered up the other night when she wasn't looking.

'No, love, it basically tells your computer to forget all the times you've been checking the Ryanair website,' she explained patiently. It's amazing what she's picking up on the computer course. 'They'll keep increasing the price if they know you're looking, the feckers.'

I hope Michael O'Leary dies screaming, I honestly do. It's now costing €230 a head just to get from Ireland to Tenerife. I'm terrified to tell the women so I've decided to absorb the increase myself. Between the thirty-two travelling from Ireland it's costing me just under €5,000, but honestly, it's a small price to pay not to listen to Aunt Shirley and co. giving out yards and I don't want anything negative getting back to Majella. I swear Fionnuala would have me done for false advertising anyway. She's so tight she used to keep her own stash of brand-name toilet roll under the bed and leave Maj and Mairead with the one-ply when they all lived together. It was practically see through.

I settle into James's couch and bite the bullet. 'Ladies, our flights and rooms are finally booked!' I type into the WhatsApp group. Aeroplane emoji. Cocktail emoji. Flamenco dancer emoji. 'I think I've managed to accommodate all your travel requests but just PM me if you have any more. Except you, Aunt Shirley!' Frazzled face emoji. 'Can anyone who still hasn't paid their deposit pop it into my account? Thanks!' Smiley face. 'Next up: the itinerary! I'm thinking "casual dinner" Wednesday night, "activity" Thursday, "mad night" Thursday night, "activity 2" Friday, "optional dinner" Friday night and "leaving" Saturday? Sound good? LOL.' Smiley emoji.

I slump back in my seat, turn my phone face down and brace myself for the reaction. I had to leave the predominantly Spanish group Pablo's relatives added me to, which is always awkward, so I set my alarm for 3 a.m. and did it then. Truth be told, I was still awake. In fact, I've barely slept the past three weeks with the stress of organising this hen and getting everything booked and confirmed in Tenerife. I'm a bit panicky about using my credit card at the best of times – it normally only comes out for emergencies or when I'm abroad – and for some reason I kept putting off booking the flights. It's my own fault it's costing me an arm, a leg and a head, and that's before I had to add on my two extra suitcases for all the props. I really shot myself in the foot ordering those light-up shot glasses you hang around your neck. Two AAA batteries in each one – the weight of them! But Maj loved Roisin Rice's so I couldn't not get them, or the hairband zogabongs, the forty-eight T-shirts or the inflatable shamrocks. You only get one hen.

The Paradise Aqua debited the money from my account mere seconds after I made the booking but I haven't seen sight nor sound of a receipt in my inbox yet. I'm sure Flo isn't trying to scam me though. She called me 'poppet' twice on the phone. And besides, I have a bloodhound nose for scams.

James kept asking me if I was sick when I couldn't finish my fillet steak last night but, sure, I couldn't admit I was stressing about the whole thing. I had to pretend my period was coming. He didn't say another word, only disappeared and came back with a tub of Ben & Jerry's Phish Food twenty minutes later. I had to take a picture and put it straight up on Facebook. The boy done good.

I take a deep breath and flip over the phone. Forty-two WhatsApp notifications. Mother of God.

'Are we wearing the Tenerifian getups to the casual dinner or the mad night?' Dearbhla, a Moran cousin, wants to know. 'When are we wearing the T-shirts?'

'Put me down for everything but the optional dinner,' Danielle says. 'I think I'll do a bit of sightseeing.' By herself on a Friday night in a place where she knows no one? She really is a strange fish.

'Is the activity costing extra? I hadn't budgeted for extras.' Two guesses who that is.

Then there's a lot of toing and froing in Spanish between Juana, Maria and Pablo's assorted relatives. I'm not too up on my *Español* – I did German, full sure we'd all be speaking it by 2005 – but the word *abuela* keeps popping up and I get the distinct impression Pablo's granny is a bit of a weapon.

'Sounds fab, hun, I'm bringing my kit so I can do our make-up and lashes xxx.' It's a small gesture from Sharon, but I immediately feel tears pricking my eyes. Everything has been so stressful lately, it doesn't take much to set me off. I'm starting to feel bad for the amount of times I've chastised Pablo for bursting into tears at the drop of a hat.

'What's the activity, Ais?' Denise Kelly wants to know. I didn't make it to her hen due to a clash with my great-aunt's ninetieth birthday party, but apparently they did archery, a cookery class, zip-lining *and* a make-up masterclass over two days. It was all anyone could talk about. Dee Ruane ended up having to leave early due to exhaustion.

'I've a few ideas lined up.' Smiley-face emoji.

'Can I get a double room, Aisling?' This is the first I've heard from Majella's cousin Bernadette. I had her in the No Hassle column in my notebook but I'll be moving her to Low Hassle now for this. If she wants her own room, who am I going to put in with Ellen? She and Teresa fell out last weekend over one of them underpaying for a Westlife comeback concert ticket and now they're not speaking. It's thrown my sleeping plan into chaos. 'Also, would you mind if I brought my new boyfriend?'

****

At 3 a.m. I'm still wide awake while James snores softly behind me, one arm casually flung over my waist, his breath warm on the back of my neck. I'm so tired I even eyed his drowsy Sudafed in the bathroom press but I couldn't bring myself to take one. Next thing you know I'd be buying poppers and yippers behind the chipper in Knock. It's a slippery slope.

I was complaining to Sharon when she was giving me a head massage on Saturday that I was having trouble switching off and she said to write out a list of my worries, stick it in a drawer and come back to it the next day. She swore blind it works for her and she gets her full nine hours every night.

Holding up James's arm, I slither out of bed and fumble around in the dark until I find my negligee on the floor. There's absolutely no heat in it but he looked so hopeful when he gave it to me, and the quality was so good, that I just kicked my Harry Potter pyjamas – €12, Penneys – into my overnight bag and threw it on.

I grab a hoodie off the chair in the corner and tiptoe out to the living room, lifting a sheet of paper and a hard A4 folder from James's desk, and sink onto the couch, pen poised over the accusingly white page. I stare at it. It gets bigger and wider before my eyes. Where do I start? I look around the room and feel the panic slowly rising in me. What if the Paradise Aqua doesn't have another double room free for Bernadette and this lad she met last weekend at a wedding? I don't know if I have it in me to tell her he can't come. What kind of hen has a man on it – apart from maybe a Gay Best Friend, but Sadhbh tells me that's an offensive stereotype, and anyway I'm probably too late to make friends with Brendan Courtney? What if Sharon's make-up weighs more than 20kg? And, worst of all, what if Majella doesn't have a good time because her cousins are fighting and her grandmother-in-law is as mad as a box of frogs? I'm the only bridesmaid, the chief bridesmaid. It's all on me.

'Ais?' James is standing in the doorway rubbing his eyes. 'What are you doing? It's nearly four.'

'Sorry. Couldn't sleep.'

'Are you … drawing something?'

I look down at the paper and realise I've been scribbling on it. Not my usual name and address or the classic 'this is a nice pen' but the full-on scratchings of a mad woman.

'Just talking the pen for a walk,' I say with a smile before getting up. 'Now, I'd better call it a night.'

CHAPTER 16

When Sadhbh suggested me and Maj come up to Dublin for a pre-Christmas girly night to see the new house and drink wine I couldn't say yes fast enough. She's hardly ever in Ireland these days, and as much as it's been nice spending every spare minute with James, I'm looking forward to a couple of days' break from the holdy-in knickers and the being nice to each other all the time. And, to tell the truth, I need a break from worrying in the wee small hours.

I grab a Going Out Top as I'm leaving the house, just in case, and then drive over to BallyGoBrunch to make sure Carol is all set for the rest of the weekend. I feel bad leaving her but I helped her with loads of prep this morning and she assures me she's got it all under control. I don't know how she does it. I don't do half as much as her and I feel like I'm drowning half the time. But she's said that she's worked hard all her life and she thrives on it. I suppose after the end of her marriage to bully boy Marty Boland she's thrilled to strive for something without him taking all the credit. Either way, she sends me off with a flick of a tea-towel, so I get back into the car and ring Majella's phone and hang up – our long-time money-saving code for 'get your arse outside'. Before we had mobile phones, we used to do it on the house phones as teenagers to signal that that had just been a particularly riveting episode of *Home and Away*. It used to drive Daddy spare, although the evening the Summer Bay stalker was revealed and the phone gave two rings to indicate that it had been a stunning episode, he sighed before declaring Maj was 'dead right'.

I've only given her one ring this time but she's down the stairs and reefing the passenger door off the Micra thirty seconds later.

'Jesus, what took you, Ais?'

'It's just gone half four. I've dragged you out of bed at this hour on a Saturday afternoon before.'

'I wasn't out last night. We stayed in to finish the guest list.'

'What's the final headcount so?' I enquire, pulling carefully out on to the Knock Road.

'Two hundred and twenty, including kids.'

'I thought you weren't having kids?'

'Pablo's mam was on to him. Said if little Juanita and Pancho and Guillermo couldn't go, the granny would kick off. I'm raging but my hands were tied. Pab really loves that granny.'

'Jesus.'

'I know,' she goes, leaning back against the headrest. 'Would you mind if we stop in to the Ard Rí on the way? I need to tell Lisa and I'd like to see her write it down, if I'm honest. It'll only take a minute.'

'No problem,' I say, mentally recalculating our arrival time at the roadworks on the N7. We'll still miss the worst of it, I'd say – if I step on it.

****

Ten minutes later, Lisa Gleeson is ushering us into her little office in the Ard Rí. 'Come in, come *in*, sit down,' she says, diving for her computer. I could barely see the screen from where I was standing but I swear she'd been watching a film.

'No problem at all,' Lisa goes when Majella explains the situation. 'I'm guessing we have a kids' menu?'

She's looking straight at me, eyebrows raised.

'You do,' I sigh eventually. Christ, she hasn't a clue. 'I think it's a choice of pasta or goujons or fish fingers.'

'That's what I thought,' Lisa says with a nod, typing away. 'It definitely sounds familiar anyway.'

'I think that's it so, isn't it, Maj?' I say, standing up and pointing at my watch. We really do need to hit the road.

'Do you think I should have more of a ... persona for this job?' Lisa says, leaning back in her chair and chewing on her pen.

'What?' Majella looks as confused as I feel. I wiggle my left wrist at her.

'I was just thinking it could be good for business if I was a bit more flamboyant. Maybe adopt an accent? The brides might like it.'

'I think you're doing fine just the way you are,' I say, lying through my teeth while putting on my anorak.

'Really, Aisling?' She sounds surprised and chuffed at the same time. 'That actually means a lot.' God, she'd believe anything.

****

We're hitting Ranelagh when my phone beeps in my bag.

'Get that will you?' I would usually ignore any and all distractions while driving, but it might be Carol with an emergency, and Majella can relay the information for me.

She reaches in and retrieves it. 'It's "Paul Oz New 2",' she says, sounding disappointed. 'I was hoping it might be James in nothing but his tool belt.'

'Maj!' My cheeks flame. 'Just read out the text.'

She clears her throat. '"Hannah is leaving in 3 days. Need to buy her something. Any ideas?"'

'Wow,' Majella says. 'It sounds like he's really fallen head over heels for this young wan.'

'You know what he's like. What do you think? She's going to be crammed into a camper van with probably fifteen other girls for months so it can't be a handbag or a scented candle or anything.'

'Something small? Jewellery?'

'Perfect. Type that out.'

'That reminds me,' Majella says, firing my phone back in my bag, 'what'll I get Pab for Christmas?'

'Hmmm. I don't really know. He's a man of few needs. A lock of your hair?'

'Gave him that last year. But that's about all I can afford at the moment so you're on the right track.'

Although all their spare cash is going towards invitations and candles and jam jars and all the bits that my voucher didn't cover, Majella and Pablo are still saving for their own place.

'Are you gone over your budget for the extra wedding bits?' I've been trying to explain the concept of budgeting to

Majella for years, but it wasn't until she started pricing gospel choirs and doves that the penny finally dropped. She's been diligently keeping track of her spending ever since, and I must say I've never been prouder.

'No, I'm on top of that. I just ordered a kilo of confetti from China, actually – saved myself a fortune.'

'You didn't fork out for the new Colette Greene Beauty Experience in Arnotts did you? €350 is too much for a blow-dry and a spray tan, Maj – I don't care if Colette herself is doing the spraying.'

'I can't say I wasn't tempted,' she admits, 'but it's school stuff. We're crowdfunding for new laptops and we were so close to making our target that I needed to donate a few bob to get us over the line. It's going to make my life so much easier in the long run.'

'Fair dues, Maj. That must have put you in Mrs O'Leary's good books.'

'Well, she's stopped calling me Marilyn, so it definitely helped. Speaking of school, did you say Fionnuala and Mairead are definitely coming to the hen?'

'I couldn't possibly say, so stop asking.'

CHAPTER 17

Don opens the door and Majella lets out an involuntary gasp. His months abroad have managed to turn even his Navan skin a fetching shade of golden, and he's kept the head shaved. A great look for him.

'Aha, the gals!' He beams, reaching for the handles of our wheelie cases and sweeping his arm out behind him. 'Welcome! Herself is in there.'

We nearly fall over each other in our rush to follow his pointed finger and get a gawk at their new place – it's one of those old Georgian houses. All renovated, of course, and looking festive with a massive Christmas tree in the front hall and fairy lights everywhere. I've seen bits of it on FaceTime with Sadhbh but now it's time for a proper inspection. We make our way down the hallway, oohing and aahing over the height of the ceilings – although, I can't help fretting about how astronomical the heating bills are going to be. We touch the nice bowls on the side table, and I notice that not one of them is full of keys and hair clips. Very swish. We compliment the art on the wall, even though it looks absolutely cracked. I always think if you're going to pay money for a painting you should at least be able to figure out what's in it.

'Ah, there you are, my lovely ladies!' Sadhbh is sitting cross-legged on the absolutely mahoosive velvet couch – a position I'd need help getting into *and* out of – and closing her laptop as we arrive into what must be the Good Sitting Room, there's that many cushions, while Don disappears upstairs with our bags like a celebrity butler. 'Sorry, just finishing off a bit of work so we have the whole evening free.'

I'm surprised to see, as she unfolds herself from the couch, her outfit is almost completely normal. Pale grey bottoms and a matching sweatshirt. They look incredibly soft and like they're straight out of the shop, of course. I have something similar but they're as bobbly as a school jumper, despite my careful attention to the washing instructions. I know all the little symbols. She comes in for a hug and my hands hit her bare back. There it is. A chic backless tracksuit. On anyone else it would conjure images of Christina Aguilera's arseless chaps – a look Majella tried to emulate with a pair of old Wranglers for Halloween 2002. Sadhbh is also wearing a whisper of a bra, if you could even call it that. A bralette, is that what they are? I could never get away with one. I need a bit of steel and at least five centimetres in strap width to feel in any way secure.

'Show us around!' Majella shrieks. 'What a house! This is even nicer than the Portobello place.'

She's right, it is. And I didn't think that could ever be topped. I was only telling a complete stranger in BallyGoBrunch about the wine fridge in our old Dublin apartment the other day. There must be money in having the number one single in the States for eight weeks in a row.

Don appears with three mimosas on a tray. Imagine having a tray in your house for carrying drinks around on! How the other half live. I make a mental note to look for one in IKEA for bringing the tea in from the kitchen. 'For the journey,' Don says, and we do a cheers to welcome him home and to toast the new house.

'Follow me so,' Sadhbh says, leading us out of the sitting room, back into the hallway and downstairs to a very swish open-plan kitchen and living room. 'You have a basement,' I gasp. I can't help it. I thought only American houses had basements – for their terrifying furnaces and teenage hangouts, the latter being my dream when I was fourteen. She also has a kitchen island – that's been on my vision board for as long as I can remember. A double sink and one of those drawers with the triple bins, and maybe even a hob right there in the middle of the room so you can baste something while entertaining your guests. Although basting seems to involve a fierce amount of butter and I'm not sure my carefully measured sprays of Fry Light would do the job.

'Lads, it's faboo,' Majella goes, draining her glass and examining the ice-cube dispenser in the fridge door. 'Are you loving it? You must be loving it – you have underfloor heating.'

'It's great,' Sadhbh says, and we settle in on another enormous couch for a good catch-up. 'I just wish we were here more. Don't say anything but The Peigs have just booked a US arena tour for next year so we're going to be based in New York for at least six months.'

Sadhbh gone again. I'll miss her. 'Well, isn't that brilliant, though,' I say. 'Think of the shopping – the outlets over there are something else.'

We chat and laugh and drink and before we know it three hours have flown by and there's a *ping* from the oven.

Don pipes up. 'Dinner is served, ladies'

****

I had my oh-yes-it's-delicious face all ready for when Sadhbh served up one of her mad dairy-free, gluten-free, taste-free buffets, but it turns out Don has taken over most of the cooking in the house. I wasn't complaining, let me tell you, when he handed me a plate of shepherd's pie. Okay, it was made with lentils and, okay, the topping inexplicably contained sweet potato, if you can even call that a potato, but it tasted bloody gorgeous all the same.

'Don, are you just good at everything? Is that it?' Majella half-accuses when we've had an hour to digest our main courses and he produces an apple crumble that was hiding in a second oven disguised as a microwave. Two eye-level ovens! My head is swimming slightly and I clock that we're on our fourth bottle of wine.

'Cooking destresses me,' Don says with a smile and my ears prick up. 'I hardly ever get to do it.'

'Really – does it, Don?' I say. Maybe I'll give it a go. Although, I spend a fair portion of my day in the kitchen of BallyGoBrunch and, if anything, being in charge of the toast only increases my stress levels. Carol has very exacting standards.

'Definitely. You should try it.' Then the phone in his pocket starts to vibrate and he backs out of the room muttering his apologies and something about Elton calling him at all hours.

We move back over to the couch and Sadhbh produces three woollen throws from a wooden chest doubling as an end table. I must add multiple spare woollen throws to the vision board.

'How are things in the café, Ais?' Sadhbh asks kindly, topping up my glass and passing it to me. I sent her something of an SOS text when I found myself having a small panic attack over settling on a new lunch special. It was very unlike me. But I've started to feel that familiar pull of anxiety more often these days, and even the smallest tasks occasionally feel impossible. Like asking if a friend's band will play at a wedding or choosing a lunch special. Next I'll be in full-blown panic when Carol asks if I want a cup of tea. I went for the darne of salmon for the special in the end. Sure you can't go wrong.

'I just have a lot going on at the minute, you know yourself.'

'Oh, I'll tell you where there's a lot going on – in James Matthews's bedroom.' Majella cackles. 'You lucky thing,' she adds with a sniff.

'Majella!' I go. But I'm fairly tipsy at this stage so I can't help myself spilling my guts. 'He's so lovely, though,' I whisper into my glass. 'And he's made such an effort to have all my favourite bits in his place for when I'm over …'

'Your Müller Lights. Even if they were the wrong flavour.' I had sent Sadhbh a picture of them. Toffee! Who buys the toffee ones?!

'That's more than John ever did after nearly nine years together,' Majella interjects with a nod, and I choose to ignore her.

'The problem is me. I just feel so wound up all the time. I'm always on edge. And I think it's because maybe he's too nice?'

'I think that's normal at the start of a relationship, before you start to get comfortable together,' Sadhbh says, putting together one of her rollies with one eye closed. 'Well, normal-ish. Are you still wearing the CC cream?'

I nod earnestly.

'I think you're having trouble relaxing in general at the moment, though – aren't you?' Sadhbh continues, and I hope she's not going to mention trying some of her crystals again. I don't understand how rubbing a lump of celestite is supposed to make me stop catastrophising over every little thing, but each to their own.

'I am a bit. Last week I brought up leftovers from the café – Carol's famous vegetable moussaka, which is always the Tuesday lunch special and a good way to use up the prepped veg from Monday. We had a lovely dinner, a glass of Pinot Greej and were just about to sit down with Netflix when a ferocious pain went through me.'

The girls look confused.

'You know, a pain. In my belly.' I nod down towards my lower half, mortified. 'A gas pain, like.'

Majella catches on and nods sagely. 'Moussaka farts. I know them well.'

Sadhbh shrieks with laughter and lies back, nearly drenching her lovely tracksuit.

Majella gives me a look. 'So? What was the problem?'

'I can't fart in front of him!' I shriek.

'You definitely can,' Sadhbh says, pulling herself together and nodding furiously. 'You're only human. I had to get Don to help me with an ingrown hair on my bikini line a few weeks ago. Guys aren't squeamish.'

'Well, that's just gross, Sadhbh.'

'So what did you do?' Maj asks.

'I panicked and ran straight out the front door and did it in the hallway. I'm surprised you didn't hear me. I ended up pretending I heard someone outside shouting "sausages" – it happens more than you'd think. And I'm shaving my legs at least once a day, sometimes twice, morning and night, which is crippling me financially – the price of razor blades! – but once you use the ones with the built-in Olay moisture bar you just can't go back.'

'I bet while you were outside he was inside doing the same thing,' Sadhbh says.

'Shaving his legs?'

'No, farting!'

I don't know about that. James doesn't fart. I'm convinced of it.

'You need to let your guard down,' she continues, opening another bottle. 'Be yourself around him. Was it not like this before, like, before you were boyfriend and girlfriend?'

'Well, I just didn't see him this much, did I? I was just sort of … in and out.'

This is out of my mouth before I realise what I've said, and the girls fall around the couches, shrieking with laughter. It really does feel like old times now, drinking wine and talking about boys. God, I miss it. I miss Dublin too, now that I'm here. I can feel the buzz and the energy of the city even through Sadhbh's fancy double glazing.

'It's still so new. I don't even fully know why he likes me. He called me "chilled out" the other day and said he likes that about me. I've never been called "chilled out" in my life, especially not at the moment. I've never actually been so tightly wound.'

'Moussaka makes me gassy too, Ais.'

I jump as my rant is interrupted. It's Don! How long has he been standing outside the door? I can feel my ears turn crimson and I'm fairly sure I've gone momentarily deaf. Maybe nobody will notice.

'Ais, you've gone bright red!' Majella roars. 'Here, Don, put on some tunes, will you? Good lad.'

Now Don Shields from The Peigs knows I fart and grow leg hair. Talk about things going from bad to worse.

'Listen, I'm a guy, I know how he thinks,' Don says, reaching for the remote while Majella mouths 'The Corrs, yeah?' at him. 'He doesn't give a shit about any of that stuff. I guarantee he wouldn't notice if you didn't shave your legs for a week. He's crazy about you. Sadhbh told me about the yoghurts.'

'Men like Müller Lights too,' I say with a shy smile.

'No, they don't.' He scoffs. 'He got them in because he luuurves you.'

I reach for one of the many cushions and bury my head in it. I'm not able for all this carry-on.

'How's your own living situation going, Maj?' Sadhbh asks, and I'm grateful for her changing the conversation. I feel safe enough to lift my head off the cushion just as she's tucking her legs under her bum and I have pins and needles just looking at her.

'Well, I caught Daddy and Shane eating one of my face masks after they crashed in from Maguire's last week, so I'll let you draw your own conclusions, bird. It's not easy.'

'In their defence,' I say diplomatically, delighted to have the focus off me, 'it was in the fridge and smelled like chocolate.'

'And what's the latest on the wedding?' Sadhbh once saw Majella drinking a bottle of cucumber eye-make-up remover while under the influence of a particularly catastrophic hangover, so she's not too fazed by the behaviour of the extended Moran family.

'It's all systems go. And, from what I hear, I'm going to have the hen party of the century.'

I feel an instant sweat go up the back of my head at the mention of the hen. I wonder should I work on lowering her expectations. I'm about to explain that there are a million and one things that could go wrong with it when my phone beeps in my bag. No matter how many times Sadhbh has begged me to get with the times and turn my ringer off, I refuse, and this is why. Who knows what I'd miss! I stumble over to the kitchen island to get it, expecting a good night message from James. But it's not James: it's Paul Oz New 2.

'Can I ring you?'

CHAPTER 18

I'm just about to text him back to warn him I'm about seven glasses of wine in when the phone starts ringing in my hand anyway, giving me a fierce fright.

'How do you manage to still have a polyphonic ringtone?' slags Sadhbh from the couch, but I just wave at Don to lower the music a bit.

'It's Paul. I better answer it,' I say, grabbing my glass of wine and heading upstairs to the fancy front sitting room. I check my watch – it's gone 11 here so it's about 9 in the morning in Melbourne.

I try to bend my legs under myself like Sadhbh but nearly fall over and spill my wine on the couch in the process. My nerves. I bet it cost more than my industrial-sized walk-in fridge in BallyGoBrunch.

'Well, P-Force,' I say, sitting down normally. P-Force was what Daddy used to call him when he fell and grazed his knees as a child. 'Everything all right?'

There's a sort of choking sound down the line. 'She broke up with me,' he eventually says in a strangled voice. 'Hannah. She said there's no point staying together while she's away.'

Poor Paul. He had seemed so happy.

'Ah, Paul, that's shite. I'm sorry to hear that.' I don't really know what else to say. We're fairly close, but we were never the best at having deep and meaningfuls. Not like Majella and her brother Shane when they get stuck into the Southern Comfort and red. They're like Oprah and Dr Phil then with their aha moments.

'I only told her I loved her the other day, Aisling.' He's sobbing and I'm a bit lost for words. I'm not used to Paul talking about his emotions and throwing around words like 'love'. It's not like him, especially when he's talking to me.

'I know it's a cliché, but there's plenty more fish in the sea. Especially where you are. Fish and sharks, isn't it? But he's not listening.

'I thought she was The One, Ais. She was perfect.'

'No one's perfect. We all fart!' I say emphatically, trying uselessly to cheer him up.

'I don't know what to do. I feel like I'm going out of my mind.' He gives a deep, shuddering sigh.

'Are none of the lads from home there to talk to? Philser Cuddihy – isn't he in the house with you?'

I'm grasping at straws here. Philser Cuddihy is a cousin of Mad Tom's and the last person you'd want near you in a crisis.

'They're gone off to play pitch and putt. Sure, I've hardly seen them in months. I was with Hannah.' He starts to cry again and I'm at a loss. 'I'm going to come home, Ais. I can't stay here without her. I want to be at home.'

'Now calm down, Paul. It was only four degrees here yesterday. Think about what you're saying.'

'Everything here is going to remind me of her. I could never go to the Tricolour again for a start.'

'Listen, I know things feel like a disaster right now, but you'll feel different soon, I promise.'

I think back to advice that gave me comfort when me and John split. 'Goodbye is a hello to a life without you.' 'When you're going through hell, keep going.' And, of course, my favourite.

'What's for you won't pass you,' I say gently to Paul. 'It's always the way.'

'Well, she's the one for me. And she's said she doesn't love me and to forget about her.'

Jesus, that seems very harsh. I've never heard Paul this upset. I could kill that Hannah one.

'Why don't you take your mind off it for the moment? You work on Sundays, don't you? Should you not be getting into your Mr Tayto costume? You must be busy with Christmas around the corner and everyone after the twenty-pack boxes.'

You can't have Christmas without a twenty-pack box of Taytos under the tree – I don't care if you're Australian or not.

'Fuck work. I'm not going. Fuck everything.' He trails off into tears again. 'I'll let you go, Aisling. I'm going to look at flights. I might need a lend.' And he's gone.

When I get back into the kitchen Majella has seized control of the remote and is standing on a kitchen chair dancing to The Peigs' forthcoming single, 'No Hot Ashes'. Don is doing his best impression of himself with a fish slice while Sadhbh is lighting a rollie off one of the gas rings on the fancy hob.

'Will I open another bottle?' she roars when she sees me and I don't have it in me to relay the Paul news. So I nod.

****

It's nearly eleven when I wake up the next morning, but I'm still wrecked. It took me ages to get to sleep, the worrying I was doing about Paul – I kept thinking about him sitting there on his own crying. I think about texting John – they are good pals after all. But would it be odd to text him out of nowhere? He wasn't mad for the texting even when we were together. I once sent him an essay about seeing who I thought was Rod Stewart on the bus (it wasn't Rod Stewart but it could have been, and I swear the woman had the same hair and nose) and all I got back from John was 'K. Will u buy milk?' I didn't talk to him for two days. But then, I suppose, there was the time he was on a stag in Antwerp and he sent me twenty-three texts in one hour trying to tell me he loved me. It's really quite something the number of times you can misspell 'love'.

I decided not to text him for the time being about Paul. Paul will be grand. He overreacts about things. Instead, I started worrying about the catering orders I left Carol to look after while I'm off gallivanting. She insisted I take the time off, and I suppose she was off for her niece's wedding last week, but I just can't stop fretting. Then I started wondering if I should put the willy straws for the hen in my carry-on in case they lose my luggage. The mattress in Sadhbh and Don's spare room wasn't to blame for my sleeplessness, anyway. It was like a cloud. And, of course, I took two paracetamol and drank a pint of water before turning in so at least I'm not completely dying. It's the only way to ward off a hangover, other than just not drinking. And I wasn't about to do that in party season, as they call December on *Xposé*.

There's no sign of anyone moving so I help myself to a tin of Diet Coke from the entire shelf of Diet Cokes in the fridge and then take a second one to hold to my head. I don't feel too bad but old habits die hard. I retrieve my phone from where I left it charging beside the couch – apparently having it in the bedroom is the last thing you need if you've trouble sleeping – and check for messages from Paul. Nothing. I fire off a text asking how he's doing now, hoping he's had a change of heart about coming home. Although, I suppose he might be a good help to Mammy with the eco farm, if it comes to that. As I'm sending it, a message from James flashes up. It's a picture of two mugs on his kitchen table.

'Got one out for you without thinking. Hope you're having fun x.'

'What are you smiling like an eejit at? And how do you look so grand?' Majella accuses me as she slopes into the kitchen. 'I'm in bits. On a scale of rice to sand I'm basically dust.'

Sadhbh follows her, heading straight for the fancy coffee machine. There's no sign of Don at all.

'You know how.' I shrug. 'I offered you some Panadol last night and you said "codeine or nothing" and wobbled off to ring Pablo. I tried, Maj.'

'Fair enough, bird.'

'Were you talking to him today yet?' Sadhbh asks her, sticking on a round of toast. 'Has he calmed down?'

Apparently when he'd answered the phone Pablo was sobbing quietly. Nothing new there, I thought – he probably just saw a nice bird or something. But Majella eventually got him to admit he's cacking it about the stag, even though it's months away. The lads have told him he needs to bring his passport, get an anti-tetanus shot and write his name and blood type on a consent form. They're only winding him up, but he's taken to googling 'Irish stag parties' and is worried they're taking him out to international waters in Chief Gittons's speedboat. I said I'd doubt it since it only has enough space for four people and a cool box for fishing bait. Besides, John would never plan anything really dangerous. He once witnessed a lad sellotaped to a lamppost in Dingle and it was so cold his mickey is said to have never recovered. A cautionary tale if ever there was one.

'Yeah, he's grand now,' Majella says, helping herself to a slice of Sadhbh's fancy seedy bread and lashing on the Kerrygold – I never leave home without it. I might be a Fry Light devotee for cooking, but when it comes to bread and butter I'm a purist and only a thick layer will do, Points be damned.

'And where are you at with the wedding prep? I bought a hat when I was in Japan.'

I notice Majella taking a deep breath and steadying herself on the kitchen island. She wouldn't be a fan of Sadhbh's mad outfits at the best of times, but the thought of her in a Japanese hat might push her over the edge, even though Maj herself was a big fan of Gwen Stefani's Harajuku phase.

'We're motoring, aren't we, Ais?'

'We are.'

We are, I tell myself. We'll be grand. I sent her on a few ideas for invitations last week, very classy, so that's another thing off my list.

'They've a new wedding coordinator in the Ard Rí who seems a bit clueless, but we're not worried.' She steals a look at me. 'Are we?'

'Not at all,' I say, shaking my head. 'Everything is under control. And we haven't said a word to anyone about The Peigs playing. It's going to be the talk of the night.'

'Excuse me?' Majella goes in mock horror.

'After how stunning the bride is, of course,' I add.

'That's more like it.'

'Does Pablo have many coming from Tenerife?' Sadhbh asks.

'Last count was forty-two and three kids, which is plenty. We have to have a Spanish priest now to keep them up to speed. Felipe from Maguire's was able to put me in touch with one.'

'I thought he was Brazilian?' Sadhbh looks confused.

'He is. But he's a great connoisseur of the Romantic languages. That's a direct quote from him. Father Fenlon is bulling, of course. He hates sharing the altar.'

'And dare I ask, what about the dress?'

'No joy yet,' Majella says sadly. 'I think I'll need a miracle to get one that I love with my current budget.'

'I actually saw an incredible dress in *Vogue*'s wedding special – well, it was a while ago now, but it just screamed Majella to me. Let me see if I can find it. I think I put all my magazines in here,' Sadhbh says quietly, walking over to a deep drawer and rummaging a bit before producing said magazine, the colour coming back into her cheeks. Nothing like a bit of fashion chat to get her blood pumping. The corner of one of the pages is turned down and she flips it over.

There's a sharp intake of breath when we see the dress. Sadhbh was right, it *is* very Majella. But in a good way. A great way!

Maj stabs at the page with her finger. 'This! This is the exact style I'm after. Just look at that boat neck.'

It's faboo. Absolutely faboo. Majella has collarbones like razor blades.

'It couldn't be more perfect,' she says. 'I have to have it! Pablo will need to be hospitalised when he sees me in this. Paramedics on standby, Ais.'

Then she looks for the price. 'Six grand! Ah, Sadhbh, what are you doing to me here?'

'Calm down, calm down,' Sadhbh says. 'Krystal Ball is the designer and I know for a fact that her dresses go on sale all the time, and they go for quite cheap. Well, comparatively. And this magazine is about six months old. Write down the style and keep your eyes peeled in January. You might get lucky.'

'Fingers crossed,' Maj says, tearing the page out. 'And if I don't?'

'And if you don't, there's this amazing girl Diva who styles Don and the lads. She also designs the most stunning gowns. I could get you an appointment if you're interested? Mates rates!'

'Deadly! Does this Aoife have a shop or something I could go into for a goo?' Majella asks.

'Diva.'

'I just wanted to have a look!'

'No!' Sadhbh laughs. 'Her name is Diva, not Aoife.'

'Oh, right,' Majella goes. 'Eh, I'll let you know then.'

CHAPTER 19

'm barely in the door when Mammy comes flying into the kitchen, the cordless phone in her hand. 'Paul was saying he was talking to you. Ah, Aisling, my heart is broken for him. The craythur.'

'Do you not think he's being a bit dramatic, Mammy? He's talking about coming home and everything,' I say, parking my wheelie bag and lifting up the kettle and then flicking it on. My white wine hangover is starting to make itself known. I nearly had to drop poor Majella at the County General on the way home – she asked for a pen and paper to write her will when we were passing the Red Cow.

'Oh, his flights are booked,' she says, going for the mugs. 'He'll be home in time for Christmas.'

'But what about the rental deposit on the house? His job?'

'Philser Cuddihy said they'll have no problem renting out his room so he gave him the deposit back. It nearly covered the flights.'

'Nearly?'

'Well, it's two weeks to Christmas. He was lucky to get a seat at all, Aisling, with the amount of Irish in Australia. I just gave him a few bob to make up the difference. I couldn't have him halfway across the world with not even a Terry's Chocolate Orange in the state he's in.'

Mammy's always been like this with Paul – nothing is ever too much trouble for her golden boy. I could be on fire in the middle of the calving shed and she'd step over me to bring him a ham and cheese sandwich with the crusts cut off.

'Well, I suppose he could give you a hand with the farm. Any new bookings since your media blitz?' I feel bad that I even have to ask that. I should be helping out more but I just don't have the headspace to take on anything else at the minute.

'Oh, did I not tell you? We're booked out for February! Constance sent John a picture of a pet lamb sucking milk from a bottle, and as soon as it went up on the website we got a school tour, two hens and a corporate retreat. Air traffic controllers from Shannon, I believe.'

'That's deadly, Mammy.'

'How's Sadhbh and himself, the rock star? Still singing about Liam Neeson, is he?'

'Well, it's Pierce Brosnan, but yeah. The place in Ranelagh is lovely. Two ovens, if you don't mind.'

'Ah, isn't that great. God, you're all so grown up now, settling down and getting married. It's starting to make me feel a bit old.' Then off she goes, humming 'Oh Come All Ye Faithful', to return the phone to its cradle – God forbid the battery gets used.

****

It's pitch dark at 6 a.m. when I pull up the shutters and open the back door to BallyGoBrunch. But the Christmas trade waits for no woman. As well as her signature mince pies and spicy gingerbread women, Carol's new limited-edition Santy Sandwich has been flying out the door. It's great for business, but it also means someone has to get in early to fire up the oven for Billy Foran's organic turkey breasts. I'm rostered on today, but I'm tired after tossing and turning all night, dreaming of monster kangaroos and oven timers that can't be turned off. I pride myself on being no slave to the demon coffee, but I whip myself up a little cup of Nescafé to keep me going – which seems criminal given the freshly ground beans not five metres away from me, but if my hand was forced I'd have to say I couldn't be bothered with all the fluthering.

Half an hour later I'm in the office making a small dent in the paperwork that's been piling up when I hear a key in the back door.

'Well, Carol,' I call out. 'Ready for another day of it?'

'Are you alright, Aisling?' she says, appearing in the doorway after a minute, a concerned look on her face.

'Why?' I ask, swinging around in my ergonomic office chair.

'It's just the trays of turkey are on the counter.'

I jump up, scooch past her and fly out into the kitchen. But she's right, of course: her carefully seasoned turkey breasts, scattered with sprigs of rosemary and thyme, are indeed sitting out catching salmonella instead of roasting in the oven, which is going full blast. I distinctly remember turning it on but I could have sworn I'd put the turkey in too.

'I ... I'm sorry, Carol. I thought I'd done it,' I stammer, mortified.

'Not to worry, love. I'll pop them in now. They'll still be done in time,' she glances at her watch, 'more or less.'

'Would it help if I cranked up the temperature?'

'And serve dry turkey in my Santy Sandwich? Over my dead body. Now go on, back to your desk. I've some party bits to assemble and the sausage rolls to put on.'

I'm on my way back to the office – it's very hard to say no to Carol when she's being uncharacteristically stern – when there's a knock on the front door. Mother of God, it's like Heuston Station here today. We're not due to open for another twenty minutes but I go out to answer it anyway in case it's a lunch order from the crew at Garbally. They've been sausage-bap stalwarts since they arrived, thanks in no small part to James's encouragement, I'm sure.

I'm expecting to see some lad in a high-vis but instead there's an immaculately turned-out woman smiling through the glass at me. She's dressed head to toe in black and has two phones in one hand and a BallyGoBrunch catering leaflet in the other.

'Hi!' she trills. 'Mandy Blumenthal. Can I come in?' She waves the leaflet at me. 'My apologies, I thought you'd be open at 6.40, but I guess things are pretty laid-back around here, huh.'

An American. Americans outside America make me nervous. They seem louder than usual and make ordering chips unnecessarily complicated and have much better raincoats than us. Although this woman isn't wearing a raincoat. It's probably in her car.

'We don't normally open till seven,' I say apologetically, opening the door and flipping the sign around. In for a penny and all that. 'I'm Aisling, the owner. What can I do for you?'

'This is your place, then? Honey, it's super-cute. I love it.'

'Thanks a million.'

We worked hard to make the place 'Instagram friendly' on Sadhbh and Elaine's advice and they were right. People are flat out posting photos of their #kale and #sausagemeat salads, although a fierce number of them seem to think there's aubergine in it if their emojis are anything to go by.

Mandy looks down at the leaflet and follows me across to the counter where Carol is walking past with a tray of sausage rolls ready for the oven. My stomach growls at the sight of them, even in their raw state.

'And this is Carol, who runs the kitchen,' I say, as Carol sort of genuflects and backs into a massive bag of spuds.

'Carol, hello!' Mandy says cheerfully. I bet she starts the day power-walking in heels on a treadmill while barking into a headset. 'Your food comes highly recommended,' she continues. 'I know I should have called ahead but I was passing and was wondering if there might be any samples available to try for an event I'm putting together?'

'Carol, the canapés,' I mutter out of the side of my mouth, and Carol immediately goes scurrying off to the back larder where there are evening platters waiting for tonight's Knock Retired Undertakers/Bowls Club joint Christmas dinner-dance. They didn't have enough people for their own individual events so they teamed up, and there are actually a few retired undertakers on the bowls team anyway. 'Where is the event on?'

'I can only give details upon signature of contracts, I'm afraid,' she says with a huge American smile. 'There is a degree of confidentiality involved.' My mind immediately goes to Garbally and the birthday party. Surely not. Although, why else would an American be in here asking about food? We get the very odd USA road tripper passing through, asking about shillelaghs and Barack Obama's cousins, but BGB's most famous ancestor is the great-great-great-grandfather of the lad who invented Skips. We're very proud but he's no Obama.

Carol re-emerges with some tiny bits and pieces that I was initially worried might be too small for the large paws of either the undertakers or the bowlers, but she assures me they're packed with flavour and don't need to be any bigger. Mini parmesan tarts, the freshly baked sausage rolls in thyme pastry, ham and Cheddar croquettes – people go wild for them. I scoot out from behind the counter and direct Mandy to the closest table while Carol places the plate and a stack of napkins in front of her. We both stand there like spares, and it's only when she politely asks for some water that I realise we're gawping at her and we retreat behind the counter and pretend to be busy.

I hold my breath as Mandy picks up a meatball-and-relish stacker and sniffs it before taking a tiny bird-like bite and sits there for a second with her eyes closed, seemingly having a religious experience. Then she pulls a small notebook out of her bag and starts scribbling. I steal a look at Carol, who gives me a wink. She's right to be confident – it looks simple but the marinade is absolute dynamite and she knows it. There's Guinness of all things in it.

As soon as she tastes the sausage roll, Mandy takes out one of her phones and punches in a number. 'Honey!' she chirps. 'You were right – it's absolutely darling. The Instagram photos almost don't do it justice. And the food is delicious. A contender for sure. I can just imagine the trays circling the orchard.'

CHAPTER 20

'The woman who came to Garbally that time, was her name Mandy? American? A heap of phones?'

I was up to James's place like a shot as soon as I saw his jeep coming in.

We were mad busy between finalising the bits for the dinner-dance and the usual café rushes and lulls, so I didn't get a chance to ring him after Mandy left BallyGoBrunch. She said she'd be in touch and asked how many people we can cater for in total and what's our lead-in time and a million and one other questions. The most we've done so far is about a hundred but I showboated and said we can adapt to any size. If she's talking about catering at Garbally, and I suspect she is, we definitely want in, no matter how much of a pain in my stomach it gives me. We'll figure it out.

'Hello to you too,' he says, kissing my cheek.

'The woman, James. The woman at Garbally. Was she American?'

He rubs his stubble and ponders for an interminable moment. 'She was. And you're right. She did have a lot of phones.'

'She was in this morning.' I beam. 'At the crack of dawn, actually. I think she's going to hire us to do some catering. She seemed impressed with Carol's canapés anyway.'

James looks confused. 'But the first event isn't scheduled until early summer. Final snags aren't due until the beginning of April.'

This is the most I've been able to get out of him about Garbally since he started. For a man who can be so flush with the compliments – I've managed to get him down to calling me stunning about twice a day, thanks be to Jesus – he can be difficult to glean information from. In the two months since my birthday, I've struggled to learn much more about him than I knew going into this relationship. He gives me only monosyllabic answers about his family or his friends back at home, as if he doesn't want to share his life with me at all. But then other times he's so loving and kind – and still a bit over the top, if I'm honest. I stayed at home in Mammy's last night and when I got up at the crack of dawn there were five texts about how much he'd missed me. We're off-balance, somehow. I need to find a way to address it with him. 'Communication is to a relationship what oxygen is to life. Without it it dies.' I took a screenshot of that one off Facebook and sent it to Maj, who was still complaining about Pablo being shy in the bedroom. Maybe I need to take some of my own screenshotted advice.

To be fair to James, though, he's more about the building and the craftsmanship when it comes to Garbally, not the parties and canapés.

'Four months is nothing to an event planner. We got an order in for a communion yesterday that's not on till next year. Nothing wrong with being organised.'

Suddenly there's a knock on the door. We both stare at each other. James doesn't often get visitors here at the apartment, especially ones that get past the intercom on the outside door.

'We know yis are in there,' roars Shem Moran after a second. 'Open up!'

'Daddy, stop!' I hear Majella hiss, and then another thud. Probably a swift kick to his ankle.

I smile at James apologetically and he opens the door. Straight in front of me are Shem and Majella alright, and between them is an absolutely massive noble fir. I'd say nine foot at least.

'To say thanks for keeping us off the streets these past few months,' Shem says to James, who looks understandably horrified. Although the Morans plus Pablo have been model tenants, James has only been charging them about half what he could be getting for the apartment. A sound gesture, no doubt about it.

'It's very big, Shem,' I say nervously. 'You didn't …?'

'Oh, you know he did, Aisling,' Maj pipes up. 'What Coillte doesn't know won't hurt them. He got one for us too.'

'They're charging €55 for them this year in Knock Garden Centre,' Shem says, shaking his head furiously and pushing the massive tree through the door towards me. 'It's daylight robbery. Happy Christmas now.' And off they go down the hall, bickering away.

'I suppose this means I'm decorating for Christmas, although I hadn't planned on it,' James says a little glumly, closing the door. We haven't talked about Christmas plans. I assume he's going home but I'm nearly afraid to ask. Instead, I embrace the festive spirit.

'Ah God, you have to throw up a few lights – sure isn't that what Christmas is about? Twinkly lights and too many Pringles and fighting over Trivial Pursuit? I can give you a hand later if you like. I have a rake of baubles left over from the tree downstairs.'

'Okay, yeah, that'd be nice. Make the place a bit more homey,' he says with a smile. 'I'll buy a bottle of wine. We can make a night of it.'

****

There are no less than five emails from Mandy Blumenthal in my inbox when I get a blessed few minutes to slip into the office the next day. According to her signature she's a 'party consultant and event engineer' based out of New York City, and they were sent at all hours of the day and night, even taking the time difference into consideration.

I scan the first one fast, half-afraid of what it's going to say. 'Farm to table', 'cocktail hour hors d'oeuvres' and '250 guests' all immediately jump out at me. Apparently she's 'obsessed' with our 'whole vibe'! 'We'd love to secure your services, honey,' she says. 'I was worried you were a small-time operation so I can't tell you how happy I was to hear you could cater to a big crowd. Looking forward to working with you.' *Yes!* I punch the air. If me and Carol can pull this off, BallyGoBrunch catering could properly break into the high-end events market. This would be a massive deal and all in under a year since my little café first opened its doors. I'm delighted, I really am. Well, I'm 70 per cent delighted. The other 30 per cent feels a lot like dread. And nausea. How are we supposed to cater a cocktail hour? Especially one that involves a big crowd and requires an event engineer from New York? I'm already feeling a bit stretched with the hen to organise. Would it be taking on too much? But I can't turn this down. At least Paul will be at home now to help Mammy when she needs it. Yes, this is a good thing. This is definitely a good thing. But what if I commit to it and somehow mess it up? The business might never recover. I decide not to think about that.

The second email is a list of Mandy's favourite canapés – the sausage rolls came out on top, naturally – and a pretty thorough questionnaire about ingredients and allergens. I'll forward that on to Carol. The third is a list of suggestions to keep vegans, coeliacs and the lactose intolerant happy, and she's gone to the trouble of copying and pasting ideas from our online menu. Very thorough. This Mandy Blumenthal is obviously at the top of her game.

The fourth email was meant for her dog walker, called Aimee. I see what happened there. She's wondering if Aimee could bring Salt and Pepa to the groomer after their doggy yoga on Wednesday morning. And the fifth email is to tell me that she'll have a contract to me by Christmas and a heads-up that I'll be expected to sign a non-disclosure agreement.

****

James is thrilled when I fill him in later in Maguire's.

'Did you say yes? Do I need to order some Romanian plonk?'

'I did,' I reply hesitantly. 'How could I not? It's a brilliant opportunity.'

'You don't sound too happy about it?'

'It's just such a huge commitment – 250 people, she said! My nerves were gone totting up how much the ingredients alone are going to cost me. This has to go off without a hitch.'

'You have months to plan, and you and Carol together are unstoppable. You'll absolutely nail it!'

And Majella's hen to execute in the meantime, and her wedding to make sure Lisa Gleeson doesn't make a hames of. And the café to run. And Paul to worry about. And Mammy.

'Do you not get nervous taking on a big job, James?'

'No.' Oh. 'Stop worrying. And, hey, we'll practically be working together. Power couple or what?'

He glances up at the telly, which is showing BBC News. This is what happens when the place is empty and Felipe lets him take control of the remote. If anyone walked in and saw we were cheating on Six One I'd be turfed out of BGB, but James is far enough away from home without taking the Downing Street cat and whatnot away from him too. The news has something on about high-street sales figures ahead of Christmas. I broke the habit of a lifetime and did most of my shopping online this time round. God forgive me, if another Dublin institution closes down because of my disloyalty I'll never forgive myself, but there's only so many hours in the day. I'm still not over the loss of A Wear and it's been years. I'll probably get a few more bits in Knock Garden Centre – there's a Le Creuset teapot in there I think Mammy would love. 'Oh, lovely, another teapot,' she said when I gave her the blue one for her last birthday so at least I know she likes them. I don't know what to get James. I'm at a complete loss. He doesn't seem to want for very much, and he's got plenty of fancy aftershaves and shirts. I'm usually top notch at choosing presents but this is a tricky one.

'What do you want for Christmas?' I nudge him.

He furrows his brow for a second, thinking, and then smiles. 'I have everything I need right beside me.'

I swear, I'm not able for his romantic lines sometimes. I'd be mortified only there's nobody looking at me. Yesterday he suggested getting a couple's massage sometime. I had to explain that it was far from couple's massages I was reared, and anyway I get very awkward in spa-type places. I never know if I'm supposed to be in the nip or wearing my good knickers or my togs or what.

'Speaking of Christmas,' James sits up and turns around to me, 'I've decided I'm going to fly home. I'll go on the twenty-third.'

'Oh, lovely. The airport will be magic,' I say, delighted he's offered up this information at least. I hadn't really considered that he might *not* go home. Who doesn't go home, like? Imagine James Matthews sitting with us in our pyjamas eating selection boxes at half nine and trying to keep That Bloody Cat away from the sausagemeat stuffing.

'Harry was insistent.' He pulls a tight smile. 'He can't possibly have Christmas without his big brother, or so he says. Actually,' his eyebrows raise, 'my dad … my parents wanted to extend an invitation to you, to come with me for Christmas. I've told them all about you and they're really keen to meet you. I suspect they think I've made you up.'

I don't tell him that I was starting to think the same about them. I don't even have to think about his offer, though. 'I couldn't. I'm sorry – I couldn't leave Mammy.'

Mammy would hate to hear me saying that, I know, but it's true. She's getting back into the spirit of Christmas this year – our second one since we lost Daddy. She has three boxes of Chocolate Kimberleys hidden in the garage, and it's a good job I'm out of the house half the time because I'm not able to sleep thinking about them when I'm there. The eco farm has been open for Christmas tours for a week now and they're absolutely flying. Only one Santa hat has been lost to an alpaca's gob, and the farm shop has to be restocked every evening.

'Even with Paul coming home?'

'I just … couldn't.'

'It's okay. I told Dad you'd probably feel like that.'

'Tell them thanks, though, won't you? It's so nice to be asked. And I'd love to meet them. Just not at Christmas.'

'How about New Year's Eve then?' he counters, raising an eyebrow and taking a gulp of his pint.

My first instinct is to say no again. I don't know why. I wasn't lying when I said I wanted to meet them – I really do, half out of nosiness. And parents usually love me. I suppose it's just a bit nerve-wracking, since they're English and probably drive a Rolls-Royce or something. I don't know what to expect. Will Mammy mind? I was at Elaine and Ruby's wedding last New Year's Eve but that was only in Dublin and, sure, she was invited herself. But going away feels different. It puts another bit of distance between us and the life we had when Daddy was still with us. New Year's Eves will be different for Mammy for evermore now. And for all of us.

'Okay,' I say, surprising myself. Carpe Diem. 'Sure, I have nothing else on. And the café will be quiet with everyone's houses being stocked to bursting.'

'Really?' he says with a wide smile. 'Great. And Harry and Natasia will be there too.'

'Brilliant. I can't wait to see how this Buckleton place compares to BGB. How many ATMs do you have?'

'Er, none, I don't think. There's just the Pig and Poddle and the village shop.'

No ATM? Amateurs.

CHAPTER 21

You could water a desert with the condensation on the windows of Strong Stuff where Sharon is executing curly blow-dries like her life depends on it, heels and all. My head is over the basin and Majella's decided that Christmas Eve is the day to get serious about Operation Wedding Hair and has a whole roll of tinfoil on her head. Fair play to Sharon, she didn't blink an eye when Maj pointed to a picture of Rosie Huntington-Whiteley in a magazine and said, 'That please.' Majella's hair has been every colour under the sun, often at her own hand and often with disastrous consequences and more than one scarlet neck. So who knows, maybe Sharon *will* have her looking like Rosie come May.

'When is Paul home?' Maj roars at me across Cillian Ruane, who's letting Caitriona loose on his eyebrows with the thread. He nearly loses one he gives such a lep with the fright. Cillian is definitely an early adopter among the BGB lads when it comes to eyebrows. He went to art school in Dublin and told Deirdre he's pansexual so he'd be fairly on the ball. Dee told him not to tell their father, but Trevor Ruane spent a summer in San Francisco in the seventies and can't be scandalised so it all went grand.

'This afternoon,' I roar back at her, as Cliodhna, the other Ó Súilleabháin twin, scalds my scalp with the water.

'A bit of cold, Cliodhna, good girl,' I encourage her through gritted teeth. Sharon says they're great workers but lack an ounce of cop-on. A crisis was narrowly averted the other day when she intercepted Caitriona on her way to apply a peach rinse to Granny Daly's tight white curls. Imagine the sight of her at mass.

'I'd say your mother is delighted, is she?' Maj roars again, just as Sharon turns off her hairdryer. Half the salon turns to look at her and she mouths a sheepish 'sorry'.

'She's already baked two apple tarts and his electric blanket has been on for hours,' I reply.

'Jesus, he must be in a bad way.'

'You know Mammy, any excuse to mollycoddle him.'

'Still,' Majella goes sympathetically, 'it's hard being newly single at Christmas, especially since all his friends are still Down Under.'

'I know,' I say, as Cliodhna nearly takes my scalp off with her acrylic nails. 'I offered to pick him up from the airport but he said he'd get the Timoney's bus and not be putting me out.'

Paul sounded fierce sorry for himself on the phone so I think he was being a martyr. I let him off because I've enough to be at and I've hardly time for the blow-dry even. Carol is doing up the last of the Christmas hampers at the café and operating a cold-food-only menu for the day, thinking it would be quiet enough with people out doing their Big Shops and Last Bits. She texted me half an hour ago to say we were out of pâté already and there was a queue nearly out the door for coffees. I must remember that for next year, assuming we're still there. Right now, the thought of making it to another Christmas at BallyGoBrunch seems like climbing a fifth flight of stairs when the previous four have burnt the lungs out of your chest.

James hit the road early this morning, not even batting an eyelid when I asked him had he booked his airport parking, declaring that he'd just 'find something in short term'. And him not back until New Year's Day. The legs nearly went from under me. I was half-expecting him to ring me to say he was still driving around Dublin Airport five hours later, but all I got was a text of a picture of a pint and a 'see you in six days', smiley face.

Cliodhna is massaging the conditioner into my hair with what feels like knives when Lisa Gleeson opens the door, letting a blessed blast of freezing-cold air in.

'Curly blow-dry, is it, hun?' Sharon calls to her from where she's examining what's going on under Majella's tinfoil, and Lisa nods in the affirmative, clocking Majella in the process and making a beeline for her. Cliodhna sits me up and wraps a towel like a vice around my head, absentmindedly asking me have I any holidays planned as she leads me to the chair beside Maj.

'I'm actually going abroad for New Year's ...'

But she's already gone back to the sinks to torture someone else.

'I still can't believe you're ringing in the New Year in a *lad's house*.' Majella's tone is a mixture of awe and disgust. This is the second year in a row I'll be missing our traditional night out in the Vortex but, to be fair, we were both at Elaine and

Ruby's wedding last year. And anyway, maybe we've grown out of the Vortex. We've been going there since we were seventeen and Jocksy Cullen let us in even though he knew well we were underage. Daddy had slipped him a tenner in Maguire's and told him we were good girls and he'd rather we were in there dancing to Justin Timberland than out drinking vodka in a field.

'I can't either, to be honest.'

Mammy took the news well. At least I think she did. It can be hard to tell sometimes.

'Sure isn't that alright, love? I'd expect you to be going out with him anyway.'

'No, I mean I'm going to spend it with his family. In England.'

She went quiet for a second and I couldn't read her face. But then she smiled. 'Well, isn't that lovely for you. You'll have to take some local honey from the farm shop with you for his mother.'

'Are you sure you don't mind me going?'

'Of course I don't, pet. Whatever makes you happy. Now bring me down your nice pyjamas and I'll iron them so you don't make a show of us.'

****

'What are you going to wear? Will you be going out?'

Majella's face has started to turn puce under the halo of tinfoil, and the noise in the salon has cranked up another notch between Cillian's yelps and the two hairdryers on the go. I shrug at Majella and make a pained face. 'James said they have a party every year – in the house.'

'Ah, shite. You can't even escape. Good job you're good with mams.'

As if on cue, the door opens and John's mother, Fran, walks in. Behind her trots Megan, who must be going with them to Midnight Mass. She has the family stamp of approval so. Fran clocks us straight away. 'Hello girls,' she says with a nod and a tight smile. 'Looks like we all had the same idea.'

'Bad hair day!' I blurt out, desperate to say something. Fran's eyes narrow and she pats the back of her hair, which is cut short in that classic do that mams love.

'Thank you, Aisling,' she says curtly, turning to Megan, while I mutter, 'I meant my own,' and try to sink as low as I possibly can into my chair. Why can't I just be normal around her?

'Majella,' Fran says sharply. 'You might tell your father the Christmas tree he provided for the church altar has already dropped every needle and a bird's nest fell out of it this morning.'

Majella nods obediently, her tinfoil wig rustling. Megan gives us a sweet smile and Cliodhna leads them to the waiting area and takes their tea order, which if it's anything like mine will be delivered catastrophically wrong. Thank God for the Lindor, although we're all supposed to be getting Trim for Tenerife. It was Maeve's idea – something to keep us on the straight and narrow over Christmas, she said. 'Don't tell on me now,' I say to Sharon, horsing into my third Lindor. She purses her lips and reaches for a comb but doesn't say anything. They must be costing her a fortune.

'Majella,' Lisa says matter-of-factly, 'I've been thinking about what you said about meaningful poems to break up the speeches.'

I've told Majella I have a folder of those on my laptop. Lovely Poems. So handy.

'Well, I came across one you might like.' She picks up her phone and swipes through her notes. Maybe I've underestimated her. 'Feck, I thought I had it here,' she says, putting back down the phone and sounding frustrated. 'You know the one, girls. He says something about stopping the clocks. And giving the dog a juicy bone?'

Me and Maj look at each other at the same time.

'Does that one not mention mourners and coffins, Lisa?' I ask tentatively. 'I think it's about funerals?'

'Fairly sure it's about funerals, hun.' Sharon has momentarily stopped all the hairdryers to correct her.

Lisa looks confused and turns to me and Maj, who nods sagely. 'Funerals, Lisa. Definitely funerals.'

Lisa goes back to the phone, furiously adding to her notes.

****

Sharon has me in the chair and six big curly brushes already in my hair before I know it, God bless her. I was afraid I was going to have to make small talk with Fran and Megan.

'This will last you to Stephenses Day,' she roars over the hairdryer.

I haven't the heart to tell her I won't be going out. It's been such a hectic lead-up to Christmas that any plans for socialising have gone by the wayside. Plus, I'll be working. No rest for the self-employed. I'm looking forward to my lie in tomorrow, though. Me and Paul used to get up at the crack of dawn when we were small, with Daddy roaring at us to go back to bed for an hour, although we could tell he didn't mean it.

'Enjoy your turkey and ham, hun.' Sharon pulls the last section of hair into a perfect coil and combs through with her fingers. She whips the cape off and up I get, squeezing past Fran and Megan to get my coat.

'Sorry now, happy Christmas. Sorry there.'

Sharon already has Lisa in the chair and is instructing Cliodhna to get Megan under the taps as I open the door, waving goodbye to Majella.

I step out onto the relative quiet of BGB's Main Street, shake out my curls and relish the silence in my ears. Another stellar job by Sharon. I sneak a look in Marty Boland's window and try to picture myself in the Matthewses' ballroom or wherever their party will be.

'Hiya, Ais.'

His voice sounds different. It's been only on the phone or on Skype for so long. I turn and Paul is standing on the street, massive GAA hold-all over his shoulder, black circles under his eyes. Beside him is John, shuffling his feet in the cold and jangling his car keys.

'John passed me at the bus stop outside Heuston. Thanks, lad.' He shakes John's hand and John gives me a nod and I sort of lurch towards him and we awkwardly half-hug, so quick that it's like we're each made of scalding oil.

He steps back, nods at Paul again and gives him a little dig on the shoulder. 'Mind yourself now. You look like a boiled shite. Go on and get a good night's sleep and some home-cooked food.' Paul manages a watery smile as John turns his attention back to me. 'Are you all finished up yourself for the Christmas, Ais?'

'I am, yeah. We've been flat out. I'm dying to get home.'

'Let me guess – new pyjamas ready to go,' he says, giving me a gentle nudge with his elbow. Of course he knows this, given he used to be the one buying them. He always had a good eye for nightwear. Cosy and functional, just the way I like it.

'Old habits,' I reply quietly. 'You can't be waking up on Christmas morning in old pyjamas.'

'Pablo says you're away for New Year's.'

'That's right, yeah. Bit of a change of scenery.'

'I suppose I'll see you next year so,' he says.

I'm no stranger to a late December 'see you next year' gag myself, but coming from John it feels weird.

'Happy Christmas,' I say. And with that he's gone into the salon and straight over to Megan.

Paul is next for the awkward hug, and with that out of the way I gesture with my head. 'Come on. The car is over here. He's right, you do look wrecked.'

CHAPTER 22

Christmas Day passes in a blur of post-mass visitors and little drops of Baileys and just the one alpaca escape. I nearly choked when James texted me from the Pig and Poddle to say he missed me and was looking forward to my visit. Imagine going to the pub on Christmas Day? The English really are a law on to themselves. After dinner I fell asleep in front of *Chitty Chitty Bang Bang* and Mammy admitted she put a spoon under my nose twice to make sure I hadn't died of a Quality Street overdose.

After all the weeks of stress and worry, I'm actually feeling more like my old self when I find Paul sitting at the kitchen table staring into space on Stephenses morning. Maybe all I needed was a good rest?

'Hellooo? Anyone home?' I say, waving him out of his trance and moving some files over to the counter. The table has been doubling as Mammy's office and there are letters and sheaves of paper everywhere. 'Where's Mammy?'

'Out in the farm shop. She said something about marking down chestnuts.'

Bloody Constance Swinford and her notions. She had Mammy convinced BGB was ready for them. 'Marian, chestnuts are simply *diviiine* in stuffing!' she had brayed, insisting she put in a big order from my Brussels sprouts contact. 'We won't be able to keep them on the shelves.'

Well, Constance was wrong. People around here don't stray far from sausagemeat or the classic sage and onion, unless under strict instructions from Neven Maguire. And Neven hasn't okayed chestnuts in stuffing yet. I wonder could Carol do something with them for the Garbally canapés? Would they keep that long? And then I stop myself. No, Aisling. You're not to panic about work stuff until you get back after New Year's Eve. January is for panicking – it's still party season. *Xposé* says so.

As such, I'm considering adding a few Roses to my Special K when Mammy appears in the kitchen, shaking raindrops off her anorak.

'Alexa, you rip, I thought you said it was going to stay dry for the day!' she shouts. There wasn't a teapot to be bought in the entire county when I eventually found the time to go looking for one so I had a brainwave and got Mammy a fancy talking speaker instead. She had no problem setting it up on Christmas morning but learning how to work it has been another story.

'I don't understand,' Alexa calls back. I can see Mammy take another sharp breath so I decide to intercede. If not, they'll be here arguing all morning.

'Jet lag still bad, is it?' I say, sitting down opposite Paul.

'Something like that,' he replies quietly. He's barely said two words since he got home. All he does is check his phone and sigh periodically. He even turned down a slice of Mammy's Christmas cake, which I know she made and iced with a little snowman in a little snowscape especially for him. She's putting his Quiksilver and Rip Curl T-shirts to air on the Aga but I can tell she has one ear on us. She's barely left Paul's side since he arrived in with a face like a slapped arse and not a single Christmas present for anyone.

'Have you heard anything from her?' I half-whisper.

'No.'

'Did you text her?'

'Yeah.'

Another sigh.

'Do you fancy some fresh air? I'm not opening the café till twelve.'

****

We're standing under my Totes umbrella in the lashing rain looking at Daddy's grave. There's a fresh holly wreath with a big red bow on the headstone with a handwritten ShayMar Farm label hanging off it.

'You have it looking well,' Paul notes. 'Although you missed a bit of bird shite there.'

'We do our best.' I give him a little dig. 'The tree is the problem.'

'You must be here all the time, are you?'

'A good bit. I come and talk to him.' I've never told anyone else that, not even Mammy. But it's true. I fill him in on my bits of news, keep him up to date with what's happening in *Home and Away*, the score of the last match. That kind of thing. 'It actually helps, I think.'

'Maybe I shouldn't have gone back to Oz. Maybe I should have stayed.'

'Not at all, he wouldn't have wanted that.'

'I suppose.'

'What do you think he'd have made of the eco farm?' I say.

'I'm not sure. He'd miss the livestock, but I think he'd like dealing with the customers. He loved the chats, didn't he?'

'He did.'

'I can't believe how well Mammy's looking. It's really given her a new lease of life.' There's just the hint of a smile on his lips, but it's definitely there. 'All he ever wanted was to make her happy.'

'That's true. Do you remember the time he wrapped up the deep freeze and tried to get it under the tree?'

'Jesus, I thought she was going to go for him.' He does his Mammy impression: '"Seamus, there'd better be a necklace or a bracelet inside that freezer or That Bloody Cat'll be getting your turkey dinner."'

I laugh at the memory of it. 'She was delighted with the frozen side of beef, all the same.' I clear my throat. 'You have to snap out of it, Paul. She's fretting about you.'

'Me and Hannah have only been broken up a few weeks.' He sounds annoyed but I keep going anyway.

'I know it's tough. Sure, I was in bits after John. But it won't last forever.'

'If you say so.'

'Mammy is flat out now between the farm shop and the yurts. She doesn't need to be waiting on you hand and foot on top of it too.'

'I've only been home three days. Will you get off my case, Ais?'

'Only if you promise to cheer up a bit for us.'

'I promise I'll cheer up a bit.'

'But you have to mean it.'

He sighs and digs at a weed with the toe of his runner.

'There'll be other girls. You should see the style around these days. The new beauty salon has done wonders for the village.'

'I'm not interested in meeting someone new.'

'Well, neither was I, and then James came along.'

'And let me guess, this is the happiest you've ever been?' His tone is bitter and accusatory. I can't tell if he thinks I'm smug or full of it.

'Something like that.'

He rolls his eyes. 'Can we go home, Ais? My feet are getting soaked.'

****

I'm flying on the thirtieth and Majella and Sharon come over the night before to 'help me pack', which is a thinly veiled excuse to finish off the last of the Christmas chocolates.

'Was that John I just heard coming in the back door?' Majella inquires on her way back from the bathroom. I heard him coming in too and had to stop myself from getting annoyed. He and Paul are pals, but it's still deeply awkward to have my ex-boyfriend walking around the house.

'Yeah. I think Paul mentioned going for a pint.'

'Any luck with the dress yet, Majella?' Sharon asks.

'Oh yeah, I found the perfect one but it costs about the same as second-hand car,' Majella wails. 'I'm so sickened.'

'Remember what Sadhbh said?' I say. Then I turn to Sharon. 'The designer does great reductions but you have to jump on them.'

'Your mother actually showed me how to set up Google Alerts, Ais,' Maj says. 'So say a prayer.'

Just then there's a blast of 'Livin' on a Prayer' from downstairs so loud that Sharon falls off the bed and knocks several of my carefully rolled pairs of knickers onto the floor. Rolling is the only way to go when you're packing. Sadhbh sent me a YouTube video about it and the girl in it was like Mary Poppins the amount she got into the case. My heart was broken earlier trying to roll up my footies. They can be very fiddly.

There's a roar from Mammy. 'Alexa! Stop playing!'

The music stops abruptly.

'Jesus, that thing is very sensitive,' Majella whispers. 'Do you think it can hear us from up here?'

There's another roar from Mammy. 'Alexa! What are the opening times for Mc. Daids. Hard. Ware?'

Without missing a beat, Alexa blasts out 'Livin' on a Prayer' again. Poor Mammy. The music stops again and I hear John laughing, that deep belly laugh of his I haven't heard in so long. Mammy must have him cornered about putting goalposts in the Far Field. She wants them there for when school tours come and said John would be just the man to help her source them. I really wish she'd come to James for things, but I suppose in this instance John is something of an expert, what with his GAA connections.

'I got Mammy and Daddy one of those speaker yokes for Christmas as well,' says Majella as she paws absentmindedly through my wardrobe. 'They've been shouting at it and getting disappointed at everything it can't do for days. Feels like my teenage years all over again. And Shane came in steaming the other night barefoot and kept swearing blind at the top of his voice that he'd left the house with "two shoes" on and, well, long story short, there's a year's supply of tissues arriving on New Year's Day.'

'They'll be handy for Pablo come wedding time, to be fair.'

Majella bites into a Coffee Escape. 'True that, Ais. True that.'

'Okay, how many nights are you staying, hun?' Sharon says, gently pushing Majella out of the way and standing in front of my wardrobe.

'Only two. But I feel like I need "outfits". I want to be prepared.'

Sharon sifts through the rail – my purple Savida dress, my good interview suit, my fleecy dressing gown. It doesn't look like much, I have to admit. I feel a stab of anxiety in my belly. I've nothing at all that's suitable. Downstairs John laughs again and for a split second I feel something close to jealousy and wish that I was downstairs laughing with them, nothing to worry about except Alexa and goalposts.

'You need something savage for New Year's Eve anyway – who cares if the party's in the house,' Majella says, swishing her not-quite-there-yet Rosie Huntington-Whiteley highlights over her shoulder.

'I don't have anything savage,' I reply, my voice going up an octave. Maybe I could buy something in the airport in the morning? I rack my brains trying to remember what shops are in Terminal One. House of Ireland? Could I dress up an Aran jumper? Fashion some kind of toga out of a Foxford wool blanket and a belt? I'm sure I've seen Sadhbh do it.

'Oh my god, you have to wear the suit – it's perfect,' Sharon says, taking it out and hanging it on the door.

'But it's only for interviews. Would the dress not be better?'

'The suit is lucky, though, Ais. It got me my job, remember?' Majella says, digging through the Roses looking for a Caramel Barrel. On 29 December? Good luck.

'But it's a party. I can't wear a suit to a party. I want to look glam, not like a receptionist!'

'Oh, you will look glam, hun,' Sharon says confidently. 'Suits are very hot right now. Did you not see Emilia Coburn in the pink one at the BAFTAs? And I'll loan you these to finish it off.' She holds up one of her sparkly gold sandals. I balk at the height of them. Why she continues to shun kitten heels is beyond me. So much easier to walk in and there was definitely something in *Grazia* about them being 'back'. Were they ever gone?

'And what'll I wear under it?' I ask, coming around to the idea. 'I've a few decent shirts in the drawer there or I've my red vest top but that's at James's.'

'Oh, hun, you don't wear anything under it except a bra, and you could definitely pull it off,' Sharon says enviously.

Majella takes another look at the suit and starts nodding emphatically. 'Yes!' she goes. 'Classy but sexy too.'

'Ah, girls,' I say. 'I'm not Emilia Coburn. She's tiny for starters. I heard she lives on lemon juice and maple syrup. I ate a block of cheese last night. I'm still trying to lose that stone from 2012, you know.'

Sharon rolls her eyes and folds her arms. 'Would you ever give over. You'll be stunning.'

'I don't know about this. I can't meet James's parents with no top on, can I?'

But Majella is already rummaging in her handbag for tit tape.

It's decided that the suit, the purple dress, my good jeans, my red shumper and the pair of fancy yoga leggings Elaine and Ruby got me for Christmas will cover all bases. Elaine spent an hour talking to Constance at my thirtieth about plans to do yoga classes at the farm, and she's convinced I'm going to be converted. After my Pilates hell? I don't think so. But the leggings and my good fleece will be a decent outfit if they spring any country walks on me. I'm only raging I won't be able to fit the Hunter wellies I won three years ago at the Ploughing in my carry-on suitcase. I feel like they'd be very Buckleton.

'Aisling. Will you tell Paul John's here?'

Mammy's stage whisper up the stairs interrupts a debate about shoes and how many pairs is acceptable for two and a half days away. Two (me). Four (Sharon). Just book another bag (Majella). I step out onto the landing and peer down the stairs, relieved to see he's not in the hall with her.

'What are you doing, Mammy? Why are you whispering?' I feel a bit annoyed with her now and her buddy-buddy carry-on with John. But I know she's worried about Paul and desperate to get him out of the house to see if it will help with his mood.

'I don't want Alexa to hear me. God only knows what she'll be at next. Will you give his door a knock there? I think he's listening to music.'

I thud on Paul's door. No response. I bang harder and hear his bed squeak and the door opens. His eyes are red.

'John's here for you.'

'Okay, I'll be down in a minute.'

'Are you alright?'

'I'm grand.'

'He'll be down in a minute,' I call dutifully to Mammy, who's still posted at the bottom of the stairs. Paul emerges from his room with his coat on and gives me a gruff 'bye', jogging down the stairs as John emerges from the kitchen, shrugging his own coat up onto his shoulders.

'Hiya.'

'Hi.'

Is this us? Destined to awkward greetings for the rest of our lives?

What tiny moment of silence that follows is broken by Majella. 'Found the tit tape!'

CHAPTER 23

'**A**re you in the bathroom, Ais? Why are you whispering?'

Sadhbh's face fills the screen as she squints and positions herself properly in front of the camera, showing me glimpses of the city skyline behind her. I really must go to Thailand sometime, although Sinéad McGrath went for three weeks last year and, God forgive me, but her face was like a beetroot in every photo she posted on Facebook. The humidity would kill me. Sadhbh isn't a bit sweaty now as I'm looking at her, but then she's probably never sweated in her whole life. Her shorn silver crop means there isn't even any hair to scrape back off her face. I'd be puce and firing up my mini fan.

'Sadhbh,' I repeat furtively. 'How does tit tape work? I can't get it to stick.'

I *am* in the bathroom. It's the en suite off James's room in his parents' house in Buckleton and everywhere I turn there's a towel – on every surface and hanging off multiple hooks and rings. If competitive towel hanging was a sport then the Matthewses would be world champions. It's the same in the other three bathrooms in the house, and my nerves are gone knowing which one to dry my hands on. James is downstairs and I'm up here 'checking in with Mammy', which is my personal code for practising my outfit for tonight's party and trying on the bra Sharon told me to buy in Victoria's Secret in the airport. I've also relieved my very nervous belly ahead of tonight's party and meeting Mrs Matthews, who has proven to be something of an enigma.

'Get one with a real plunge. You've lovely boobs,' Sharon said somewhat wistfully and, of course, I had to tell her that I have a terrible arse and child-bearing hips to make up for them. I'm thrilled to have a bit of me called lovely, but I've never met a compliment I didn't instantly deflect. I was going to ask her what colour I should get the bra in, but she actually went into a bit of a mood, so I had to go with my instinct in the end and went with purple and black, but unless I can sellotape the suit to my chest everyone will be able to see it so I've entered crisis mode. I have the purple dress as a back-up, of course, but I met James's twin cousins, Bryony and Georgia, last night and they seemed super glamorous so I feel like it will have to be the suit. Why didn't I bring the nice red vest top?

'Are you sweating, Ais? You look like you're sweating. You need to be dry as a bone for it to stick.' This feels like an attack from Sadhbh, to be honest. She knows how I get. Meanwhile, she's leaning back on her lounger looking like she might even be a bit cold. I'd be wiping the Nile off my top lip.

'Okay, feck it, I'll worry about it later.' Maybe I'll go and stand outside for an hour and get really cold and apply the tit tape while I'm still a bit blue.

'So how's it going? Tell me everything!'

James picked me up from the airport in a Land Rover and we drove through flurries of snow and miles of countryside into the so-called village, which is almost aggressively picturesque with its cobblestone streets, quaint stone cottages and pastel shopfronts. I'd call it a town myself. The place was buzzing with people wearing wax jackets and expensive fleeces and generally looking posh, although I did spot one random lad outside a pub called the Drunken Sailor in a dressing gown and a pair of flip-flops holding a box of kittens. I suppose even Buckleton has its Mad Tom.

As we drove over a cute little hump-back bridge, James pointed out the Pig and Poddle and the village green, where the local fête is held every year, and the little gift shop where I can pick up something small to bring home to Mammy. To be honest, ATM or no ATM, Buckleton puts BGB to shame. There was the huge Christmas tree outside the post office, for starters, and then the truly alarming number of galleries and antique shops on every corner. I once got very into *Cash in the Attic* when I was off work for a week with the flu and became convinced we were sitting on a fortune, but it turns out Great-Uncle Brendan had been a terrible spoofer and his spoon collection was actually from Roches Stores.

James also pointed out the local school and revealed that he hadn't gone there because he started boarding school at the age of eight. I was momentarily floored by the thought of tiny little James being sent off on his own so young, but he already seemed a bit on edge, so instead I grilled him about whether it was like Mallory Towers and St Clare's. To my disgust, he didn't even mention one midnight feast, which was my absolute dream as a child. Me and Maj and Sinéad

McGrath once stole a packet of Rich Teas and two litres of Rock Shandy from Mrs Moran's press at a sleepover but we were caught eating them at ten o'clock. Didn't even make it to midnight and not a ginger cake or potted-meat sandwich in sight.

The Matthews have a driveway long and windy enough to be a pain in the hole for the postman – Pat Curran wouldn't stand for it at all – and enough ivy covering the house for me to be worried about its structural integrity. And while it's definitely big and rambling, it's not the castle Majella had me convinced I'd be arriving at. It's teeming with such high-end notions, though, that I'm afraid to put my hand anywhere in case I break a china pheasant or brush up against some family-heirloom tapestry.

'I swear to God, when we arrived inside his father was standing beside the roaring fireplace with a brandy like something out of an ad for aftershave.'

'No way!' Sadhbh leans forward, loving the detail. 'What's he like?'

'He's nice, although he's a bit scary – sort of booming rather than talking. He checked twice that he was pronouncing my name right, though.' It was a tonic after enduring two 'Ayes-leengs' and an 'Eileen' in the pub last night, to be honest. 'He asked me was I the girl keeping James across the Irish Sea, which was a bit mortifying, so I had to use up my Irish granny material straight away,' I whisper to Sadhbh, exiting the bathroom and sweeping the phone around James's bedroom to give her a quick look.

James's mother's mother was born in Dublin, so I made him tell me everything about her on the drive from the airport so I could have the chat with his parents. I pride myself on being a hit with them. Even Fran couldn't resist my top-tier specialist Mammy topics: interesting supplements in the newspaper and the subsequent hoarding of them in case someone might find them useful, poor dead Eva Cassidy, draught excluders, evening primrose oil and its many uses. James's granny sounds like no granny I've ever met, though. She was from a wealthy Dublin family who he doesn't really know much about, but she lived a lot of her life in their holiday home in the west of Ireland. He didn't exactly say the word 'banished' but that was the vibe I got. I was agog in the Land Rover beside him. It's the most he's ever talked about his family and I got the feeling some of it was a bit of a warning. He said he was only ever in his granny's Connemara house twice as a child and it was a bit like a commune. Lots of candles and scarves and artists and bottles of wine and port. His mother grew up there but came to England for school and never really went back, which sounds a bit sad.

'And what about the mum?' Sadhbh is eager for more details.

'I haven't met her yet.'

'What? Where is she? That's a bit weird.'

It *is* a bit weird. When we arrived, James asked, 'Where's Celine?' which threw me completely because the only other person I've known to call their parents by their first names was a girl called Esther who was in college with John. She was an only child and said she smoked weed with her dad and went on clubbing holidays with her mam. I got stuck talking to her at a party once and ended up making up something about Mammy and Daddy going to Woodstock. She got really interested and I had to make my excuses and hide in the bathroom.

'Do you not call her "Mum"?' I whispered as his dad turned around to stoke the fire.

'No, she never wanted that,' he whispered back. 'Said it made her feel old.'

Anyway, George told James that Celine was 'away with the gang' and that she'd be back this afternoon. I did meet Marie the housekeeper, though, who came out of the kitchen to give James a bear hug, and I could see instantly that my time spent weeding the herbaceous borders with Daddy over the years was going to come in handy. Over her mauve skirt and high-necked silk blouse she was wearing an apron that read 'gardeners spend all day in their beds'. It looked new. A Christmas present, no doubt. She gave me a hug too, which was a surprise. James had warned me that the Matthewses aren't really an affectionate family – which I can sort of relate to, having never really hugged anyone until I was about nineteen. It's just not the country way. I suppose Marie isn't a Matthews, though.

'Okay, show me more of the house,' Sadhbh encourages and I give her another go around James's room. 'It's very … floral. And frilly.'

Sadhbh is right. James's room is teeming with rose patterns. He swears blind he had posters when he was a teenager, but Marie likes to keep the house looking its best so she had the paint testers and the fabric samples out the second he left for university, and from the looks of things, she just had the entire room upholstered. Mammy has never touched my sacred Forever Friends wall-hangings and I know she never would. I gently asked James if his parents didn't mind Marie doing the decorating and he just shrugged and said his mother isn't into it and his father would barely notice. The house belonged to his father's parents and hadn't changed too much since they lived there. We were lying in bed last night when I asked him, and I noticed how flat and cold his voice was talking about it. I didn't really know what to say so I just gave him a massive squeeze and gently ran my fingers through his hair until his breathing got slow and steady. I lay awake for hours after that, listening to the sounds of the big posh house and thinking about little eight-year-old James in the far-away school with no midnight feasts.

'Show me more,' Sadhbh says. 'Is there a gym? A garage full of cars? How many sitting rooms?'

'No gym, although the housekeeper did tell me there are two exercise bikes in the sunroom if I wanted to do a workout.' I can't imagine doing a workout on my holidays, but thank God I packed the leggings in case someone forces me into it. The mysterious Celine, maybe?

'Sunroom. Ooh-la-la.'

'It's about the size of Knock Town Hall – I'll have to get you a look.'

I crack James's bedroom door open and peer out. James and his dad sound like they're in the study – a proper study too, not just a spare room full of bits of shite, one of which happens to be a desk – judging by the rise and fall of their voices. Marie is in the kitchen dealing with caterers for tonight's party. I must go down and see how they operate. I might even pick up some hors d'oeuvres tips. This seems like the kind of house that's seen its fair share of hors d'oeuvres.

'But the dad is nice anyway? And show me more of the bathrooms. I bet there are toilet-roll covers.'

Sadhbh lives for minimalism, so any kind of frou-frou carry-on at all and it's like she's watching an episode of *Hoarders*. She'd get sick if she knew about the boxes under my bed containing the teenage diaries and every note me and Majella ever passed in school and every birthday and Christmas card I'd ever received. You just never know when I might need them again.

I tiptoe across the landing and bring Sadhbh into the main bathroom for a goo, making sure to pause on the massive sink and the Jacuzzi bath. 'He's very nice. He's insisting I call him George but, you know me, Sadhbh. I just can't get it out. He gave me a tour of his wine collection and I was forced to choke down a glass of red.'

Sadhbh gasps and pauses in her humming appraisal of the bidet. 'But you hate red. I tried to get you to taste a lovely Malbec so many times.'

'It's just not for me, Sadhbh. It's very rich and I'm just very loyal to the white.' I'm also fairly sure I read something years ago about the Points in red wine being through the roof so, just like avocados and Elaine's beloved nut butters, I can't bring myself to enjoy it.

'A wine collection is very swank.'

'I know. James opened a white for me last night and when I said it was quite sharp he opened another one straight away. Fancy bottles, like!'

It was sharp but I would have drunk it out of a welly. I'm from the eight-euro-deal-in-Centra school of wine drinking, so who am I to judge a sharp unpronounceable French bottle?

'What else did you do yesterday so?'

'We walked down to the Pig and Poddle and met James's cousins.' I felt absolutely cat not helping with the party prep, but James looked at me like I had two heads and said it was all being looked after. 'They had more hair than I've ever seen on a person's head,' I continue.

'Rich hair.' Sadhbh nods knowingly. 'What about his brother? Oh, and won't your friend Natasia be there?'

'They're coming this evening. Flying in from Reykjavik.' Natasia went on to be a pilot with KLM so she's literally flying them in herself. I'm delighted there's going to be a friendly face at the party, truth be told. Being on best-guest behaviour is exhausting, and if the tit tape goes arseways she can be my lookout.

I hear the study door open and James's voice gets louder.

'Sadhbh, I've to go.'

'Okay, send me an outfit pic and have fun!'

I can't resist it. 'See you next year!'

CHAPTER 24

After throwing on a heap of talc and fanning myself with James's 2002 *Beano* annual for twenty minutes I eventually get my body temperature low enough for the tit tape to stick. It's working overtime, to be fair, but Majella assured me it's jiggle-proof, and she'd know since she still does the odd set-dancing display for any American tourists that have ended up in the Mountrath on Paddy's Day. The tips are legendary, even if she's considered way over the hill on the 'circuit'.

A familiar knot of anxiety is tightening in my stomach. James casually mentioned this morning that his ex-girlfriend will be coming. This was the first I'd heard of her, and once again I'm struck by how little I actually know James. I pressed him for more information, and apparently her family are pally with the Matthewses and growing up they were practically like brother and sister until they went away to college, or uni, as he insists on calling it, and fell in love. He said they were together for a few years before she moved to Bury St Edmunds to work in an art gallery. I didn't ask him, but I bet she wears mad glasses.

'Aisling?'

It's James. I'm eyeing the purple dress longingly when he walks into the bedroom.

'Wow! You look … amazing. That's different!'

I pull at the lapels of the blazer to see if they'll come in any further over the exposed bit of my chest. 'Is it too much? It's not very me.' I'm not in the habit of asking James how I look, although, to be fair to him, he often tells me. I was always asking John and he just said the same thing no matter what – that I looked 'lovely' – and it started to lose all meaning. It makes me a bit shy to have James looking at me. It's like being scrutinised by a stranger, somehow.

'You look great. Super festive.'

Is that a good thing? Who knows?

'Ready to come down? Celine has finally arrived.'

'Shite, she hasn't, has she? I'm on the way.' I scramble for Sharon's sandals and fire my Heather Shimmer and some other bits into my clutch bag.

'Just a heads-up, Rose has arrived too …'

Rose is the ex. 'Oh right.'

'… and she can't wait to meet you.'

He holds out a hand and I wobble towards him to grasp it. He's wearing a suit tonight too, as it happens, but his is navy. And he's wearing a shirt under it, the lucky article.

I'm expecting to hear music and voices and maybe even the odd clang of a fork hitting the floor when I open the bedroom door, but it sounds suspiciously sedate downstairs.

'People have definitely arrived, have they?' I ask. Mammy and Daddy only ever had the one New Year's Eve party, when I was about ten. The whole of BGB was mad into line dancing that year, and my only memory is rows of old people doing kick-ball-turns and stomping around the yard as midnight approached. I'll never forget the sight of

Daddy in jeans and a Stetson swinging Mammy around and Shem Moran's illegal fireworks nearly taking the arm off him while myself and Majella watched out the spare-room window.

'Oh yes, I think half of Buckleton is in the sunroom.' James laughs. 'Dad is in the drawing room holding forth with his cricket club mates. Best to avoid them until you've had at least two glasses of wine.'

'Right you are,' I say, trying my best to remember how to walk in heels as he steers me through the foyer towards a stony-faced couple in their sixties holding tiny glasses.

'Aunt Isabelle, Uncle Bert, this is Aisling,' he says, leading me over to them while I paste on a smile and try to concentrate on not sweating or tripping.

'Aisling, hello,' Uncle Bert says to my bust while his tongue hangs loosely out of the corner of his mouth. 'We heard James had someone new. And an Irish girl at that. Honouring his mother's heritage. Lovely to meet you.'

'Lovely to meet you … too,' I say, extending my hand while Aunt Isabelle gives me the once-over out of the corner of her eye. I'm tempted to tell her I was coerced into wearing the suit and I've a perfectly nice wrap dress upstairs that I'd much rather be in, but James is already leading me down the hall and away from them.

'Sorry about him,' he whispers into my ear. 'He's a bit of an old letch. Let's get you a drink.'

As we round the corner, a woman in her late fifties wearing a long, floaty dress breaks away from a small group by the door of the sunroom and comes towards us, arms outstretched.

'James, darling. And this must be Aisling?' She goes in for the two cheek kisses. She smells like Duty Free in Dublin Airport Terminal Two. Rich face creams and exotic scents.

James smiles tightly at her. 'Aisling, this is Celine, my mother.'

This is not what I was expecting. I was expecting pearls and high-necked blouses and a woman who maybe looked like one of the toilet-roll covers upstairs. Celine is wearing necklaces but they look more like Sadhbh's crystals than pearls. She has delicate silver rings on her fingers and her naturally greying hair is piled up on her head like Katherine Hepburn's in that Africa film.

'You look darling, my dear,' Celine says, taking a glass of champagne from a passing tray. 'Did James tell you my mother's side of the family is Irish? From Ranelagh.'

'He did of course. My friend actually just bought a house around the –'

'And you came all this way to Buckleton for our James. Such serious young people. You do amuse me.' And with that she floats away.

What an incredibly cracked thing to say. I steal a glance at James, who looks a little annoyed and a little bored by his mother. He breaks a smile, though.

'Shall we?' He points towards the sunroom door, behind which is the hum of conversation and music. My belly does a jump towards my throat and I take a deep breath and smooth down the lapels of my jacket, half-wishing I was in the Vortex throwing shapes to some Ed Sheeran banger.

Just as James drops my hand to push the heavy double doors open and I walk through, my heel catches in a loose flagstone and I stumble and fall on one knee, cursing under my breath. It all happens in slow motion. My forehead is just about to hit the deck when a pair of hands extends from behind me and grabs me under the arms just in time.

'It's okay, I've got her,' the woman helping me up says in a husky voice, and I know before I even turn around that it's her. It's Rose. And I was right – she's wearing glasses with thick black frames and, no, God no, a suit. Except hers is white and baggy and she's got a little red top on underneath and a high ponytail swishing around her shoulders. Rich hair. I'm puce and clutching my jacket lapels together to contain my dignity. What am I doing wearing four-inch heels in someone's house anyway? Nobody else is teetering around like me. I should be in my Crocs.

'Ais, are you hurt?' James gently pulls me towards a seat while the guests get back to their conversations. It's mostly an older crowd with a smattering of people in their twenties and thirties. I spy James's cousin Bryony and she gives me a wave. Most of the older people are women. Maybe they're all widows? A teacher in Majella's school lost her mam on Stephenses Day and Majella made the quite chilling observation that 'we're at that age when parents start dying' and I suppose she's right. Well, she's definitely right in my case. Just then, though, the sunroom doors open again and a great gale of male laughter comes from the direction of what James has called a drawing room but anyone with eyes can see is the Good Front Room. Ah yes, that's where the men are. Cricket widows, maybe, rather than actual widows. Marie comes speeding into the room. News of me going on my ear has obviously travelled.

'Do you need some ice for that knee?' she says, discreetly removing some china figurines and a large poinsettia from my general vicinity.

'I'm fine, I'm fine, thanks very much now,' I babble, trying to shrink down to the point of invisibility.

'I'll get you that drink. Sit tight,' James goes. 'Champagne, Rose?' he calls over his shoulder.

'Please,' Rose calls back. 'That's happened to me before,' she whispers, sitting down beside me. 'These old floors. Anyway, hi. I'm Rose.'

'Aisling,' I say with a nod. 'Thanks for … that.' I smile brightly, trying my best to take in the room.

'Those heels are something else – I love your outfit,' Rose says kindly as I do my best to keep my bra inside it.

'Thanks a million.'

She laughs. 'I love that saying, "thanks a million". Your accent is so soft.'

'Thanks … a million.'

She laughs again. 'When did you arrive?'

'Just yesterday.'

'Did James give you a tour of the village yet?'

'Yeah, he showed me a few of the sights alright. It's lovely here. I can't believe there's no ATM, to be honest.'

Rose glances over to the bar where James is chatting to a woman wearing a turban. 'So, you and James? He seems happy.'

God, she's getting right into it. 'Does he? That's good.'

It dawns on me that James always seems fairly happy. Nothing much seems to stress him out or set him off. In fact, the only time I've really seen him in anything approaching a mood was on the drive here from the airport. There was just an air of tension around him that even Mammy's present of six loaves of soda bread couldn't shift. And again, just now in front of his mother. He was like a different person.

'He's a good guy. Very loyal. Very … I don't know, just very James.' She looks a bit wistful and I wonder if she gearing up to fly over to him and declare her love. I bristle a little. He's my James. She might have the better suit but I have a new Daniel Wellington watch. I push up my left jacket sleeve in case she's missed it.

'He's one in a million,' I say, somewhat sharper than I had intended but feeling territorial. I don't want her getting ideas.

She just laughs, though. 'How long have you been seeing each other?'

'About four months. Nearly five, actually.' I don't tell her that only two of those months have been 'official' – she doesn't need to know that. It dawns on me that it hasn't actually been very long at all, but I suppose things move a bit faster when you hit your thirties. Nobody has time to be hanging around.

'Have you met Celine?' Rose asks with interest.

'I have – just there, actually.' I try to keep my voice neutral.

'She's an enigma,' Rose goes. I find myself nodding in agreement as Celine walks into the sunroom and joins a group of women by the wicker chairs, and even from where I'm standing I can see her greetings are disingenuous. Meanwhile, George has emerged from the drawing room holding a tumbler of brandy and is greeting a man whose name appears to be Bumbo with an enormous handshake.

'Are they ... still together?' I haven't asked James this outright and he hasn't offered any more detail. But I can tell from my brief encounters with both of them that they're like chalk and cheese. Celine is a like a cheese you might not have even heard of yet. One from the fancy section in a larger Tesco.

Rose purses her lips. 'Well, she lives here some of the time, I guess. Which wasn't always the case. I suppose they've never had much of a relationship. Especially after she left them. And James and Harry spent so much of their lives in boarding schools and ski camps and French colleges.'

James has never mentioned anything to me about his mother leaving, but Rose obviously thinks I know so I babble to her that my only experience with skiing was the dry slopes in Kilternan on a transition year day trip and it lashed rain and Catherine Mulloy hydroplaned right into a bin. Rose just laughs.

'You know, I'm so glad James has met you. He's got a lot of love to give. I always said I'd like to see him settle down with someone lovely.' She squeezes my hand. 'And you seem to be someone lovely. And when he's into someone, he's really into them. I mean, who could blame him? He hasn't had the most stable upbringing.' With that she nods towards Celine on one side of the sunroom and then towards George outside the door.

'We're still sort of getting to know each other,' I say, wishing James would extract himself from that conversation and get back over here. 'He's great, though. Not like any of the lads at home. Ha!'

'Really? Why do you say that?' Rose looks amused.

I think for a second. 'He's just ... very different.'

'Different good?'

I pause for a second, not wanting to be disloyal to the lads. 'Ah sure, you know yourself,' I say finally. 'A change is as good as a holiday.'

A commotion kicks off over by the door and I recognise Natasia's voice above the chatter. Getting to my feet is like trying to get up out of a bean bag, such is the height of the heels, but I manage and follow Rose out into the hall, looking back for James, who catches my eye and excuses himself from Turban and Top Hat to come out with us. I break into a smile and lean back against James's arm as Harry and Natasia bundle in out of the cold, waving hello to Natasia and feeling so thankful to see her friendly face. She and Harry join me, James and Rose back in the sunroom and he regales them with tales from BGB and the big homecoming while Natasia tells us about the drunkest and most hungover people she's seen getting on an aeroplane. I'm surprised Majella's infamous hungover return from Puerto Banus in 2014 isn't somehow in her repertoire. She managed to convince the flight staff that she had a tummy bug and they considered making an emergency landing.

'God, James, that reminds me of the time you and I were coming home from Stockholm after you ate that suspect shellfish,' Rose says with a tinkly laugh. Then she turns to me. 'He threw up in my handbag, Aisling. I could have killed him.'

'It wasn't a Michael Kors, was it?' I gasp, giving James a horrified look.

'Mulberry,' she whispers to me.

'I hope this new chap you're with can handle his lobster,' Harry says with a laugh, and I laugh along too because I've never had lobster. It looks far too complicated.

'I didn't know you were seeing someone, Rose,' James says, taking a sip of his champagne.

'It's only been a few months,' she replies with a smile. 'Thanks for that, Harry.'

'I thought it was public knowledge.' Harry shrugs. I feel James's arm tense slightly around my waist when suddenly the call goes up.

'Ninety seconds to go. Outside everybody, outside!'

I fire my texts off to Mammy and Maj and Sadhbh, eager to get them sent before the phone lines jam at midnight. I would always text Mammy and Daddy from the Vortex at a quarter to, not wanting to leave the all-important 'Happy New Year' to chance. I stuff my phone back into my clutch and teeter out to the hall after James, Harry, Natasia and Rose just in time to hear James drop the bombshell that he and his parents hadn't opened any Christmas presents until 4 p.m. What the hell were they doing?! I'd nearly have something returned by four on Christmas Day.

There's a box of blankets laid out by the door and James takes one and hands it to me before running to grab two glasses of champagne. Rose walks on ahead with Harry, and Natasia links my arm as we navigate the pebbled driveway towards the neatly manicured lawn at the side of the house. It's so green I half-expected it to be fake, but when my heel sinks into it I know it's the real deal alright. Impressive.

'It's so nice to see you here. Imagine us both ending up in this place to ring in the New Year.' Natasia and I spent much of the formative days and weeks of our teenage friendship wondering how many sweets we could get in Filan's for fifty pence and teaching each other the Irish and Ukrainian for 'shifting' and 'two Loop the Loops, please'.

She nods over towards Rose and says, 'You met her? Isn't she a doll?'

'A doll,' I agree. 'Can I ask you something?'

'Uh huh.'

'Rose mentioned something about James's parents and their relationship – well, about his mother leaving?'

Natasia sighs sadly. 'George took the boys to Wales for a holiday when Harry was ten and James was, what, eleven years old? When they came back, Celine was gone. Moved back to her mother's place in Ireland. She was with an artist for a few years and then a poet, I think Harry said. They didn't really see her again until Harry was sixteen.'

'Oh God.'

'It wasn't a happy house. She met George when she was young and never took much interest in her family. Harry says Marie is more of a mother.' She squeezes my arm. 'I'm so glad James is happy again. You're perfect for him.'

I smile in the darkness but feel a twinge of something in my stomach. Everyone wants the best for James so much. It all seems to be resting on me and I hope I can give it to him.

Before I can answer, a glass is pressed into my hand and another blanket whooshed over my shoulders as James gathers me into him and covers his own shoulders too. I give him the tightest hug I can, imagining him coming home to find his mother gone. The poor craythur.

'Fifteen, fourteen, thirteen ...' George calls out as everyone turns to gaze into the middle distance where we've been promised a fireworks display awaits. Celine is nowhere to be seen.

'Eight, seven, six ...' James joins in and tightens his grip on my shoulders as the tit tape starts to give way, peeling slowly but surely away from my skin.

'Four, three, two ...' He smiles and looks down into my eyes as I give praise and thanks for the blanket covering the purple and black plunge bra from the eyes of Buckleton's lords and ladies.

'One! Happy New Year!' they shout and the first fireworks shoot into the air and James kisses me soundly and softly on the lips.

'I love you, Aisling.'

CHAPTER 25

A split second of looking into his eyes and only a whisper of hesitation later I say it.

'I love you too.'

It's such a perfect moment, as rockets and Catherine wheels erupt in the sky above us, how could I not say it back to him? A whole new year is yawning out in front of us, full of hope and possibilities. Maybe we *will* get a couple's massage! And I do feel so much love for him, this poor little lost boy who came to BGB and swept me off my feet. As George Matthews starts bellowing 'Auld Lang Syne' into the night sky like Pavarotti himself, I think back to how Celine was so dismissive of us earlier. A flicker of doubt flashes somewhere at the back of my mind but I ignore it. I've never said 'I love you' to any man other than John. Of course it's going to feel a bit strange and foreign, especially the first time. I snuggle deeper into him, inhaling his James Matthews scent, feeling content and safe despite being so far from home.

Standing there looking up at the fireworks, I catch myself wondering what he's doing tonight. John. He's probably in the Vortex with Megan and the gang. Paul too, I hope. They do a legendary drinks deal on New Year's Eve – two vodkas and a can of Generic Energy Drink for €10 – and things tend to get out of hand early in the night.

James and I turn in shortly afterwards in a bit of a love bubble. Celine is nowhere to be seen, and James predicts she's taken over the study with whatever members of her crew came to Buckleton with her from wherever they were. I ask James where that might be and he shrugs and says, 'Probably at some castle in Scotland.' I save this information for Majella. She'll be delighted.

I'm grateful to be leaving the party. I was bored making small talk with the likes of Bumbo and his sisters, Buffy and Hedge. And I couldn't risk exposing myself any more than I already had done.

'James?' I whisper when we get into bed and are lying face to face in the dark listening to cars crunching up and down the driveway. I feel like I should talk to him about it. I know it's not a secret to him, but it's a secret that I know about it.

'Yeah,' he says, his voice sleepy.

'You can talk to me about anything, you know? Anything at all.'

'Uh huh.'

'I mean, we could talk about our childhoods or ...'

He sits up, turns on the bedside lamp, props himself up on his elbow and looks into my eyes. 'Is this about my mother?'

'Well, Natasia said –'

'I knew it was either Rose or Natasia. Look, it's not a big deal. She wasn't a very hands-on mother. She and Dad were never close. He was older. She travelled a lot. She made art with people.' A few people there this evening looked like they'd made some jewellery or pottery in their time alright. 'My father was fine but not that interested in looking after small boys. The end.'

'Okay.'

He turns off the light and lies on his back.

'James?'

'Yes?'

'Why did you and Rose break up?'

He sighs and then laughs. 'Okay, I suppose I was asking for this,' he pokes me in the side, 'telling you I love you like I did.' He lifts his arm and I duck under it and lay my head on his chest. 'We just wanted different things, I guess. It was all fine. A long time ago. Water under the bridge.'

We lie in silence for a bit and then he talks into the darkness. 'So I get to ask the same question then. Why did you and John break up?'

I answer quickly, parroting back what he'd said to me. 'Same as you. We wanted different things.'

Although, in truth, John and I just grew apart in the end. We broke up, we hurt each other and then we got back together and it just wasn't the same.

'We outgrew each other,' I admit to James. I've learned more about him in the past forty-eight hours than in all the time I've known him. I can return the favour.

'Well, aren't I the lucky man who got to claim the newly grown-up Aisling?' he teases, tightening his arm around my shoulder, and I'm instantly and unfairly reminded of all the work and responsibilities waiting for me at home. I squeeze my eyes shut and try to stay in the moment.

'James?'

'Yes?'

'That castle in Scotland. How many rooms do you think?'

****

I've already been awake for hours when James stirs at eight the next morning.

'Hi.' He smiles, turning to me. 'I love you.'

This is what I've been thinking about, watching him sleep. How do you know you love someone? With John I just knew. I felt it deep in my bones. I wanted the very best for him. He was my best friend. We shared everything. When it was good, it was really good. And when it went bad, it broke my heart to pieces. That's how I know it was love. As I watched James's long eyelashes flutter in his sleep, I wondered if we would be best friends. Would we share everything? Would he ever be able to break my heart?

'Love you too,' I say back to him, hoping he can't hear the strain in my voice. I'm just tired. That's all.

****

Our flight isn't until 6 p.m. so there's plenty of time to kill before we're due to leave, even allowing for the fact that I like to be there a good three hours early. Who knows what Southampton Airport has to offer? There might be a Gordon Ramsay restaurant or somewhere to buy a little Harrods bag. James decides to go for a run, and it's brand new information to me that that's something he does. I tried Couch to 5K with Majella a few years ago, but we made it as far as the second tree before we gave up completely. Fast walking is more my style – I don't even run the mini marathon. I hope James doesn't suggest couples jogging.

I don't fancy getting caught talking to Celine by myself. She's not like other mammies I've managed to charm. There's no warmth to her. I can't even imagine her having small kids, although James and Harry *must* have been small at some stage. The poor little yokes. So instead I snuggle under the duvet – goose down, very swish – and reach for my phone. Just five more minutes. Then I'll go ask Marie for a few cuttings from her gardenias. If I can't charm a mammy, I'll do the next best thing.

I've a total of six Happy New Year texts that must have got clogged up in the midnight rush and filtered through overnight. When will they learn? There's the usual suspects – Mammy, Carol, Sadhbh, Elaine and Ruby, one from Maj declaring 'I'm getting married this year' – and then one from John, which surprises me. 'Happy New Year' it says, same as the others. He probably forwarded it to everyone in his contacts list.

I'm checking my email – still nothing from Flo at the Paradise Aqua confirming our rooms – when there's a sharp rap on the door, and I instinctively pull the duvet up around myself even though I'm wearing my good Harry Potter pyjamas ironed by Mammy.

'I'm decent!' I shout.

'Aisling, it's Celine. We're heading out for a walk shortly. See you in the driveway in twenty minutes?'

Great, I escaped the running but now I'm stuck going on a family walk. I would have sworn Celine wasn't the walking type. I hope I don't get stuck with her.

'Er, great. I'll be down in a minute,' I call, scrambling out of bed. After a quick shower I close my eyes, spin around and grab the first towel I lay my hand on. It's a bath sheet. Are they all bath sheets? Even for hair? The luxury of it. These people know how to live.

James is standing inside the front door with his hands in his tracksuit pockets when I come down the stairs fifteen minutes later. He looks like he barely even broke a sweat.

'There you are,' I whisper. 'I thought you were still out running and I was half-afraid to leave the room in case I got lost. Or ran into Uncle Bert by myself.'

'I'm so sorry. I got a work call as soon as I arrived back,' he says, helping me into a waxed jacket. There's a rack of them at the front door in a selection of sizes, as well as assorted wellies and walking sticks. 'There's a problem on the site. I think it should be okay till I get back, though. I'm just hoping we don't end up losing a couple of weeks over it.'

'Is time that tight?'

'Unbelievably so.'

'James, you're not talking about work are you?' Harry says, coming around the corner and slapping him on the back. 'You're supposed to be showing Aisling a good time.'

'Is Natasia not with you?' I ask, saying a silent prayer that she hasn't abandoned me in my hour of need.

'Still in bed, I'm afraid,' Harry goes. 'She has a flight this afternoon and woke up with a migraine.'

'Who? Your mother?' It's George Matthews, striding across the foyer wearing what looks suspiciously like a Sherlock Holmes get-up, complete with hat.

I feel James bristle beside me but he doesn't say anything. Harry takes a deep breath. 'Mum won't be joining us either.'

'But she just knocked on my door?' I say. 'Is she okay?'

'She's fine. She likes to change her mind,' George bellows. 'Now, let's make a move. Aisling, after you.'

****

'She'll actually take a third one too,' James says, passing me three little bottles of Pinot Greej while the air hostess – although according to Sadhbh I'm supposed to say 'steward' – looks on bemused. 'She's earned them.'

'James!' I protest. 'The flight's only an hour and a half.'

He's right, though, I have earned them. Hook them up to my veins, Deborah, to be quite honest. I thought the walk would never end. George insisted on showing me every inch of property he owns and then gave an impassioned speech about why Ireland was lucky to have been colonised in the first place. A thought crept into my head that maybe Celine had the right idea jumping ship, but I chastised myself right away.

'You must admit things are better here on the mainland, Aisling,' he said when I mentioned it's often very wet in Galway, giving a mini hint that I know something of Celine's background. But he was barely listening. 'And what's this I hear about Potato Park? Is it some kind of joke?'

Well, I took umbrage at that one and I just couldn't hold my tongue. 'It's actually *Tayto* Park,' I said in a tone I wouldn't normally unleash on a parent, especially not a boyfriend's parent. Fran would have turned me into a pillar of salt if I'd so much as tried it with her. 'And it has a rollercoaster and a zoo and you can get a guided tour of the real Tayto factory. Like, the actual working one, where Taytos are made.'

'Aisling, calm down,' James whispered, pulling my sleeve gently.

'No, James,' I said indignantly. 'Too many people think Tayto Park is a joke but it's actually one of the country's top attractions.' Then I added under my breath, 'Have a bit of respect,' and I'm pretty sure Mr Matthews heard me too.

The rest of the walk was fairly subdued, save for when Harry spotted a beaver and made an inappropriate joke.

****

'It was nice to see your ma – mum before we left,' I say to James when we're halfway across the Irish Sea and I've had my first few gulps of wine. I didn't think Celine was going to surface again at all, but then, just as we were putting on our coats, she appeared in another floaty ensemble and pecked us on the cheeks in a cloud of expensive perfume. Marie watched on with a seasoned and unimpressed eye. It was like something out of an old film.

'What did she mean when she said "you do amuse me" at the party?' I suspected Celine was talking directly to me when she said that.

'Oh, she finds relationships amusing. The very idea of monogamy or settling down or … marriage. She finds that all very amusing.'

'Right.' I'm truly dumbstruck.

'I don't tend to listen to her. She's not exactly a ringing endorsement for healthy relationships.'

This is the most jaded I've ever heard James. His parents seem to truly depress him.

I think back to how it used to be when Daddy was alive. Him and Mammy's relationship wasn't perfect – there used to be war over what match to listen to on our aimless Sunday drives – but they were always solid. I don't mean kissing and hugging and saying 'I love you' or any of that craic. I mean the unsaid stuff. The flasks of tea left out during lambing season. The hours he spent sitting outside the supermarket so he could help her with the bags. The dancing around the house to Abba and Big Tom and the Mainliners.

'Actually, I've been thinking,' he says, snapping me out of my trance. 'I have a proposition for you.' A proposition? I pour out another little bottle of Pinot. What kind of a proposition? Myself and Mammy awkwardly watched *Indecent Proposal* on RTÉ One the other night and I start panicking that he wants me to do the deed with one of his friends for a million dollars. Who could it be? Not Uncle Bert, surely …

'Instead of you going home to Ballygobbard and leaving all your stuff at your house and spending all your time at my house …'

Oh my God.

'I think you should move in with me,' he says confidently.

Stunned silence. I'm suddenly very conscious of how tightly I'm holding the plastic cup in my hand and the roaring of nothing in my ears.

'If you want to, that is,' he says quickly, his confidence wavering ever so slightly.

I'm so shocked my hands start moving independently, picking up the little wine bottles off my tray table and putting them down again.

'You spend so much time at mine anyway, and you're always saying your clothes are all over the place, and we're not kids. I like having you around, and … I hope you feel the same.'

He finishes his sales pitch and I look up and catch his warm brown eyes, hoping the mild panic isn't visible in mine as I grapple with my first instinct, which is no, I can't move in with you. Not after a few months and not without a ring. I always thought there'd be a ring, truth be told.

'You still haven't said anything.'

But then I snap out of it. It's 2019, Aisling. This is what I've always wanted, what I never had with John, despite all the years together – a grown-up man to live with. James to live with. He's practically perfect in every way. The height. The manners. The respect for my tea-bag preferences. Okay, the family is a bit of a hurdle, but they're in another country and haven't they made his life hard enough?

'And if I'm going to stay in Ireland long term …'

This is the first time he's really said this out loud. He's dropped suggestions of picking up work in Dublin when Garbally is finished and made noises about this project and that, but he hasn't actually said anything concrete about staying long, long term. I've daydreamed about maybe moving to England with him, but after the couple of days I've just had, with the Tayto Park abuse sprinkled on top, I don't know if I'd be able for it, and I really am so fond of the euro. Home is home.

'You *still* haven't said anything.'

I smile, suddenly flooded with warmth and surprising myself. 'You'll have to get a few more mugs.'

****

By the time we land in Dublin I've panicked and calmed down about it around seventeen times. I hardly know him. What if he leaves? But he said he's staying. When will I do my moussaka farts and my Big Toilets? But sure, he has to do his too. He has no idea how to properly stack a dishwasher. But then again, I am partial to a chair full of clothes in the corner of the room. What will Mammy say?

CHAPTER 26

'**N**ow will you take a few plates with you? And have you enough pillows?'

Mammy is flat out trying to add items to the latest box of stuff I'm transporting to James's. I'm not bringing that much – the apartment isn't that big and is already fairly well kitted out, although I know for a fact there's no whizzer for doing soup and I'm really trying to get Trim for Tenerife now that it's January. Colette Green has been posting a lot of New Year, New Me recipes, and I saw another influencer posting about carrots helping with feeling anxious – I'll give anything a go. After taking a bit of a break for Christmas, I'm back with hen prep and keeping things going at BallyGoBrunch and now I'm moving on top of it all.

'I'm already overloaded as it is,' I say, swatting away the stack of tea-towels she's trying to sneak under my good bedside lamp. I've been running around the house for the past hour packing up my last bits and my head feels as full as the box I have on the kitchen table.

'Has Paul said anything to you, Aisling?' Mammy's following me everywhere, tidying everything I lay my hand on. I won't miss this when I move into James's place, that's for sure.

'I'd say he's said about six words to me since Stephenses Day, Mammy. You know the way he is.'

'I saw a sign in Dr Maher's surgery. For men. About opening up. You wouldn't see if you could sit him down for a chat, would you? I've tried but –'

'Have you seen my spare phone charger, Mammy? I could have sworn I left it on the counter there. I have to check my email.'

'I put it up beside your bed, love.'

'Ah, Mammy!'

To be fair, she barely batted an eyelid when I told her I was moving out.

'I knew it was on the cards as soon as James said he was staying on, pet,' she'd said, feeding a bit of brandy to a leftover Christmas cake and wrapping it tightly in parchment. 'Sure you're always there. It makes sense.'

'Are you sure you don't mind, Mammy?'

'Aren't you thirty, Aisling? My big girl!'

Still, though, the guilt sat in my stomach like a bowling ball. There's me, shacking up in my lover's nest (Majella's words, all of them) leaving my poor widowed mother in the empty house. Well, Paul is there, but he may as well not be, the moping he's doing.

'I know you're thinking about me, and I appreciate it, Aisling, but I'll be fine, honestly. And isn't James just the bee's knees? You landed on your feet there,' Mammy said as I followed her into the spare room where she pulled a clothes-horse out from under the bed and shoved the cake in in its place.

'Actually, Mammy, about James, I was wondering …' I saw my chance and went with it. 'If you've jobs that need doing around the farm and William or whoever can't manage, will you make sure you ask James?'

Earlier that day I had called into her and caught John just as he was leaving.

'Thanks again for your help with the chicken wire, John. And I must photocopy that banana-bread recipe for you,' Mammy had called out after him. 'Megan loves banana bread,' she said to me by way of explanation. I'm partial to a bit of it myself, truth be told. It's practically like eating salad.

'What was he doing here with chicken wire?' I asked her, surprised at how annoyed I felt by all this cosiness.

'We needed to go deeper with the wire around the coop because, I swear to Jesus, those foxes will dig down to Australia one of these days. Paul and William Foley couldn't manage it between them so John gave a hand when he was down during the week,' she replied, somewhat defiantly, picking up on my tone.

And so when I asked her to ask James instead, she was ready for me.

'Isn't James fierce busy, though, Aisling? And John doesn't mind.'

'Mammy, maybe you could not be as pally with John? James is my boyfriend now and it's just a bit awkward. You had John here looking at a wonky sink in the yurt shower block last Sunday. What does John know about sinks?'

She looked ever so slightly ashamed, so I think she knew she'd been favouring John. I'd like to think it's just because she knows him so well and she still thinks James is a bit like Prince William or one of the *Downton Abbey* lads. When she asked me about his family I was vague enough. I don't need Mammy taking against Celine this early on.

'Sorry, Aisling. I thought you were all friends. John has just been a great help with the online stuff and he and Paul are friends anyway so I thought there was no harm in it. And, sure, he's like part of the family.'

'Well, he's not really any more.'

'I know, love. Okay, message received.' She thought for a second. 'Actually, do you know what would be very helpful? I need a yoke – a scarecrow, I suppose – for the vegetable patch. Could James knock one up, do you think? He's very handy.'

A scarecrow. That's what she gave me to take to him. I sighed. 'Alright, Mammy, I'll ask him.'

Now, as she forces the clothes-horse onto me, telling me, 'I don't want to see you in a damp jumper,' I hope she'll be heeding my request and leave John out of things. After meeting Rose with her swishy ponytail and effortless laugh, I'm not sure I'd like her hanging around the whole time, and James deserves the same courtesy.

Majella's been having a better time of it. She came roaring into BallyGoBrunch off the Timoney's bus on Wednesday, waving her phone at me and repeating 'oh my God, oh my God, oh my God'. It was quiet enough but she still managed to take the cream off Eileen Kelly's scone as she whipped past with her coat flying and bag full of books and papers ricocheting off tables and chairs. It turned out the dress, *the* dress, the Krystal Ball one, was going to be on sale in a bridal boutique in Tipperary on Friday – a first-come first-served kind of deal. The second she told me, I could feel my adrenaline start to pump. It felt like a job I was always destined to do: get a 70-per-cent-off wedding dress out of the hands of some other thirsty wagon who wanted it too. I'd draw blood if I had to.

'It's this Friday, Ais. I know it's short notice, but … can you come? I'm going to take a course day from school. I have to get this dress.'

I looked her dead in the eye 'Majella, we are *going* to get this dress.'

****

'These aren't very nice, Ais.'

Majella rolls her tongue around in her mouth in distaste, shoving the packet of sweets into the passenger-side door pocket. 'They're very chalky. Wouldn't be for me now.'

She swigs from her collapsible reusable coffee cup once and then again, before shrugging and digging the packet out a second time and tipping more into her mouth, turning the newspaper on her lap over and tutting at a headline about corruption in local councils.

'I like your cup. It's very earth conscious.' I'm cruising along the motorway at a solid eighty-five and tut as a jeep as big as a tractor zooms past. 'It's a speed limit, not a speed target,' I call after him. 'Did you see that, Maj? Absolutely flying.'

'Flying, Ais,' agrees Maj, examining the back of the bag of snacks. 'Is this recyclable, I wonder?'

'God, you're going to save the whole world at this rate.'

'It's school.' She sighs. 'The kids are up to ninety about global warming so we've made it a staff-wide priority to make a proper effort. There was a child crying in the corridor yesterday about the ice caps, and there was war in one of the fourth class parents' WhatsApp groups about a child bringing a plastic straw in her lunchbox. I'm doing as much as I can to keep the peanuts out, Ais. I can't be the straw police too, can I?' She pours most of the rest of the bag into her mouth and chews thoughtfully. 'They've grown on me. Very tasty.'

Traffic isn't as bad as I had anticipated, and I think we'll actually be at the dress shop well before it opens. 'Did you check the website again this morning?'

'I did. And it's still there, in my size.'

It's four months to the wedding and I won't have her in anything bar her dream dress on the Big Day. If all goes to plan today, she'll have saved over four grand on the Krystal Ball dress. It will still be eight hundred euro over her budget, but she and Pablo discussed it and he said he would pay ten thousand to see her in a potato sack, so that was that decided. I double checked with her last night that she didn't want her mother to come with us, but Majella claims Pablo is rubbing off on her and she'd be too emotional. I also think that Mrs Moran has been agitating for Majella to just wear her old wedding dress, which might explain her absence. I've seen the pictures and, while she looked fabulous on the day in 1982, I don't think puffed sleeves and lace up to her ears is really the look Maj is after.

I've ordered three more potential bridesmaid dresses online – one strapless, two with straps, so we have options. Melanie in the little post office in Filan's told me she has no idea how I'm keeping track of them all. She's actually become deeply invested in the search for the dress. Last time I was in she produced pictures she'd printed off the internet. Let's just say I'm glad Melanie isn't picking the dress for me. Of the latest ones I've ordered, the strapless one looks the nicest but I'm already having premonitions of hoiking it up all night. Last time I wore strapless was to my debs and I've my hands clamped to the top of the dress in every picture. I also don't have the elegant neck required for strapless. Majella said she just wants me to be comfortable, but I won't have her looking back on the pictures in five years and wishing I'd worn the pale pink rather than the lavender. She'll be looking at those photos forever.

She's so excited and I'm so happy for her that my eyes unexpectedly start to prick with tears and I have to give my head a little shake and focus back on the road. I've drifted over ninety kilometres an hour. Next thing you know I'll be over the limit and hauled into court. Paul was forced to admit to me this week that he flew through a speed camera in the Micra just after Christmas, after a letter arrived to inform me I now have three penalty points. His licence lapsed while he was in Oz so now I have to live with the shame of the points. I could barely look at him. It's for the best I moved out last week. I slow down to a more respectable speed, ignoring the angry flashing lights of an impatient tractor behind me.

'Do you need a hand with more of your stuff this weekend?' Majella looks up from her phone where she's checking the website and the shop's Facebook page once again to make sure the dress hasn't magically vanished since she last looked. We've been keeping track of the 'likes' on the picture to try to gauge how many bloodthirsty bitches might be gunning for the same one.

'No, I'll be grand. I'm not bringing that much for now. James's place isn't that big and, sure, I still have my room at Mammy's. I'm only moving a mile up the road.'

'How was she about the move?'

'She was grand. Not a bother on her.' This sticks in my throat a bit but, sure, I'm just being soft. 'She's mostly concerned with how I'm getting on living somewhere with no washing line. She's been losing sleep over it, I can tell, so I'm bringing over a few things later to put in the hot press for an hour.

'Actually, speaking of Mammy, stick on Skippy there. He's giving away a weekend at the eco farm as a prize on the show and I want to hear who rings in.'

Majella jabs at the dial as I take my exit off the motorway and Garth Brooks fills the car. She throws her head back and bellows along. '"If tomorrow never cooomes, will she know how much I love her …" This is a contender for first dance, you know, Ais? It was number one the summer I was born! Pablo hadn't a balls notion who Garth Brooks was a year ago but I caught him looking up cowboy boots on the internet last week. A convert!'

I can already imagine the weeping if he has to whisk Majella around the dancefloor in the Ard Rí to this. Maybe we can get The Peigs to learn it, although I'm not sure if Don Shields and co. might be as devoted to Garth as us. I still know every word to 'No Fences' and Maj and I once won a karaoke competition in Majorca duetting on 'Unanswered Prayers'.

'Ninety-seven-point-six FM. This. Is. Solas. Eff. Em. I'm Skippy Brennan and you're tuned into the home of the Six Word Traffic Report sponsored by Hennegan's Liver Fluke

Blastex: Matty Kiernan, your headlights are on! Coming up we'll be looking at the shocking number of people who've mistaken the cat treats given away with today's *County Chronicle* for human treats. We'll talk to one woman who says she might sue.'

Majella takes out the packet and examines it more closely and shrugs. 'I've had worse.' She tips the remaining few into her mouth.

'What's Google Maps saying there, Maj? We must be close now.'

'It looks like ETA is twenty-five minutes, although there's a red line not far ahead. What does that mean?'

'Feck it. Traffic.'

We've transitioned quickly from three lanes to a narrow country back road and I'm struggling to imagine why there'd be a traffic jam ahead. And then I see it, the telltale sign: sheep shit. I know Majella's seen it too because she's shaking her head vigorously.

'Ah no. No, Ais. No, it can't be. If we're not there by 9 a.m. someone else is going to get it!'

'And we were making such good time.'

But I round the corner and there in front of me is a herd of sheep. At least a hundred head. Some of them in lamb too, by the looks of their low-hanging bellies. Within seconds the car is surrounded and we grind to a halt. Majella nudges her door open and stands on the doorjamb.

'The oldest man in Ireland is herding them into a field,' she calls back in to me. 'Ten minutes, at least.'

That will have us cutting it very fine, but what can we do? Majella nudges a particularly nosy ewe out of her way and settles back into the car, jigging her legs with nerves and looking at her phone.

'Oh, I forgot to tell you, Mammy wanted me to ask you did you see Aunt Shirley's message about her back?'

'Oh, balls!'

'On the WhatsApp, is it?' Majella smiles and nudges me and then jumps as a sheep lets out a particularly loud bleat right beside her open window.

I did see Aunt Shirley's message about her bad back but forgot to respond. In my defence, all it said was 'Just lettin you know Aisling, I have a very bad back' so I was at a bit of a loss and set it aside to reply later. I dig out my phone and swipe open the group, and then put it down again and turn off the car engine. You never know where there might be a guard hiding. Returning to the phone, I see that Aunt Shirley has already got a few sad face emojis in sympathy from the rest of the hens and one bomb emoji from Juana who I presume misunderstood the message.

'No worries, Shirley,' I respond. 'I'll keep it in mind for activities and let the hotel know.'

To be honest, I'm not sure if the Paradise Aqua is the kind of place that has a mattress or pillow menu, but anything to keep the peace. I follow it up with, 'Thanks to everyone who already paid deposits. Here are my bank details again in case anyone misplaced them.'

I copy and paste them in and add a smiley face, smiley face, blessed hands, starburst so it doesn't come off too aggressive.

'We have movement, Ais! Go, go, go!'

I look up and, save for a few stragglers, the road is mostly clear. Quarter to nine. If I go now at a brisk but responsible pace we should make it. I turn the key in the ignition and set off, giving the obligatory wave to the ancient man as we pass. Straight on, around the corner, and another and …

'Ah shite.'

Shite is right. A slurry truck. A glacially slow slurry truck. And we're stuck behind it.

CHAPTER 27

We peel into the little car park at seventeen minutes past nine, practically on two wheels. Majella has the door open before I even have the handbrake on and is flat out running for the entrance of Bridal Sweet. I race around to the boot and fish out the bag with the plastic champagne flutes and bottle of Buck's Fizz. This could be the day Majella gets her dress and I don't want to be taking chances that the boutique might not have any bubbly. Plus, the Buck's Fizz is only 3 per cent alcohol so half a glass won't hurt.

I make it to the door a good two minutes after Majella has disappeared inside, pulling it open and fully expecting to see a near-fatal crush. Maybe two women fighting over the same dress, ripping off sleeves. A bride-to-be sitting under the rails crying, possibly eating some doughnuts. A frazzled yet glamorous store owner with a clipboard, begging for mercy and order.

Instead, there's just Majella, already methodically flipping through the hangers in the section marked 'Sale' in black marker on a heart-shaped cardboard sign. There's not a sinner in the shop besides her and a bored-looking and distinctly unglamorous teenager sitting at the till painting her nails, the stench of the polish filling the small space.

'Are we too late?' I ask both of them, panic rising in my belly. The teenager looks up from her nails and smiles like her life depends on it. 'Welcome to Bridal Sweet, where we make dreams come true,' she drones, and then the smile drops like a lead balloon and her attention goes back to the lurid red nails.

'We're the first ones here, Ais!' Majella calls excitedly from behind the sale dresses. 'The only ones.'

'Is it not the first day of the sale?' I ask the teen, making her once again lift her head, which she does like she's on her deathbed and being forced to open her eyes to say a final farewell.

'We have a sale, like, every month. It's never that busy.'

This is news to me. I used to be fairly well up on the comings and goings of all the bridal boutiques in a four-county radius, between keeping an eye out for my own theoretical Big Day and assisting various friends and acquaintances in finding The One. The one dress, that is. But I'm out of practice and Majella is new to the circuit so Bridal Sweets wasn't on my radar. A hidden gem, I suppose I'd have to call it. I make a mental note to add that detail to my bridesmaid's speech. I already feel sick at the thought of it, but Majella has begged me to do one – I think mostly because she wants the story of how she brought the entire town to tears the time she performed 'The Streets of Ballygobbard' to the tune of 'The Streets of Philadelphia' at the Pride of BGB ten years ago. She was narrowly beaten by Simon Ruane who – to be fair to him – had trained his dog to say 'hup BGB', but it was a memorable day. I'm the only one who can truly do it justice and Maj knows that.

I drop my bags on the artfully banjaxed chaise longue. I recognise it as the same one I got for BallyGoBrunch in IKEA but someone has gone to the trouble of ageing the MDF frame with some gold spray paint and vigorous rubbing. It's a technique I'm considering for the flower crowns I'm planning on making for Majella's hen. I can forage for some pliable twigs and branches and fashion them into forty-eight crowns and boho them up with some spray paint and steel wool. I saw something similar on Colette Green's blog and noted that Maj had given it a like. That reminds me, I must see about getting a bigger case. Between the flower crowns and the Prosecco pong and the hangover recovery bags I'll be bursting at the seams.

Majella is still rummaging when I find her amid the layers of froth and lace. 'You know the one, right, Ais?'

'It's seared into my brain.' I start to pull back hanger after hanger.

'No. Nope. No.'

'Nope. Nope.'

We both work methodically, flip, flip, flipping through dresses. I almost go past it but suddenly the beaded neckline catches my eye and I backtrack. 'Maj. I think I have it.'

She stops mid-flip and her eyes widen. 'Go on so.'

I reach in deep and grasp the top of the hanger, pulling the fullness of the dress towards me, catching sight of the Krystal Ball tag. We both gasp as I reef it all the way out.

'Oh my God, it's gorgeous, Maj.'

'It is,' she replies tearfully, 'it's gorgeous.'

'Gorgeous,' the teen drones from her spot behind the counter, not looking up from the nails. I breathe in deeply through my nose to stop myself from roaring and turn my back on her.

'Well. Go on. Try it on.'

****

'Are you wearing the good knickers I got you?'

Part of this dress-shopping experience I planned for Maj was getting her some new holdy-in knickers and a strapless bra to wear for the fitting. No point putting a new dress over old pants, was my reasoning. And, anyway, it's just what you do. It's special.

'Of course I am.' Majella huffs and puffs from behind the curtain. We managed to rouse the teen from her stupor long enough to show us where the changing room was and hang the dress up for Maj to try on. 'It's off the rack so try not to get tan on it,' were her only words of encouragement.

'As if I'm wearing transferable tan like some kind of amateur,' Majella hissed after her, and I pulled the curtain across and asked Shannon, who had grudgingly given up her name, would she not light the nice scented candle on the counter and to bring out any veils she might have in the back.

'How's it going in there?' I call nervously to Majella. All our hopes are pinned on this dress fitting and suiting. She doesn't answer but instead the curtain is pulled back and my breath is taken. She looks so beautiful. My eyes instantly fill with tears. 'Oh, Maj. It's gorgeous.'

'Is it really? Will you do up the back for me?'

The back is a long line of tiny buttons and she spins around and I set to work, cursing my fingers as they battle with the delicate little pearls. I give up trying to do them all and settle for every fifth one, reaching the top and turning her back around to me. Shannon makes a reappearance and throws some boxes down onto the chaise longue. Without being asked, she pulls a box forward and instructs Majella to stand on it, like a ballerina in a jewellery box, and flings a pair of heels at her and then slouches back to her post.

Maj holds onto my hand and steps into the heels and up onto the box and looks at herself in the full-length mirror for the first time, smoothing and twisting. The boat neck sits across her collarbone and the slightly full skirt swishes as she turns.

'Ais,' she whispers, peering around at the desk where Shannon is carving something into the counter. 'Take a few snaps there.'

Taking photos in bridal shops has always truly tested my moral compass. The signs tell me it's not allowed because they don't want you going off and getting the dress made by somebody's auntie for a third of the price. But I must admit I have whipped out the phone for a sneaky photo in the past, beads of sweat running down the back of my neck in fear of getting caught. I have a strong feeling Maj is going to buy this dress, though, and I know that Shannon couldn't care less if she just walked out of the store wearing it, so I slip my phone out of my pocket and surreptitiously slide it into position.

As if Satan himself was watching me, no sooner have I snapped the first photo than the bell on the shop door tinkles and a woman bustles in with armfuls of garment bags, hissing at Shannon as she does. 'Shannon, a hand, please?'

As soon as Shannon has sullenly relieved her of her burden, the woman's face transforms into smiles and warmth as she sails towards us, arms outspread. She's got a real Cilla Black-in-her-sixties vibe and is wearing a pussy-bow blouse and tight black trousers, and if she's Shannon's mother then the apple has fallen kilometres from the tree.

'Oh, sweetheart, you look gorgeous, give me a twirl there.' She flits around Majella, tucking and pulling and expertly doing up the buttons on the back that I missed.

'I think …' I look at Maj with my eyebrows raised. 'I think we're going to take it?'

Maj takes one more look at herself in the mirror as Mrs Bridal Sweet fixes a veil to the top of her head and spreads it out behind her. This is the kind of treatment I was after. I hope Shannon is out the back somewhere preparing a bottle of bubbly.

'We'll take it,' Majella announces with a sigh.

'Excellent choice,' the woman declares as she whips the price tag off the back of the dress and scurries over to the till, rabbiting, 'Now, it's a sale dress so no returns, no exchanges, no alterations, sold as seen, full payment due immediately.'

Majella steps off the plinth and rummages in her handbag for her wallet. 'Give her my card there, Ais, you know the number.' Majella has such a history of losing her card and forgetting her PIN that every time she gets a new one she tells me the details as a security measure.

Madame Bridal Sweet has the payment processed before Majella even has the dress off. As she hands me the receipt, I hover, hoping a pair of flutes might appear, inwardly raging that this woman isn't falling over herself to mark this special moment. However, she just busies herself getting a garment bag ready for the dress, so I dig out the Buck's Fizz and the two glasses and clink them together as Maj emerges from the changing room.

'You don't mind, do you?' I challenge your one, who cluelessly chirps, 'Work away, darling,' and I make a mental note to find Bridal Sweet on TripAdvisor and let loose. They didn't even try to gussy Majella up in an overpriced headpiece and then give her the hard sell on it. They didn't even try to persuade her to invest in the dreadful shoes. These are rites of passage for a bride. Even a dress-on-sale bride.

I squeeze the cork out of the bottle and get Majella to hold the glasses while I pour the Buck's Fizz. She smiles as we cheers.

'Thanks, Ais, you're the best. This is the best.'

It's far from the best but it makes me even more determined to make the rest of Majella's bridal journey as perfect as possible.

'You'll have a fab day,' Bridal Sweet goes as she zips up Majella's garment bag. 'And you're in good company. Did you hear Emilia Coburn is renting a French chateau for her wedding to the James Bond lad? I heard it on the radio on the way in.

'Go 'way! The glamour. That will be some do!' Maj is on a high as she slings the dress over her shoulder, bottle of Buck's Fizz in her other hand. I throw a cold 'bye' over mine as we exit and head for the car.

****

'Your dress is next, Ais. Then we're sorted.' Maj sinks into the passenger seat contentedly as the email tone sounds on my phone.

'Sorry, I'll just get that before we head off.'

I fish it out and see Mandy Blumenthal's name on the screen. The NDA and the final contract! She said she'd be sending it this week. Majella is flat out sending pictures of the dress to Sadhbh so I open the email and click on the document, scanning it quickly.

'This Non-Disclosure Agreement is entered into by BallyGoBrunch Catering of Ballygobbard and Mandy Blumenthal Inc. of New York City … confidential information … sensitive nature … held in the strictest confidence for the sole and exclusive benefit of the Disclosing Party (Miss E. Coburn) …'

My eyes go past the name and then fly back to it. E. Coburn. Emilia Coburn. Is Emilia Coburn having a birthday party? And I'm doing some of the catering? Oh my God!

'What is it, Ais?' Majella swigs from the bottle and puts her feet up on the dashboard.

'Eh, nothing. Just Mammy wanted to know about, eh –' I cast my eyes wildly around '– about, eh, air fresheners for, eh, goats.' Luckily Maj is too preoccupied to notice. I drive home right at the speed limit, frantic for a chance to read it all properly, feeling like my heart is going to beat right out of my chest.

CHAPTER 28

I read it again, just to make sure.

'This NDA shall remain in effect until the confidential information pertaining to the event, the nature of the event, the bridal party and their guests no longer qualifies.'

It's their wedding. Emilia Coburn and Ben Dixon are having their wedding at Garbally and I'm the only one who knows it. Well, the only one around here anyway, it seems. Even James seems to think the first event there is a birthday party, and I'm afraid to probe any deeper because am I even allowed to say that I've signed an NDA? Won't that reveal that I know something about it? Better to say nothing at all. Mandy has prepared less detailed agreements for Carol, Noel and Karla, so all they know is that we're preparing food for an event at Garbally. I open the calendar on my phone and I'm about to put the date into it when I freeze. Maybe it's best not to. You never know who's watching. I'll hardly forget it anyway, though – 27 April. Exactly one week before Majella's wedding.

'Honey, I'm home,' James calls into the apartment as he closes the front door with a swing of his hip. He's done it every night since we moved in together and is just thrilled with himself. It's cute but also wearing a bit thin. Plus, he's started coming in covered in cement dust every day. They're pouring floors at Garbally apparently. Pity they wouldn't pour themselves into washing machines at the end of the day. James is carrying shopping bags. He must have gone to the New Aldi to get ingredients for the toad in the hole he's promised to make me. Or threatened, more like. I couldn't say anything over breakfast, of course, but it sounds God-awful, with the exception of the sausages.

'Honey, you're home.'

I said this back to him the first night he did it, and now it's a little ritual. He smiles at me in his work fleece with his bag of groceries in one hand and some post in the other. It's mad how quickly this has all happened. I survey our little place. I must say, it's looking a lot better since I went to Knock Garden Centre the other day. As well as a lovely cosy throw for the couch, I picked up a Colette Green reed diffuser, a bottle of fancy hand soap for the bathroom, eight baskets in varying sizes, a set of Joseph Joseph chopping boards, three stepping-out mats for the shower, a silver picture frame, four succulents, two mugs that say 'Love', a knitted pouffe for the living room and two hundred tea lights. You can never have enough tea lights, especially in your first proper home with a boy.

Carol nearly fainted when the receipt fell out of my purse in the café, and it's very unlike me to be so flaithiúlach, but I must admit, firing the stuff into the little wheelie basket they give you there made me feel quite calm. The calmest I've felt in ages. Maybe that's why Sadhbh likes shopping so much? Maybe I need another shopping spree after the shock of this NDA stuff.

'Well, did she get the dress?' James is unpacking stuff in the kitchen and I stop myself from going in to make sure he's putting everything on the right shelf in the fridge.

'Oh, she did. One thing knocked off my to-do list.'

He waves a square white envelope at me. 'Look! Addressed to both of us. Our first post.'

I reach out and take it from him, running my finger over our two names. It looks so grown up. I slip my finger under the flap and open it.

'It's a card! "Home Sweet Home" with a picture of a cottage. Aw.' I flip it open. '"Congrats Aisling and James! Love Elaine and Ruby, and Dexter." "Dexter is our new puppy," it says in brackets. Ah, they got a puppy! I thought it would have been cats, to be honest.'

'That was very nice of them,' James says, going back to his groceries while I move some of the smaller baskets and succulents around on the mantelpiece to make room for the card. Of course there's only an electric fire in the hearth, given that it's an apartment, but it's better than nothing, and the 'real' effect is so convincing James had to stop me flinging a sod of turf on it for the first few weeks.

'Remind me to tell them about the new mugs,' I say, arranging the baskets by size. 'They were designed by Ellen DeGeneres, you know.'

'Huh?' He's looking at his phone.

'The mugs. Ellen designed them herself. She has her own range of delph now. I'm sure the girls are all over it.'

'Sorry, Ais … it's just this email. Gah!'

'Everything okay?' I walk over to the kitchen and run a hand up his back, feeling bad for being annoyed at him when he came in. As I know only too well myself, the curse of being self-employed is you have to be reachable at all times. There's just no escape. It's not like sitting in an open-plan office and being paid whether you process those pension claims or not, and more's the pity. Hindsight is 20/20, but I didn't know how good I had it back at PensionsPlus.

'It's about that event that's scheduled for Garbally. The planner is nitpicking about finishes when we're not even close to that stage yet. So bloody clueless. It's that woman, Mandy, the one you met. What's the latest with that, anyway?'

I start to panic. Can I tell him anything? Can he even know we're doing food for this 'event'? Will I get sued? I decide to err on the side of caution. 'No, she's gone very quiet. They must be going with someone else.'

'You're probably better off.' He flings his phone onto the counter and I gather up the butter and milk and head for the fridge, avoiding his eyes.

'Well, you know the way it is with … some people,' I stammer. 'They probably want everything to look perfect. For the pictures, I mean. The … eh … birthday pictures.'

I nearly said wedding pictures. I really need to stay on top of this. To be fair, though, everybody does love looking at wedding pictures. Denise Kelly has her album on a sort of stand in the corner of her sitting room. More of a podium, really. She turns a page every day like the Book of Kells. It's a good idea, really, when you factor in the price of a wedding photographer. She's only getting her money's worth.

James looks at me through narrowed eyes. 'Are you okay?'

'Of course I am. Why wouldn't I be?' I pick up the *RTÉ Guide*. 'Oh, look, the repeat of *Dancing with the Stars* is starting. I'm dying to see Marty Whelan's tango. Majella said Pablo was very impressed with his rhythm.' I slide down onto the couch and flick on the telly, grateful to have my back to him.

I still can't quite believe BallyGoBrunch will be doing the canapés for Emilia Coburn and Ben Dixon's wedding. On the one hand, it's doing nothing for my already sky-high stress levels, but on the other, it's likely to be a star-studded affair. What if their pictures get into magazines, what with all their celebrity friends? Imagine Amy Huberman being papped eating a Carol Boland sausage roll? Or George and Amal going bananas for our ham and cheese croquettes? The café could be catapulted onto the international stage. I can feel my heart pounding in my chest. Everything will have to be perfect. I take out my phone again and open the document, swooshing my finger around to draw my signature before I change my mind. I hit Send and sit back on the couch, thinking about all the ways I could possibly make a balls of this.

Sadhbh sent me a link last week to an article about compartmentalising. She said it would help me get my cortisol levels down, and at this stage I'll try anything. Well, anything but 'smudging'. This was her other idea: that I wrap up a little pile of sage, set it on fire and walk around the apartment waving it till all the negativity is gone from my life. I ask you. No, compartmentalising makes more sense. With that, I just visualise keeping every problem in its own box and not letting them all spill out together and joining up like one giant, mega problem, which is how I'm feeling at the moment, and it's starting to show, even with Majella's dress now under control.

Carol had a huge pot of chicken carcasses and vegetables and herbs on the hob for three days to make a stock, and when she asked me to strain it yesterday, I poured the lot down the drain and kept the pot of bones. She had to explain to me three times what I'd done wrong. I'm half-thinking of going to Dr Maher and asking him for a prescription or something, but I don't know if I can bring myself to confess to anyone that I'm feeling so overwhelmed. Would they even believe me? I should probably tell James first, since he's my boyfriend. My 'partner', as Mammy's taken to calling him. I always thought 'partner' was for glamorous women whose first husbands died in mysterious circumstances but here I am, a 'partner'. James's partner.

I can hear him whisking away goodo in the kitchen and I know I'm lucky to have him. I had to go to the cash and carry yesterday morning, and when I got to the Micra I noticed he'd poured boiling-hot water on my windscreen to de-ice it. A lovely gesture, even though it's highly dangerous and he could have shattered the whole thing. Still, though, it's the thought that counts.

I can't help but think back to his parents in that big house in Buckleton, how they can barely stand to be in the same postcode as each other, and how you'd think that would have completely messed up his idea of what love really is. But no, he's behind me making me toad in the hole. He's staying in Ireland because of me. He loves me.

'Hey, I was thinking.' He slams the oven door, throws himself down beside me on the couch, and nuzzles my neck. 'We should have a little housewarming in the next few weeks, now that you're all unpacked. What do you think? I know you've been non-stop with wedding-dress shopping and all that. It'll be a chance to let your hair down and relax. You can invite all your friends and I can bring some of the work crew.'

Oh God, as if I haven't enough to be doing without adding a party. I'm about to object when he cuts me off. 'You can show off your new mugs. And those candles you're so fond of. Maybe get another throw.' He raises his eyebrows and he knows he has me, the crafty shite. I must ring Knock Garden Centre and get them to hold two of the Colette Green cushions for me. If we're going to have a party, we're having it in turquoise-velvet style.

CHAPTER 29

I know being fashionably late is a thing, but it's a quarter past eight and there's still not a sinner here. I thought I could count on Majella and Pablo to be early, or at least on time. They're only coming from upstairs.

'If you look in the freezer one more time the ice will have actually melted.' James laughs, opening a bottle of Bishop's Finger with my Las Vegas fridge-magnet-slash-bottle-opener. 'Relax, Aisling.'

That's the third time he's told me to relax and it's getting more and more like a red rag to a bull.

'I was just making sure it's definitely there,' I reply as evenly as I can, adjusting China's finest silver-foil helium balloons that spell out 'cheers' and karate chopping the velvet cushions. He's probably spent his whole life hosting effortless parties for people who are used to just holding out their glasses and having them refilled as if by magic, but this is my first grown-up party and I'm in ribbons trying to get it right. 'You remembered the lemons, didn't you? I won't have it said that we didn't have slices of lemon for people's gins.'

'They're in a bowl. And I did some cucumber too, just in case. *Relaaax*, Ais. They're all on the bar cart.'

The fourth 'relax' sets my teeth on edge and I spy a patch of concrete dust on the edge of the couch and go for it with my hand, whacking it far longer than necessary.

The bar cart was my idea. I saw it mentioned in *House and Home* magazine as a 'must-have' for any party so I immediately ordered one online. So far we have three different bottles of gin, a bottle of vodka and a bottle of Tia Maria on it, as well as the lemons and cucumber and just the one basket. The Tia Maria is for Cyclops – he won't drink anything else. I got six litres of milk as well.

'Oh, you can tell your mum I've made a start on her scarecrow. State of the art, it's going to be. I've done my research.'

God bless him. He's taking it so seriously. I accept the drink he's handing to me and resolve to go easier on him. 'I'm sure she's going to love it.'

I go to the front door and look into the apartment, pretending to be someone else, not the person who's been hoovering and dusting it all evening and artfully arranging succulents on every available surface. It looks good. I think my new 'If Life Gives You Lemons, Add Gin' print adds a certain *je ne sais quoi*. The place smells great too. I panic-bought two more reed diffusers and have a Yankee Candle in Home Sweet Home the size of a tractor tyre going in the bathroom.

I'm about to stick my head into the freezer one last time, just to be sure, when there's a sharp knock on the door. As I near it I can hear the faint sound of voices bickering on the other side.

'I don't think I'll ever get over this … this betrayal,' Majella is hissing at Pablo when I open it.

His eyes are screwed shut like a man in pain. '*Mijo, mi amore*, you know I would never plan it like this. Please forgive me. I beg you.'

'Oh, what's all this?' I say, standing back as Majella storms in in a cloud of Alien. 'A lover's tiff?'

'James,' she says, nodding at him. Then she turns to me, tears in her eyes. 'It's the bloody stag, Aisling. You'll never guess when it's on.'

'No idea,' I say, pasting on a smile. 'Welcome to our home. Drink?'

'Bloody Valentine's Day,' Majella screeches, ignoring me, while Pablo buries his head in his hands and sinks to his knees. 'I can't believe my fiancé would do it to me. Who has their stag on Valentine's Day?'

'It is not my fault, *mi amore*! Javier and Miguel, they used the Google and found the best deal to come to Ballygobbard that they could. That is 14 February at the Mountrath.'

I stifle a laugh. I know that deal – they run it every year. I hope Pablo's brothers enjoy their complimentary bottle of fizz and rose petals on their double bed. It's very romantic altogether.

'Something from the bar cart, Majella?' James says, trying to defuse the situation. 'Do come in.' Thank God Carol's gone down to Ballymaloe for the night. It's shaping up to be a noisy one if the first two guests are anything to go by.

'I won't go! I will take you to Ballygobbard's finest restaurant,' Pablo wails, and I assume he's talking about BallyGoBrunch since the only other 'restaurant' is the Chinese takeaway. I'm flattered, to be honest. James looks a bit taken aback but I suppose he's only used to Majella and Pablo's public displays of affection, not their raging fights.

There's another knock on the door.

'Can you keep it civil, lads?' I say, making a beeline for it. 'This is our housewarming, remember? Go look at the bar cart. It's rose gold.'

Sharon and Cyclops are the next to arrive, clutching bottles of champagne.

'The place looks stunning, hun,' Sharon says, pressing a bottle at me and handing me a bag from Avoca. Swish! 'Ooh, is that a bar cart?'

'It is,' I say, delighted. I should have known Sharon would cop it immediately. She's very up on her interiors and is no stranger to a decorative houseplant herself, real or otherwise.

'That smell is unreal,' Cyclops says, patting me on the shoulder.

'Just a few candles,' I say with a smile. 'Go get yourself a Tia Maria, Cy. Plenty of milk in the fridge.'

'Sound, Ais.'

The next twenty minutes are basically a blur of me opening the door, firing coats at James to throw onto the bed and showing people to the bar cart.

'You and James are such a fab couple,' Dee Ruane says when I join some of the girls in the kitchen. 'I told Titch about the yoghurts. He said James is putting them all to shame. Good, I said. It might make you pull your socks up. Sumira Singh shouldn't be the only woman in the village getting help with her shopping.'

'Ah, stop,' I reply, folding my arms and leaning back against the counter, all the 'relaxes' from earlier forgotten. 'He has his faults.'

'Like what?' Sharon goes.

'He has no idea how to load the dishwasher. I always have to redo it. He puts building-site muck all over the apartment.'

'*Pfft*,' Denise goes. 'Liam doesn't even know where the dishwasher is. Fair dues, Ais. He's some catch.'

'And he has bad taste in films.'

'Don't they all,' Dee says, rolling her eyes. 'I'll never understand Titch's loyalty to Jason Statham.'

'How are you and Cyclops getting on above the salon, Sharon?' Denise asks. 'I heard he got a bit of slagging at training for the back wax.'

'We're in a bit of a bubble,' she says with a smile. 'It's been lovely, hun.'

'I remember those days,' Denise chimes in. 'I put on nearly a stone after the wedding. All we did was sit on the couch and order food from the Chinese. I couldn't even fit into my O'Neills until I started doing Zumba with Mags.'

'God, I'm right there with you,' I say, pinging the waistband of my holdy-in knickers, which is just below my bra. I swear I see Sharon rolling her eyes.

'You have the place very cosy. You know we still have two free Thursdays this summer?' Lisa Gleeson, who's here because she's Maeve's first cousin, is waggling her eyebrows at me. I know what she's getting at, but it would kill me to get married on a weekday. Especially with her doing the organising – who knows what I'd get. And anyway, marriage is the last thing on my mind. Living together is all the rage now. Look at Sadhbh and Don.

'Maybe you should try to get Emilia Coburn,' laughs Maeve. 'She could have a BGB wedding instead of swanning off to France.'

I almost drop my glass at the sound of her name and pray to God nobody noticed, but nobody seems to. Sharon is staring at the floor and I wonder what's annoyed her. She was in great form when she arrived.

'I was half-thinking of tweeting her from the Ard Rí account,' Lisa goes, oblivious to my panic. 'What do you think, girls? I know she has two million followers but, I mean, it would make sense for them to do it here since her granny was from Knock.'

'Ballygobbard!' Dee and Maeve roar together.

'Right, whatever,' Lisa says while I sweat quietly and rearrange the apples in the fruit bowl, praying they change the subject.

'Skippy Brennan thinks they're actually doing it in Canada, since that's where they're filming the new James Bond,' Maeve says. 'According to him they've got some fancy wedding planner. She did Kim and Kanye's.'

Well, I know for certain that's not right. I googled Mandy and there was no mention of Kim and Kanye.

'She's the best in the business, apparently,' Dee says, nodding. 'Charges something like 100K a go.'

'Is that what I could be earning if I went independent?' Lisa asks, her eyes widening. I can almost see the dollar signs. Well, euro signs. 'Because I was thinking I could promote myself to "wedding consultant" if I went out on my own.'

'What exactly would you be doing?' Maeve asks, looking sceptical.

'Giving expert advice and that,' Lisa says with a wave of her hand. 'You know there are men who go to weddings just to drink the free booze and score vulnerable women? It's actually shocking. Wedding crashers. I could tell brides and grooms how to spot them.'

'I can count on one hand the number of weddings I've gone to with a free bar,' Sharon finally speaks up. 'I don't think wedding crashers are a big problem, hun.'

'Do you miss home at all, Ais?' Sharon asks. I think about it for a second while watching James talking to Cyclops, Titch and Pablo across the room.

'Not really. I still see Mammy nearly every day. And Paul is there now in the evenings to keep her company, which is keeping my guilt at bay.'

'How is he doing, Ais? I heard he's not great. He's in Maguire's a lot at the bar on his own,' Maeve says.

That's news to me. I must take him out for a drink one of these weeks and check up on him. 'He'll be grand, I'm sure. Mammy is looking after him.'

****

'Hey, not a bad turn out,' James whispers in my ear later when I'm queuing outside the bathroom and praying to God forty spare toilet rolls was enough.

'People are so good,' I say, smiling up at him. 'We got six more Ellen DeGeneres mugs!'

'Lads, I'm sorry to interrupt.' It's Majella not looking sorry at all. 'But Pablo is up the walls about this bloody stag.'

'I don't think they'll be able to change the date at this stage,' I say. 'It's only three weeks away. These things don't organise themselves, you know.'

'Ah, I'm over that. In fact, he was delighted when I lost the rag. He actually wants to get out of it.'

'Why?' James asks.

'He's scared shitless, James,' Majella says flatly. 'And I'm starting to get a bit worried myself, if I'm being honest. Remember when Con Rice broke both his elbows paintballing? They had to get a new suit jacket specially made for him. I don't want Pab coming back to me with no eyebrows or only one testicle. We're planning on having kids, you know.'

'He'll be grand, Majella. Sure isn't John organising it? He won't let it get out of hand.'

I steal a glance at James to see if there's any reaction to me mentioning John. But nothing. He's as cool as a cucumber that lad.

'I know what the Rangers lads are like when they get together, Ais. And you do too. It's like a pack mentality – they lead each other astray. I need someone to go and keep an eye on things. Someone … impartial.' I follow Majella's gaze – she's looking pointedly at James. And then the penny drops.

'But James isn't going on the stag,' I say.

'He isn't yet.'

'What do you mean … yet?' James asks hesitantly. 'I was planning to make Aisling a special dinner. And that spotted dick I loved at school. It'll be our first Valentine's Day. I wanted it to be special.'

'Actually, maybe you have a point, Maj,' I say quickly. 'Someone should be there to mind Pablo. We don't want a repeat of what happened to Tiny Hands Turlough in Prague.'

Majella visibly pales. 'Oh, shit. I'd forgotten about that.'

'Would you do it?' I say, batting my Colette Green eyelashes at him. 'For me?'

James smiles sweetly. 'I would, but unfortunately I'm not invited.'

'Not a problem,' Majella says, draining her G&T. 'Aisling can ask John to sort that out. He won't say no to her.'

I glare at Majella. What a thing to say in front of James. It's not like I have John wrapped around my finger.

'Go on, Ais, ring him. Please?'

****

'Ah, you're not serious, Aisling?' John says, when I ring him from the bedroom five minutes later. Majella wasn't going to stop hassling me until I did, and it would be nice for James to be included. I think because Pablo works for him and he's kind of a big man around town, he's a bit isolated.

'Ah, go on, you'll barely notice him. He's very polite. Please?' I'm buoyed by the booze and feeling tenacious.

'Who is it?' I hear Megan go in the background. It sounds like they're in the pub. Although it must be fairly empty since everyone who's anyone in BGB is here. I probably should have invited them.

'It took me weeks to get all the money off people. I finally got everything sorted yesterday, and then Paul changed his mind and said he wasn't coming so my numbers are off.'

'Our Paul?'

'Yeah. He said he's just not up to it.'

Between this and going on his own to Maguire's, it all sounds a bit worrying. I was hoping the stag might be something for him to look forward to. But I seize on this piece of information. 'That means you have an extra spot, right? James can take Paul's place? Majella just really wants him there to look after Pablo.'

'Do you really think we're that irresponsible? That we need James to mind us?'

I can already feel this backfiring but it's too late now. 'I don't know, maybe you should ask Turlough?'

There's silence on the other end.

'Please, John,' I urge. 'I really need a dig out here. Please.'

'Oh, alright then,' he says with a sigh. 'Send me his number and I'll add him to the WhatsApp group.'

'Who is it, John?' I hear her go again.

'You're a lifesaver!'

'Ais, before you go, do you know his blood type?'

CHAPTER 30

'I knew this stag, it would get out of the hand. I have seen enough *Ibiza Unconscious* to know this.'

'*Uncovered*,' I mutter, without thinking, but Majella silences me with a touch on my arm.

'Shhh, Ais, he's very shook. They gave him seventeen Jägerbombs.'

I've seen Pablo standing on a table singing 'Hips Don't Lie' after two pints so this is truly alarming. John and James were supposed to look after him. I'll kill them.

We're sitting on the couch in the Morans' apartment, which is mercifully otherwise empty. James fell in at 3 a.m., went straight to sleep and left first thing this morning with barely a word. I texted Majella to see how Pablo got on and she summoned me in, where I found him with his head in her lap, clutching a tea-towel and a banana.

'Why did you drink so much, Pablo?' I've read two *Stellar* articles now about victim blaming so I don't want to be pointing the finger, but surely he could have just said no. I bet Titch was the ringleader. He's a danger to everyone when it comes to shots.

'It wasn't the lads,' Majella says quietly. 'There was a hen in the Vortex. Down from Dublin. They attacked Pablo with feather boas.'

As if on cue, a solitary pink feather dislodges from Pablo's hair and sinks to the floor.

'That must be the gang Mammy had in the yurts! They're supposed to stay again tonight but she found an alpaca wearing a negligee this morning and asked them to leave. There was a goat in one of the beds too. Mammy said he had the good grace to look ashamed.'

'Sounds about right.' Majella purses her lips. 'They fed Pablo full of drink. He says he was powerless to resist.'

'They were so many,' Pablo keens. 'They say, "You're our Valentine, Pablo. Don't let us down, Pablo. You make the bride cry, Pablo." I don't want to make the bride cry.'

'Oh, you're such a dote. A soft, foolish, dote.' Majella kisses his forehead and he grips his tea-towel and his banana even tighter.

'My brothers, my Javier, my Miguel, they were laughing. They laugh and they laugh.'

The absolute lousers.

'But where were the lads? Why didn't they save you?' I don't know why they would let this happen. John knows how impressionable Pablo is, and James was sent explicitly to look after him.

Pablo looks from me to Majella and then back to me again, his large brown eyes full of uncertainty and red with the hangover.

'Go on,' Majella encourages. 'Tell her.'

'They were smashing up the fight.'

'Breaking up,' I say reflexively. 'What fight?'

'John and James.'

'What?' A sick feeling hits my stomach. 'What were they fighting about? They weren't hitting each other, were they?'

Pablo looks as panicked as I feel. 'I do not know. They had the words and Cyclops and Baby Chief Gittons they took them outside and I think that one pushed the other one. And The Truck said after that maybe one caught a fist.'

'Who … caught the fist, Pablo?' Whichever one of them was hit or did the hitting, I feel sick.

'I do not know, Aisling. I like John. I like James. I do not want my friends to fight. A misunderstandment, I think.'

I catch Majella's eye and give her the 'what's going on?' eyebrows but she just shrugs. 'You'll have to ask James.'

****

'I know as little as you, Ais,' Sharon shouts over the roar of the hairdryer. 'But we can ask him as soon as he comes down.'

I was going to skip my blow-dry appointment, I feel so sick over what Pablo's told me, but I reckoned that Sharon might be able to shed some light on the situation, via Cyclops. I sent James a text the second I left Majella and Pablo's but there's been no reply. I can't face ringing him just yet. I was so distracted that I let Cliodhna Ó Súilleabháin put a treatment in my hair even though I only got one last week. They're only a racket but I have more important things to worry about.

The salon is mercifully quiet for a Saturday morning so I can roar back at Sharon to my heart's content. 'Did he say anything at all about it?'

'Just that it was eventful. But, sure, I thought he meant Pablo got a lap dance or something.' Jesus, Pablo would expire. 'He didn't mention anything about a fight.'

Just then the beaded curtain behind the counter parts and Cyclops slopes out, bleary eyed and fresh from the shower. Sharon beckons him over and he nods when he sees me, resignation on his face.

'Well, Ais, I suppose you've heard?'

'Well, not really. Only from Pablo. What happened?'

'Well, I hate to have to tell you this, but … James started on John.'

'What?' I can't believe my ears. 'What did he say to him?'

'I'm not sure, to be honest, Ais, but he squared up to him inside the Vortex, and then when we took him outside to cool off and John followed. Titch says he swung for him. I put James in a taxi and sent him home.'

'What did James say, Ais?' Sharon looks at Cyclops with concern in her eyes.

'Nothing. He was working today. He left first thing. I haven't talked to him.'

Sharon has long since turned off the hairdryer, and when I turn my head the Ó Súilleabháin twins are hanging on our every word. Great.

****

'Aisling! Hey, Ais!'

Someone calls my name as I leave Strong Stuff, checking my phone again for any word from James and debating ringing John. It's Turlough McGrath, looking a bit worse for wear. He's coming out of Filan's with a roll the size of my head in his tiny hands. He jogs towards me but has to stop after about ten paces, bending down and breathing deeply.

'Are you alright, Turlough?'

'Heavy night. You know yourself.' He regains a bit of colour and stands up straight. 'I just wanted to check if James is okay? I don't have his number and he left awful quick last night after John –'

'What happened, Turlough? Do you know?'

'I just saw John having a go at him, Aisling. Which isn't like him at all, to be fair.

'I thought it was the other way around?'

'Well, that's what it looked like to me. John's a good friend of mine so I don't want to chat shit about him at all, but James was buying rounds and, well, he seems like a good lad. I hope he's okay.'

****

'Why didn't you answer your phone all day?'

James, with the faintest shadow of a bruise under his left eye, pulls the door of his site office closed behind me and points me towards a chair. 'It's barely even lunchtime, Aisling.' But he can't quite look at me.

I nearly had to hand over a kidney to be allowed onto the Garbally site. The same monster of a Nordie security man as before checked my driving licence against my name on the list about seven times, and I got so flustered that I started explaining that I had been on holidays the week before the photo was taken and my freckles might be disfiguring but it's definitely me in the picture. I even reminded him about the quiche.

Eventually the brute let me through and I raced the Micra towards the site office, avoiding potholes and stacks of pipes the size of a house. James was right: there *is* a lot of work to do here.

'What happened with you and John?'

'Who told you?'

'Pablo. Cyclops. Turlough. It was the talk of the stag, naturally.'

'Look, I'm not proud of it but I wasn't going to let him push me around and not defend myself.'

'So he did push you around?'

'Yes, of course.' But he doesn't meet my eye.

'Oh. But why were you fighting at all? What was said?'

James is avoiding my eye again. 'Nothing. I can't remember. There were a lot of shots.'

'You honestly don't remember why you and John were going for each other?'

'Look, all I know is it's all sorted now. Can you leave it? I'm not feeling the best.'

He does look fairly ropey. They all did. There might be a better time to do this.

'Sorry. I'm just stressed. Mammy has been on to me about groups causing hassle at the farm, and I'm supposed to be on a day off but there's been a big delivery so I have to go back to the café.'

As well as the hens, Mammy had what she thought was a group of nature artists during the week. She assumed they were there to draw the wildflowers, but actually they were naturist artists there to draw each other. They kept threatening to shed their clothes but, thank God, the icy February chill isn't conducive to it. Constance had her hands full directing them away from the polytunnel, according to Mammy, who kept me on the phone for half an hour going on about it – she was just launching into talking about Paul when I had to cut her off. And then there's the delivery of some of the non-perishable stuff I've ordered for the Coburn wedding canapés. Carol and I are trying to get on top of as much as possible in order to minimise the stress coming up to both the Garbally wedding and Majella's. Carol and the BallyGoBrunch staff have all signed their NDAs but I still have to guard the Coburn –Dixon wedding info with my life.

A voice outside calls James's name and his eyes dart to the window and then back to me.

'Okay, well, I'll see you later then.'

There's a knock on the door and a woman in a hard hat reefs it open and sticks her head in. 'James. Problem with the pointing on those upstairs interior walls.'

'Be right there.'

He kisses the top of my head, picks up his own hard hat and heads out the door calling behind him. 'Don't worry, Aisling. Everything is fine. Relax.'

CHAPTER 31

I'm exhausted the following morning as I head towards the eco farm. James came home late from the site and announced he was wrecked before heading straight to bed, so I got nothing more out of him about the stag. To be fair, he looked dead on his feet and my heart went out to him. He was fast asleep when I was leaving so I left him to it. I say a little prayer that I can get five minutes alone with Mammy. Apart from the odd badly timed phone call, I feel like it's been weeks since I've seen her properly, and they've been really busy with the first of the school tours starting to come in and then the naturists and the hens. She and Constance weren't expecting the uptake in school tours so early in the season but they're not complaining. Keeping a keen eye for any exposed flesh, I pull into the driveway of the house and around the back, hoping and expecting to see Mammy's car. In its place, however, is John's, with a trailer hooked up to the back.

'What the blazes …?' I mutter. What is he doing here? I specifically asked Mammy not to keep asking him for things. I debate turning back and going instead to BallyGoBrunch where I have a million and one things to be doing. But a part of me wants to see what John has to say for himself after the stag. Fighting with my boyfriend outside the

Vortex. The tiny horrible voice in my head telling me that I actually like the idea of it doesn't get much of a chance to speak up. Instead, I focus on being mad. James is such a nice man and has been so good to everyone in BGB and beyond. How dare John make him feel unwelcome. With my hackles good and high, I get out of the car and march to the back door, swinging it open and nearly taking the nose off John, standing on the other side. He looks less than pleased to see me.

'Hiya.'

'Hi.'

'What are you doing here?' My voice is ice cold.

'I'm just collecting something. I'm leaving.' It's a bit of a stand-off, me on the step, him inside the door. He goes to push past me. 'I better go.'

'What did you say to James on the stag?'

He stops in his tracks, fiddling his car keys between his fingers. He speaks quietly. 'Nothing.'

'So why were you fighting in the Vortex? What the hell was that all about?'

'Just a few too many drinks. It's nothing, Aisling.'

'Cyclops says he started it. Turlough says you started it. Pablo was nearly hospitalised for his nerves. What the hell happened?'

He's saved by the crunching of tyres on gravel and Mammy swinging around the corner. I've never seen anyone look so relieved.

'Don't make a big deal of it, Ais. It's nothing. I'll text him and sort it out,' he mutters as Mammy gets out of the car, reefing a few bags for life with her.

'Well, there's a surprise. Hiya, Aisling. I had to race over to the New Aldi for more burger buns.'

'I better go,' John says.

'You're blocking him in, Mammy.' I take the bags from her and she goes to get back into the car but John is over in a flash.

'I'll move it. No worries. I'll drop in the keys.'

'Well, now, aren't you a gentleman, John? Thanks very much.' He's already in and reversing, eager to get as far away from me as possible.

I bring Mammy's bags into the kitchen and she follows, looking sheepish.

'He was just collecting something, Aisling. He wasn't doing any work or anything.'

'Okay, Mammy.'

'But do you know, it was just like old times seeing the two of you standing there chatting. Isn't it great you can be friends?' She obviously didn't pick up on any of the ice-cold tension.

'Sure,' I sigh, unpacking the shopping for her and quizzically holding up some curiously posh-looking cat food.

'That contrary old b-word has stopped eating the regular stuff so I have to feed her like a queen now.' As if on cue, That Bloody Cat strolls into the kitchen, gives a snide meow and strolls back out again. 'She has some attitude since your father died. I think she misses him,' Mammy deduces, and I nod in solidarity.

John finishes his manoeuvres outside and, with his car freed, he knocks gently on the door, holding up Mammy's keys and placing them on the counter with a small wave. He doesn't meet my eye and is gone.

****

'John texted me.' James is barely in the door when he offers up this information. I know John said he would but I took it with a pinch of salt and definitely didn't think he'd do it that very evening.

'Oh?'

'So it's all fine. We both said sorry and it's water under the bridge.'

Just like that. If it was girls there'd probably be a tribunal followed by a candlelit ceremony of hope and reconciliation. We had a particularly crusty religion teacher in second year who instigated a candlelit ceremony of hope and reconciliation after Claire Conrad's gang starting picking on Majella after Titch Maguire gave Majella a Valentine's card even though he had been Claire's first shift two weeks previously. (I must remember that one for the wedding speech too.) It ended up developing into something of a civil war between the second year girls, and Mrs Kinsella made us sit in a circle and say what we liked and admired about each other. Majella really struggled with what she liked and admired about Claire, finally settling on 'you're good at French', which sounded like a cop-out to me but Mrs Kinsella seemed to accept it. She was straight out of her seat to gather up all the candles and cushions and get the desks back in order for Mr Burke's double Geography. I always had a soft spot for Mrs Kinsella because she was very supportive of me and Maj's earnest harmonising to 'Dreams' by the Cranberries at the St Brigid's Cross retreat in first year. I still have the cross I made in one of the boxes under my bed.

James collapses on the couch, puts his head back and closes his eyes, and he looks so wrecked I feel sorry for him. I sit down beside him and tuck my legs up under me – not quite Sadhbh levels of tucking but I manage – snuggling in to him. He smiles with his eyes closed and puts his arm around me and we sit like that for a few minutes. I try to clear my mind and just relax, and I'm just about getting there when there's a racket in the hallway – a jumble of Spanish and the bashing of cases against the walls. Pablo's brothers are finally leaving.

James's eyes open slowly and he looks slightly pained. 'Should we help?'

The shouting intensifies, somehow Willy the dog gets involved and there's a high-pitched scream and some definite sobbing.

'Nah,' I say. 'They'll be grand.'

CHAPTER 32

Five weeks pass in no time and the week of Majella's hen is suddenly upon me like a ton of bricks. The stag drama dissipated fairly easily, although things were a little bit tense between me and James for a while. We're both stressed out, though, so I try not to worry. He's under pressure to get Garbally finished before the big 'party', and I feel like my shoulders are nearly up around my ears with the tension of trying to keep the details of Emilia Coburn's wedding under wraps. It's a weird, lonely feeling, being the only one who knows. But I feel proud that she's chosen our local BGB café to feed her guests. I wonder who's doing the main meal. Some big celebrity chef with their own NDA, I'm sure. Mandy communicates only via me, and Carol and the gang still think it's a birthday party they're working towards – and their NDAs prevent them from even talking about that, even though the whole town is buzzing with speculation about whose party it is. Mandy has told me that Ben and Emilia have been so hounded by paparazzi they're determined to keep the whole thing a secret until the Big Day if they can. They've even rented a chateau in France, which seems like a fierce waste, but Mandy says they're also selling their wedding pictures to *Hello!* and donating the two million euro fee to charity so I suppose I can't really judge.

I've booked Maguire's for the night before Majella's wedding. She really wanted to have a few 'send-off' drinks and I said I'd organise it, as if I haven't enough on my plate. I was hoping her parents would want to do it in the house, since it's almost finished being renovated and they're due to move back into it in a week or two, but no such luck. I'm going to need a holiday after all this, despite the fact that I'm going to Tenerife in two days.

And with that in mind, I've arranged for the girls to head into Strong Stuff to get our nails and tan and all the rest of it done. Well, it'll just be a pedicure for me. As much as I enjoy the freedom of wearing sandals, my feet are in no condition to be seen in public now that I'm pretty much on them twelve hours a day. I've never had a pedicure before, but Sharon assures me it will change my life. I don't think Majella will let me wear my footies with my bridesmaid dress anyway – it'll be strappy sandals all the way. I finally found the perfect dress among the thirty-seven-odd I ordered online. A simple blue chiffon tea dress with cap sleeves and a sash that's almost the same ivory as Majella's dress. It's perfect. I still have about fifteen others I need to return, though. I must remember to do that tomorrow.

Sharon said we could come in after closing time so we have the run of the salon. Everyone – Maj, Dee, Denise, Sinéad and Maeve – is there when I tip in at ten past seven. They're all huddled around the computer on the reception desk, screaming and gesturing at the screen.

'That's her, that's definitely her,' Dee is saying. 'She was standing at the pump talking on the phone but she had two more in her other hand. That's what caught my attention in the first place. I thought to myself, why would anyone need so many phones? And at the pump, too. It's no great shakes.'

I'm about to point out that the decorative pump, and the Tidy Towns committee's controversial decision to paint it red, is one of the reasons Ballygobbard was commended in the Pride of Place Competition, Population 300 –1,000, in 2015. But I say nothing. It's not the time.

'Ais, it's that celebrity party planner! She was in BGB the other day. The Indo has pictures online.'

I nod and try to look interested. I actually knew Mandy was in BGB but obviously hadn't said anything. I didn't see her myself but James had had what he described as a 'challenging' meeting with her.

'I could just tell she was American,' Dee says knowingly. 'Even though I was going nearly forty.'

When will she respect the thirty kilometres per hour speed limit in the village? That's what I want to know.

'Has James said much about it?' Maeve asks as I shrug off my anorak.

'No, we, eh, we don't really talk much about work. He's just involved in the building side of it, sure.'

'He must know something,' Maeve insists, frustrated.

'So are we going to start the treatments now or …?' I say, absolutely desperate to change the subject. I'm about to fake some kind of seizure – anything – when there's a knock on the glass door and I breathe a sigh of relief. It's Lisa Gleeson, waving frantically.

'Sorry,' Maeve goes, 'she lost a nail trying to glue a hurl back onto a cake topper and I said you'd be open late tonight, Sharon. I didn't know it was just for us.'

Cliodhna Ó Súilleabháin jumps up from the chair at the reception desk. 'I'll do it. I only put them on her yesterday.'

'Skippy Brennan was saying on the radio the other day that he's convinced it's Emilia Coburn's birthday party, but I looked it up and her birthday's in November,' Sinéad says.

'Maybe it's Ben Dixon's?' Dee suggests before Sharon lets out an uncharacteristic roar.

'Will everyone decide what they're having done and we can try to get out of here by midnight?'

The girls start studying the nail books intently as Cliodhna opens the door and lets Lisa in.

'I've news,' she says conspiratorially. Oh God, not her too. The girls all lean forward in anticipation as she sits down and prepares to deliver her gossip.

'Well, I heard from Martin Kelly's cousin – she was in the hotel today pricing a communion – that Dicey Kelly was caught taking money out of the church collection basket last week. He had hundreds in two euro coins.'

The girls all sit back, disappointed.

'Who hasn't taken a fiver to get milk and bread on the way home, to be fair?' Majella says, holding out her hands for Cliodhna to get to work. Lisa's gossip is shite but I'm delighted that she's distracted them all from talking about Emilia.

'I'm sort of disappointed Emilia Coburn's getting married in France,' Sinéad goes. Jesus, Mary and Joseph. There's no escape.

'I was hoping she'd have a winter wedding,' Denise says, staring wistfully out the window. 'She has that colouring that would look good in the snow. Imagine she wore a fur cape? Stunning. You'd love that, Sharon.'

Sharon has an extensive collection of faux fur, a coat for every occasion. Weight Watchers Maura always told us to avoid it since it 'adds unnecessary volume', but truth be told, I'd love a little stole for a wedding now and then. Sharon's very focused on Dee's nails, though, and just gives a nod.

'How's everyone's Trim for Tenerife going?' Denise asks. Denise was like a rake before she had baby Cumhall and she stayed much the same after she had him, so I don't know why *she's* going on about Trim for Tenerife. The girls chat about how they've 'been good', and Sinéad reveals she tried eating celery for a week but gave up after two hours because she just really hates celery. I can't help but mention my steps are off the charts at the moment, what with all the running around I'm doing.

I notice that Sharon is still very quiet and I wonder is she thick with me for landing the whole hen party in on top of her like this. I've definitely felt a bit of a vibe off her this past while, but I know I'm feeling a bit sensitive about everything and stressed about leaving BallyGoBrunch for the weekend. Carol assures me everything will be grand. I ordered the tiny racks of lamb last week for the wedding, and Carol's been practising in the meantime cooking them to pink perfection to slice into little chops. She promised me we won't be giving them food poisoning, but I won't be happy until we're twenty-four hours the other side of that wedding.

'I've more news, actually,' Lisa pipes up, looking put out that her Dicey Kelly revelation wasn't the bombshell she was hoping. 'The date is confirmed for that big party in

Garbally. Someone I know who works in a fancy restaurant in Dublin said half their part-time staff are taking 27 April off to work at it.'

'Jesus, that's only a month away!' Dee squeals. 'The excitement.'

'And it's only a week before your wedding, Maj,' Sinéad adds.

'I know, God!' Majella laughs. 'Imagine it was the same day? I'd go spare. All eyes on me, please!' The girls laugh and move on to chatting about what they're packing for the hen, and I finally relax.

'Are you all set for Tenerife, Maj?' Maeve asks.

'Oh yeah, I have a different white dress for every day.'

Lisa jumps off her chair, nail fixed, and heads for the door. 'No ethnic food, okay?' she says seriously. 'You don't want to be getting the shits in the middle of the street and destroying one of them.'

CHAPTER 33

I 've now sent four increasingly desperate emails to Flo at the Paradise Aqua to confirm our rooms and have heard nothing back. The website is still down and I can't find a phone number online for love or money, but I'm trying to stay positive. I consider giving Interpol a buzz but they probably have enough on their plates. Despite the name, it wasn't anything close to paradise the time I stayed there with John – the itchy blankets and feral cat situation still haunt me – but when I made the initial enquiry Flo had promised it was getting a huge facelift, as well as saying she'd give us a rock bottom rate. I'm afraid to think about what will happen if we arrive and it still has bars on the windows. Majella deserves so much better.

My hands are actually shaking when I pick up my phone to open the hen-party WhatsApp group. Our flight leaves in nine hours and the last time I checked certain people were just starting to pack and were unaware that you can't bring bottles of liquid over 100ml on a plane.

I scan the list of unread messages. Thirty-six. Aunt Shirley is incredulous over the liquid ban and some of the cousins are trying to explain it to her.

'But it's only a litre of Tresemmé?' she's arguing. 'It's not a bomb???'

'Put it in your checked bag if you want to bring it so much, Shirley,' Dearbhla advises.

'I'm sure they have Tresemmé in Tenerife,' Bernadette adds.

'Have you never heard of travel sizes?' That's Ellen.

'Tresemmé, it is no *bueno*,' Juana chimes in. 'Bring Pantene, *guapa*.'

'I think I'll chance it in my handbag. Sure they'll never know,' Shirley says, followed by a shush-face emoji.

There follows – I count them – twenty-four different messages explaining the ins and outs of airport security to Shirley. It turns out she didn't know about the X-ray machines. Or taking off your shoes. And she'd never even heard of *Nothing to Declare*. She'll probably try to bring a shrub in her handbag and introduce a deadly parasite to the farms of Tenerife.

'When was the last time you were on a plane?' Danielle asks.

'The year I went to Lourdes – 1979.'

Well, that explains it. I might have to turn to the Virgin Mary for salvation myself before the weekend is out. Shirley is going to get some land when she's charged for her mid-flight cup of tea.

'Cluck, cluck, hens,' I type into the group. Chicken emoji. Martini emoji. 'This time tomorrow we'll be at our "casual dinner" at Emilio's Tavern. Table booked for eight. Hope everyone likes tapas, it's one of the bride's faves!'

I take a deep breath and close my eyes. When I open them the question is already there, and in record time too.

'What's tapas? It sounds foreign.' Carmel. A second cousin once removed. Majella was highly surprised she decided to come since she hasn't left Headfort in fifteen years and is starting to prep for the apocalypse.

'Tiny bits of dear Spanish food.' How did I know Fionnuala wouldn't be impressed? She has a point about the portions, though. I got some land when Majella and I accidentally ended up in a tapas bar on a long weekend to Budapest. We got Ryanair flights for forty quid each and Majella thought we were going to Romania until the flight touched down and the captain welcomed us to Hungary. In her defence, Budapest does sound very like Bucharest. But once you get past the disappointment of the 'small plates' of tapas the grub is actually dynamite. Maj took to it in a major way, horsing into calamari and manchego and prawns pil pil like her life depended on it. She was never the same after, so I just had to bring her to Tenerife's finest tapas bar on our first night. Emilio's is highly rated on Yelp, save for the three one-star reviews it got because Emilio didn't contribute to the street's Christmas lights fund two years ago. The louser.

'Just get three portions of patatas bravas like you always do, Fionnuala.' Smiley face.

Mairead! It's not like her to be so snarky. To be fair, I was going to suggest the same thing. I'll be bulk ordering the patatas myself.

'What's the plan for Thursday's activity, Ais?' Maeve asks.

It was hard to think of something that would combine Majella's favourite things – drinking and acting the maggot, basically – but I eventually found it online one night a few weeks ago after I stayed up till 3 a.m. smudging the apartment. Desperate times.

'We're taking a pedi-bus to an Irish pub where we're booked in for an hour of knickers customisation over cocktails. I'll distribute the T-shirts in the morning. Any questions?'

I have to plug in my phone five minutes later after it nearly dies under the weight of the messages that flood in. Even Sadhbh is stumped.

'What's a pedi-bus? Just boarding now in JFK. See you all soooon xx.' There follows at least fifteen variations of the same query from the others.

'It's an open-top pedal-powered bus that seats ten,' I say, and attach a picture I found online in an article on TheJournal. ie on the rising number of public order offences in Temple Bar. 'We can bring booze and play our own tunes! Leave the playlist to me. I have flower crowns.' Winky face.

I made the playlist on Spotify earlier during a quiet spell in the café. Noel gave me a hand and stopped me just putting 'Maniac 2000' on repeat. He explained that, although Maj would definitely get a kick out of it, the rest of the hens might get sick of her screaming 'oggie oggie oggie, oi oi oi' through the streets of Tenerife since we'll be pedalling for an hour. I conceded, although it's not like we're all going to fit on the same bus – I had to order six in the end. The price of them.

Thursday night is the officially sanctioned 'mad night', so I've given us three hours to go home and change into the traditional Tenerifian outfits and then we're booked into another Irish pub, Fibber Magee's, for platters of mini fish and chips and dares and generally terrorising the other patrons. The stripper is booked for one. It has to be done. Wearing the new customised knickers is optional.

I've downgraded Friday's 'activity 2' to a pool day at the Paradise Aqua since I blew the budget on the pedi-buses and the plain knickers. That's assuming there *is* a pool. That night's optional dinner is going to be at the pizza place next door, which has promised us free shots on arrival, but to be honest, I can't see many making it. I have the Prosecco pong set and a How Well Do You Know Maj? quiz just in case.

There are a few other random questions – 'Does Tenerife have the euro?' 'Will there be films on the plane?' 'Has anyone seen my passport?' – which I answer as best I can before saying goodnight and reminding them to bring sandwiches for the morning unless they want to be stung paying airport prices.

When I stand up to go weigh my suitcases of props, I notice I've been absentmindedly scratching my left forearm, which is dotted with angry-looking hives. Probably my own fault for switching to generic washing powder, but with the amount this hen is costing me, Fairy Non Bio seems like an unnecessary luxury.

CHAPTER 34

I didn't get a wink of sleep all night. Not a one. When my alarm goes off at 3 a.m. I'm already up and dressed and checking my email. Still nothing from Flo, although the airport transfer company has been on to say the bus driver's name is Diego and I won't be able to miss him in Arrivals. I don't like the sound of that but it's the least of my problems, to be honest.

I'm trying my best not to wake James, but as soon as I go for one of my three suitcases – the prop situation is truly out of control – he's out of bed like a shot, being his usual helpful self.

'Are you sure you can manage?' he asks, wedging the last one into the passenger seat of the Micra, the exhaust pipe practically scraping the ground.

I fight the urge to admit that I can't manage at all, that I'm worried all thirty of us Irish are going to be sleeping on the street, that the activities are going to be disastrous, that I'm going to ruin Majella's hen, that what I really want is to go back upstairs, crawl into bed and never come out again, but instead I say, 'I'm grand, I'm grand. I'll text you when we arrive,' and hop into the driver's seat.

I can barely see over the suitcases when I push the trolley into Departures after hauling them three miles from the

QuikPark. I couldn't pass up the online deal. Majella, her mam and a selection of the more affable cousins stayed in the Airport Maldron last night to ensure they wouldn't be late, while the BGB girls got a minibus this morning. In hindsight I should have gone with them, but Tony Timoney was being very relaxed about our departure time. We booked him to bring us to Slane for Bon Jovi in 2013 and we missed the first three songs as well as all the support acts. I don't think I could trust him with something as important as this.

I check the board – FR 7122 to Tenerife is leaving on time. Well, that's something, I suppose. I have everyone's boarding passes – all twenty-nine of them – printed out and in a folder in my backpack. I've already emailed Sadhbh hers. I also have a lumbar support pillow for Shirley, some vegan energy balls to keep Joyce out of McDonald's and a bottle of Prosecco and sashes for the bride, the mother of the bride and myself. Well, I am a bridesmaid, after all.

A quick scan of the WhatsApp group reveals that everyone is either on the way or parking up – even Danielle, who is wrecked by the sounds of things. She seems to be very unlucky with late-night punctures.

'Here comes the *briiide*!'

I swing around and there she is. Majella. My best friend in the world. She's wearing a white wrap dress and wedges and strutting through Departures like she owns the place, flanked by miscellaneous relations. It's not even 6 a.m. and she's carrying a plastic champagne flute, looking absolutely radiant, happiness and highlighter oozing out of every pore.

While most of us dream about our wedding day, Maj has been just as excited about the hen and unapologetically so.

Not that she's not looking forward to taking Pablo down the aisle, but she's very partial to a stripper when she can get her hands on one.

'How's the best bridesmaid in the world?' She pulls me in for a hug and I squeeze her back. 'I'm already having the time of my life. You're the best, Ais,' she whispers into my ear. 'Can't wait to see what you've got up your sleeve for us.'

I mutter something about patience being a virtue, pass out the sashes and scuttle off in the direction of the Bag Drop. I should really try to stop worrying and just enjoy the weekend but, well, easier said than done. While Majella introduces me to Joyce, Teresa, Ellen and the gang, Fionnuala and Mairead come at us from the other direction with inflatable pillows already around their necks, followed by Elaine and Ruby, who is wearing a leather jacket despite the forecast saying we're in for highs of nineteen degrees. Total fashion victim.

Maj cracks open the bubbles and I start handing out boarding passes like a blackjack dealer and suddenly it's feeling very much like a party. Until I look at my watch, that is. Five forty-five. Our flight leaves in an hour and forty-five minutes and there's still no sign of the BGB contingent and loads of bags need to be checked. We'll have to get our skates on.

****

By the time we get through security, Sadhbh has joined us direct from the States in a flurry of hugs and kisses, and I've taken to doing a headcount every ten minutes, just to be sure Aunt Shirley hasn't wandered off again. She was seduced by a Bailey's stand earlier and had to be dragged away from the free samples. So did Mairead, to be fair. Fionnuala has her work cut out for her.

I check my watch again, throwing one eye over at Majella who's trying to sweet talk her way into the Emirates first-class lounge with Bernadette, who hasn't let the break-up slow her down, and Karen, her sister egging them on. Still no sign of the BGB crew. I emailed them their boarding passes when we went through, but I haven't seen hide nor hair of them and I'm getting worried. I'm heading into a quiet corner to try ringing Maeve again when I hear a screech and the familiar clatter of heels on lino. Just in the nick of time.

'Sorry we're late, hun,' Sharon gasps, followed by Dee, Sinéad, Denise and Maeve, all carrying bags from Filan's. 'We stopped for rolls in the village and they ran out of coleslaw so Eamon had to do up another batch. You'd think he'd be quicker at it by now.'

Majella spots them and there's more squealing and screeching and before I know it I'm up and queuing to board our flight to Tenerife.

CHAPTER 35

'By any chance, are you Diego?' I ask the moustachioed man wearing an inflatable penis hat and wrapped in an Ireland flag in Arrivals at Tenerife Sud Airport.

He bows deeply. '*Si, señorita*. You are Mrs Ayes-Ling? Welcome to Tenerife, good lady.'

'Aisling. Miss,' I say, leaning out from behind my tower of suitcases and shaking his hand. I fire off a quick text to James to tell him we all got here in one piece – well, pretty much – before getting back to the job at hand.

'Now, Diego, I'd just like to apologise in advance. Some of the women are a bit rowdy. It's Sadhbh's fault. You see, she bought three litres of Jose Cuervo in the Duty Free in JFK and, well –'

Before I can finish, the swinging double doors fly open and Aunt Shirley slides out of the baggage-claim hall on her knees singing 'Come On, Eileen' at the top of her lungs, followed closely by Ruby, Danielle and Carmel careening around on a luggage trolley and nearly taking the ankles off a group of seven-foot Scandinavians in the process.

Diego gives me a knowing look. 'Miss Aisling, we specialise in transporting your hen parties.' He gestures to his headgear. 'I have seen it all, I assure you.'

There's more screaming from baggage claim before Majella emerges behind the wheel of a golf cart. Her mother is in the passenger seat pouring tequila straight into her mouth while Sadhbh, Elaine, Sharon, Fionnuala and Joyce chant 'Mad-Jella! Mad-Jella! Mad-Jella!' and twerk in the back. The rest of the hens are not far behind them in a conga line led by Mairead, who has a bottle of Bailey's in each hand. It turns out giving free samples really does work.

I swear I see Diego falter, but he takes a deep breath and steels himself. 'Who is the bride?' he roars. 'Show yourself to Diego!'

When Majella's hand shoots up, the whole airport cheers, and the roars only get louder when Diego puts a studded leather collar and leash around her neck and leads her towards the exit.

****

My heart is pounding so loudly I'm sure it's going to wake up Shirley, who's fallen asleep on my shoulder and is snoring contentedly despite Diego's erratic driving. I check my phone one last time. Still nothing from Flo. The Paradise Aqua is only two minutes up this road and I have no idea what we're going to find when we get there.

'Any sick bags, Ais?' Dee appears beside me on her hunkers, confirming my worst fears. The cocktail of Baileys and tequila didn't sit well with Mairead, and by the sounds of things, I'll need to dip into my Dioralyte stash to get her ready for later. I anticipated this carry-on and brought three boxes, spread out between my suitcases in case one went missing. There was no such mishap, though, thank God.

'Of course,' I say, going into bridesmaid mode and handing her a stack of the little bags. I was even able to get them and the hangover recovery bags personalised with 'Majella's Bride Tribe'. The internet is great all the same for things like that.

Dee disappears off down the back of the bus and I hear the faint clicking of Diego's indicator. I screw my eyes shut. This is it, I think to myself, scratching my hives. The last time I was here the fountain out the front hadn't seen water in years and the pink facade was faded and crumbling. And don't get me started on the situation with the itchy blankets. Is it going to be the same this time? Worse? Is there just going to be a giant hole where the Paradise Aqua used to be? I'm struggling to catch my breath.

'It has been a pleasure to transport you Irish ladies, but now you are arrived at your accommodations,' Diego announces sadly into a little microphone and I swear I hear a crack in his voice. Majella had introduced him to Ellen before we'd left the airport car park and the two of them hit it off famously on the twenty-minute journey. Tenerife certainly does an excellent line in charismatic drivers.

'A woman is like a tea-bag – you can't tell how strong she is until you put her in hot water.' It's one of my all-time favourite inspirational quotes and I'm repeating it to myself when I eventually pluck up the courage to open my eyes.

Diego is standing up, holding out his penis hat, presumably for tips.

I look out the window to my left as the women start shaking each other awake and trying to find their handbags.

Where the jaded block once stood is now a gleaming white six-storey building surrounded by towering palm trees. The fountain is gone, no great loss there, and in its place is a lush flower bed with PARADISE spelled out in vibrant red hibiscus flowers. I can't believe it. Flo wasn't lying and she didn't skim my bank account – they really did renovate the place! And not a minute too soon. I'm positively weak with relief, so much so that I accidentally lean on Diego for support and get a filthy look from Ellen.

Majella sits bolt upright from where she was stretched out on the back seat. She has tears in her eyes. 'Ais, it's *stunning.*'

****

Unfortunately, not everyone made it to Emilio's for tapas in the end. I don't want to name names but one or two of Majella's relations took to their air-conditioned rooms as soon as we checked in and didn't surface again. I can't say I blame them, to be honest – the new beds are *that* comfortable and the thermostat was a cinch to use. You don't want to know how many times one of those little panels has beaten me and I've gone to bed in a hotel room either blue from the cold or sweating bullets.

And Flo was very apologetic about the whole lack of contact thing. Apparently their email server has been down for months and they have to do all their correspondence through a local man with a donkey.

Majella had been a bit nervous about meeting Pablo's mother, the two sisters, six aunts and eight cousins, but being in the tapas bar was the perfect ice-breaker since there was loads of translating to do and the local vino was flowing for anyone on their second wind. After half an hour they were doing some serious wedding chat over albondigas and sending selfies back to Pablo in BGB. I can only imagine the floods he was in.

'I have to say, I didn't really know what to expect from this,' Sadhbh admits, casually helping herself to one of my churros while I pretend not to notice, 'but this is great craic, Ais. Some of the women are really letting their hair down.'

She's talking about Bridget, another of Majella's aunts, who's sitting on Emilio's lap while he mops his brow with a red hanky. A livid-looking woman, who I can only assume is Mrs Emilio, is giving him daggers from behind the small bar.

'I just want to make sure Maj has a good time. It's a lot of pressure being the only bridesmaid,' I say.

'I can imagine. I did think you looked a bit tired when I saw you this morning. Did the smudging help at all?'

'Ah yeah, a bit, I think.' I hope I sound convincing.

'Don't forget to have fun yourself too, right? And if there's anything I can do to help, let me know. You can borrow my crystals.'

'Thanks, Sadhbh, but I have it all under control.' At least I hope I do.

CHAPTER 36

I'm standing in the foyer of the Paradise Aqua with the box of customised T-shirts, forty-eight pairs of blank white knickers (varying arse coverage), the zogabongs, the flower crowns, the flashing shot-glass necklaces and thirty inflatable shamrocks, tapping my foot impatiently. My hives had all but disappeared last night but the heat now isn't doing them any favours. The pedi-buses will be here soon, and so far only about half the women have surfaced and are standing around comparing sunburn, even though the only time they were outside was walking in from the bus yesterday. It's impressive, really.

I have my phone in my hand ready to send Maj a hurry-up text – we're on a schedule, like – when the lift doors open and she comes skulking out looking unimpressed. My hackles are up immediately. Did she not sleep well? Did things go south with Juana? Does she need a Nurofen Plus? Or a shot of sambuca? I have both on me.

'Everything all right, Maj?' I ask casually. That's when I realise she's wearing a coat. It's already sixteen degrees in the shade. She's going to melt. 'You'll be roasting once you start pedalling, you know. There are a few steep hills on the route,' I say, digging out the I'm the Bride fluffy zogabongs and handing them over along with the shot-glass necklace.

'I can't, Ais.'

'Why not?'

'My T-shirt. I have to hide it.'

'But I got you the one you wanted,' I say, rooting in the box for it. 'One Last Ride for the Bride on the front and It's All About Me on the back. Size small.' I hold it out to her but she just shakes her head.

'I can't. Pablo snuck this one into my bag. And I promised him I'd wear it.'

She opens the coat. The T-shirt is neon yellow, with a giant picture of Pablo's beaming face on the front. 'This Is My Fiancé,' reads the text. 'I Don't Want Your Burger, I Have Steak at Home.'

****

It takes the pedi-bus man twenty minutes to explain to us how to make the yokes go. His name is Clive and he's actually from Canada, so we can't even blame the slow uptake on a language barrier.

'I have a bad knee. What if I need to stop for a break?' Shirley asks, rolling up her sleeves and climbing on to the last available seat.

'As long as everyone else keeps going, the bus will continue to move,' Clive says, looking exasperated. 'It's a group effort, remember?'

'How do we steer it again?' Bridget asks.

'Once again, ladies, I'll be looking after the navigation,' Clive replies, rolling his eyes.

'Come on, women, I want to get moving,' Liz Moran shouts from two buses back. I don't think the three sisters have spent this amount of time together since they were kids, and I can see why. They don't get along very well.

Majella is sitting across from me wearing the Pablo T-shirt over her proper bride one. I thought it was a decent compromise. I nipped out this morning and bought plenty of water as well as more Prosecco, so she has a plastic flute in her hand again. At this point I'm afraid to look at my bank balance, which is a new concept to me. I normally know exactly how much is in there at all times.

'Can you plug in my phone there, Clive, and we'll get going,' I say, passing it up to him. There's a short pause and then the opening bars of the Proclaimers' seminal hit 'I'm Gonna Be (500 Miles)' blares out of the speakers.

'*Yeow!*' shrieks Majella, and we start pedalling.

****

We're thirty minutes late pulling up to the Claddagh Bar, and Clive had the foresight to have an ambulance waiting for us on arrival. 'This isn't my first rodeo,' he mutters, loading the pedi-buses onto the back of a flatbed truck and screeching off into the Tenerifian sunset.

Another reason to be glad I made sure everyone packed their European Health Insurance cards. You can't take any chances when you're abroad.

Despite my best efforts pushing bottles of water on people, Dee, Mairead, Danielle and two other cousins need intravenous rehydration and Shirley has to be treated for mild sunstroke. I couldn't stop her flinging her Roscommon Ladies Golf Club sun visor at a crowd sitting outside a café as we trundled past so she only has herself to blame.

I check my phone while the rest of them head into the bathroom of the pub to reapply their faces.

There's a text from James. 'How's it all going? Miss you xx.'

I meant to give him a ring last night, but after I'd poured Pablo's relations into a taxi, got the rest of them out of the restaurant and fixed up with Emilio it was far too late in the end. And then I had to get everything ready for today.

'Grand,' I say back. 'Rooms are great and everyone still alive, I think. Just waiting for the granny now.'

The meeting between Majella and Pablo's Abuela Sofia has been a source of concern for both families. From the bits of conversation I overheard last night, the matriarch sounds like a formidable woman and, according to Paola, Pablo is her golden grandchild. She's fairly devastated he's marrying a 'gringa', especially one as pale as Maj, and there was even talk of her sitting out the wedding as a form of protest. I didn't want to inflict the pedi-bus on her, what with her being ninety-six, but Maj asked me to seat them near each other for the knicker decorating so she can show off the *Español* she's been learning on Duolingo. She's the bride so I couldn't say no, but I'm sincerely hoping nothing kicks off. I had an Abuela Up for It T-shirt made up so she'll feel included.

'Do you have the pants, Aisling?' Elaine goes, once the women are all sitting around the long rectangular table. 'Pass 'em over – myself and Ruby can give them out.'

'Thanks a million, girls,' I say gratefully, before heading to the bar to make sure the signature cocktails I preordered weeks ago over email are ready. First we're having Mango Majellatinis, then it's Majitos, then Majaritas and finally a round of Long Island Iced Majellas.

Once everyone has their knickers, I put out baskets of glue, scissors, lace, ribbons, googly eyes, sequins, rhinestones, letters and a load of other bits. China really came through for me in this instance, and I'm delighted to see Majella getting stuck in straightaway and the rest of them following suit. By the time the cocktails are served, the craic is up to ninety and I'm actually very impressed with some of the designs. Teresa has fashioned an elegant peephole into the back of her classic briefs while Maria did a sparkly Spanish flag on the front of her boy shorts. I'm actually in awe of Maj, though, who managed to spell out Pablo in glittery letters on the back of her thong – especially since she dropped down to pass Home Ec for her Junior Cert and missed all the sewing. The less said about what Shirley did with the crotch of her control pants the better.

'They look fab, hun,' Sharon says on the way to the bathroom, pointing at the pink sparkly J I'm sticking on to my Brazilian briefs with sequins. 'I can't believe you've organised all this on your own. Majella is having the time of her life over there.'

I follow Sharon's gaze and it's true. Maj is having a ball talking to Paola and Ellen, Majarita in one hand, glue gun in the other. Once I get through today, I'll be over the worst of it, and I can focus on the weddings. Then I see Majella's face fall and she puts down her glass. I look over to the front door of the Claddagh and there she is, the abuela, looking around the pub and clutching her handbag close to her chest. She has a face on her that would make an onion cry.

Juana jumps up and starts babbling in Spanish and gesticulating wildly while Majella sits there, her arse rooted to the seat. Apart from Liz, who's keeping an eye on things while stitching Up Rangers on to her hipsters, no one has noticed anything amiss. Juana is saying something to the abuela while pointing over at Majella, but the abuela isn't moving. In fact, she's shaking her head. Of course, I can't understand a word of what's being said but I know it's time for me to intervene.

'Abuela,' I say, grabbing her T-shirt and curtsying before her. She just looks at me. 'Please join us in the ceremony of knicker decorating.' Then I turn back to Juana with a look that I hope says, 'Can you translate that there, please?' She gets it, thankfully, and reels off a load of Spanish. Again, I haven't a clue what's being said. I can feel Majella's eyes boring into the back of my head.

I proffer the T-shirt to the abuela. 'From Ireland, a gift to you,' I say, again hoping Juana translates, which she does. This time the abuela actually takes the T-shirt with a muttered 'gracias'. She unfolds it, and for a minute I'm not sure if she hates it or if she just has one of those resting bitch faces I keep reading about in women's magazines. Juana points at the text and whispers something to her in Spanish. Then the abuela throws her head back and roars laughing before walking over to Majella, dragging her out of her seat and giving her a massive, all-encompassing hug.

CHAPTER 37

I can't really remember the rest of the day, to be honest – probably because the Long Island Iced Majellas basically blew the heads off us. And we had more than one of them to celebrate Abuela Sofia joining the party. Many more. My original plan had been to get everyone back to the Paradise Aqua to change into the traditional Tenerifian rigouts, but once Sofia got going there was no stopping her. When Juana said she was 'formidable' what she meant was she's mad. Wild! She's basically a tiny Spanish Majella and, naturally, the two of them got on like a house on fire.

So we stayed at the Claddagh until it was time to go to Fibber Magee's, which is where John and I spent the bulk of our time during our own Tenerifian holiday. It's also where he met a camogie-playing temptress called Ciara, but the less said about her the better. I'm delighted that I don't recognise her or anyone else when we arrive, but there's a framed picture of us behind the bar with the rest of their most loyal customers, which I thought was a nice touch. Anyway, we basically took over the place. Well, there were forty-eight of us, to be fair, and it's not a big pub. I don't know how many little cones of fish and chips we got through but it was a lot. Then it was time for karaoke. Sofia and Majella set the standard with a haunting rendition of 'Ebony and Ivory', followed by Liz Moran who nearly brought the house down with 'Country Roads, Take Me Home'. Again, my memory is hazy, but I know me, Maj, Sadhbh, Elaine and Ruby did 'Wannabe' by the Spice Girls because there are pictures to prove it. Christ. Ruby insisted on being Mel C and did a back-flip. I was Baby, obviously. And then the dares – oh my god, the dares. The dares are why I woke up with some Dutch fella's boxers in my backpack. But nothing was worse than when the stripper arrived. In hindsight, the fact that the website had no pictures of him should have been a red flag. But I just can't resist a deal, and he was 40 per cent off for the month of March. Cris el Oficial de Policia – Cris the Cop. He sounded perfect for Majella's needs. I even brought along a pair of pink furry handcuffs in case Cris didn't have any. You can't have a hen party with a stripping guard and not have pink furry handcuffs. Long story short, Cris was short for Cristina. But Maj sat there and took her lap dance like the pro that she is because I'd paid for it in full and the email said there were no refunds. Cris was very good to stop mid-thrust and wait while we took my phone out to read the fine print.

What I remember most, though, was Majella's speech. It was after closing time and we'd all drank ourselves sober but were refusing to leave while the Fibber's staff cleaned up around us and tutted loudly.

'Ladies,' Maj had slurred into the mic. It wasn't even on. 'I can't feckin' wait to marry Pablo.' We'd all cheered, of course – no one more than Sofia, who is adamant that the happy couple comes back to live with her. 'I can't wait to be his wife and you know why? It's because I *looove* him. I do. I love him.

And I tell him everything. And he knows me better than I know myself, which is how I know this is the real deal. I can't get anything past him.' That's when the tears started. 'And I'm just so in love and so happy and Mammy –' Liz's head shot up from where she'd been resting it on the bar, obviously asleep '– I'll be sorry to leave you, but I can't wait till me and Pab have our own place because, well ... And Sadhbh! Where's Sadhbh?' Sadhbh was reclining on the pool table. 'I fancy Don Shields something rotten but I'd still pick my Pab over him any day – I don't care how famous he is.' Sadhbh just gave her a thumbs-up and lay back down. At this point, Majella was crying so much she was almost incoherent, and I was about to pick her up and throw her over my shoulder when she said, 'And Aisling?' I sat up straighter in my chair, waiting for her to heap praise on me. Maybe even call me up to say a few words myself. 'Let's all raise a glass to Aisling, the best bridesmaid ever in the world ever ever. I can't wait to marry Pablo and I can't wait for you to marry John.'

I froze momentarily and the girls from home – everyone who knows John, basically – all looked to me for a reaction while the others whooped and cheered because, well, why wouldn't they? It's a nice sentiment, except John is not my boyfriend. I didn't want to make a scene on Majella's big night so I pretended nothing had happened, hopped up and started firing discarded knickers and T-shirts into my massive suitcase.

'Come on, girls, time to call it a night,' I said, avoiding Majella's eye. We got separate taxis home and that's where we left it.

****

There are only a handful of other guests at the Paradise Aqua so I have no trouble securing thirty sun loungers at the pool the next morning, especially at 8 a.m. I'm not expecting to see the others until much later but I didn't want to run the risk of us not having enough umbrellas. I've already shoved the hangover recovery bags, which have sachets of Dioralyte and little paracetamol duos in them, under everyone's doors because I'm still in charge of this hen party for the next twenty-four hours and never let it be said that I shirk my responsibilities just because I'm hanging.

'Hey.'

It's Majella looking sheepish with a tin of Diet Coke in each hand. I'm very surprised to see her in direct sunlight at this hour.

'I knocked in for you but there was no answer so I guessed you'd be down here –' she nods at the thirty sun loungers draped in thirty towels '– doing this.'

'Well, I don't want a repeat of what happened yesterday. Ambulances aren't cheap here.'

She smiles. 'Are you okay, Ais? You've been very quiet. You seem preoccupied or something.'

'I'm grand, grand. Just very busy with everything, that's all. Are you having a good hen?'

'The best.'

'Great stuff.'

'About what I said last night,' she says, sitting down beside me and handing me a tin. It's freezing cold and dripping with condensation. Manna from heaven. 'I'm sorry. I was locked. I just got confused. I meant James, obviously.'

The weird thing is, after she said it, I couldn't get the idea out of my head, but I was just being a sap. Those Long Island Iced Majellas have a lot to answer for.

'It's grand,' I say, cracking the tin open, 'I'm happy with James, so it's all good.'

****

I feel like I've aged about forty years when we're queuing to board our flight back to Dublin. Majella and I didn't mention her speech again during our pool day, which was just what everyone needed after all the madness. Abuela Sofia even came over for a dip and to give Majella her something borrowed to wear for the wedding. It's a delicate gold locket that belonged to Pablo's great-great-grandmother. You can imagine the waterworks. It was a lovely moment.

The pizza dinner afterwards was surprisingly good craic too. Very low-key. Everyone came except Danielle, who was last seen behind the wheel of a rented Smart car heading in the direction of some local hills. Still wearing that bandeau dress, brazen as you like.

It's amazing how hen parties create the most unlikely bonds. Me and Aunt Shirley went halves on a sixteen-inch Hawaiian and she ended up explaining that the reason she went buck-wild this weekend was because her best friend died eighteen months ago and she hadn't let herself have fun since.

I can't even describe the feeling of relief when we got to the airport. I'd been worrying for weeks about how I'd pull this hen off, but everyone ended up having a deadly time – no one more so than Maj, who kept saying she'll need a holiday to recover, but in a good way. Have you even gone on a holiday if you don't need a holiday to recover? I feel like I've just finished the last exam of my Leaving and I allow the beautiful waves of relief to wash over me as I browse for fridge magnets with Elaine and Ruby. It's a good feeling. I go for a little donkey holding maracas in his front hooves for Mammy.

Waiting for our flight to be called, I take out my phone to text James when I see the new email notification and click into my inbox. It's from Mandy Blumenthal, and as soon as I see her name I feel my blood pressure rise again.

'Aisling,' it starts, 'I've just learned that our event is being pushed back by seven (7) days. We still need your hors d'oeuvres, honey. Now more than ever. Can you reply to confirm you're good for 4 May? Different day, same menu. Any questions I'm on my cell. M.'

Oh, shite. Emilia Coburn is getting married on the same day as Majella.

CHAPTER 38

'Hello, Mandy? Hiya, it's Aisling. Aisling. From BallyGoBrunch? From the ...' I lower my voice and glance furtively around my immediate vicinity. Who knows what ears are listening in Tenerife Sud Airport? There's an auld one by the magazines looking very suspicious and I'm nearly sure that cleaner already emptied that bin. 'The Coburn –Dixon wedding? Aisling, the caterer?'

There's silence on the other end of the phone for what feels like an eternity before Mandy places me. 'Aisling, honey. Can you give me a minute while I take a Xanax? I've been on my cell for twelve hours straight. "Can you move the wedding back a week, Mandy?" they asked me. "Can God move mountains?" I asked them back. "Not really but I'll make it happen."'

She goes silent again and I presume she's gone to take the Xanax, which I know Ruby used to keep a stash of in the Dublin apartment to 'take the edge off' a heavy weekend of partying. She offered me one once when I was particularly anxious about my tax disc failing to arrive within three to five days and was watching the post like a hawk. I declined, though. 'Xanax' sounds like something out of *Breaking Bad* and I would definitely end up in a ditch somewhere.

'Aisling, honey. You got my email?'

Mandy's back.

'I did, Mandy. And I have to admit I'm alarmed. Very alarmed.'

'Tell me about it. His shoot is running over because the director went AWOL for a month in a vintage Aston Martin. "You can't reschedule two-hundred-fifty people," I told them. "Try," they said. So here I am, less than five weeks out, rescheduling a wedding.'

'Mandy, I can't … I just don't think I can do it. I have my best friend's –'

'I don't want to hear "can't" and "don't" from you, Aisling.' Mandy is using a soft sing-songy voice but it has an edge like a razor blade.

'My best friend's wedding is the same day. I'm her chief bridesmaid. Her only bridesmaid.'

'You signed a contract, Aisling. I need that food. Emilia wanted local. I'm getting her local.'

'I signed a contract, exactly. For work on 27 April, not 4 May!'

'It's all in there, tootsie roll, in your contract. Change of dates is covered.'

My panic rises and rises and I fan my passport across my face and neck, which are now pulsating with heat. I read the whole contract, didn't I? Of course I did. Did it say something about dates changing? I was so focused on the NDA, did I miss something in the fine print? It all happened so quickly I can't remember. I've never signed anything without reading it in my life. My iPhone updates are like murder.

'I just – I can't be there, though.'

'No offence, honey, but I didn't hire you for your pretty face – although you do have that "sad Saoirse Ronan crying on the back of a ship and shittin' in a bucket" look going for you. I just need the food – 4 May, Garbally House. We done here? We're done here. Laters, honey.'

And she's gone. Sweat prickles the back of my neck even though the air conditioning in the airport is gloriously efficient. How am I going to do this? When am I going to do this? I'll have to call in some favours, push back the food orders. Even if I could get Mandy to let me off the hook, I've spent so much money pre-ordering ingredients I'd have to go ahead with it. These bloody NDAs – if it wasn't for them I could hire an army of extra staff to help us out.

'Aisling.' Sadhbh touches my arm and I jump a country mile. I turn around to her, trying to calm the crazed look I'm sure is in my eyes. She looks almost as worried as I do.

'What's wrong?'

'I've got bad news. I just got a text from Don, and he … we … He can't go to Majella's wedding. The Peigs can't go, I mean. They can't play.'

'Mm-hmm.' I feel my legs start to go from under me, and I lean towards the nearest chair, which some clown has claimed with his backpack. 'You wouldn't move that, would you?' I growl at him, shoving it to the side with my arse.

'I'm so sorry, but something's just come up. A work thing, sort of. I'm supposed to go with him but maybe I can try to do both?'

I eye her suspiciously. This all sounds very familiar, but I can't ask her if it's Ben and Emilia's wedding without breaking my NDA.

'This "work thing",' I whisper, doing air quotes with my fingers, 'is it in BGB, by any chance?'

She starts to smile. 'You know, don't you?'

'The … the E and B wedding?'

'Yes!' she whisper-shrieks, before looking around and composing herself. 'You can't tell anyone but they're doing the song for *Scarlet Fever*, the new Bond film. The Peigs, I mean. Don wrote it. It's called "Sex Martini".'

'*What!*'

Sadhbh can't help a flush of pride and excitement, even in this moment of my dire need, and I don't blame her.

'They're doing *what*?'

'I know. It's mad. Completely mad. Like, Madonna's done one! Adele!'

'This is all so mad.'

'Anyway, they're basically contractually obliged to be at the wedding because of the film company and the record company, and Don has actually gotten quite close with Ben.'

The reality of the situation is starting to hit me now and I'm feeling a bit faint. My stomach does an involuntary gurgle and I scan the terminal but I can't see any sign for *los baños*.

'No, of course, of course. I understand.' The Peigs can't play. Majella's going to throw herself in front of a Boeing 747 when she finds out. 'Majella will be fine. I'll break it to her.'

'I'm going to do whatever I have to do to be at both,' Sadhbh says, teeth gritted in determination. 'I'll clone myself if I have too.'

'You're a good friend, Sadhbhy,' I reply.

'So how did you know about the wedding? Did James tell you? Don and the lads had to sign NDAs. He wasn't even supposed to tell me what we were going to until the day before, but obviously he understood my need to think about outfits so he told me anyway.'

Oh, to have a rock star's flagrant disregard for the law.

'Don't breathe a word of this,' I say, trying not to pass out, 'but BallyGoBrunch is actually doing the passed food for the drinks reception.'

'Aisling, that's amazing! What a coup.'

'Yeah but ...'

Sadhbh's eyes widen with realisation. Then it hits her. 'Oh, shit,' she gasps, sitting down heavily on her little wheelie case. 'It's now on the same day as Majella's wedding.'

'What am I going to do, Sadhbh?' I wail. 'I can't break the contract or I'll be sued and I've already spent every penny I have on the food order.'

'Majella will understand,' Sadhbh says, sounding very much like she did back in her HR days. 'You'll just explain it to her and she'll probably be happy for you.'

'But the NDA. You know she couldn't sit on a secret like this. And I'm her only bridesmaid. I can't just not show up on her wedding day.'

'Fuck, Ais, this is a nightmare,' Sadhbh says helplessly, throwing her hands in the air. 'Don and the guys will be sorry to be missing it too.'

'I'll figure it out.'

Majella has told anyone who'll listen about The Peigs playing. I tried to get her to keep it under wraps and get Lisa on board to do the same, but sure Lisa has been worse than Maj. I'm surprised it isn't on the Ard Rí website somewhere. Lisa will definitely be putting it in her wedding-planning portfolio even though she had literally nothing to do with organising it.

'Maybe they could ... play at both, somehow?' I suggest, my eyebrows high with hope. But they fall almost immediately. Who'd want to leave a celeb-studded affair at Garbally for the ballroom with the second-nicest chair covers in the Ard Rí?

Just then Majella, Deirdre, Sharon and Elaine come clattering over with their Duty Free spoils. Majella is proudly sporting her T-shirt from Pablo and Elaine seems to have become deeply connected to her penis zogabongs. The man with the backpack gathers up his belongings with a look of sheer disgust and goes to find somewhere else to spread out, and Majella sinks into his seat gratefully, her bag clinking.

'I got Pab some Tenerifian coffee to keep him going and four giant Toblerones for school ...' I don't even have the energy to tell her not to bother and just to get them in Dunnes. She reaches into the bag. 'I got *you* this.'

She hands me a box wrapped in a smaller plastic Duty Free bag. 'For being the best bridesmaid in the world and organising the best hen in the world.'

I hold the bag in my lap, feeling like the worst bridesmaid in the world.

'Go on, open it.'

I shake out the top of the bag and peer inside, then clasp it shut again when I see what she's bought. 'Ah, Maj, it's too much.'

'It's not at all. You deserve it.'

'Open it. Open it,' chorus Deirdre and the girls and I reach in and pull out the limited-edition Clinique Happy.

'And it's the big bottle and all,' I gasp.

'And …' Majella digs into her bag again. 'Your special gift.'

I gasp again. I'm always very up on whatever toilet bag and tiny bits are on offer with your purchases in Brown Thomases or Debenhams, but this one is a style I'm unfamiliar with and comes with – I zip it open – a mini mascara and a generously sized Dramatically Different Moisturiser.

'I kept the exfoliator for myself,' Majella admits. 'Have to look about twelve for the wedding.'

I nod dumbly and glance at Sadhbh, who gives me a nudge of encouragement. 'Maj. I have some … news.'

She sees my face and clutches at my arm. 'What is it? Is it Pablo? Oh God, what is it? I can't be a tragic bride. I'm too old. You have to be in your early twenties for that to be truly sad.'

I think Majella's been spending too much time sitting in Strong Stuff striving for the Rosie Huntington-Whiteley hair and reading *Chat* and *Take a Break* and the new Irish one simply called *Tea!* Lots of tragic young brides and husbands running away with donkeys and ghosts showing up in mobile homes.

'Is it Mammy? Daddy? Not Willy? Not my little hero Willy?'

I know it's her hangover sending her into overdrive but the hysterics aren't helping me one bit. Would it be better to tell her now when my blood is 99 per cent adrenaline or put it off till we land and I'm wrecked? I don't think I could enjoy the flight with it hanging over me. Michael O'Leary might be my arch-nemesis, but I'm very partial to Ryanair's little in-flight snack boxes and the tune that plays when the plane lands on time. I put my hand over hers and take a deep breath.

'The Peigs can't play at the wedding.'

****

I only need to offer a brief synopsis of what's happened to the air steward and she agrees to furnish Majella with a G&T before the plane doors are even closed. In fairness to Majella, she took it quite well. She went through a range of emotions. As we were queuing to board, she was telling me that it was grand and she and Pablo could soldier on without The Peigs and maybe they could get Love Hurts to play one of their songs instead.

By the time we were showing our passports she was crying, saying it wasn't going to be the wedding she dreamed of and maybe she should call the whole thing off.

Sadhbh broke the news that she might not be able to come to the wedding either while we were going up the steps of the plane, and I did think Maj might tip herself over the steel bannister. Elaine floated the idea of The Peigs recording a video for Majella's wedding, which cheered her up for a bit, but then Lisa Gleeson texted Maeve to say the birthday party at Garbally had been pushed back a week and now both events were happening on the same day. Apparently the Garbally party planner had been straight on to the Ard Rí to try and secure rooms for some celebrity guests. She even went so far as to offer double the rate for the honeymoon suite, but thankfully that came as part of the Effortless Elegance package. I'll say one thing about Mandy Blumenthal, she has some neck. Luckily everyone was too caught up in the drama to put two and two together and suspect The Peigs were going to this 'party' instead.

Majella started fretting about Garbally stealing all the good staff for the celebrity party and her wedding dinner being 'flung at her by amateurs', which was right around the time the G&T arrived, so not a minute too soon. I placated her by saying Lisa Gleeson wouldn't let that happen, and the subsequent laugh we had was a brief moment of respite. Most of the hens, including Majella, mercifully passed out for the majority of the flight, but I got my notebook out and started planning what food could be made safely in advance and how we might store it and how I could plot out the night before and the morning of the weddings to make it all work. But as preoccupied with the logistics as I was, I couldn't stop my mind wandering back to what Majella had said about John, and James, and how uncomfortable the whole thing was making me feel.

****

By the time we're queuing for our bags in Dublin Airport, everyone has gotten more excited about the prospect of the big celebrity party and they've all got their theories about whose it might be. Puff Daddy. Mariah Carey. A Hemsworth. Majella even gets into the spirit of things and suggests either Kim or Kanye.

'They went on their honeymoon to Portlaoise so anything's possible,' reasons Denise.

Deirdre Ruane, always with her estate agent hat on, poses a very good question. 'Aisling, there isn't much accommodation at Garbally, is there?'

'There's some in the main house and the stable yard and those bubbles around the place. Not a heap, though.'

Majella pipes up. 'Well, the Ard Rí is the only other decent hotel, and I have most of it block booked.'

'So,' Deirdre muses, 'where is everyone going to stay?'

CHAPTER 39

Naturally, word about the party's change of date and the resulting scramble for accommodation spread like wildfire around BGB and beyond. Suddenly every spare room in the village was straight up on Airbnb, with entrepreneurial locals hoping to snag a celebrity guest or, at the very least, one of Pablo's relations. I nearly came to blows with Mandy about her robbing beds straight out from under the Tenerifians, but she reminded me that I should 'stick to the hors d'oeuvres, honey'. It seems Mandy isn't completely omnipotent, though, and hadn't reckoned on another very big wedding in the area on the same day, so her back-up accommodation plans were sent somewhat haywire. Most of the rooms at the Mountrath had been booked for months for an oil-fired boiler convention so there wasn't much leeway there either and the management had no time for her sweet talking. She put a notice in the parish bulletin and send missives out to every house in a ten-mile radius looking for 'quality luxury accommodations available to rent'. I heard Sumira Singh in the shop saying they were thinking of skipping town for the weekend and renting their three-bed semi to the Clooneys if they wanted it. They have a see-saw out the back for the twins.

Lisa Gleeson wasn't much use after it emerged that any of Majella's guests who hadn't paid their room deposits to the Ard Rí were having their bookings cancelled. She insisted beds would somehow turn up for the twenty-odd people who were suddenly roomless. I suppose they could all bunk in together if worst came to the worst. Sure you hardly see your bed at a wedding anyway. I did feel like her follow-up questions, which seemed to veer widely away from the issue at hand and appeared to suggest Pablo could potentially fall in love with her, were a bit out of order. Pablo's only met her twice and, despite Lisa's insistence that she looks a bit like Jennifer Lopez (she doesn't) and Pablo looks a bit like Matthew McConaughey (he *really* doesn't), I had to put her in her place and ask her to please make sure everything else was going to go smoothly.

One person who took full advantage of the situation was Maj's father, Shem. The family were only back in their completely renovated bungalow a few hours when he shoved a double bed into the wooden shed at the bottom of their garden and listed it as an 'artisan panelled dwelling' with mountain views. It worked too, which inspired Dr Maher to chance charging €150 a night for the consultation bed in his surgery. When that got snapped up, every shed and outhouse within a twenty-mile radius was magically converted into a 'bijou annexe', and there was a queue of jeeps out the road when camp-beds went on special in the New Aldi. Mammy was up the walls trying to squeeze extra beds into every nook and cranny of the eco farm and had already asked Elaine and Ruby if they wouldn't mind sharing the one yurt with Fionnuala and Mairead. I was mortified, but the girls said they didn't mind, especially when Mammy said they could have it for free. The yurts were hot property and she was trying to get as many extras for the wedding weekend as Gantulga could supply. I tried to corner her one morning to see if she could recommend anything for my hives, but she was too busy trying to cajole Paul out of his room and into the farm shop. I know break-ups are hard, but Mammy said he's barely getting out of bed most days. I feel bad that I haven't had a chance to give him another of my pep talks, but there are only so many hours in the day.

'If I were you I'd stick an air mattress in the office there,' Carol had suggested while practising making her sausage-meat-stuffed button mushrooms completely symmetrical. 'You could get €200 for it because there's a lock on the door.'

As if I had time to become a landlord on top of everything else! Majella was, understandably, bulling about all the commotion and rightly felt like her wedding was being somewhat overshadowed – although, I'm still at her beck and call and doing my best to protect her from it. I think she thought she might get her pictures into *RSVP*, what with the Peigs connection and all that, but that'll hardly happen now. And I know she had her eye on the garden shed for one of Pablo's sisters and her kids.

And I still couldn't tell her about the work I was doing for the Garbally 'event', as much as I wanted to. My stress levels were off the charts and, because James was working day and night to get Garbally ready, I didn't have anyone at all to talk to. We'd just been falling into bed at night, and the last time we managed to sit on the couch together he'd snapped at me for scratching my hives, which are back with a vengeance.

I felt like we were a couple who'd been looking at each other for thirty years, not a couple barely six months into a relationship. He'd said sorry and made me a cup of tea, and later in bed tried to get something going, but I just couldn't unwind enough. He said, 'I love you,' but I pretended to be asleep already and waited until I was sure he'd drifted off to scream into my pillow. Maybe we need a holiday.

****

They say time flies when you're having fun, but it flies even faster when you're trying to keep a seemingly infinite number of balls in the air. Before I know it it's the last Saturday before the wedding and Majella has asked me to come over and help write out two-hundred-and-twenty names on two-hundred-and-twenty place cards. She and Pablo are going to stay on in the Moran's apartment above BallyGoBrunch for a month or two at least so they don't have to start married life sharing with the entire Moran clan, although the house is like new, to be fair. Two-hundred-and-twenty place cards doesn't sound like a lot, but Maj has sent me a picture of them and all laid out like that it actually looks like a gargantuan task. I should never have told her I ordered that calligraphy pen from China. But it was so cheap. And Ruby said that writing in script was a great way to practise mindfulness and unwind, and I was desperate to get out of my head and away from my spiralling thoughts and ever-increasing number of hives.

But first I'm dropping Mammy over a loan of my power washer. Apparently three goats and an alpaca escaped last night, trashing the place, and the all-weather playground needs some immediate attention before the influx of guests. I tried to tell her I barely have time to sit down at the moment, let alone drive around the country with power washers, but she'd already moved on to the latest speculation about who's having the birthday party at Garbally so I just let her talk and quietly hung up.

'Do you want a hand with that?'

It's John, coming out of the alpaca shed carrying a sprong.

'Oh. Hi. What are you doing here?' I can't keep the edge out of my voice. He's the last person I want to see when I'm like this, especially after what Majella said at the hen. I can't stop thinking about it, despite the calligraphy.

'The extra yurts are due this afternoon. Your mam asked me to help. It's all hands on deck trying to get everything ready.'

Mammy had actually sent me a text to tell me John would be helping since it was an emergency situation and asking me if that was okay. I didn't even get a chance to reply.

'Where's Paul?'

He looks at his feet. 'He's still in bed, I think.'

I glance at my watch. It's nearly half ten. The farm shop opens at eight. 'Is Mammy in the shop?'

'Yeah,' John says. 'Do you want a hand with that box?'

I look down. I thought I'd taken the power washer out of the Micra but instead I'm carrying the box of porcelain teardrop spoons I had to get for Carol's miniature pork belly bites. Apparently Ben Dixon is big into his pork belly.

'Fuck it,' I shout, furious with myself, heading for the car. 'I'll have to go back for the power washer,' I add, scratching the hives on my shoulder.

'Go inside and get a cup of tea, Ais,' John says, jogging after me. 'You look like you need it. I'll come out for the power washer in a while, honestly.'

'Are you sure you don't mind?' I say. 'I've to run over to Maj for some wedding prep. Another all-hands-on-deck situation.'

'Have a cup of tea. Go on.'

'No time,' I say, shaking my head.

'There's always time for tea,' he says and we both smile. He gave me a mug with that saying on it back when I started in PensionsPlus. It was a great mug – good and big, but not heavy. A reliable, sensible mug. No airs or graces. It was so popular I had to put an 'Aisling's mug – hands off :)' label on it so people wouldn't keep taking it. A few noses were out of joint over it, if I recall. While he was never flashy, John did give me a fair amount of really thoughtful presents when we were together. I wish I hadn't been so focused on the one present he didn't give me: the ring. But that's all in the past now.

I drop the box into the boot and follow him over to the house. Inside, he sticks the kettle on then opens the drawer where Mammy keeps the shoe polish and produces a twenty-four-pack of Penguin bars like a man who's been successfully looking for Good Biscuits in this house for years.

'Bingo,' he says with a smile as I go to take out the mugs. 'No, let me,' he says gently. 'You sit down there and chill out. How's Majella?'

'Mad busy. She's coordinating a massive reading drive at the school and it's taking up loads of time so a lot of wedding stuff has been left to the last minute'

'Fair play to her. She really seems to have taken to the job.'

He's right. She has. She's so capable. Something I feel anything but at the moment. 'And Pablo?'

'Currently trying to write his speech but he keeps having to take crying breaks so he's not getting far,' he says, sitting down and passing me the steaming mug. 'You know the way he is.'

'I do,' I say quietly. 'They're some pair.'

We both take sips of tea and I realise I can't remember the last time someone made me a cuppa. I've never been so tempted to break the NDA. If I could just tell John what's been going on he'd know exactly what to say or do to help me. I feel a lump forming in my throat so I take another deep sip to swallow it down and reach for a Penguin.

'How's Megan?' I can't help myself. I feel like if I don't say her name I might get carried away.

He looks momentarily startled and then relaxes again. 'Great, yeah. Looking for a new job at the moment, actually. She's subbing in a school in Donegal and can't understand a word anyone is saying to her.'

'Oh. I'll tell Majella to keep an ear out. She gets the emails.'

'Thanks.'

We take another sip. I can hear Paul moving around upstairs and I pray to God he comes down and interrupts us. John's so easy to talk to that I'm half-afraid of what I might say – about Emilia Coburn's wedding, about James, about everything. Then the toilet flushes and I hear Paul creaking back towards his bedroom.

'Did you get a bite off something?' John says, gesturing towards my neck. I instinctively put a hand over the latest cluster of hives to cover them.

'No, no, I don't think so,' I say, trying to sound casual. 'Just hives. According to Google I'm dying, but I think it might be just stress. Roll on next week.'

'Don't take this the wrong way, Ais, but are you okay?' He looks so concerned that my heart jumps in my chest.

'Why wouldn't I be okay?' I ask, clutching the mug with both hands.

'You just seem to have a lot on your plate at the moment. Is it Paul?'

'Paul? What about him?'

'Well, he's not doing great from what I can see.'

I glance around the kitchen and my eyes fall on the freshly baked apple tart cooling on the counter. I feel protective and guilty at the same time. 'Don't worry about Paul. He's being well looked after.'

I scratch my neck again. I thought the hives were going down yesterday but they were as bad as ever when I got up this morning.

'And who's looking after you?'

The question catches me off guard. Who *is* looking after me?

'James, of course.'

'Is he?'

I laugh ruefully. 'Since when were you so concerned about James? Last I heard you were throwing digs at him.'

John looks embarrassed for a split second. 'Is he looking after you, though?'

'I'm grand.'

'Are you sure?'

'I'm grand, John. I'm always grand.'

CHAPTER 40

I can't believe I'm going to Majella with more bad news, but as I'm heading over to her to work on the calligraphy, I get a call from Mikey Maguire to say he can't accommodate drinks next Friday night before the wedding.

'What?' I shriek down the phone as he explains that the food safety people had been in and told him he had to have the seats reupholstered as they're holding 'noxious fumes'. We've been complaining about the smell of Guinness farts rising out of them for the past ten years, and now he's decided that this Friday is the day he's going to replace them?

'It's Majella's wedding drinks, Mikey,' I plead as I arrive at BallyGoBrunch and stick my head in to Carol to give her a thumbs-up. She smiles back at me and wipes a bead of sweat off her forehead. I don't know how she does it – she's been here day and night the past few days, working off a detailed spreadsheet. Apparently Mammy was able to give her a crash course in the basics of Excel and then off she went inputting times and amounts and everything we need to get these bloody canapés out the door. Just the sight of the kitchen has started to give me such anxiety about next weekend. Mikey isn't budging about the drinks and I'm forced to give up. I only hope they'll be able to squeeze us in at the bar in the Ard Rí.

****

I knock on the door of Majella's apartment and walk in. It feels so cavernous now that the other Morans and Willy have moved back to the bungalow. She's sitting in the middle of mounds of cards, black ink all over her hands.

'Oh, thank God, Ais, I keep making a balls of the Spanish ones,' she says, getting up and stretching her legs.

I drop my bag on the floor beside the door and take a deep breath. 'I think you should sit back down, Maj.'

Her eyes instantly widen and she reaches for the table to steady herself. 'Jesus Christ, what is it *now*? I'm not able for any more bad news, Ais. I'm starting to think this bloody building is on an Indian burial ground or something.'

'Well, it's not good news,' I admit.

'Let me guess! The church is gone up in flames? My father's broken his two legs? Pablo has cold feet?'

I laugh. I just can't help it. As if anything could stop Pablo from marrying her.

'It's not the wedding – it's about Friday,' I continue. 'I was just on to Mikey Maguire. They're closing for the night.'

She twists her face in disbelief. 'They don't even close on Good Friday any more! What reason did he give you?'

'He's getting the seats done. Finally.'

She sighs. 'That's something at least. The bang of farts can't be healthy.'

We set to working through her guest list and writing out the place cards as fancy as we can, mostly in silence with the low hum of Coldplay in the background.

'Nobody said it was easy …' Majella sings along absentmindedly, and I realise this is the calmest I've felt in weeks, maybe months. It's nice to be focused on just one task.

'Oh take me back to the sta-aaart,' I join in with her and we laugh.

'We're like larks,' she says and I smile in agreement and we fall silent again.

'Aisling?' Maj says, interrupting my daze of lettering and ticking names off the list. 'Are you okay? You're nearly taking the arm off yourself.'

I didn't even notice how much scratching I was doing.

'Helping with the wedding isn't too much for you, is it?' she asks. 'I know the café is busy at the moment and you must have been months planning the hen. Don't be afraid to say no to me.'

I know Majella means this, but she also wanted the best hen in the world and I wanted to give it to her, same with the wedding. And she deserves the best too. She's looking at me with so much concern in her eyes that I almost blab about Emilia Coburn and the food, The Peigs and everything.

'Not at all, I'm grand,' I say, sitting on my hands.

'How are things with you and James?'

How *are* things with me and James? Not great, if I'm honest with myself. I'm niggling at him about things around the house. The dishwasher. The way he keeps turning off the shower switch while I'm in the shower. He's trying his best but there's something off. It's so hard to put my finger on it, though, because he's so nice. My poor lost boy.

'We're okay,' I say tentatively and shift awkwardly in my seat. 'He's been so busy I've barely seen him.'

'You should book a holiday.'

'That's what I thought.' Nowhere near Buckleton, though. Christ, the thought of ever going back there again.

'And the café?'

I grimace.

'Aw not that too?' Majella looks concerned.

'I've just started to dread it,' I explain. 'It's nothing like I thought it would be. I love a spreadsheet as much as the next person, possibly even more, but I'm drowning in the admin. I feel like I'm sinking. Carol is so capable but I forgot to put payroll through last week. One of Karla's standing orders bounced. She was bulling, and rightly so. '

'You definitely need a holiday, bird. You need to get away from all this for a while. You'll come back feeling way better, I swear.'

'Yeah, maybe.' The thought of fleeing is actually blissful. I'm mad to take flight and have been fantasising about packing it all in. Even a light coma sounds appealing at this stage.

'I was thinking,' I say to her, trying to change the subject to something a bit more positive. She's the bride, after all. 'You have your something borrowed?'

'The locket from Abuela Sofia,' she confirms.

'You have your something new and your something blue?'

'Dress, and a corner from Pablo's blue boxers sewn into the lining.'

'Well, I'm going to give you your something old.'

'Aw, Ais, really?'

'Of course. I'm your one and only bridesmaid.'

'Are ... you going to tell me what it is?'

'You'll find out on the Big Day.'

CHAPTER 41

'Aisling, can I just double and triple check some of these instructions from Mandy?'

It's the day before the weddings and Carol and I have been at BallyGoBrunch since 4 a.m. I'll say something for Mandy, she's thorough – she's provided detailed lists and inventories for how each dish should be stored and plated and served. We're actually learning a lot from her, but the way I'm feeling now it will be some time before I can truly forgive her or Emilia Coburn or Ben Bloody Dixon for steamrolling in on the weekend of Maj's wedding. Double-oh-seven? Double-oh-bollox more like it. I won't be at Garbally for the plating and serving so I'm determined to make sure everything is ready for Carol and Noel and Karla to send the food out when the time comes.

'Go ahead, Carol. We need everything to be perfect.'

'Okay, first thing is when she was in the other day she kept talking about "a-loo-min-um" and I just wanted to check ...'

'Tinfoil. It's tinfoil.'

'Okay, grand. And just so we're clear, the small fries ...'

'Little cones of chips. Not tiny full Irishes.'

'But then the chocolate chips ...'

'Not actually chocolate chips, but crisps coated in chocolate.' Emilia wanted to recreate the taste of childhood summers with that one, apparently. The perfect mouthful of cheese and onion and a square of chocolate. I'm not normally into culinary fusion but this I can get on board with.

'And then the Koran wrap ...'

'Saran wrap.'

'Of course. The Saran wrap ... is the cling film.'

'That's the one.'

I'm glad we have it sorted. I know Carol knows the menu inside out but we're both a bit on edge and it's better to be safe than sorry.

We've agreed that BallyGoBrunch will have to close for the day. We'll take a hit, but the income from the catering will cover it, and at this stage I just want to break even and do a good job. And Carol has said she'll nip in and open up Sunday morning for any heads that miss the Ard Rí breakfast. We always have a steady little stream of them after a wedding, and while I don't know what breakfast arrangements there are at Garbally, it seems like there could be people crawling out of sheds and from under couch cushions to beat the band come Sunday. I must actually tell Carol to put in an extra order of sausages, if she hasn't thought of it herself. I add it to my long, long, long to-do list

At around half eight I see James's jeep pull out of the car park and I leg it upstairs. If I'm honest with myself, I'm avoiding him. Things have still felt off this week. I've lain in bed and listened to him drifting off, barely touching, definitely not doing anything else. I've been telling myself we're stressed and busy but we're not even together a year. The knot in my stomach – the James knot – has been winding tighter and tighter. It's jostling with the Maj knot and the

Paul knot and the work knot and the Mammy knot and even a tiny little John knot. Between them, they're pushing up into my chest and throat. I'm finding myself clawing my hands through my hair and across my head, trying to push the anxious feeling away, but it comes back over me like a poxy misty rain. I'm clawing at my hives still too, getting out of bed at 4 a.m. to sit on the couch and have a good scratch. I allow myself to imagine crawling into my little single bed at home – Home Home, as anyone who's ever left BGB to live elsewhere would call it. Maybe I could move Home Home for a while. The thought comforts me.

Standing in the shower, I fantasise about what I'll do when it's all over. A holiday, definitely. Me sitting alone under an umbrella with the latest Marian Keyes in one hand and a Long Island Iced Majella in the other. Although, when will everything be done? After the weddings there's summer and beyond at BallyGoBrunch to plan for. Carol has an idea for evening events, to make more use of the space. She came to me ages ago with it, back when I was trying to figure out sleeping arrangements for Majella's hen and I thought that was the biggest worry I had. I haven't even sat down with her about it. She'd knocked on the door of my little office early one morning, nearly lifting me out of my skin.

'Sorry, Aisling, I thought you'd heard me starting up the mincer,' she'd said, poking her head around the door. She's down every morning at 6.30 a.m. like clockwork (apart from this morning, when it was 4 a.m.) to start prepping for the day.

'I was miles away, Carol. How are things?'

'All good, all good,' she said, tying the apron around her waist. 'I've been thinking. We could hold some events here of an evening. I was talking to Mags after Zumba with Mags last night and she had a fantastic suggestion to get us going: speed dating! What do you think?'

Mags is the closest thing we have to a cougar here in BGB. Ever since her divorce was finalised two years ago, she has men on the brain and she doesn't care who knows it. She's hard to miss in her selection of neon Lycra outfits and is best friends with Geraldine from Geraldine's Boutique. They make quite the pair power-walking on the Rathborris Road. I've donned my walking gear of colourdy runners and a high-vis armband many times and swung my arms up and down it. I wasn't sold on the speed-dating idea, though.

'Ah, Carol, half the village is already on Tinder and spending all their time swiping left on their cousins and their old maths teachers and people they shifted in the handball alley in second year. Do you really think anyone apart from Mags would go for it? Geraldine has a husband last time I checked.'

Carol thought for a second. 'I think the older crowd might, and we could pull people in from surrounding areas. Give them a few nibbles to get them back in for the lunchtime trade. Not everyone is on, what did you call it, Spinster? Mags said we could advertise it at her class anyway.' I barely answered her and we haven't spoken about it since.

I feel a bolt of realisation now that adds a Carol knot to my stomach. Was she talking about herself, maybe? And being ready to move on? She was bullied and controlled for years by Marty Boland. Maybe she wants to find love. When I think about how broken she was before she plucked up the courage to leave him, and just look at her now. I make a pledge to myself to bring it up with her again as soon as we're over this weekend. And then I add shampoo to my hair for the fourth time, or it could be the tenth. Who knows at this stage? I tried to shave under my arm with toothpaste yesterday.

****

Back down in BallyGoBrunch Carol and Noel have the kitchen under control and I'm checking off my list of things I need to remember to bring with me from the apartment to the Ard Rí this evening. I'm going to stay with Maj in the bridal suite tonight and Pablo will stay in the Morans' old apartment. John and a few of the lads are calling over for some drinks, he said, and I wonder will James join them. I haven't even asked him.

A noise at the door of the café brings me out to the front counter. A young one in a baseball cap and oversized denim jacket is pushing on the door. I wave to get her attention. 'Sorry, we're closed. Sorry now.'

She waves back, pointing inside in a 'can I come in?' fashion and I have a quick look around for a weapon of some sort, just in case. I've listened to enough murder podcasts to know never to underestimate anyone. I peer out at her as I walk slowly towards the door. Something about her looks familiar. Maybe she's one of the Ruane cousins. She's smiling anyway so she must know me. I'm usually a whizz with the names so it's killing me as I turn the lock and pull the door open. She lifts up her face towards me with a shy, 'Hi, I'm –'

I help her finish her sentence. 'Emilia Coburn.'

'It's so nice to finally meet you,' she says, pulling the cap off her head and shaking her hair out, with a practised glance out the windows. I suppose she's used to being looked at. 'Is there somewhere we could talk in private?' She's small and young looking. Totally unrecognisable. I guess I'm used to seeing her glammed up to the nines. She posted a picture on Instagram last week at a premiere and tagged her 'glam squad' in it. Fiesty Morganstergen Something-or-other and a man whose name seemed to be simply Blu.

I check that the coast is clear and rush her into my office and close the door, pushing mounds of paper off the second chair so she can sit down.

'Aisling, isn't it?'

I nod mutely. This is how Mammy must have felt coming face to face with Skippy Brennan that time.

'I just wanted to thank you for all the work you've put in. I know the change was at the last minute and you've been very accommodating. It was important to me to have local flavour at the wedding. My granny …' She clears her throat and pauses for a second. 'My granny was from here, you know?'

I nod ferociously. Kitty Coburn. Definitely from BGB and not Knock.

'Well, she pretty much raised me down here every summer when I was a little girl, and she used to talk so much about growing up here and the hay fields in the autumn and feeding spring lambs and dancing in the courtyard of Maguire's pub.'

'Oh, that's still there! Well, it's the smoking area now and there's a pool table but it's a courtyard alright.'

Emilia nods, her eyes bright. 'When Granny passed away last year I was devastated. My mother died when I was twenty and I don't really know my dad so she was kind of all I had.

She had always wanted to see me get married, and she always said I should do it in Ballygobbard. I met Ben shortly afterwards and just fell head over heels. Are you married, Aisling?'

'No, no. I'm … I have a boyfriend.'

'Well then, you know what I mean.'

I don't really, but I nod anyway.

'Anyway, I just wanted to thank you for accommodating the change in schedule. Between Ben's work and my work and contracts and … ugh!' She throws her arms up in frustration. 'Between everything, it's been really stressful. It means so much to me to do it here at this time, and with all the food sourced locally. I hope it hasn't been too much bother.'

It has actually been a colossal bother, but between the granny and the work and the contracts, sure don't we all have our problems?

'No bother at all. My friend Sadhbh and her boyfriend Don are actually going to –'

Oh, balls. She's going to know Sadhbh told me. The NDAs!

But Emilia's face lights up. 'You know Sadhbh? I've only met her a couple of times but she's a doll. And The Peigs are playing at the wedding tomorrow, you know? We're so excited.'

I nod and grin ruefully. 'Oh, I know.'

'Ben just loves them. Wait until you hear the song they've done for the film. And I just love …' She breaks into their most recent hit, 'Absolutely Tapped', and I'm slightly pleased that even gorgeous movie stars have flaws. She sounds like a crow. She laughs as though she knows she does and puts the cap back on her head.

'Anyway, I was just passing and wanted to drop in to say thanks. You came so highly recommended, I was just sorry you couldn't do *all* the food.'

The thought of catering an entire wedding is enough to bring blood rushing to fresh hives around my ears so I just smile. 'No problem.'

Emilia pulls her cap down further and I open the office door and give her an all-clear sign. She scurries to the café door as a black SUV with tinted windows pulls silently around the side.

I can't believe I've just met Emilia Coburn and I can't even tell anyone about it. For half a minute I allow myself to fantasise about checking us both in at BallyGoBrunch on Facebook and the avalanche of Likes that would roll in. I didn't even get a selfie with her. Majella would be disgusted with me.

CHAPTER 42

I just have to drop into Mammy's for two minutes to collect my bridesmaid dress and Majella's something old, and then I can head to the Ard Rí in time for the wedding-eve drinks the hotel was luckily able to accommodate. I had dropped the precious garment bag in weeks ago in a rush and asked Mammy to hang it up for me. For luck it's not the type of material that creases badly so it shouldn't need to be steamed or anything. For some reason special dresses like these – bridesmaid, wedding, communion, maybe even debs – have to be stored in other houses. It's like an unspoken rule. God forbid I might have my bridesmaid dress in my own wardrobe at James's. And of course, it would be criminal if Majella's wedding dress was in her own house. What if Pablo suddenly somehow developed X-ray vision and could see it? What if he lost the run of himself and looked? No, Majella's dress had actually been in my wardrobe until she collected it earlier.

Mammy's car isn't there but the back door is open and I let myself in, looking over the wall and noting the new scarecrow standing tall and proud over the vegetable patch. James must have found the time to get it finished – fair play to him. He never said. I take the stairs up to my room two at a time, and as soon as I push the door I sense something is different. Wrong. The atmosphere is … off. As I walk in, I see that my little single bed is still there but everything else is different. The walls are bare and a larger desk has replaced my ancient one, and on it stands a new computer, printer and stacks of Mammy's paperwork and files for the eco farm. Where is all my stuff? It hits me like a punch in the stomach. I go to the wardrobe and fling it open. Almost empty apart from a few Good Coats and the one garment bag. My bridesmaid dress. At least that's still there. I sit on the bed, trying not to cry, and reach under it, feeling for my boxes. My hand claws the air, though. There's nothing there. I get down on my hands and knees and peer under the bed but the empty space yawns back at me. Not even a ball of dust. I scream. I can't help it. What has she done? All my things. My memories. My photos Blu-Tacked to the mirror and my posters and my Irish dancing medals. All gone. Why didn't she tell me? Can I never come home again? I stay on my knees for a minute or two, fighting back the tears, and then remember I was supposed to be at the Ard Rí twenty minutes ago and pull myself together. I stand up, take out the garment bag and head back downstairs. I hear Mammy's car pulling into the driveway and look out the kitchen window to see her unloading bags from the boot. The yurts are completely booked out for tomorrow night so she has a busy weekend ahead. I don't even go out to help her, I'm that annoyed. She bustles in the back door, her arms laden, getting a fright when she sees me standing there.

'Aisling. Jesus, you nearly put my heart through the roof.'

'My car is outside.'

'I know, but you're just standing there like the grim reaper. Will you grab a few bags for me, good girl?'

'I don't really have time.'

She's barely listening, though, and rushes back out to the car, calling behind her. 'There's some activity going on at Maguire's this evening. Fierce coming and going, out and in.'

Out of nowhere a ghostly voice booms, 'Playing. Blowing in the Wind. By. Bob Dylan.'

Mammy comes back into the kitchen and drops more bags. 'ALEXA. WILL YOU GIVE OVER?'

She stops and looks at me. 'Aisling, what's wrong.'

'My room, Mammy.'

She hits her hand off her forehead. 'Jesus, of course. You haven't seen it.' Then she beams. 'Well, what do you think?'

She looks delighted with herself but her face soon falls. 'What's wrong, love? Do you not like it? You were only complaining recently about having too much stuff.'

She's right, I suppose, I was. I was feeling frustrated with myself for not fully embracing the move into James's place and still having so much stuff at home. I didn't think she'd do this, though.

'I needed an office, pet,' she says gently. 'I can't keep all my paperwork for the farm in the kitchen. It was Tessie's idea – she has me roped into moving up a level in the computer course. I needed a proper desk and a good chair and your old room, well, it's the perfect space for it. Sure aren't you all grown up with your own place now?'

My eyes fill with tears and I rub at them angrily. 'Where is my stuff, though?' I wail, scratching at my hives. 'I need one of the boxes from under the bed. Did you throw them all out? There was one with a red lid.'

'Of course not, love. They're all in the attic. Paul helped me put them up there. I was delighted to see him up and about actually, he was –'

'Mammy, I need that box! It has Majella's something old in it.'

'Don't panic. We can get it down.'

'I don't have time now. I'll make do.'

'You got the dress, though?' She nods at the garment bag.

I feel bad for being angry with her. But she could have just asked me before doing it. 'I did. Thanks.'

'It's a lovely dress. A most unusual colour, that dusty pink.'

'What? It's not pink.'

I reef the zip on the bag down and, sure enough, a swathe of pink fabric comes into view. 'Mammy. This isn't the one I gave you.'

'It is, Aisling. There was only one dress in that bag.'

I stare at the offending pink number trying to figure out what's happened. I had so many deliveries coming and so many of the same coloured bags that I must have lost track and sent the wrong dress – well, the *right* dress – back.

'This isn't my bridesmaid dress. I've kept the wrong one.'

I can feel a cold sweat working its way over my shoulders and up the back of my head and my breathing gets shallower and shallower. I start to cry but it just comes as heaving breaths.

'Aisling, pet, sit down here and calm down and have some water.'

I sit in the chair she offers me, still clutching the garment bag, and do my best to calm down like she says. She waits a few minutes for my breaths to return to normal.

'You were panicking, Aisling. It's only a dress. Can't you wear that one?'

'It's way too small. And it's strapless.'

'Have you nothing else? An old one you can wear? There's something long in the back of that wardrobe, I'm sure of it.'

'It's Majella's wedding, Mammy. I'm the only bridesmaid. I can't show up in my debs dress.'

I realise I'm now mad late for the Ard Rí and Majella is going to kill me because she wants to do a little practice with me and her walking up the aisle and then back down with Pablo and John. I bundle the pink dress into the bag.

'I'll figure something out.'

I grab my keys and Mammy calls after me. 'Will you go easy, Aisling? Go easy, pet.'

I race out the back door and, with her words ringing in my ears, force myself to stop for a second and take a few deep breaths before walking over to the Micra. I'm just getting in when Paul rounds the corner, his phone in his hand.

'Hey,' I call over. I've been so busy I can't remember the last time I actually spoke to him. 'Come here for a sec, will you, Paul?'

He ambles across the yard slowly, flipping his phone over in his hand.

'Well, what's the craic?' I ask, leaning against the car and trying to push the dress saga out of my mind for a minute.

'Not much,' he replies. 'Just restocking the farm shop. She was at me all evening.'

I resist the urge to make a quip about earning his keep. He drinks about two litres of milk with every meal! 'You're looking better than the last time I saw you anyway,' I say. He's not really. His face is pale and drawn but who doesn't like to be told they're looking well.

'Sure I do,' he replies sarcastically, staring out over the Far Field.

'Ah, Paul, don't be like that.'

'Be like what?'

'Smart with me. I'm only asking how you are.'

'I feel like shit, if you really want to know. I should have stayed in Oz.'

'What are you talking about? Mammy is running herself ragged looking after you, as well as getting everything ready for this weekend. What more do you want?'

He shrugs and sets his jaw, still looking into the distance.

I feel the anger bubbling up inside me. I can't help it. 'Maybe you should stop thinking about yourself for five minutes,' I say sharply, scratching my forearm. 'You're not the only one with problems.'

He looks at the ground and shakes his head. 'You don't know what you're talking about, Aisling.'

'What's that supposed to mean?'

'I should never have come home. You'd all be much happier if I wasn't around.'

'Ah, Paul, don't be so silly.' I feel such a pang of guilt and sadness for him.

'I just – I don't feel like I belong anywhere. I don't know. Doesn't matter.' He scuffs his foot on the ground then turns and walks away.

Before I can stop him my phone goes in my pocket. Majella! She's going to murder me if I don't go now. 'Paul!' I shout after him. '*Paul!*'

But he's gone in through the back door.

CHAPTER 43

'I can't believe I'm saying this, but I don't think it looks that bad.'

Majella stands back and takes a good look at me. She makes another few adjustments and appraises her work. I wish I could get Sadhbh to weigh in but she hasn't arrived in BGB yet. I haven't said anything to Maj but there's a good chance I'll see her before we go up the aisle. James is still at Garbally putting finishing touches to the orchard and the bubbles and whatever other madness they have going on. I can only imagine what it looks like now that it's all finished. I hope James is proud of his work, even though the idea of him makes me feel sad. It's all fallen apart so badly.

I turn around and look at myself in the mirror. I thought the colour would be a disaster but I've worn worse to be honest.

Majella had managed to hold it together when I eventually got to the Ard Rí and explained the dress fiasco to her. 'We'll figure something out,' she said. 'Someone will have something.' Then a look of inspiration crossed her face and she excused us and dragged me upstairs and produced it.

'I kept it as … I don't know, a kind of good luck charm. The first wedding dress I ever bought.'

And now the decision is made. I'll wear the mint-green monstrosity from China tomorrow. My heart aches for the lovely blue dress but there's nothing we can do about it now. Me and Maj head back downstairs to see out her final day as a single woman, and to make sure Pablo isn't making his face swell too much with the crying. I manage to relax and have a few drinks and a catch-up with the Tenerifian gang from the hen, and it's 2 a.m. when I eventually get Majella to sleep after a pint of room-service champagne and half a sleeping tablet her mother passed me earlier. When I think of all the years I spent fantasising about sleeping in the bridal suite of the Ard Rí, I didn't imagine it would be like this. Majella chants 'I'm getting married in the mooorning' for a few minutes with her Wifey eye mask on before drifting off, a huge smile on her face. Then I lie staring at the ceiling until my alarm goes at a quarter to three: 4 May. My Everest. I swear to God, I'm this close to turning to … well, God.

I throw my fleece and O'Neills tracksuit bottoms on over my personalised Chief Ridesmaid nightie and sneak out of the room. Driving to the café, I go through the list of stuff I have to do before Majella wakes up. There's pork belly to cube, apple garnishes to slice, the potatoes for the croquettes to boil and mash, pastry to roll, herbs to chop, things to stack, fry, cream, ball, whisk, flake, froth and bake. Carol is the most organised person on the planet, and her timetable for this morning is military grade, but time is going to be tight no matter what way you look at it.

Space is one of our main issues, and when I come blustering into the café, every available surface already has a tray or a pot on it and Carol is dancing between them like Katie Taylor herself.

'Are we on track?' I say, reaching for a hairnet. The windows are dripping with condensation and between the ovens, boiling water and extractor fans I can barely hear a thing.

'Six minutes ahead of schedule but who's counting.' She opens the oven and flips a tray of sausage rolls around then sets the timer again and closes the door. They smell unreal. 'Karla is outside pulling up the pansies.'

'Did Mammy drop over the honey?'

'It was on the back doorstep when I opened up, along with Constance's purple carrots and the white asparagus.'

'Does she suspect anything?'

'I don't think so. I said we were expecting a rush tomorrow.'

'And the eggs?'

'I'd say they haven't even been laid yet.'

Mandy Blumenthal wants fresh and fresh is what we're giving her.

****

It's as bright as day and coming up to six when I slip back into the bridal suite. There was a helicopter doing the rounds above the village on the drive over and I wonder if Mad Tom has eaten another dishwasher tablet and is being airlifted or if it's paparazzi looking to catch a glimpse of a few celebrities. Apparently it's in a couple of the tabloids this morning that Ben was spotted arriving into Dublin Airport, and Skippy Brennan was more than happy to give them a few quotes. I wonder who his sources are. He always knows everything. Only a few hours to go now until all will be revealed anyway and I can go back to living free from the shackles of the NDA.

I check my phone just as I'm pulling the duvet over me. There's a text from Sharon. 'One of my sunbeds exploded, hun. Glass everywhere. Have to bring the bridal appointments forward to nine. Call me when you're up xxx.'

Oh God, is she for real? She was supposed to be coming at eleven to do our hairs and make-up here in the suite. The photographer is due at one to take pics of her at work, but we obviously need to be finished and looking our best by then. Majella won't be happy. And I can say with absolute certainty that I'll have sweated any foundation right off me by the time the ceremony starts at two if it's put on at nine o'blasted clock. Long-wear, my eye.

Majella stirs in the bed beside me and I lie as still as I can.

'Ais?'

'Mmm,' I go, in the manner of someone who's in a deep sleep, not someone who's been out grating garlic all night.

'Oh my God. I can't believe I'm getting married today,' she screeches, sitting bolt upright and ripping off the eye mask. 'What time is it?'

'Just gone six. You should try and get another couple of hours' sleep so –'

My phone starts to ring on the bedside locker.

'Who's ringing you at this hour?' Maj asks looking suspicious.

I look at the screen. It's Mandy Blumenthal.

'It's James,' I say, lepping out of the bed. 'Just going to …' and I leg it into the en suite and lock the door.

'Aisling speaking!' I whisper brightly.

'Honey, just checking we're all on schedule?'

'Yes. All good here. We'll be ready to go.'

'You can start bringing the food up now. The kitchen is ready for it.'

Shite, this wasn't supposed to happen until nine, and I thought I'd be able to go and be back before Sharon got here. If I go now, though, I can be back in time but I'll have to rush.

When I slink out of the en suite Majella is sitting at the dressing table in her ridey bride nightie looking at herself.

'Only seven hours of singledom left,' she muses. 'Hard to believe isn't it, Ais?'

'It is,' I say, pulling back on my fleece and O'Neills. 'It really is.'

'Where are you going?' She swings around.

'Nowhere. I've to get something from the car.'

She turns back to her reflection. 'I had a good run, to be fair. No regrets. I did it my way.'

'Oh, by the way,' I say. 'Sharon was on a while ago. She has to come at nine now. Something exploded in the salon. Will you tell your mother and Juana to be here?'

'Nine? My Rosie Huntington-Whiteley hair! It'll be flat as a pancake.'

'Not at all. She's bringing extra Elnett, she said. The big tins. Hop into the shower there and I'll be back in a minute.'

I race down the stairs to the restaurant where the early risers are just starting to drift down for breakfast. I recognise one of Pablo's aunts at the toast rotisserie and I swear a woman at the pink grapefruit is the head of Kate Moss.

'Aisling, I knew you'd be down early for the breakfast. Good woman.' That's Lisa Gleeson. I feel relieved to see she has a clipboard. She's wedding ready. At least somebody is.

I race out of the hotel, into the car and back to BallyGoBrunch as fast as the speed limit will let me. Carol catches me when I fall in the door of the café.

'What time is it?' I gasp.

'Five to eight.'

I sit on a crate of tomatoes to catch my breath before explaining that I need her to give me the first trays ready to go so I can bring them to Garbally. She helps me carry them out and I fumble in my bag for the pass Mandy sent me to gain access to the grounds. I make sure the trays are secure and belt towards Garbally, sweating and mumbling bits of my wedding speech to myself. I reach the gates and pull out the pass, shaking it at the burly security man who waves me through. I'm only going in the back entrance but I can see glimpses of the orchard and the bubbles as I drive up the driveway. It looks stunning. James has done some job. I haven't even talked to him since he dropped in briefly to the drinks last night. As I trundle up the driveway, a familiar-looking figure striding at high speed down one of the glass walkways connecting the various parts of the Garbally buildings catches my eye. Was that ... Sharon? No, it can't be. Sharon wouldn't be caught dead in the flats this woman is wearing. I pull up by the catering entrance and leap out and ring the bell. The young fella who answers the door has no choice but to take the trays I'm pushing into his arms, and after some small talk about how this whole thing is mad and isn't it great they got the weather, I'm racing straight back to the car. Just as I round the corner to where the Micra is my foot catches on a bag of something and I go head over heels, dragging whatever it is with me and feeling a fine powder settling on my skin. I open my eyes and spit the offending stuff off my lips. Cement. Of course. Just perfect. I stand up, brush myself off and leap into the car to reverse back out to head to the Ard Rí.

I screech into the car park and race back into the hotel. With the adrenaline coursing through my veins, I don't have the patience to wait for the lift, so I run up the stairs to the bridal suite. It's the penthouse and, needless to say, I'm puce by the time I arrive. Four storeys is a lot, and there's absolutely no arch support in my Crocs. Everyone turns around when I walk in.

'There she is,' Liz Moran says, while Sharon backcombs her hair aggressively. 'Not like you to abandon a bride in her hour of need, Aisling.'

'I … I …' I gasp. 'I was only gone twenty minutes. I had to get something.'

'You were gone an hour. And where is whatever you were supposed to be getting?' Majella asks, her eyes narrowing. If I'm not careful she's going to twig that I'm double jobbing. I say a prayer to St Anthony and put my hand into my fleece pocket. It lands on a packet of spearmint Extra.

'Here,' I say, pulling it out. 'You want to be minty fresh for Pablo, don't you?'

'Aw, Ais,' Majella goes, spraying Alien on her ankles and up her nightie, 'you really think of everything.'

CHAPTER 44

'How long have you had the hives, Ais?' Sharon asks as she starts to buff and contour and highlight my face. I try not to worry about looking like a toffee apple and instead fire a text off to Carol to see how everything is going back in the café. She replies very quickly for a woman with as much going as she has. It's all under control. But I scratch at the hives as soon as Sharon mentions them – there aren't too many today, thank God.

'Ah, they flare up every now and then. You know yourself. Stress. Can you cover them?'

'Of course. You should look after yourself a bit better, you know? It's better to get to the root of the problem than just hide the symptoms.'

Honestly, I don't think hairdressers get enough credit for what they do. I'm going to suggest that Sharon officially retrains as a therapist one of these days. She's a great listener.

'I think I'm a bit run down. I must get myself a tonic when all this is over.'

'Definitely,' she says, searching frantically for my cheekbones. 'You can't pour from an empty cup.' She puts a friendly hand on my shoulder and I smile in the mirror at her gratefully. Then I remember her doppelganger from Garbally.

'Hey, I saw someone the absolute spit of you out at Garbally this morning.' The words are out of my mouth before I realise what I've done. All these months I've managed to keep it a secret and now I fall at the last hurdle.

'What?' says Majella.

'What?' goes Liz Moran from under a set of heated rollers.

'*Que?*' says Juana, who has been struggling to keep up at the best of times – we've been talking that fast all morning.

'What were you doing at Garbally this morning?' demands Majella as Sharon refuses to meet my eye in the mirror.

'I just had to drop something off.'

Majella roots around on the bed and pulls a copy of *The Sun* out from under a pile of hair extensions. 'Drop something off for this?'

Splashed across the front page is the headline 'Emilia Coburn to Wed 007 in Swish Country Bash', accompanying an aerial picture of Garbally. I think I can make out James's jeep. Must have been taken yesterday. I just stare at it, and I'm spent. I can't pretend any more. If Mandy wants to come for me, she can come for me. The jig is officially up.

'Yes, dropping something off for that.'

It feels so good to let the cat out of the bag.

Majella gasps and rushes to my side, taking care not to smudge her fresh French mani. 'What. The. Fuck? Tell me everything, bird.'

'BallyGoBrunch is doing a few nibbles for the reception. That's all. Emilia wanted local stuff and so we got the call.'

'Oh, "Emilia", is it? Best friends, are you?' Majella's eyes are like saucers.

'I wish – I've only met her once. She'd fit in your pocket, the little size of her.'

'You've met her?' Majella is so shook her fake eyelashes nearly come off. 'Why didn't you tell me? This is huge! And you knew all this time that her wedding was on the same day as mine?'

'I had to sign an NDA. I wasn't allowed tell anyone. And the wedding was supposed to be last week. They moved it. The stress nearly killed me.' I gesture at the hives, or what's left of them after Sharon's careful concealing.

'An NDA? The glamour!'

'I know. I felt like I was the only person in the world who knew.'

Sharon clears her throat. 'Well, actually, I knew.'

Now it's my turn to nearly shake off the make-up she's just applied with the turn of my head. 'What?'

'I signed one too. They had me on retainer for any emergencies that might pop up and –'

I gasp. 'Oh my God, that *was* you this morning at Garbally!' That's when I notice her feet – she's wearing flats. At last! She'll never go back to the heels now. Next thing I'll have her in Crocs.

'Yep.' She cops me looking at her feet. 'The size of the place, hun! I was running around all morning. I got back here just before you. I was sweating!'

'Who did you see?' Majella shrieks.

'Let's just say a certain A-lister decided he needed a quick trim.'

'Oh my God, who?' Liz is hanging on our every word and poor Juana is gasping along, but who knows how much she's really picking up.

Sharon laughs. 'I'm not supposed to say anything, but I guess I could tell you he's,' she starts singing The Peigs' break-out hit from last year, 'so far from Naaaavan.'

'Oh my God, Pierce Brosnan. Another Bond. Of course.'

'He definitely has that sexy-older-man thing going on,' Sharon says wistfully. 'And his hair is in mint condition. No sign of Ben though, unfortunately.'

A few things start to fall into place. So that means when I was trying to dodge Emilia Coburn wedding chat, Sharon was too. I thought she was acting odd and definitely thought she was annoyed with me a few times.

'So the reason you had to move our appointment this morning ...?' Majella asks.

'I'm so sorry, Maj. They need a nail technician on standby and the money is whopper. If my phone goes, I'll have to leg it back.'

There's a pause as everyone turns to look at Majella. I see Juana examining her own nails out of the corner of my eye and pray she doesn't kick up a fuss.

But Maj shrugs good-naturedly. 'Ah, that's okay. I'd nearly go myself and it's my wedding day. If you meet Brad Pitt, send me a selfie.'

That's very sound of Majella. I don't know how I'd be if I found out a massive celebrity wedding was happening up the road from mine. Her face suddenly looks stricken, though.

'You don't have to go back up there, do you, Ais? I really need you with me today. Maybe I should have listened to Denise and had more than one bridesmaid.'

'No way – Carol has the rest of it under control, and I've told Mandy you are my top priority.'

'Mandy? Oh my God, Mandy Blumenthal. She did Kim and Kris Humphries.' It's no Kim and Kanye but it's close enough.

There's a knock on the door and it's room service with breakfast. Majella, Juana and Liz head out into the little living room, Majella protesting that she doesn't think she can eat a thing but changing her tune fairly lively when she sees the pancakes.

Sharon goes back to doing my face and checks her watch. 'We're doing well for time. Liz and Juana are done and I'll leave Maj to the very last.'

'Did I tell you about what happened with the dress? Oh God, I didn't.' I fill Sharon in on the whole fiasco. 'Of course, I look like a bit of a hound in it. It's very clingy around the middle.'

Sharon doesn't answer me and when I try to catch her eye in the mirror she looks annoyed. That same annoyed expression I've been seeing for months.

'Sharon, is everything okay?'

She takes a breath and then looks me in the eye. 'Aisling, how do you think it makes me feel when you go on and on about getting fat and counting points and doing steps and "being good" and dresses "clinging around the middle"?'

My eyes widen. I was not expecting this.

'I'm a big girl, right? I'm fat?'

'You're not fat,' I say reflexively and she holds her hand up.

'I wear a size twenty, Aisling. I know that probably horrifies you but I do. And you going on and on about Weight Watchers and "Trim for Tenerife" and – Jesus. I'm just sick of it.'

I'm dumbstruck. Sharon is a bigger girl, but she wears her clothes with such confidence and always looks so sexy, I just never thought ... I just never thought.

'When you talk like that it makes me feel you'd rather die than look like me,' she says in a small voice. 'You and the girls do it all the time.'

Her statement sinks in and I realise she's right, we *do* do it all the time. I feel worse than I have done in months. 'Sharon, I'm so sorry. I just ... I'm just so used to doing it. I don't even notice.'

Sharon lifts her head up high again. 'Well, maybe start noticing. Not everyone wants to hear about how many Points are in their bloody Lindor.'

I nod. 'I will. I promise.'

She holds my eye in the mirror and then squeezes my shoulder. 'I know you will.'

Sharon spends the next hour perfecting Majella's face. Honestly, the things she can do with make-up. I've never seen Maj's eyes look greener or her skin so glowy. She's gone for a simple half-up, half-down look for her hair and she's just stunning. I'm taking the three hundredth picture of her on my phone when there's another knock on the door. I jog over to answer it and am surprised to see Mammy standing there. I've barely had time to think about our run-in in the kitchen last night.

'Hiya, Mammy.'

She has a box in her hands. 'I found it. I went digging in the attic.'

I could cry with relief. 'Thanks, Mammy.'

'Look at you. My grown-up girl.' Majella comes to the door to see who it is and Mammy smiles and takes each of our hands. 'My two grown-up girls. I'll see you in the church.'

'Is Paul driving you, Mammy? Tell him traffic is going to be bad, what with everything happening at Garbally.' I'm glad Paul's coming today – it'll cheer him up a bit.

'He told me this morning that he'd make his own way, pet. Constance is bringing us in the Range.'

The Range! Honest to God. She'll be wearing the Camilla Parker Bowles hat next.

I say goodbye and retreat into the bridal suite. I'm just sitting on the couch firing off another few texts to Carol when Majella rounds the doorframe, hair backcombed to within an inch of its life.

'Sadhbh just texted me. She said she'll see us in the church and later at the afters. Does that mean The Peigs are in BGB, but they're playing at Garbally?'

I n for a penny, in for a pound, so I confirm straight away to Majella that, yes, The Peigs are playing at Emilia's wedding and Sadhbh is going to be there with them, but she's determined to see Maj walk down the aisle. Plus, she's not missing the Ard Rí's legendary 11 p.m. Tayto-sandwich buffet.

'She couldn't say anything earlier because they all had to sign NDAs too,' I explain diplomatically.

'Is there anyone who *didn't* sign an NDA?'

It would be Majella's dream to be so far into an inner celebrity circle that she'd have to sign an NDA, so I know this must be hard for her. And on her wedding day of all days. I wonder could I get Mandy to rustle up something for her to sign. Maj'd be thrilled. I placate her with tales of the day Emilia came to BallyGoBrunch, going into minute detail about what she was wearing and answering detailed questions about whether or not I thought she had hair extensions and how much money, roughly, did I suspect her earrings cost.

Before we know it it's twenty to two and time to head to the church. Shem Moran is driving us in his father's old Morris Minor. In hindsight, maybe we should have ordered another car, but luckily Juana decides to go with her daughters – which is probably for the best because she started crying about her *bambino* at around half twelve and I haven't been able to get her to stop. Paola and Maria seem well able for it, though. They have half of Tenerife on FaceTime when they come to the room to collect Juana, and there's a lot of shrieking and *te amo* and twirling by Majella, who looks absolutely stunning. Like, truly stunning. I've nearly ruined my good eyes several times looking at her. I was doing the usual 'the state of me' putting on the back-up green dress, but I remembered what Sharon had said and thought about how I really looked and felt and decided that I looked and felt quite nice, actually.

We bundle Maj into the back of the tiny car and I get in beside her. Liz and Shem are in the front and I sneak one last look at my phone to get the latest from Carol. Almost all the grub is up at Garbally, and Mandy has an army of young lads and girls ready to pass them out. According to Carol, Mandy was low on staff because of the date change and so recruited anyone in the locality with a white shirt as late as yesterday in a bid to keep things under wraps for as long as possible. They've been given a crash course in tray carrying and napkin placement and not accidentally calling Aidan Gillen a sap. I stick my phone into my tiny satin bag and take Majella's hand and squeeze it.

'Done with work now, I promise. Nearly time.'

She smiles. 'Nearly time.'

We pull up to the church just a few minutes after two and I'm impressed, to be honest. I had visions of us being two hours late and nobody getting their dinner until midnight. Shem opens the car door and takes Majella's hand, and I stick my head in the door of the church and give the nod. The music starts – an acoustic version of Ricky Martin's 'She Bangs' – and away I go. I hadn't even thought about getting nervous, but now, as I take my first steps up the aisle, I am. Everyone turns to look and I'm the first one their eyes land on. I see familiar faces from the hen: Ellen and Carmel and Teresa; Abuela Sofia, dabbing her eyes with a tissue. I see Mammy and Constance, her plus-one for the day. I see Cyclops and Titch, red in the face from too-tight ties. Sadhbh and Don, looking too cool for school. I search for James and see his tired face peering out from one of the pews. I can tell when Majella comes into view, a parent on each arm, because there's a collective *ahhh* from the congregation. On I go, one foot in front of the other, walking up the aisle. And then he turns around … John. I feel my bottom lip start to tremble as he smiles at me, and I remember how I used to dream about walking up this very aisle towards him. He looks handsome in a bow-tie. He got his hair cut. Then Pablo turns around and on sight of Maj he crumbles. Full-blown bawling. He looks smashing, considering. Majella reaches the top of the aisle and I take her bouquet and Father Fenlon and Padre Iago step forward and we're off.

****

The service is long. Nobody is going to deny that. Padre Iago repeats everything Father Fenlon says in Spanish, including the readings and the prayers. People start to wilt at about half three but a rousing rendition of 'To Make You Feel My Love' wakes everyone up again. I'm not sure we were supposed to join in, but I think people need something to live for, to be quite honest. Then we're on the home stretch, and before we know it it's half four and I'm up signing the register with Majella and Pablo and then out the door of the church for the shaking of the hands and the chat about how starving everyone is. Sadhbh and Don race past to their car so they can boot it over to Garbally for their second wedding of the day. I find James standing alone by a shrub, and he drives us in almost complete silence to the Ard Rí in the jeep, which is spotless. Something has definitely changed between us, but now is not the time. When we arrive at a quarter past five, Lisa Gleeson's anxious head bobs around the front entrance.

'Thank God,' she hisses at me through her teeth. 'I thought ye would never get here. The chef is threatening to throw the beef down the toilet if he can't start getting the dinner ready soon.'

'Sorry, Lisa, the ceremony ran long. They'll all be here any minute.'

She'd want to get used to this, to be quite honest. I've been at weddings where the goat's cheese and beetroot salad wasn't served until half nine.

****

Half six and the Prosecco reception is nearly over. Majella and Pablo get the photos done and Javier and Miguel surprise everyone by pulling out two guitars and flamencoing away to their heart's content. It's a good ice-breaker for at least some of the forty-two Tenerifians who had made the journey. They had formed their own little enclave and I was worried they might never integrate when Majella made the controversial decision to mix up some of the tables, putting people together who don't know each other. Wouldn't be for me, now. I was at a wedding once with John where I knew nobody and I wasn't even sitting with him. I was like a bull. Although, I did meet a very nice woman called Eleanor, who I'm still friends with on Facebook and I'm not entirely convinced isn't one of the naturists who showed up on Mammy's eco farm. Some of her hedgerow shots looked very familiar. The guitar playing proves to be a good mixer, though, and before long a very pretty señorita – Juana's neighbour's niece, I think – has Murt Kelly up doing a few moves. As I'm watching Murt turning various shades of maroon, James sidles up with a glass of white and points to the empty chair beside me. I nod and he sits down, watching Murt slowly dislocate his hips.

'Can we talk, Aisling?'

Before I can answer him, Lisa Gleeson appears in the ballroom doorway ringing the dinner bell. Deirdre Ruane sweeps past us on her way to her table and gives me a thumbs-up. 'Can't wait for your speech, Ais.'

Ugh. I had managed to forget about the bloody speech for about a minute. I have bits of it written down on a scrap of paper in my tiny handbag, and I know what I want to say in my heart, but will I be able to get it all out? Maj is having the speeches in between courses so at least people will be a bit distracted. Shem is going to go first after the starters and then it's me and John after the mains.

I give James's arm a squeeze. 'Talk later, okay? Enjoy your dinner.'

I feel bad that James won't be sitting at the top table with us but Majella has put him with Cyclops and Sharon so he should be fine. Megan's with them too. Lisa rings the bell again but everyone's already forgotten their table numbers, despite having had a nosey when they first arrived, so there's a huge gathering of people around the table plan and a lot of confusion. I have images of the chef stuffing heads of broccoli down the sink in petulance.

Finally, everyone is seated and the starters and Shem's speech – complete with a dissection of every hickey Majella came home with from the ages of sixteen to twenty – come and go all too quickly, and by the time they're clearing away the plates my nerves are eating away at the lining of my stomach and every last hive on my body is screaming. John seems to be faring a bit better and says he's keeping his speech 'short and sweet'. Pablo is doing his after dessert and I'm wondering how many bathroom breaks I'll need during it.

'Aisling? Ais.' Majella comes up behind me and sinks into the chair John has just vacated to answer his phone. 'I'm worried about table twenty-three.'

Table twenty-three is a mix of her father's side of the family and Pablo's mother's cousins. It was a risky move but Majella thought that a shared love of films about Don Quixote would unite them. She was wrong. I take a look and there are a number of sour pusses and not much chat. 'What'll we do? I just want everyone to have a good time.'

Lisa Gleeson has obviously noticed too because I see her heading straight over, beckoning Javier and Miguel to follow her. Then she leans in and whispers something to them. Before anyone can figure out what's going on, the brothers pick up their instruments and start playing. Within three seconds it clicks. I know what she's at. I leap up from my chair and head over there, joining in with her just as she begins to sing.

'The moment I wake up, before I put on my make-up ...'

Within thirty seconds the entire wedding is gathered around table twenty-three roaring 'Forever, forever, you'll stay in my heart and I will love you,' while those seated wave their hands in the air. It's quite the moment.

'Thanks, Lisa, you really pulled that out of the bag,' I say admiringly, following her out of the ballroom and back to her office at her request. '*My Best Friend's Wedding*, right?'

'Yep. What a movie! I picked up so many tips. I have a groom convinced to surprise his bride with karaoke at a wedding next week.'

That sounds like an absolutely terrible plan but I say nothing. She seems so pleased with herself. I glance around the room and so many things start to make sense. *Father of the Bride, Four Weddings and a Funeral, The Wedding Planner* and *Bridesmaids* are just some of the DVDs lined up against the wall. Hey, at least she does her research.

I sink into a chair opposite her desk, glad of the bit of peace and quiet and a chance for a scratch. I'm trying not to go for the visible hives but the ones on my legs under the dress are just asking for it.

'You've allergies too, huh?' Lisa asks sympathetically. 'It's such a pain in the arse. My brother is covered in hives just like that. He's been working out at Garbally and he's allergic to whatever cement dust they've been using out there. Mammy had to put socks on his hands like a baby.'

I stop mid-scratch. 'Allergies? I thought they were from stress.'

'Oh, well, that wouldn't help either. A third of my hair fell out during my Leaving Cert even after I dropped to pass French,' Lisa says. 'The body has a way of telling you things.'

Yeah, like when your boyfriend is literally giving you hives.

'Aisling.' Lisa turns to me with a concerned frown. 'I asked you in here because I've bad news.'

'What now?'

'Michael Coleman, the lead singer of Love Hurts?'

'Yeah, what about him?'

'I just got a phone call. He's broken his right wrist doing an energetic "Rock the Boat" at a communion in Offaly and can't play tonight.'

'You are joking me.'

'I'm not.'

'What are we going to do?'

'He said his brother Brendan can stand in for him, but he said, and I quote "he hasn't got the" –' she struggles to finish the sentence '– "the Mickey Magic that the ladies love".'

First The Peigs pull out and now bloody Love Hurts are banjaxed?

'What are we going to do?' I ask her again. Before she can even answer John sticks his head around the door.

'Aisling. You don't know where Paul is, do you?'

'No, why?'

'He's not here. No one's seen him all day.'

CHAPTER 46

'Shit, Ais.' John's using the tone he normally reserves for when Rangers are ten points down with only two minutes left on the clock and he's watching the match through his fingers. I know it well, although I haven't heard it in a while.

'What? What is it, John?' I follow him back out into the hallway, trying to keep my voice level, but the panic inside me is rising. John looks so worried and Paul's been so down. And now he's been missing all day and I didn't even notice. All I can think about is what he said yesterday about belonging nowhere.

'Why are you so panicked, John? Mammy said he'd make his own way to the wedding. Maybe he just changed his mind?' Even as I'm talking John is shaking his head.

'I rang him the other night to say hello. He'd just found out Hannah was going out with some new lad. He was in bits. Crying. The works. I'm really worried, Ais. I asked your mother casually as I could where he was today and she said he got an offer of work doing some bricklaying with Titch's father but I checked with Titch and that's not true.'

I catch Tessie Daly waving frantically out of the corner of my eye. She's on her way in to the ballroom and is pointing at her handbag and mouthing 'card here'.

'I'll come over in a minute,' I mouth back, pasting on a smile.

'Why didn't you tell me, John,' I hiss, swinging back to him, although I know in my heart that I should have put all this together myself. I desperately try to remember if I saw Paul at any stage during the day.

'You have enough going on yourself,' John says. 'I didn't want to worry you. I asked him if he wanted to go for a pint, but he said he was trying to stay away from the beer because it was making him maudlin.'

'You didn't call over to him or anything, no?' I feel rotten saying this to John, nearly accusing him of neglecting Paul when really it's myself I should be blaming. Didn't he try to talk to me loads of times? At least John listened.

'I was going to but your mother told me not to be calling around so much. She said William Foley was worried there'd be no work left for him on the farm if I was doing all the jobs for free.'

Oh no. This is all my fault. I was so caught up in my bloody James and John drama that I didn't even notice that John is really Paul's only friend here. And I cut them off. And had Mammy lying for me. I walk back towards the open double doors of the ballroom, which is buzzing with chat and the sound of cutlery hitting plates. They've started serving the mains. Majella will be wondering where me and John are. I stand at the door and scan the room. 'Is his phone ringing?'

John shakes his head silently. I scan again, desperately trying to figure out what to do. Mammy is over there talking to Father Fenlon but I don't want to worry her unless I absolutely have to. Then I clock Lisa Gleeson waving her arms at me frantically and pointing at her watch. Balls. The speeches. I turn back to John, hiding behind him so I don't have to make eye contact with her. 'I have to find him.'

'Now?'

I'm afraid to even think it, let alone say it out loud. I feel like my throat is closing. 'What if he's done something stupid, John? I don't know. I have a bad feeling. The way he was talking yesterday …'

He sticks a hand in his trousers pocket and pulls out his keys. 'I've Daddy's car,' he says.

'Have you not had a drink?'

'I was afraid to before the speech.'

We lock eyes. 'Are you sure?'

He nods. 'We'll be back before they even miss us. And if we're not, they can just … wait.'

The swinging kitchen doors are just feet away from us, so I put my eyes down, grab John's arm and we speed walk towards them. We make it, dodge through the kitchen and leg it out the back entrance just as Lisa Gleeson comes sprinting after us. 'Where are ye going?'

'We're just going to get something. We won't be long. Stall for us, will you, Lees?'

****

'Which way?' John asks when we pull up to the front gates of the Ard Rí. 'Left or right, Ais? Come on!'

'I don't know, I don't know,' I say, raking my hands through my hair. It doesn't give an inch. Sharon really is at the top of her game. Where could he be? Should we go straight to the garda station in Knock? To the County General? Think Aisling, think!

A BMW pulls up behind us and flashes its lights.

'For feck's sake. Left,' I mutter, and we go screeching off.

'Where are we going?' John asks, putting his foot down as fields and ditches fly by.

'I don't know. Let me think for a minute.'

Most of the lads Paul was pally with ended up going to Australia around the same time, so it's not like there's a friend in the village he could be with. And all the Rangers lads are back in the Ard Rí. John really is his only pal here. How could I be so oblivious?

We're booting down the Ballygobbard Road now and the crossroads is about two miles straight ahead. On the left is the new sign Mammy and Constance had done for the eco farm. It's massive – so big that three complaints were lodged anonymously at the county council suggesting it should have required planning permission. 'ShayMar Eco Farm and Yurt Resort, next left, 10km. Come pet a lamb!' it says in three-foot letters.

I turn to John just as we get to the cross. 'Right! Go right here! I think I know where he might be!'

The car hasn't even come to a full stop when I bail out the passenger door and run, holding up my dress in case it slows me down. I turn around and John is running too. Please be here. Please be here. Please be here. And that's when I stumble on a rock.

'Shite,' I groan. 'These bloody heels!'

'Are you okay?' John pants as he reaches me but I wave him on.

'Keep going, keep going,' I shout. 'We've wasted enough time as it is.'

John runs off and I tentatively put weight on my left ankle. I think I've done one of those twists that makes you feel for about four minutes like you've broken it, but then it goes back to normal and you're mortified that you made such a scene. I just need to walk it off. I limp on until I get to the gate, which is still open from when John barrelled through it just a minute ago. I take a breath and keep going, teeth gritted, holding the wall for support.

When I see him the relief floods through me so much so that my body starts to convulse and I think I might puke. Instead I cry. Big fat tears. I cry because I'm happy and I cry because I'm sad. And I cry because I don't know what else to do. I'm wrung out. There's Paul sitting cross-legged at the bottom of Daddy's grave, with John on his hunkers beside him, a hand on his back. I've never been so happy to see the back of his head in my life.

'You inconsiderate little shite,' I roar across the graveyard.

Paul turns around and clocks me then puts his head back down. John is talking in his ear but they're so far away I can't make out what they're saying.

When I eventually get to the grave, I plonk myself down on the other side of Paul, and the three of us sit in a row, side by side, staring at the headstone. It needs a good wipe down. Bloody birds.

'You can't just do that, Paul,' I say softly. 'Not when you've been so out of sorts. It was scary.' My voice starts to wobble but I keep going. 'You had me … had me … thinking the worst after what you said yesterday.'

'Ah, Ais. I was only talking about going back to Melbourne. I'm going out of my mind here. And you're so busy and important and making something of yourself. I just feel a bit spare.'

Jesus, if only he knew how spare I feel sometimes. And busy and important is one thing, but so is family and talking and, I don't know, just taking it easy.

'John told me about Hannah,' I tell him gently. 'I know you're upset and I understand, really I do. And I'm here if you want to talk about it. Any time.'

'You don't understand at all really, though, Aisling.' His tone is sharper now. 'Daddy had just died. I was ten thousand miles from home and not taking it well, if I'm being honest. She knew that. She knew I needed her and she just dumped me like I was nothing. And now she's going out with someone else? Fuck that.'

'People break up,' I say gently. 'Life goes on. People move on.' The words hang in the air and it's so quiet I can hear the Daniel Wellington ticking on my wrist.

'Listen to me, lad,' John says, 'you can't keep blaming Hannah. It wasn't her job to fix you, or to mind you, or to stay with you because she felt sorry for you. Sure, neither of you could be happy carrying on like that. And anyway, you deserve better for yourself. You nearly made the senior team – there's plenty of girls around here that haven't forgotten that.'

Since when did John get so wise? He's right too, of course. I can understand how trapped Hannah felt, knowing Paul's happiness all hinged on her, especially since he was away from home, afraid of what might happen if she changed her mind. It's a lot of pressure on one person. Maybe I'll send her a message on Facebook. She really did seem very nice.

'And another thing,' John continues earnestly, 'it's okay to admit you want to talk or that you need help. I've spent the last twenty-four hours with Pablo and his two brothers and, Jesus, but they're not afraid to cry, and you know what? They're all the better for it too, mentally speaking.'

'Would you think about maybe going to see Dr Maher?' I suggest, adjusting my legs, which are both fast asleep. I have no idea how I'll ever get up. 'Just for a chat. I don't know. It might make you feel a bit better.'

Paul nods. 'Yeah, maybe I will.'

'Good lad.'

'And you won't go missing again?'

'I wasn't missing, Aisling. I was here. Filling him in on my news, that's all. I had a lot to say. It's been a while.'

And then he starts to cry. I put my arm around him, accidentally meeting John's, and we both recoil like we've been given an electric shock.

After a minute Paul's shoulders stop shuddering and he sighs deeply. 'Hey,' he sniffs, 'does the Ard Rí still do that Tayto-sandwich buffet?'

'There'd be a riot if they stopped,' John says. 'I'd lead the charge myself.'

'I'd be right behind you,' I add.

'We should probably head so,' Paul says quietly.

'You could say that,' John says with a grimace. ''Mon Aisling,' he says, helping me up.

The three of us are heading for where John abandoned the car when he puts an arm out to slow me down, letting Paul go ahead.

Christ, what now?

'Ais, before we head on.' His voice is low. 'I just wanted to say that I'm glad we never fell out, you know? After the break-up. And I think what you've done with your café and everything … it's deadly. I've said it before and I'll say it again, but you're some woman. And all that stuff I was saying to Paul, about minding yourself. I hope you were listening?'

I was listening. I was hanging on his every word. Because I suddenly realise that John could be reading the phone book and I'd still be mesmerised.

'Lads,' Paul shouts before I can get a chance to respond. 'Will you get a move on?'

****

'Majella is going to have a conniption,' I whisper when we're all in the car. 'She's never going to forgive me for this.'

'I'm in the same boat with Pablo.'

'How can we make it up to them?'

'I don't think we can. This is their wedding. Weddings are a big deal, or so I'm told.' He glances over at me, smiling, and is just pulling out onto the road when I remember what Lisa Gleeson said about the Love Hurts singer.

'Turn right.'

'But the Ard Rí is left?'

'I have an idea.'

CHAPTER 47

'Sadhbh, Sadhbhy, hiya, can you talk?'

'Oh God, yes please.' She sounds so thankful on the phone. I thought she'd be up the walls with craic. Literally.

'I need a favour. The biggest favour I've ever asked of you.'

'Where are you?'

'I'm outside Garbally. Can you come and get me?'

I tried to get in using the pass Mandy had given me but apparently it expired at midday. Sadhbh is my plan B.

'I can try. Why aren't you at Majella's wedding?'

'I'll explain. Just come and get me. Use Don if you have to. Or get Emilia. She knows me, kind of.'

'Okay, I'll try.'

We sit at the gate for what seems like an eternity when suddenly there's a buzz on the security guard's radio and he listens, nods twice and then leans down to the car window. 'In you go.'

I squeal as the gate opens and John moves slowly up the driveway towards the main entrance while Paul sits in the back looking completely baffled. Another security guard tells us to follow the 'valet' sign and we do, pulling up to a very familiar face: Eamon Filan, of Filan's shop, garage and everything else in between.

'Aisling, John, Paul,' he says, as if seeing the three of us at this Hollywood wedding is the most natural thing in the world. 'Fine evening for it.'

'Wasn't expecting to see you here, Eamon,' I say.

'Ah, I couldn't tell anyone. Signed what they call in the business a non-disclosure agreement.'

Who didn't? 'Oh, I see.'

'Hop out there now and I'll park it for you.'

We do as we're told and walk along a beautifully lit walkway towards the main entrance and my teeth start to chatter with nerves. What am I at? Walking into this ... whatever it is I'm about to walk into. My relief when I see Sadhbh skipping towards the entrance is such that I have to grip John's arm. Is she? Yes she is. She's changed into cycling shorts and a blazer. And there was me fretting about the green dress.

'*What* are you guys doing here? What's going on?' she demands after a quick hug.

'There's been a disaster with Majella's band. The singer broke his wrist in a "Rock the Boat" accident.' Sadhbh giggles and I don't even take the time to shush her, even though we all know the dangers that come with 'Rock the Boat'. I take a deep breath. 'Do you think there's any way The Peigs would be able to come down, even for an hour? I'm in such bad books with Majella – I'll explain all that later. But is there any way do you think?'

Sadhbh looks behind her and shrugs. 'Ordinarily I would have said no, but this wedding is so dull. Like, catastrophically dull. I was about to sneak out myself. I'm dying to give Maj a proper squeeze.'

'Really?' I say, craning my neck towards where I presume the action is happening. I can hear some tinkly piano music but that's about it.

'It's just a weird mix of kinda stuffy movie execs and lots of really old people, friends of Emilia's granny. They'll all be in bed by eleven.'

'But what about Emilia and Ben's friends?'

'Oh, they're here. But the atmosphere isn't. Everyone's afraid to touch anything.' She gestures towards an admittedly terrifying piece of sculpture made of glass and what appear to be spears near us in the lobby. 'There's just no craic.'

No craic at a wedding. The greatest of all insults. Just then another familiar face rounds the corner. Mikey Maguire. In a black shirt and trousers and a barman's apron.

'Ah, hello, Aisling.'

'Mikey. Wasn't expecting to see you here.'

'Likewise.'

'Are you working or …?'

'Indeed and I am. My services were engaged for the weekend, in fact.'

'I thought you were refurbishing the pub last night?'

'Eh, no.' He has the good grace to look ashamed. 'We hosted a small party for young Miss Coburn and her friends.'

'And let me guess, you signed an NDA?'

'Months ago. I kept the biggest secret in Ballygobbard.'

I nod knowingly while Sadhbh whispers, 'Let me go and find Don.'

'Can I come in for a look?' Paul asks with a small grin, and I swear it's the first time I've seen him smile in weeks.

'Why not?' Sadhbh replies, and the pair speed walk off.

John and I stand there like spares, and what he said to me back at the grave is swirling around in my head, and so is him asking if James was looking after me when I saw him at Mammy's that time. So I just go for it.

'John?'

'Yeah?'

'Why did you and James fight at Pablo's stag?'

He scuffs his shoes on the marble floor and says nothing.

'You don't have to tell me, but I just keep imagining awful things –'

'It was the scarecrow.'

'Sorry, what?' I splutter.

'The scarecrow. That your mother asked me to make.'

'She asked James to make it, though.'

'She asked me first. Then she came back to me and said James would do it instead. But I had it pretty much done at that stage so I ...' He looks ashamed. 'I went ahead and put it up for her anyway.'

'Oh, I see. And then James ...'

'Yep, he was making one too, so there was a row about it.'

I can kind of see why neither of them wanted to tell me about it. Fighting over a scarecrow is neither of their finest hours.

'Is that what you were collecting that time I saw you at the house?'

'Yep.'

'And it's James's scarecrow that's up there now?'

'I guess so.'

I burst out laughing. I just can't help it. All that over a scarecrow? James had a black eye! John looks at me suspiciously for a second and then he starts laughing and suddenly the two of us are creasing ourselves, our roars echoing around the foyer.

Why didn't Mammy tell me? Did I make her feel so bad about the whole John and James situation that she felt she couldn't? And her making up lies about William Foley worried John was stealing his farm job. What a silly mess. And yet my heart is warmed by both of them – James wanting to do something for Mammy and John refusing to give up his tie to her.

'Well, thanks for making her that scarecrow,' I say softly and he lifts his big kind eyes up to meet mine and for a second I think he's going to –

'Aisling!' It's Sadhbh, skidding back across the tiles in her high heels and Lycra with Paul hot on her heels, a bottle of champagne in each hand. 'Head back to the Ard Rí. We'll be right behind you.'

CHAPTER 48

'I've seen some effort go into getting out of things – I've put a lot of that kind of effort in myself – but to actually leave my wedding to avoid doing your speech? Wow.'

Majella isn't really that angry. I had relayed more or less what had happened with Paul to Sharon on the phone when we were on the way to Garbally and she had passed on the message to the top table. I don't know how it was explained to the rest of the wedding, but I find James's face in the crowd and he looks hurt. I don't blame him. I should have asked him to help me find Paul, not left him in a room of people he barely knows. What does it say about us that I didn't even think about turning to him for help? He looks done. I don't blame him for that either. I think I'm done too. What John said to Paul in the graveyard is still in the back of my mind – it's not my job to fix James or be the antidote to his family problems. I can't be everything to everyone, as much as I'd like to be.

I spent the drive back to the Ard Rí with John in contented silence. It just felt right. And I know James is here and Megan is here but I feel open. Open to whatever happens. I feel at peace for the first time in ages.

'I have a surprise coming for you, Maj.' I smile at her and she looks at me quizzically just as there's a loud hooting of a horn from the front of the hotel.

Lisa Gleeson runs into the ballroom, flushed and shouting. 'It's a bus full of Peigs!'

'Oh my God,' roars Majella, and she gathers up her skirt and races out to the lobby, where Sadhbh meets her in a huge hug. I run out too and see Don and the lads and Paul and about ten strangers unloading from a Timoney's minibus.

Don clocks me and gives me a hug. 'Sorry we're so late.'

'Better late than never! Where did you get the bus?'

'Oh, he was just outside Ben and Emilia's wedding waiting to ferry people to wherever they're staying. Everyone is so spread out. Did I hear David Tennant saying he has a room with an Indian family?'

'Must be the Singhs,' I say, nodding. 'He'll get a great breakfast there.'

I look up at Tony Timoney sitting in the driver's seat of the minibus and nod. 'Let me guess – an NDA?'

'The very one, Aisling. Now, I'd better go back for the rest of them.'

I go back into the lobby and catch Sadhbh's elbow. 'There's more coming? Who are the stragglers?'

'Oh, a couple of mates. I hope you don't mind? When we said we were leaving they begged us to take them with us.'

'And did Emilia … did she mind?'

'She gave us her blessing. She was stuck talking to some movie producer and looked bored to death.'

'At her own wedding? That's shocking. Was the food nice, at least?'

'Oh my God, people were raving about your canapés. I should have brought you in to meet Ben. I never thought.'

'Ah, it was mostly Carol anyway.'

'Don't do that. You put so much work into it. Take the compliment.'

'Okay.' It nearly kills me to accept it. But I do, because she's right, I've worked bloody hard enough for it. 'Thank you, Sadhbh,'

There's the unmistakable sound of an amp being plugged into a guitar from the ballroom and she grabs my hand and we race towards it. The Peigs are setting themselves up with the Love Hurts equipment, and I must say they've been very graceful to let them use it. In fact, Brendan Coleman looks downright relieved not to have to try to recreate the Mickey Magic. Majella is front and centre with Pablo right beside her, and I can see Mairead fanning Fionnuala's face with a napkin. Tickets for The Peigs are probably the only things Fionnuala's ever spent money on, so an intimate free gig will be like a dream come true for them. Megan and John seem to be having words. Civilised words but words nonetheless. I suppose she's not thrilled that he disappeared for an hour and a half with his ex-girlfriend from a wedding where he's the best man. Not a jury in the land would convict her. Seeing them having the words gives me hope. It's not a feeling I like admitting to myself, but it does. Maybe I don't want them to work out. Maybe I want –

'There you are.'

I don't know how long James has been standing beside me, looking at me looking at John and Megan. He looks pissed off. And why wouldn't he be? I basically abandoned him.

'Sharon told me what happened.' He's looking over at Paul, who's pouring champagne into a pint glass for The Truck. 'I'm glad he's okay.'

'Me too,' I say.

'Look, Aisling, it's been a long week. I think I might head home.'

This is where I should stop him. I should ask him to stay, tell him we'll have a great night. Make it all better. He's so nice – he doesn't deserve this.

'Do you have time for that talk before you go?' I ask him, not willing to let it drag on for another moment. He nods and I take his hand and slip out into the hallway and through a side door into a quiet courtyard. James talks before I have the chance to.

'So the job is more or less finished. The Garbally job, I mean. Eh, obviously.' He doesn't often look flustered or fall over his words. My heart breaks for him a bit. 'So I was thinking about jobs in Dublin, or maybe something locally, but I wanted to check …'

I'm already shaking my head and he nods and pulls his mouth into a tight line.

'I'm so sorry, James. I don't think you should stay here just for me. It's just – it's not working out, is it?'

He shrugs. 'I stayed here just for you until now, didn't I?'

Ouch. 'I know. I'm sorry. I really did hope it was going to be something special. And, James,' I take his hand, 'it was, so many times. But it's not right. You can't feel like it is either?'

He shrugs again. 'You're easy to love, Aisling. And this place, with its bonkers people and your warm family and …' He trails off, and I want to tell him that my family is far from perfect. Far, far from it. But he doesn't need to hear that, not James Matthews, little lost boy of George and Celine. I can't fix him – it's not my job. I repeat that to myself as we stand in silence.

'I suppose I was in love with the idea of being in a relationship again. I missed it,' he says finally.

'I probably was too, if I'm being honest,' I admit, thinking back to that night of my thirtieth and the options before me.

'I did love you, Aisling.' He looks up at me.

'I know.'

****

As I arrive back into the ballroom I don't even feel sad. I feel … light. Don strikes the first chord of 'She's the Business' and the room erupts in screams.

Four hits in a row later, Don finally takes a breather and speaks into the microphone. 'I understand we haven't had a first dance yet here tonight – is that right?'

Everyone roars '*Nooo*' and Majella and Pablo are pushed into the centre of the room as Don croons, 'Sometimes late at night, I lie awake and watch her sleeping …'

It strikes me that 'If Tomorrow Never Comes' might not actually be the most romantic song for a first dance but, to be fair, Pablo probably does lie awake and watch Maj sleeping, fretting she's going to die, so leave them off. Shem Moran strides over to Juana and pulls her onto the floor and John does the same to me as Don sings, 'Did I try in every way, to show her every day, that's she's my only ooone?'

I place my hand on his shoulder and bring myself in close to him, inhaling and expecting that familiar smell, but it's different. No Lynx Africa. No hint of whatever shampoo someone else bought. But a manly smell. A woody smell. A purposeful smell. He grips my hand tightly and my back even tighter. I feel at home. I remember the last time we danced at a wedding and how far we've both come. I feel him move back from me a little and I do the same, feeling like I might say something I may or may not regret. He beats me to it, though.

'So, I have something to tell you.' He's not looking me in the eye, but staring over my shoulder. We're fairly front and centre so to be gazing at each other might be a bit much, to be fair.

'Okay.'

'I'm leaving. We're leaving.'

'What?'

Where is he going?

'Megan, she got a job in Dubai, teaching. So we're off in a few weeks. And … we're engaged.'

The roaring in my ears is so loud I feel like I might fall over. Don's singing becomes sort of far away and a fright goes through my body like a sword. I can feel that cold sweaty feeling coming over me, and the breathlessness. I concentrate hard on my breathing, trying to hide it from him and also very conscious that I haven't answered.

'We did it yesterday but, obviously, we didn't want to overshadow Majella so we said nothing,' he continues.

I get my breath back enough to force a laugh. 'She'd kill you.'

He laughs too, and pulls back to look at me, seeming relieved. 'So, yeah. I just wanted you to know.'

I'm afraid to say anything in case I burst into tears. So it turns out he does want to get married, he just didn't want to marry me. Across the room I see Megan chatting to Maeve. She's holding out her left hand but she's looking straight at us.

Thankfully, I don't have to say anything because Don interrupts his final chorus, announcing to the room, 'I believe we have another pair of first dancers in our midst. Majella and Pablo, would you mind?'

I look up and follow Don's pointed finger to the door of the ballroom, and who's standing there only Emilia Coburn, Ben Dixon and a gaggle of other strange yet familiar faces. Grateful for the interruption, I detach myself from John and force myself to smile up at him. 'Ask Megan to dance, I'm just going to get a drink.'

As Majella clocks Emilia and Ben, screams and drops Pablo to run into Emilia's arms, I push through the throng and sink into the first seat I find. I watch as Maj drags Emilia onto the dancefloor and Ben follows – James Bond an afterthought, like. Emilia is wearing a red dress, definitely not a wedding dress, and I wonder if she changed before she came. Deeply sound of her if so. Sharon is jumping up and down screaming at the edge of the dancefloor. She's a big fan of Ben's, always was. The Peigs start up again on one last chorus and I close my eyes for a second.

'Will you be alright, Aisling?'

It's a voice I wasn't expecting to hear. Fran – John's terrifying mam. She must have come for the afters. No one can resist the Tayto-sandwich buffet, it seems. I open my eyes and she's beside me, smiling at me kindly, like she knows.

I smile back at her. 'Yes, Fran, I'll be alright.'

CHAPTER 49

I feel like the Ard Rí were really shooting themselves in the foot refusing Emilia Coburn, Ben Dixon and countless other A-listers access to their residents' bar.

'They're not residents,' the manager told Lisa Gleeson when she asked him to think of the social media content, and that was that.

'What's our plan B?' demanded Majella, and I loved her so much in that moment. She could have just carried on her own session, but she knows a proper hooley when she smells one.

'What about Maguire's?' suggests Emilia, leaning on Pablo's Uncle Mateo for support. Even celebrities' feet kill them in heels.

'It's a bit late, no?' I go, and there's a hum of agreement. Two a.m. is very late to be expecting Mikey Maguire to start a lock-in.

'I bet I could sweet talk him.' Emilia smiles. 'We spent a lot of money in there on Friday night.' She digs out her phone and dials a number. Expectation hangs heavy in the air.

'Hey, Mandy. I know it's late, but can you do something for me?'

Forty-five minutes later and Mandy Blumenthal is bending my ear at the bar in Maguire's. The blinds are down and

Mikey has spotters outside looking for any sign of passing gardaí. The nearest garda station is twenty-five kilometres away, so I'd say we're grand, but Mikey says he got a stern warning a few months back when Garda Staunton filed a report that he'd heard 'mysterious shushing and whispering' coming from Maguire's very late one Sunday night.

'I'm just glad she had a great day in the end,' Mandy barks. I swear she's only had two drinks but Americans are notorious lightweights.

'She did, Mandy, she did. And she said you did everything she asked of you. Sometimes the vibe just isn't there.' The word 'vibe' doesn't roll off my tongue very easily, but I'm just repeating what Emilia said to me in the toilets ten minutes ago, just after Majella collared the two of us for a selfie.

'I'm checking us in. Fuck the guards!' she'd roared as she exited the bathroom, having the absolute time of her life.

'I did my job,' Mandy says definitively and I agree with her again. She did do her job and, sure, look, it's ended in a colossal lock-in in Maguire's, and I'm fairly sure Don has just about convinced Pierce Brosnan to get up and perform 'Pierce Brosnan' with them. Majella and Pablo are shifting in the corner and table twenty-three are doing shots with the lad from *Star Wars* over by the cigarette machine.

I slip my phone out of my bag to check for a text from James. He said he'd let me know he got home alright. I'll go to my grave making people – even people I've just broken up with – let me know they got home alright. He has sent the text and I let go a little sigh of relief. It will be good to be in my own bed tonight – one of the few empty ones in BGB – my own bed in Mammy's. And even though my room is different, I can't wait to feel the walls of home around me. And to escape the ever-present cement dust.

Mandy is still talking at me as I put my phone back in my bag.

'And if you ever need a job or a good word, you let me know, honey. I'll give you references up the wazoo. You'd be a huge hit in New York with that cute accent combined with your business acumen.'

I stick my fingers into the inner pocket of my bag looking for a twenty euro note I'm certain is in there, and I touch the little envelope I fished out of the box that Mammy dropped off at the Ard Rí for me. I never gave it to Majella! Well, no time like the present. I touch Mandy on the arm and indicate I'm just nipping over to the other side of the pub – and as luck would have it, I find Majella alone in her corner, briefly abandoned by Pablo in favour of a cry with Javier and Miguel, who don't seem to recognise the woman from *Eastenders* they're singing to.

I sit down on the stool beside her and nudge her. 'Not a bad day in the end, eh?'

'The best.'

'I have something for you. Your something old. Sorry it's so late.'

'Sure, aren't you my something old? *Ahhh-hahhh!*' she squeals before I have a chance to admonish her. She takes the envelope and opens it, lifting out the yellowed foolscap paper. 'No way! What's this?'

She unfolds it and reveals a drawing. Two oddly proportioned brides, one with red lips and one without. One with a veil and one without. One in a gigantic princess dress and one in a short sweetheart number.

'I remember! It's from that double history class when Mrs Foley didn't show up and we wrote notes to each other promising we'd be each other's bridesmaid. The skitting we used to do in that class.'

Well, Majella used to do the skitting and I would kick her under the table, afraid to get in trouble.

'See?' I say. 'I drew you and you drew me. And turn it over.'

Printed on the back is the sentence 'I solemnly swear that I'll be your bridesmaid and you'll be mine' and both our names are signed in our best penmanship underneath the declaration. Right beside it reads 'Majella luvs Cillian Ruane 4eva tru love never dies.'

'You snake!' I laugh. 'You knew I loved Cillian Ruane.'

'Thanks for being my bridesmaid. My *rides*maid.'

'Thanks for asking me.'

'Hey,' she says, 'I signed on the dotted line.'

'I'm sorry I missed my speech.'

'What were you going to say?'

'I was going to back up everything Shem had to say about every one of those hickeys.'

'Jesus, if looks could kill Juana would be refused bail.'

'I was going to tell them about the sheep and the dress. I was going to remind you of the time you and Titch Maguire nearly caused war with the Valentine's card. I was going to reveal that it was you who put the tampon in the hole in the window of the sacristy that time.'

'You wouldn't.'

'Oh, I would. I was going to say how much Pablo loves you and how much you love Pablo and how proud I am of all the work you're doing in school and how you're going to single-handedly save the coral reefs.'

'Well,' she says, smiling through some tears, 'there's a prediction to live up to. Niamh from Across the Road will be sickened.'

We're quiet for a second and then she says, 'I haven't seen James in a while?'

'He went home.'

'Are you guys okay?'

I shake my head and she sighs.

'Ah, I'm sorry Ais. James is a nice guy. And such a ride.'

I laugh.

'But I wasn't convinced about him for you, you know that?'

'Really? You were so into us being together!'

'At the start, yeah. I just wanted you to be happy. And he was nice. A nice guy. But that's about it.'

'And I'm literally allergic to him.'

She looks confused.

'The hives? Cement allergy.'

Majella hoots. 'You couldn't make that up, bird!' She's right, you couldn't.

'Anyway, I was mostly trying to force something that wasn't there this past while, you know? I just didn't want to get left behind again.'

She sits up and looks at me. 'Who's getting left behind? You have a fabulous life and don't you forget it.'

'I know. It's just Colette Green put this thing up on her Instagram about –'

'Ah, look, forget bloody Colette Green and her bloody inspirational quotes.'

How could she? Majella has more CG at Home candles than anyone I know. Such sacrilege. And we've met her and she's sound.

'Colette Green has a perfect life on Instagram, but she sits down to take a shite like the rest of us. Sadhbh told me she was engaged twice before she met the lad she's with now, and when she first started out she used to pay her little sister to write her blog posts because she had no good ideas.'

My God. My beloved Colette.

'She does a great pair of jeans, though.' Majella nudges me and we laugh.

'I think I bit off more than I could chew the last while,' I say quietly.

'Understatement of the century! I didn't want to say it, but I've never seen you look so wrecked, bird. Why do you do it to yourself?'

I shrug. 'I just find it so hard to say no to anyone. I want everyone to be happy, and happy with me. But I think I need to start putting myself first for a change. And talking about things a bit more. And listening a bit more.'

Majella holds out her glass and we clink. 'Now you're talking sense.'

'I need to book that holiday. And not set my alarm clock for a week.'

'Delighted to hear it. And … you heard about John and Megan?' she asks hesitantly.

'I did. I did.'

She lets it sit. She knows there's no need to ask any more about that.

'Will you move back home?' she says after a while. 'I hope not. James will surely leave and you could stay in the apartment. So handy for work.'

'I don't know, Majella, I really don't know.' About any of it. All I want to do is enjoy this night and go home to my own bed and sleep and sleep and wake up without the weight of the world on my shoulders. That would be nice.

In another corner Don has picked up a guitar and started strumming the chords of a familiar song. Sadhbh is sitting beside him and starts to sing in a surprisingly sweet voice that I didn't know she had.

'Somebody said you got a new friend ...'

Next thing they'll be touring together. A star is born. Majella and I sit side by side and listen to them, surrounded by friends old and new.

'I'm giving it my all but I'm not the girl you're taking home.'

Majella turns and smiles sadly at me, but my foot is tapping and I can't help but get up off my stool and sway and twirl as Sadhbh sings.

'I keep dancing on my own.'

ACKNOWLEDGEMENTS

Thanks to everyone who's picked up an Aisling book and let us know how much they love her. We read every message, every DM, every tweet, and we can't believe our luck.

To our families and friends for all the love and support, and especially to India, Esme and new arrival Felix for making us laugh and for sleeping at the right times.

Special thanks to the team at Gill Books who continue to make Aisling the best she can be, particularly Conor Nagle and Catherine Gough for the kitchen-table brainstorming and Teresa Daly and Ellen Monnelly for the good humour and great ideas. To Paul Neilan and Nicki Howard also at Gill Books, and to Maxine Hitchcock, Clare Bowron and Rebecca Hilsdon at Michael Joseph for their invaluable input and open hearts for Aisling.

To Marian Keyes, Sarah Maria Griffin, Paul Howard, John Boyne and all of the authors who have made us feel so welcome and supported.

To Chelsea Morgan Hoffman, Rory Gilmartin and all at Element Pictures for trusting us with the screenplay.

Big thanks to everyone at Curtis Brown, especially our agent Sheila Crowley who's probably the most fabulous woman we know. Thanks too to Luke Speed, Emily Harris and Sabhbh Curran at CB.

Thanks to our early readers and constant supporters: Aine Bambrick, Breda Gittons, Deirdre Ball, Gavan and Ciara Reilly, Eoin Matthews, Louise McSharry, Sophie White, Roisin Ingle, Abbie Greaves, the Naas gals, the Phantom gals. Thanks to Sarah Kisch, Richard Toner and Baby C for flying the OMGWACA flag way out east, and to Fiona Hyde for the title. Special thanks to Vicky Phelan for being an inspiration.

To Lin-Manuel Miranda, who's been more supportive than he could ever know.

And finally to Louise Keegan, who's been there since the start, wine in hand.